DENNIS LEHANE is the author of *A Drink Before the War*, which won the Shamus Award for Best First Novel; *Darkness, Take My Hand*; *Sacred*; *Gone, Baby, Gone*; and *Prayers for Rain*. A native of Dorchester, Massachusetts, he lives in the Boston area with his wife, Sheila, and their two English bulldogs, Marlon and Stella.

Acclaim for Dennis Lehane:

'Discovering Dennis Lehane is a bit like finding a Mondrian in the attic: surprise followed by ecstasy . . . Lehane manages to combine sentimentality and hard-boiled cynicism, handling the loss of loved ones and gun battles with equal ease, and delivering a brilliant ending where the law prevails, but, sadly, justice loses. Take my advice and catch up with Lehane soonest.' *Independent on Sunday*

'He dares the reader to accept his clever misconceptions and moulds it into a crime story as chillingly compelling as a car crash. Lehane's world – excellent.' *GQ*

'His stories are strong, taut with suspense . . . His characters are vulnerable personalities, with a plethora of doubts and anxieties, who have known the downside – just like us.' *Irish Times*

'The well-oiled plot mechanics, edge-of-the-knife dialogue and explosive bursts of violence are polished and primed.' *New York Times Book Review*

ALSO BY DENNIS LEHANE

A Drink Before the War

Darkness, Take My Hand

Sacred

Gone, Baby, Gone

Prayers for Rain

MYSTIC RIVER

DENNIS LEHANE

BANTAM PRESS

LONDON • NEW YORK • TORONTO • SYDNEY • AUCKLAND

TRANSWORLD PUBLISHERS
61–63 Uxbridge Road, London W5 5SA
a division of The Random House Group Ltd

RANDOM HOUSE AUSTRALIA (PTY) LTD
20 Alfred Street, Milsons Point, Sydney,
New South Wales 2061, Australia

RANDOM HOUSE NEW ZEALAND
18 Poland Road, Glenfield, Auckland 10, New Zealand

RANDOM HOUSE SOUTH AFRICA (PTY) LTD
Endulini, 5a Jubilee Road, Parktown 2193, South Africa

Published 2001 by Bantam Press
a division of Transworld Publishers

Grateful acknowledgment is made to reprint the following:
Excerpt from *God's Pocket*, copyright © 1983 by Peter Dexter.
Reprinted by permission of the author.
Excerpt from "Pirates" (Rickie Lee Jones) copyright © 1981 by Easy
Money Music. All rights for Easy Money Music administered by the
Haber Corporation, used by permission. All rights reserved.

A catalogue record for this book is available
from the British Library.
ISBNs 0593 047508 (cased)
0593 044762 (tpb)

Printed in Great Britain
by Mackays of Chatham plc, Chatham, Kent.

1 3 5 7 9 10 8 6 4 2

For my wife, Sheila

[He] did not understand women. It wasn't the way bartenders or comedians didn't understand women, it was the way poor people didn't understand the economy. You could stand outside the Girard Bank Building every day of your life and never guess anything about what went on in there. That's why, in their hearts, they'd always rather stick up a 7-Eleven.

—Pete Dexter, *God's Pocket*

There is no street with mute stones
and no house without echoes.

—Góngora

ACKNOWLEDGMENTS

THANKS to Sergeant Michael Lawn, as always, of the Watertown Police Department; Boston City Councillor Brian Honan; David Meier, chief of the Suffolk County District Attorney's Homicide Unit; Teresa Leonard and Ann Guden for catching my errors; and Tom Murphy of James A. Murphy and Son Funeral Home in Dorchester.

A particular debt of gratitude is owed to Trooper Robert Manning of the Massachusetts State Police, who put the ball in play and answered all my questions, no matter how stupid, with a straight face.

Deepest thanks to an extraordinary agent, Ann Rittenberg, and a brilliant editor, Claire Wachtel, for guiding me through.

I

THE BOYS
WHO ESCAPED FROM
WOLVES
(1975)

1

THE POINT
AND THE FLATS

WHEN SEAN DEVINE and Jimmy Marcus were kids, their fathers worked together at the Coleman Candy plant and carried the stench of warm chocolate back home with them. It became a permanent character of their clothes, the beds they slept in, the vinyl backs of their car seats. Sean's kitchen smelled like a Fudgsicle, his bathroom like a Coleman Chew-Chew bar. By the time they were eleven, Sean and Jimmy had developed a hatred of sweets so total that they took their coffee black for the rest of their lives and never ate dessert.

On Saturdays, Jimmy's father would drop by the Devines' to have a beer with Sean's father. He'd bring Jimmy with him, and as one beer turned into six, plus two or three shots of Dewar's, Jimmy and Sean would play in the backyard, sometimes with Dave Boyle, a kid with girl's wrists and weak eyes who was always telling jokes he'd learned from his uncles. From the other side of the kitchen window screen, they could hear the hiss of the beer can pull-tabs, bursts of hard, sudden laughter, and the heavy snap of Zippos as Mr. Devine and Mr. Marcus lit their Luckys.

Sean's father, a foreman, had the better job. He was tall and fair and had a loose, easy smile that Sean had seen calm his mother's anger more than a few times, just shut it down like a switch had been flicked off inside of her. Jimmy's father loaded the trucks. He was small and his dark hair fell over his forehead in a tangle and something in his eyes seemed to buzz all the time. He had a way of moving too quickly; you'd blink and he was on the other side of the room. Dave Boyle didn't have a father, just a lot of uncles, and the only reason he was usually there on those Saturdays was because he had this gift for attaching himself to Jimmy like lint; he'd see him leaving his house with his father, show up beside their car, half out of breath, going "What's up, Jimmy?" with a sad hopefulness.

They all lived in East Buckingham, just west of downtown, a neighborhood of cramped corner stores, small playgrounds, and butcher shops where meat, still pink with blood, hung in the windows. The bars had Irish names and Dodge Darts by the curbs. Women wore handkerchiefs tied off at the backs of their skulls and carried mock leather snap purses for their cigarettes. Until a couple of years ago, older boys had been plucked from the streets, as if by spaceships, and sent to war. They came back hollow and sullen a year or so later, or they didn't come back at all. Days, the mothers searched the papers for coupons. Nights, the fathers went to the bars. You knew everyone; nobody except those older boys ever left.

Jimmy and Dave came from the Flats, down by the Penitentiary Channel on the south side of Buckingham Avenue. It was only twelve blocks from Sean's street, but the Devines were north of the Ave., part of the Point, and the Point and the Flats didn't mix much.

It wasn't like the Point glittered with gold streets and silver spoons. It was just the Point, working class, blue collar, Chevys and Fords and Dodges parked in front of simple A-frames and the occasional small Victorian. But people in the Point owned. People in the Flats rented. Point families went to church, stayed together, held signs on street corners during election months. The Flats, though, who knew what they did, living like animals sometimes, ten to an apartment, trash in their streets—Wellieville, Sean and his friends at Saint Mike's called it, families living on the dole, sending their kids to public schools, divorcing. So while Sean went to Saint Mike's Parochial in black pants, black tie, and blue shirt, Jimmy and Dave went to the Lewis M. Dewey School on Blaxston.

Kids at the Looey & Dooey got to wear street clothes, which was cool, but they usually wore the same ones three out of five days, which wasn't. There was an aura of grease to them—greasy hair, greasy skin, greasy collars and cuffs. A lot of the boys had bumpy welts of acne and dropped out early. A few of the girls wore maternity dresses to graduation.

So if it wasn't for their fathers, they probably never would have been friends. During the week, they never hung out, but they had those Saturdays, and there was something to those days, whether they hung out in the backyard, or wandered through the gravel dumps off Harvest Street, or hopped the subways and rode downtown—not to see anything, just to move through the dark tunnels and hear the rattle and brake-scream of the cars as they cornered the tracks and the lights flickered on and off—that felt to Sean like a held breath. Anything could happen when you were with Jimmy. If he was aware there were rules—in the subway, on the streets, in a movie theater—he never showed it.

They were at South Station once, tossing an orange street hockey ball back and forth on the platform, and Jimmy missed Sean's throw and the ball bounced down onto the tracks. Before it occurred to Sean that Jimmy could even be thinking about it, Jimmy jumped off the platform and down onto the track, down there with the mice and the rats and the third rail.

People on the platform went nuts. They screamed at Jimmy. One woman turned the color of cigar ash as she bent at the knees and yelled, Get back up here, get back up here *now,* goddamnit! Sean heard a thick rumble that could have been a train entering the tunnel up at Washington Street or could have been trucks rolling along the street above, and the people on the platform heard it, too. They waved their arms, whipped their heads around to look for the subway police. One guy placed a forearm across his daughter's eyes.

Jimmy kept his head down, peering into the darkness under the platform for the ball. He found it. He wiped some black grime off it with his shirtsleeve and ignored the people kneeling on the yellow line, extending their hands down toward the track.

Dave nudged Sean and said, "Whew, huh?" too loud.

Jimmy walked along the center of the track toward the stairs at the far end of the platform, where the tunnel opened gaping and dark, and a heavier rumble shook the station, and people were *jumping* now, banging fists into their hips. Jimmy took his time, strolling really, then he looked back over his shoulder, caught Sean's eyes, and grinned.

Dave said, "He's smiling. He's just nuts. You know?"

When Jimmy reached the first step in the cement stairs, several hands thrust down and yanked him up. Sean watched his feet swing out and to the left and his head curl and dip to the right, Jimmy looking so small and light in a big man's grasp, like he was filled with straw, but tucking that ball tight against his chest even as people grabbed at his elbow and his shin banged off the edge of the platform. Sean felt Dave jittering beside him, lost. Sean looked at the faces of the people pulling Jimmy up and he didn't see worry or fear anymore, none of the helplessness he'd seen just a minute ago. He saw rage, monsters' faces, the features gnarled and savage, like they were going to lean in and bite a chunk out of Jimmy, then beat him to death.

They got Jimmy up onto the platform and held him, fingers squeezed into his shoulders as they looked around for someone to tell them what to do. The train broke through the tunnel, and someone screamed, but then someone laughed—a shrieking cackle that made Sean think of witches around a cauldron—because the train burst through on the other side of the station, moving north, and Jimmy looked up into the faces of the people holding him as if to say, *See?*

Beside Sean, Dave let out this high-pitched giggle and threw up in his own hands.

Sean looked away, wondered where he fit in all this.

THAT NIGHT Sean's father sat him down in the basement tool room. The tool room was a tight place of black vises and coffee cans filled with nails and screws, piles of wood stacked neatly beneath the scarred counter that split the room in half, hammers hung in carpenter belts like guns in holsters, a band saw blade dangling from a hook. Sean's father, who often worked as a handyman around the neighborhood, came down here to build his birdhouses and the shelves he placed on the windows for his wife's flowers. He'd planned the back porch here, something he and his friends threw up one blistering summer when Sean was five, and he came down here when he wanted peace and quiet, and sometimes when he was angry, Sean knew, angry at Sean or Sean's mother or his job. The birdhouses—baby Tudors and colonials and Victorians and Swiss chalets—ended up stacked in a corner of the cellar, so many of them they'd have had to live in the Amazon to find enough birds who could get use out of them.

Sean sat up on the old red bar stool and fingered the inside of the thick black vise, felt the oil and sawdust mixed in there, until his father said, "Sean, how many times I have to tell you about that?"

Sean pulled his finger back out, wiped the grease on his palm.

His father picked some stray nails up off the counter and placed them in a yellow coffee can. "I know you like Jimmy Marcus, but if you two want to play together from now on, you'll do it in view of the house. Yours, not his."

Sean nodded. Arguing with his father was pointless when he spoke as quietly and slowly as he was doing now, every word coming out of his mouth as if it had a small stone attached to it.

"We understand each other?" His father pushed the coffee can to his right, looked down at Sean.

Sean nodded. He watched his father's thick fingers rub sawdust off the tips.

"For how long?"

His father reached up and pulled a wisp of dust off a hook embedded in the ceiling. He kneaded it between his fingers, then tossed it in the wastebasket under the counter. "Oh, a good while, I'd say. And Sean?"

"Yes, sir?"

"Don't be thinking about going to your mother on this one. She never wants you to see Jimmy again after that stunt today."

"He's not that bad. He's—"

"Didn't say he was. He's just wild, and your mother's had her fill of wild in her life."

Sean saw something glint in his father's face when he said "wild," and he knew it was the other Billy Devine he was seeing for a moment, the one he'd had to build out of scraps of conversation he'd overheard from aunts and uncles. The Old Billy they called him, the "scrapper," his uncle Colm said once with a smile, the Billy Devine who'd disappeared sometime before Sean was born to be replaced by this quiet, careful man with thick, nimble fingers who built too many birdhouses.

"You remember what we talked about," his father said, and patted Sean's shoulder in dismissal.

Sean left the tool room and walked through the cool basement wondering if what made him enjoy Jimmy's company was the same thing that made his father enjoy hanging out with Mr. Marcus, drinking Saturday into Sunday, laughing too hard and too suddenly, and if that was what his mother was afraid of.

A FEW SATURDAYS LATER, Jimmy and Dave Boyle came by the Devine house without Jimmy's father. They knocked on the back door as Sean was finishing breakfast, and Sean heard his mother open the door and say, "Morning to ya, Jimmy. Morning, Dave," in that polite voice she used around people she wasn't sure she wanted to see.

Jimmy was quiet today. All that loopy energy seemed to have gone coiled up inside of him. Sean could almost feel it beating against the walls of Jimmy's chest and Jimmy swallowing against it. Jimmy seemed smaller, darker, as if he'd pop with the prick of a pin. Sean had seen this before. Jimmy had always been a little moody. Still, it got to Sean every time, made him wonder if Jimmy had any control over it, or if these moods came like a sore throat or his mother's cousins, just dropped in whether you felt like having them over or not.

Dave Boyle was at his most aggravating when Jimmy was like this. Dave Boyle seemed to think it was his job to make sure everyone was happy, which usually just pissed people off after a while.

As they stood out on the sidewalk, trying to decide what to do, Jimmy all wrapped in himself and Sean still waking up, all three of them fidgeting with the day hanging out in front of them but bordered by the ends of Sean's street, Dave said, "Hey, why's a dog lick its balls?"

Neither Sean nor Jimmy answered. They'd heard this one, like, a thousand times.

"Because it can!" Dave Boyle shrieked, and grabbed his gut like it was so funny it hurt.

Jimmy walked over to the sawhorses, where city crews had been replacing several squares of sidewalk. The work crews had tied yellow CAUTION tape to four sawhorses in a rectangle, created a barricade around the new sidewalk squares, but Jimmy snapped the tape by walking through it. He squatted at the edge, his Keds on the old sidewalk, and used a twig on the soft pavement to carve thin lines that reminded Sean of old men's fingers.

"My dad don't work with yours anymore."

"How come?" Sean squatted by Jimmy. He didn't have a stick, but he wanted one. He wanted to do what Jimmy did, even if he didn't know why, and even though his father would strap his ass if he did.

Jimmy shrugged. "He was smarter than them. He scared them because he knew so much stuff."

"Smart stuff!" Dave Boyle said. "Right, Jimmy?"

Right, Jimmy? Right, Jimmy? Dave was like a parrot some days.

Sean wondered how much anyone could know about candy and why that information would be important. "What kind of stuff?"

"How to run the place better." Jimmy didn't sound real sure and then he shrugged. "Stuff, anyway. Important stuff."

"Oh."

"How to *run* the place. Right, Jimmy?"

Jimmy dug in the cement some more. Dave Boyle found his own stick and bent over the soft cement, began drawing a circle. Jimmy frowned and tossed his own stick aside. Dave stopped drawing, looked at Jimmy like, What'd I do?

"Know what would be cool?" Jimmy's voice had that slight rise in it that made something in Sean's blood jitter, probably because Jimmy's idea of cool was usually way different than anyone else's.

"What?"

"Driving a car."

"Yeah," Sean said slowly.

"You know"—Jimmy held his palms out, the twig and cement forgotten—"just around the block."

"Just around the block," Sean said.

"It would be cool, wouldn't it?" Jimmy grinned.

Sean felt a smile curl up and break wide across his face. "It would be cool."

"It would be, like, cooler'n anything." Jimmy jumped a foot off the ground. He raised his eyebrows at Sean and jumped again.

"It'd be cool." Sean could already feel the big wheel in his hand.

"Yeah, yeah, yeah." Jimmy punched Sean's shoulder.

"Yeah, yeah, yeah." Sean punched Jimmy's shoulder, something rippling inside him, racing, everything getting fast and shiny.

"Yeah, yeah, yeah," Dave said, but his punch missed Jimmy's shoulder.

For a moment, Sean had even forgotten Dave was there. That happened a lot with Dave. Sean didn't know why.

"Fucking serious fucking cool." Jimmy laughed and jumped again.

And Sean could see it was already beginning to happen. They were in the front seat (Dave in the back, if he was there at all) and moving, two eleven-year-olds driving around Buckingham, tooting the horn at their friends, drag-racing the older kids on Dunboy Avenue, laying rubber in screeching clouds of smoke. He could smell the air rushing through the window, feel it in his hair.

Jimmy looked up the street. "You know anyone on this street who leaves their keys in their car?"

Sean did. Mr. Griffin left them under the seat, and Dottie Fiore left them in her glove compartment, and Old Man Makowski, the drunk who listened to Sinatra records too loud all hours of the day and night, left them in the ignition most times.

But as he followed Jimmy's gaze and picked out the cars that he knew held keys, Sean felt a dull ache grow behind his eyes, and in the hard sunlight bouncing off the trunks and hoods, he could feel the weight of the street, its homes, the entire Point and its expectations for him. He was not a kid who stole cars. He was a kid who'd go to college someday, make something of himself that was bigger and better than a foreman or a truck loader. That was the plan, and Sean believed that plans worked out if you were careful, if you were cautious. It was like sitting through a movie, no matter how boring or confusing, until the end. Because at the end, sometimes things were explained or the ending itself was cool enough that you felt like sitting through all the boring stuff had been worth it.

He almost said this to Jimmy, but Jimmy was already moving up the street, looking in car windows, Dave running alongside him.

"How about this one?" Jimmy put his hand on Mr. Carlton's Bel Air, and his voice was loud in the dry breeze.

"Hey, Jimmy?" Sean walked toward him. "Maybe some other time. Right?"

Jimmy's face went all saggy and narrow. "What do you mean? We'll do it. It'll be fun. Fucking cool. Remember?"

"Fucking cool," Dave said.

"We can't even see over the dashboard."

"Phone books." Jimmy smiled in the sunlight. "We'll get 'em from your house."

"Phone books," Dave said. "Yeah!"

Sean held out his arms. "No. Come on."

Jimmy's smile died. He looked at Sean's arms as if he wanted to cut them off at the elbows. "Why won't you just do something for fun. Huh?" He tugged on the handle of the Bel Air, but it was locked. For a second, Jimmy's cheeks jiggled and his lower lip trembled, and then he looked in Sean's face with a wild loneliness that Sean pitied.

Dave looked at Jimmy and then at Sean. His arm shot out awkwardly and hit Sean's shoulder. "Yeah, how come you don't want to do fun things?"

Sean couldn't believe Dave had just hit him. Dave.

He punched Dave in the chest, and Dave sat down.

Jimmy pushed Sean. "What the hell you doing?"

"He hit me," Sean said.

"He didn't hit you," Jimmy said.

Sean's eyes widened in disbelief and Jimmy's mimicked them.

"He hit me."

"He hit me," Jimmy said in a girl's voice, and pushed Sean again. "He's my fucking friend."

"So am I," Sean said.

"So am I," Jimmy said. "So am I, so am I, so am I."

Dave Boyle stood up and laughed.

Sean said, "Cut it out."

"Cut it out, cut it out, cut it out." Jimmy pushed Sean again, the heels of his hands digging into Sean's ribs. "Make me. You wanna make me?"

"You wanna make him?" And now Dave shoved Sean.

Sean had no idea how this had happened. He couldn't even remember what had made Jimmy mad anymore or why Dave had been stupid enough to hit him in the first place. One second they were standing by the car. Now they were in the middle of the street and Jimmy was pushing him, his face screwed up and stunted, his eyes black and small, Dave starting to join in.

"Come on. Make me."

"I don't—"

Another shove. "Come on, little girl."

"Jimmy, can we just—?"

"No, we can't. You a little pussy, Sean? Huh?"

He went to shove him again but stopped, and that wild (and tired, Sean could see that, too, suddenly) aloneness pummeled his features as he looked past Sean at something coming up the street.

It was a dark brown car, square and long like the kind police detectives drove, a Plymouth or something, and its bumper stopped by their legs and the two cops looked out through the windshield at them, their faces watery in the reflected trees that swam across the glass.

Sean felt a sudden lurch in the morning, a shifting in the softness of it.

The driver got out. He looked like a cop—blond crew cut, red face, white shirt, black-and-gold nylon tie, the heft of his gut dropping over his belt buckle like a stack of pancakes. The other one looked sick. He was skinny and tired-looking and stayed in his seat, one hand gripping his skull through greasy black hair, staring into the side-view mirror as the three boys came around near the driver's door.

The beefy one crooked a finger at them, then wiggled it toward his chest until they stood in front of him. "Let me ask you something, okay?" He bent at his big belly and his huge head filled Sean's vision. "You guys think it's okay to fight in the middle of the street?"

Sean noticed a gold badge clipped to the belt buckle beside the big man's right hip.

"What's that?" The cop cupped a hand behind his ear.

"No, sir."

"No, sir."

"No, sir."

"A pack of punks, huh? That what you are?" He jerked his big thumb back at the man in the passenger seat. "Me and my partner, we've had our fill of you East Bucky punks scaring decent people off the street. You know?"

Sean and Jimmy didn't say anything.

"We're sorry," Dave Boyle said, and looked like he was about to cry.

"You kids from this street?" the big cop asked. His eyes scanned the homes on the left side of the street like he knew every occupant, would bag them if they lied.

"Yup," Jimmy said, and looked back over his shoulder at Sean's house.

"Yes, sir," Sean said.

Dave didn't say anything.

The cop looked down at him. "Huh? You say something, kid?"

"What?" Dave looked at Jimmy.

"Don't look at him. Look at me." The big cop breathed loudly through his nostrils. "You live here, kid?"

"Huh? No."

"No?" The cop bent over Dave. "Where you live, son?"

"Rester Street." Still looking at Jimmy.

"Flats trash in the Point?" The cop's cherry-red lips swiveled as if he were sucking a lollipop. "That can't be good for business, can it?"

"Sir?"

"Your mother home?"

"Yes, sir." A tear fell down Dave's cheek and Sean and Jimmy looked away.

"Well, we're going to have a talk with her, tell her what her punk kid's been up to."

"I don't . . . I don't . . ." Dave blubbered.

"Get in." The cop opened up the back door and Sean caught a whiff of apples, a sharp, October scent.

Dave looked at Jimmy.

"Get in," the cop said. "Or you want I should throw the cuffs on you?"

"I—"

"What?" The cop sounded pissed now. He slapped the top of the open door. "Get the fuck inside."

Dave climbed into the backseat, bawling.

The cop pointed a stubby finger at Jimmy and Sean. "Go tell your mothers what you been up to. And don't let me catch you shits fighting on my streets again."

Jimmy and Sean stepped back, and the cop hopped in his car and drove off. They watched it reach the corner and then turn right, Dave's head, darkened by distance and shadows, looking back at them. And then the street was empty again, seemed to have gone mute with the slam of the car door. Jimmy and Sean stood where the car had been, looked at their feet, up and down the street, anywhere but at each other.

Sean got that lurching sensation again, this time accompanied by the taste of dirty pennies in his mouth. His stomach felt as if a spoon had hollowed it out.

Then Jimmy said it:

"You started it."

"He started it."

"You did. Now he's screwed. His mother's soft in the head. No telling what she'll do two cops bring him home."

"I didn't start it."

Jimmy pushed him, and Sean pushed back this time, and then they were on the ground, rolling around, punching each other.

"Hey!"

Sean rolled off Jimmy and they both stood up, expecting to see the two cops again but seeing Mr. Devine instead, coming down the front steps toward them.

"The hell you two doing?"

"Nothing."

"Nothing." Sean's father frowned as he reached the sidewalk. "Get out of the middle of the street."

They reached the sidewalk beside him.

"Weren't there three of you?" Mr. Devine looked up the street. "Where's Dave?"

"What?"

"Dave." Sean's father looked at Sean and Jimmy. "Wasn't Dave with you?"

"We were fighting in the street."

"What?"

"We were fighting in the street and the cops came."

"When was this?"

"Like five minutes ago."

"Okay. So, the cops came."

"And they picked Dave up."

Sean's father looked up and down the street again. "They what? They picked him up?"

"To take him home. I lied. I said I lived here. Dave said he lived in the Flats, and they—"

"What are you talking about? Sean, what'd the cops look like?"

"Huh?"

"Were they wearing uniforms?"

"No. No, they—"

"Then how'd you know they were cops?"

"I didn't. They . . ."

"They what?"

"He had a badge," Jimmy said. "On his belt."

"What kind of badge?"

"Gold?"

"Okay. But what'd it say on it?"

"Say?"

"The words. Were there words you could read?"

"No. I don't know."

"Billy?"

They all looked up at Sean's mother standing on the porch, her face tight and curious.

"Hey, honey? Call the police station, all right? See if any detectives would have picked up a kid for fighting on this street."

"A kid."

"Dave Boyle."

"Oh, Jesus. His mother."

"Let's hold off on that. Okay? Let's just see what the police say. Right?"

Sean's mother went back inside. Sean looked at his father. He didn't seem to know where to put his hands. He put them in his pockets, then he pulled them out, wiped them on his pants. He said, "I'll be damned," very softly, and he looked down to the end of the street as if Dave hovered at the corner, a dancing mirage just beyond Sean's field of vision.

"It was brown," Jimmy said.

"What?"

"The car. It was dark brown. Like a Plymouth, I think."

"Anything else?"

Sean tried to picture it, but he couldn't. He could see it only as something that had blocked his vision, not entered it. It had obscured Mrs. Ryan's orange Pinto and the lower half of her hedges, but Sean couldn't see the car itself.

"It smelled like apples," he said.

"What?"

"Like apples. The car smelled like apples."

"It smelled like apples," his father said.

AN HOUR LATER, in Sean's kitchen, two other cops asked Sean and Jimmy a bunch of questions, and then a third guy showed up and drew sketches of the men in the brown car based on what Jimmy and Sean told them. The big blond cop looked meaner on the sketch pad, his face even bigger, but otherwise it was him. The second guy, the one who'd kept his eyes on the side-view, didn't look much like anything at all, a blur with black hair really, because Sean and Jimmy couldn't remember him too well.

Jimmy's father showed up and stood in the corner of the kitchen looking mad and distracted, his eyes watery, weaving a bit as if the wall kept moving behind him. He didn't speak to Sean's father, and no one spoke to him. With his usual capacity for sudden movement muted, he seemed smaller to Sean, less real somehow, like if Sean looked away he'd look back to find him dissolved into the wallpaper.

After they'd gone over it four or five times, everyone left—the cops, the guy who'd drawn on the pad, Jimmy and his father. Sean's mother went into her bedroom and shut the door, and Sean could hear muffled crying a few minutes later.

He sat out on the porch and his father told him he hadn't done anything wrong, that he and Jimmy were smart not to have gotten in that car. His father patted his knee and said things would turn out fine. Dave will be home tonight. You'll see.

His father shut up then. He sipped his beer and sat with Sean, but Sean could feel he'd drifted away on him, was maybe in the back bedroom with Sean's mother, or down in the cellar building his birdhouses.

Sean looked up the street at the rows of cars, the shiny glint of them. He told himself that this—all of this—was part of some plan that made sense. He just couldn't see it yet. He would someday, though. The adrenaline that had been rushing through his body since Dave had been driven away and he and Jimmy had rolled on the street fighting finally flushed out through his pores like waste.

He saw the place where he, Jimmy, and Dave Boyle had fought by the Bel Air and he waited for the new hollow spaces formed as the adrenaline had left his body to fill back in. He waited for the plan to re-form and make sense. He waited and watched the street and felt its hum and waited some more until his father stood up and they went back inside.

JIMMY WALKED BACK to the Flats behind the old man. The old man weaved slightly and smoked his cigarettes down to pinched ends and talked to himself under his breath. When they got home, his father might give him a beating, might not, it was too close to tell. After he'd lost his job, he'd told Jimmy never to go to the Devines' house again, and Jimmy figured he'd have to pay up for breaking that rule. But maybe not today. His father had that sleepy drunkenness about him, the kind that usually meant he would sit at the kitchen table when they got home and drink until he fell asleep with his head on his arms.

Jimmy kept a few steps behind him, just in case, though, and tossed the ball up into the air, caught it in the baseball glove he'd stolen from Sean's house while the cops had been saying their good-byes to the Devines and nobody had even said a word to Jimmy and his father as they'd headed down the hallway toward the front door. Sean's bedroom door had been open, and Jimmy'd seen the glove lying on the floor, ball wrapped inside, and he'd reached in and picked it up, and then he and his father were through the front door. He had no idea why he'd stolen the glove. It wasn't for the wink of surprised pride he'd seen in the old man's eyes when he'd picked it up. Fuck that. Fuck him.

It had something to do with Sean hitting Dave Boyle and pussying out on stealing the car and some other things over the year they'd been friends, that feeling Jimmy got that whatever Sean gave him—baseball cards, half a candy bar, whatever—came in the form of a handout.

When Jimmy had first picked up the glove and walked away with it, he'd felt elated. He'd felt great. A little later, as they were crossing Buckingham Avenue, he'd felt that familiar shame and embarrassment that came whenever he stole something, an anger at whatever or whoever made him do these things. Then a little later, as they walked down Crescent and into the Flats, he felt a stab of pride as he looked at the shitty three-deckers and then the glove in his hand.

Jimmy took the glove and he felt bad about it. Sean would miss it. Jimmy took the glove and he felt good about it. Sean would miss it.

Jimmy watched his father stumble ahead of him, the old fuck looking like he'd crumple and turn into a puddle of himself any second, and he hated Sean.

He hated Sean and he'd been dumb to think they could have been friends, and he knew he'd hold on to this glove for the rest of his life, take care of it, never show it to anyone, and he'd never, not once, use the goddamn thing. He'd die before that happened.

Jimmy looked at the Flats spread out before him as he and the old man walked under the deep shade of the el tracks and neared the place where Crescent bottomed out and the freight trains rumbled past the old, ratty drive-in and the Penitentiary Channel beyond, and he knew—deep, deep in his chest—that they'd never see Dave Boyle again. Where Jimmy lived, on Rester, they stole things all the time. Jimmy had had his Big Wheel stolen when he was four, his bike when he was eight. The old man had lost a car. And his mother had started hanging clothes inside to dry after so many had been ripped off the line in the backyard. You felt different when something was stolen as opposed to simply misplaced. You felt it in your chest that it was never coming back. That's how he felt about Dave. Maybe Sean, right now, was feeling that way about his baseball glove, standing over the empty space on the floor where it had been, knowing, beyond logic, that it was never, ever, coming back.

Too bad, too, because Jimmy had liked Dave, although he couldn't put his finger on why most times. Just something about the kid, maybe the way he'd always been there, even if half the time you didn't notice him.

2

FOUR DAYS

AS IT TURNED OUT, Jimmy was wrong.

Dave Boyle returned to the neighborhood four days after he'd disappeared. He came back riding in the front seat of a police car. The two cops who brought him home let him play with the siren and touch the butt of the shotgun locked down beneath the dash. They gave him an honorary badge, and when they delivered him to his mother's house on Rester Street, reporters from the papers and TV were there to capture the moment. One of the cops, an Officer Eugene Kubiaki, lifted Dave out of the cruiser and swung Dave's legs high over the pavement before placing him down in front of his weeping, giggling, shaking mother.

There was a crowd out on Rester Street that day—parents, kids, a mailman, the two roly-poly Pork Chop Brothers who owned the sub shop on the corner of Rester and Sydney, and even Miss Powell, Dave and Jimmy's fifth-grade teacher at the Looey & Dooey. Jimmy stood with his mother. His mother held the back of his head to her midsection and kept a damp palm clamped to his forehead, as if she were checking to make sure he hadn't caught whatever Dave had, and Jimmy felt a twinge of jealousy as Officer Kubiaki swung Dave above the sidewalk, the two of them laughing like old friends as pretty Miss Powell clapped her hands.

I almost got in that car, too, Jimmy wanted to tell someone. He wanted to tell Miss Powell more than anyone. She was beautiful and so clean, and when she laughed you could see that one of her upper teeth was slightly crooked, and that made her even more beautiful to Jimmy. Jimmy wanted to tell her he'd almost gotten in that car and see if her face would fill with the look she was giving Dave now. He wanted to tell her that he thought about her all the time, and in his thoughts he was older and could drive a car and take her to places where she smiled at him a lot and they ate a picnic lunch and everything he said made her laugh and expose that tooth and touch his face with her palm.

Miss Powell was uncomfortable here, though. Jimmy could tell. After she'd said a few words to Dave and touched his face and kissed his cheek—she kissed him *twice*—other people moved in, and Miss Powell stepped aside and stood on the cracked sidewalk looking up at the leaning three-deckers and their tar paper curling up to expose the wood underneath, and she seemed younger and yet harder to Jimmy at the same time, as if there was something suddenly nunnish about her, touching her hair to feel for her habit, button nose twitching and ready to judge.

Jimmy wanted to go to her, but his mother was still holding him tight, ignoring his squirms, and then Miss Powell walked to the corner of Rester and Sydney and Jimmy watched her wave desperately to someone. A hippie-looking guy pulled up in a hippie-looking yellow convertible with faded purple flower petals painted on the sunbaked doors, and Miss Powell climbed in the car and they drove off, Jimmy thinking, No.

He finally wrenched free of his mother's hold. He stood in the middle of the street, watching the crowd surround Dave, and he wished he'd gotten in that car, if only so he could feel some of the adoration Dave was feeling, see all those eyes looking at him like he was something special.

It turned into a big party on Rester Street, everyone running from camera to camera, hoping they'd get on TV or see themselves in the morning papers—Yeah, I know Dave, he's my best friend, grew up with him, you know, great kid, thank the good Lord he's okay.

Someone opened a hydrant and the water jetted out onto Rester like a sigh of relief, and kids tossed their shoes to the gutter and rolled up their pants and danced in the gushing water. The ice cream truck rolled in, and Dave got to pick whatever he wanted, on the house, and even Mr. Pakinaw, a nasty old widower who fired a BB rifle at squirrels (and kids, too, sometimes, if their parents weren't looking) and screamed all the time for people to just be fucking quiet, will ya—he opened up his windows and put his speakers up against the screens and next thing you know, Dean Martin was singing "Memories Are Made of This" and "Volare" and a lot of other shit Jimmy would normally puke if he heard, but today, it fit. Today the music floated down Rester like bright streams of crepe paper. It mixed with the loud gush of water from the hydrant. Some of the guys who ran the card game in the back of the Pork Chop Brothers' store brought out a folding table and a small grill, and pretty soon someone else carted out some coolers filled with Schlitz and Narragansett, and the air turned fat with the smell of grilled hot dogs and Italian sausage, the wafting, smoky, charred smell and the whiff of open beer cans making Jimmy think of Fenway Park and summer Sundays and that tight joy you got in your chest when the adults kicked back and acted more like kids, everyone laughing, everyone looking younger and lighter and happy to be around each other.

This was what Jimmy, even in the pit of his blackest hates after a beating from the old man or the theft of something he'd cared about—*this* was what he loved about growing up here. It was the way people could suddenly throw off a year of aches and complaints and split lips and job worries and old grudges and just let loose, like nothing bad had ever happened in their lives. On St. Pat's or Buckingham Day, sometimes on the Fourth of July, or when the Sox were playing well in September, or, like now, when something collectively lost had been found—especially then—this neighborhood could erupt into a kind of furious delirium.

Not like up in the Point. In the Point they had block parties, sure, but they were always planned, the necessary permits obtained, everyone making sure everyone else was careful around the cars, careful on the lawns—Watch it, I just painted that fence.

In the Flats, half the people didn't have lawns, and the fences sagged, so what the fuck. When you wanted to party, you partied, because, shit, you sure as hell deserved it. No bosses here today. No welfare investigators or loan shark muscle. And as for the cops—well, there were the cops now, partying along with everyone else, Officer Kubiaki helping himself to a hot-'n'-spicy sausage spuckie off the grill, and his partner pocketing a beer for later. The reporters had all gone home and the sun was starting to set, giving the street that time-for-dinner glow, but none of the women were cooking, and no one was going inside.

Except for Dave. Dave was gone, Jimmy realized when he stepped out of the hydrant spray and squeezed out his pant cuffs and put his T-shirt back on as he waited in line for a hot dog. Dave's party was in full swing, but Dave must have gone back in his house, his mother, too, and when Jimmy looked at their second-story windows, the shades were drawn and lonely.

Those drawn shades made him think of Miss Powell for some reason, of her climbing in that hippie-looking car, and it made him feel grimy and sad to remember watching her curve her right calf and ankle into the car before she'd closed the door. Where was she going? Was she driving on the highway right now, the wind streaming through her hair like the music streamed down Rester Street? Was the night closing in on them in that hippie car as they drove off to . . . where? Jimmy wanted to know, but then he didn't want to know. He'd see her in school tomorrow—unless they gave everyone a day off from school, too, to celebrate Dave's return—and he'd want to ask her, but he wouldn't.

Jimmy took his hot dog and sat down on the curb across from Dave's house to eat it. When he was about halfway through the dog, one of the shades rolled up and he saw Dave standing in the window, staring down at him. Jimmy held up his half-eaten hot dog in recognition, but Dave didn't acknowledge him, even when he tried a second time. Dave just stared. He stared at Jimmy, and even though Jimmy couldn't see his eyes, he could sense blankness in them. Blankness, and blame.

Jimmy's mother sat down beside him on the curb, and Dave stepped away from the window. Jimmy's mother was a small, thin woman with the palest hair. For someone so thin, she moved as if she carried stacks of brick on each shoulder, and she sighed a lot and in such a way that Jimmy wasn't positive she knew the sound was coming out of her. He would look at pictures of her that had been taken before she'd become pregnant with him, and she looked a lot less thin and so much younger, like a teenage girl (which, when he did the math, was exactly what she'd been). Her face was rounder in the pictures, with no lines by the eyes or on the forehead, and she had this beautiful, full smile that seemed just slightly frightened, or maybe curious, Jimmy could never tell for sure. His father had told him a thousand times that Jimmy had almost killed her coming out, that she'd bled and bled until the doctors were worried she might never stop bleeding. It had wiped her out, his father had said. And, of course, there would be no more babies. No one wanted to go through that again.

She put her hand on Jimmy's knee and said, "How you doing, G.I. Joe?" His mother was always calling him by different nicknames, often made up on the spot, Jimmy half the time not knowing who the name referred to.

He shrugged. "You know."

"You didn't say anything to Dave."

"You wouldn't let me move, Ma."

His mother lifted her hand back off his knee and hugged herself in the chill that was deepening with the dark. "I meant after. When he was still outside."

"I'll see him tomorrow in school."

Her mother fished in the pocket of her jeans for her Kents and lit one, blew the smoke out in a rush. "I don't think he'll be going in tomorrow."

Jimmy finished his hot dog. "Well, soon, then. Right?"

His mother nodded and blew some more smoke out of her mouth. She cupped her elbow in her hand and smoked and looked up at Dave's windows. "How was school today?" she said, though she didn't seem real interested in an answer.

Jimmy shrugged. "Okay."

"I met that teacher of yours. She's cute."

Jimmy didn't say anything.

"Real cute," his mother repeated into a gray ribbon of exhaled smoke.

Jimmy still didn't say anything. Most of the time he didn't know what to say to his parents. His mother was worn out so much. She stared off at places Jimmy couldn't see and smoked her cigarettes, and half the time didn't hear him until he'd repeated himself a couple times. His father was pissed off usually, and even when he wasn't and could be kind of fun, Jimmy would know that he could turn into a pissed-off drunk guy any second, give Jimmy a whack for saying something he might have laughed at half an hour before. And he knew that no matter how hard he tried to pretend otherwise, he had both his father and mother inside of him—his mother's long silences and his father's sudden fits of rage.

When Jimmy wasn't wondering what it would be like to be Miss Powell's boyfriend, he sometimes wondered what it would be like to be her son.

His mother was looking at him now, her cigarette held up by her ear, her eyes small and searching.

"What?" he said, and gave her an embarrassed smile.

"You got a great smile, Cassius Clay." She smiled back at him.

"Yeah?"

"Oh, yeah. You're gonna be a heartbreaker."

"Uh, okay," Jimmy said, and they both laughed.

"You could talk a little more," his mother said.

You could, too, Jimmy wanted to say.

"That's okay, though. Women like the silent type."

Over his mother's shoulder, Jimmy saw his father stumble out of the house, his clothes wrinkled and his face puffy with sleep or booze or both. His father looked at the party going on in front of him like he couldn't imagine where it had come from.

His mother followed Jimmy's gaze and when she looked back at him, she was worn out again, the smile gone so completely from her face, you'd have been surprised she knew how to make one. "Hey, Jim."

He loved it when she called him "Jim." It made him feel like they were in on something together.

"Yeah?"

"I'm real glad you didn't get in that car, baby." She kissed his forehead and Jimmy could see her eyes glistening, and then she stood up and walked over to some of the other mothers, kept her back to her husband.

Jimmy looked up and saw Dave in the window staring down at him again, a soft yellow light on somewhere in the room behind him now. This time, Jimmy didn't even try to wave back. With the police and reporters all gone now, and the party so deep in swing no one probably remembered what had started it, Jimmy could feel Dave in that apartment, alone except for his crazy mother, surrounded by brown walls and weak yellow lights as the party throbbed on the street below.

And he was glad, too, once again, that he hadn't gotten in that car.

Damaged goods. That's what Jimmy's father had said to his mother last night: "Even if they find him alive, the kid's damaged goods. Never be the same."

Dave raised a single hand. He held it up by his shoulder and didn't move it for a long time, and as Jimmy waved back, he felt a sadness weed its way into him and go deep and then spread out in small waves. He didn't know whether the sadness had something to do with his father, his mother, Miss Powell, this place, or Dave holding that hand so steady as he stood in the window, but whatever caused it—one of those things or all of them—it would never, he was sure, come back out again. Jimmy, sitting on the curb, was eleven years old, but he didn't feel it anymore. He felt old. Old as his parents, old as this street.

Damaged goods, Jimmy thought, and let his hand drop back to his lap. He watched Dave nod at him and then pull down the shade to go back inside that too-quiet apartment with its brown walls and ticking clocks, and Jimmy felt the sadness take root in him, nestle up against his insides as if finding a warm home, and he didn't even try to wish it back out again, because some part of him understood that there was no point.

He got up off the curb, not sure for a second what he meant to do. He felt that itchy, antsy need to either hit something or do something new and nutty. But then his stomach growled, and he realized he was still hungry, so he headed back for another hot dog, hoping they still had some left.

FOR A FEW DAYS, Dave Boyle became a minor celebrity, and not just in the neighborhood, but throughout the state. The headline the next morning in the *Record American* read LITTLE BOY LOST/LITTLE BOY FOUND. The photograph above the fold showed Dave sitting on his stoop, his mother's thin arms draped across his chest, a bunch of smiling kids from the Flats mugging for the camera on either side of Dave and his mother, everyone looking just happy as can be, except for Dave's mother, who looked like she'd just missed her bus on a cold day.

The same kids who'd been with him on the front page started calling him "freak boy" within a week at school. Dave would look in their faces and see a spite he wasn't sure they understood any better than he did. Dave's mother said they probably got it from their parents and don't you pay them any mind, Davey, they'll get bored and forget all about it and be your friends next year.

Dave would nod and wonder if there was something about him—some mark on his face that he couldn't see—which made everyone want to hurt him. Like those guys in the car. Why had they picked him? How had they known he'd climb in that car, and that Jimmy and Sean wouldn't? Looking back, that's how it seemed to Dave. Those men (and he knew their names, or at least the names they'd called each other, but he couldn't bring himself to use them) had *known* Sean and Jimmy wouldn't have gotten into that car without a fight. Sean would have run for his house, screaming, probably, and Jimmy—they'd have had to knock Jimmy cold to get him inside. The Big Wolf had even said it a few hours into their drive: "You see that kid in the white T-shirt? Way he looked at me, no real fear, no nothing? Kid's gonna fuck someone up someday, not lose a night of sleep over it."

His partner, the Greasy Wolf, had smiled. "I like a little fight."

Big Wolf shook his head. "He'd bite your thumb off just pulling him into the car. Clean off, the little fucker."

It helped to give them dopey names: Big Wolf and Greasy Wolf. It helped Dave to see them as creatures, wolves hidden under costumes of human skin, and Dave himself as a character in a story: the Boy Taken by Wolves. The Boy Who Escaped and made his way through the damp woods to an Esso station. The Boy Who'd Remained Calm and Crafty, always looking for a way out.

In school, though, he was just the Boy Who Got Stolen, and everyone let their imaginations run as to what had happened during those four lost days. In the bathroom one morning, a seventh-grader named Junior McCaffery sidled up to the urinal beside Dave and said, "Did they make you suck it?" and all his seventh-grader friends had started laughing and making kissing noises.

Dave zipped his fly with trembling fingers, his face red, and turned to face Junior McCaffery. He tried to put a mean look in his eyes, and Junior frowned and slapped him across the face.

You could hear the sound of it echo in the bathroom. One seventh-grader gasped like a girl.

Junior said, "You got something to say, queer? Huh? You want me to hit you again, faggot?"

"He's crying," someone said.

"He *is,*" Junior McCaffery shrieked, and Dave's tears fell harder. He felt the numbness in his face turn into a sting, but it wasn't the pain that bothered him. Pain had never bothered him all that much, and he'd never cried from it, not even when he'd crashed his bike and sliced his ankle open on the pedal as he fell, and that had taken seven stitches to close. It was the range of emotions he could feel pouring from the boys in the bathroom that cut into him. Hate, disgust, anger, contempt. All directed at him. He didn't understand why. He'd never bothered anyone his whole life. Yet they hated him. And the hate made him feel orphaned. It made him feel putrid and guilty and tiny, and he wept because he didn't want to feel that way.

They all laughed at his tears. Junior danced around for a moment, his face twisted up in rubbery contortions as he aped Dave's blubbering. When Dave finally got it under control, reduced it to a few sniffles, Junior slapped him again, the same place, just as hard.

"Look at me," Junior said as Dave felt a fresh burst of tears explode from his eye sockets. "Look at me."

Dave looked up at Junior, hoping to see compassion or humanity or even pity—he'd take pity—in his face, but all he saw was an angry, laughing glare.

"Yeah," Junior said, "you sucked it."

He feinted another slap at Dave and Dave dropped his head and cringed, but Junior was walking away with his friends, all of them laughing as they left the bathroom.

Dave remembered something Mr. Peters, a friend of his mother's who slept over occasionally, once said to him: "Two things you never take from a man—his spit or his slap. They're both worse than a punch, and a man does that to you, you try to kill him if you can."

Dave sat down on the bathroom floor and wished he had that in himself—the will to kill someone. He'd start with Junior McCaffery, he supposed, and move on to Big Wolf and Greasy Wolf, if he ever ran into them again. But, truth was, he just didn't think he could. He didn't know why people were mean to other people. He didn't understand. He didn't understand.

After the bathroom incident, word seemed to come down from on high or something and spread through the school, so that everyone from the third grade on up had heard about what Junior McCaffery did to Dave and how Dave had responded. A judgment was arrived at, and Dave found that even the few classmates who'd been his sort-of friends after he'd first returned to school started treating him like a leper.

Not all of them muttered "Homo" when he passed in the hall or used their tongues to push against the insides of their cheeks. In fact, a good number of Dave's fellow students just ignored him. But in a way, that was worse. He felt marooned by the silence.

If they ran into each other as they left their houses, Jimmy Marcus would sometimes walk silently alongside him to school because it would have been awkward *not* to, and he'd say, "Hey," when he passed him in the hall or bumped into him on the line heading into class. Dave could see some odd mix of pity and embarrassment in Jimmy's face those times their eyes met, as if Jimmy wanted to say something but couldn't put it into words—Jimmy, at the best of times, never having been much of a talker unless he was suddenly itching with some insane idea to jump down on train tracks or steal a car. But it felt to Dave as if their friendship (and Dave wasn't sure, in truth, that they'd ever *really* been friends; he remembered with a small shame all those times he'd had to press his companionship on Jimmy) had died when Dave climbed in that car and Jimmy had stayed planted on the street.

Jimmy, as it turned out, wouldn't be in school with Dave much longer, so even those walks together could eventually be avoided. At school, Jimmy had always hung out with Val Savage, a small, chimp-brained psycho who'd been kept back twice and could turn into this spinning, whirling dust storm of violence that scared the shit out of just about everyone, teachers and students alike. The joke about Val (though never spoken if he was around) was that his parents didn't save for his college fund, they saved for his bail fund. Even before Dave had gotten in that car, Jimmy had always hung with Val once they reached school. Sometimes he'd allow Dave to tag along with them as they raided the cafeteria kitchen for snacks or found a new roof to climb, but after the car Dave was even shut out of that. When he wasn't hating him for his sudden exile, Dave noticed that the dark cloud that sometimes seemed to hover over Jimmy had become a permanent thing, like a reverse halo. Jimmy just seemed older lately, sadder.

He'd finally steal a car, though. It was almost a year after their first attempt on Sean's street, and it got Jimmy expelled from the Looey & Dooey and bused halfway across the city to the Carver School so he could find out what life was like for a white kid from East Bucky in a mostly black school. Val would get bused along with him, though, and Dave heard that the two of them soon became the terror of the Carver, two white kids so crazy they didn't know how to be scared.

The car was a convertible. Dave heard rumors that it belonged to a friend of one of the teachers, though he never found out which one. Jimmy and Val stole it off the school lot while the teachers and their spouses and friends were having a year-end party in the faculty lounge after school. Jimmy was driving, and he and Val took it for a hell of a spin around Buckingham, beeping the horn and waving to girls, and gunning the engine until a police cruiser spotted them and they ended up totaling the car against a Dumpster behind the Zayres in Rome Basin. Val twisted an ankle getting out of the car, and Jimmy, already halfway up a fence that led to a vacant lot, came back to help him, Dave always seeing it in his mind as part war movie—the valiant soldier going back to rescue his fallen buddy, bullets flying all around them (though Dave doubted the cops had been shooting, it made it seem cooler). The cops got both of them right there, and they spent a night in Juvie. They were allowed to finish sixth grade, since there were only a few days left in the year, and then their families were told they had to look elsewhere for the boys' schooling.

Dave hardly saw Jimmy after that, maybe once or twice a year until they reached their teens. Dave's mother wouldn't let him leave the house anymore, except to go back and forth from school. She was convinced those men were still out there, waiting, driving that car that smelled of apples, and homing in on Dave like heat-seeking missiles.

Dave knew they weren't. They were wolves, after all, and wolves sniffed the night for the nearest, lamest prey, and then they hunted it down. They visited his mind more often now, though, the Big Wolf and the Greasy Wolf, along with visions of what they'd done to him. The visions rarely attacked Dave's dreams, but they slipped up on him in the terrible quiet of his mother's apartment, in the long stretches of silence during which he'd try to read comic books or watch TV or stare out the window at Rester Street. They came, and Dave would try to shut them out by closing his eyes, and trying not to remember that Big Wolf's name had been Henry and Greasy Wolf's name had been George.

Henry and George, a voice would scream along with the rushing of visions in Dave's head. Henry and George, Henry and George, Henry and George, you little shit.

And Dave would tell the voice in his head that he was not a little shit. He was the Boy Who'd Escaped the Wolves. And sometimes to keep the visions at bay, he'd replay his escape in his head, detail by detail—the crack he'd noticed by the hinge in the bulkhead door, the sound of their car pulling away as they went out for a round of drinks, the screw with the missing head he'd used to pry the crack open wider and wider until the rusty hinge snapped and a chunk of wood in the shape of a knife blade cracked away with it. He'd come out of the bulkhead, this Boy Who Was Smart, and he'd scrambled straight off into the woods and followed the late afternoon sun to the Esso station a mile away. It was a shock to see it—that round blue-and-white sign already lit for the night, even though there was still some daylight left. It stabbed something in Dave, the neon white. It made him drop to his knees at the place where the woods ended and the ancient gray tarmac began. That's how Ron Pierrot, the owner of the station, found him: on his knees and staring up at the sign. Ron Pierrot was a thin man with hands that looked like they could snap a lead pipe, and Dave often wondered what would have happened if the Boy Who Escaped the Wolves had actually been a character in a movie. Why, he and Ron would have bonded and Ron would have taught him all the things fathers teach their sons, and they would have saddled up their horses and loaded up their rifles and gone off on endless adventures. They would have had a great old time, Ron and the Boy. They would have been heroes, out in the wild, conquering all those wolves.

———

IN SEAN'S DREAM, the street moved. He looked into the open doorway of the car that smelled like apples, and the street gripped his feet and slid him toward it. Dave was inside, scrunched up on the far side of the seat against the door, his mouth open in a silent howl, as the street carried Sean toward the car. All he could see in the dream was that open door and the backseat. He couldn't see the guy who'd looked like a cop. He couldn't see his companion who'd sat in the front passenger seat. He couldn't see Jimmy, though Jimmy had been right beside him the whole time. He could just see that seat and Dave and the door and the trash on the floor. That, he realized, had been the alarm bell he hadn't even realized he'd heard—there had been trash on the floor. Fast-food wrappers and crinkled-up bags of chips and beer and soda cans, Styrofoam coffee cups and a dirty green T-shirt. Only after he'd woken up and considered the dream did he realize that the floor of the backseat in his dream had been identical to the floor of the car in real life, and that he hadn't remembered the trash until now. Even when the cops had been in his house and asked him to think—really think—about any detail he might have forgotten to tell them, it hadn't occurred to him that the back of the car had been dirty, because he hadn't remembered it. But in his dream, it had come back to him, and that—more than anything—had been why he'd realized, without realizing it, somehow, that something was wrong about the "cop," his "partner," and their car. Sean had never seen the backseat of a cop car in real life, not up close, but a part of him knew that it wouldn't be filled with trash. Maybe underneath all the trash had lain half-eaten apple cores, and that's why the car smelled as it had.

His father would come into his bedroom a year after Dave's abduction to tell him two things.

The first was that Sean had been accepted to Latin School, and would begin seventh grade there in September. His father said he and Sean's mother were real proud. Latin was where you went if you wanted to make something out of yourself.

The second thing he said to Sean, almost as an afterthought, when he was halfway out the door:

"They caught one of them, Sean."

"What?"

"One of the guys who took Dave. They caught him. He's dead. Suicide in his cell."

"Yeah?"

His father looked back at him. "Yeah. You can stop having nightmares now."

But Sean said, "What about the other one?"

"The guy who got caught," his father said, "he told the police the other one was dead, too. Died in a car accident last year. Okay?" His father looked at him in such a way that Sean knew this was the last discussion they'd have on the subject. "So wash up for dinner, pal."

His father left and Sean sat on his bed, the mattress lumpy where he'd placed his new baseball glove, a ball wrapped inside, thick red rubber bands wrapped tightly around the leather.

The other one had died, too. In a car wreck. Sean hoped he'd been driving the car that had smelled of apples, and that he'd driven it off a cliff, took that car straight down to hell with him.

II

SAD-EYED

SINATRAS

(2000)

3

TEARS
IN HER HAIR

BRENDAN HARRIS LOVED Katie Marcus like crazy, loved her like movie love, with an orchestra booming through his blood and flooding his ears. He loved her waking up, going to bed, loved her all day and every second in between. Brendan Harris would love Katie Marcus fat and ugly. He'd love her with bad skin and no breasts and thick fuzz on her upper lip. He'd love her toothless. He'd love her bald.

Katie. The trill of her name sliding through his brain was enough to make Brendan feel like his limbs were filled with nitrous oxide, like he could walk on water and bench-press an eighteen-wheeler, toss it across the street when he was finished with it.

Brendan Harris loved everyone now because he loved Katie and Katie loved him. Brendan loved traffic and smog and the sound of jackhammers. He loved his worthless old man who hadn't sent him a single birthday or Christmas card since he'd walked out on Brendan and his mother when Brendan was six. He loved Monday mornings, sitcoms that couldn't make a retard laugh, and standing in line at the RMV. He even loved his job, though he wouldn't be going in ever again.

Brendan was leaving this house tomorrow morning, leaving his mother, walking out that shabby door and down those cracked steps, up the great wide street with cars double-parked all over the place and everyone sitting on the stoops, walking out like he was in a goddamned Springsteen song, and not the Nebraska-Ghost-of-Tom-Joad Spring-steen, but the Born-to-Run-Two-Hearts-Are-Better-Than-One-Rosalita-(Won't-You-Come-Out-Tonight) Bruce, the *anthem* Bruce. Yeah, an anthem; that's what he'd be as he walked right down the middle of the asphalt whether bumpers rode the backs of his legs and horns honked, going right up that street and into the heart of Buckingham to take his Katie's hand, and then they were leaving it all behind for good, hopping on that plane and going to Vegas and tying the knot, fingers entwined, Elvis reading from the Bible, asking if he took this woman, and Katie say-ing she took this man and then—then, forget about it, they were married and they were gone and they were never coming back, no way, just him and Katie and the rest of their lives lying open and clean before them like a lifeline scrubbed of the past, scrubbed of the world.

He looked around his bedroom. Clothes packed. American Express traveler's checks packed. High-tops packed. Pictures of him and Katie packed. Portable CD player, CDs, toiletries packed.

He looked at what he was leaving behind. Poster of Bird and Parrish. Poster of Fisk waving that home run fair in '75. Poster of Sharon Stone, sheathed in white (rolled up and under his bed since the first night he'd snuck Katie in here, but still . . .). Half his CDs. Fuck it; he hadn't listened to most of them but twice. MC Hammer for Christ's sake. Billy Ray Cyrus. My Gawd. A pair of kick-ass Sony speakers to supplement a Jensen desk-top system, two hundred watts total, paid for last summer when he'd done some roofing for Bobby O'Donnell's crew.

Which is how he'd first come close enough to Katie to strike up a conversation. Jesus. Just a year ago. Sometimes it felt like a decade, in a good way, and other times it felt like a *minute*. Katie Marcus. He'd known *of* her, of course; everyone in the neighborhood knew of Katie. She was that beautiful. But few people really knew her. Beauty could do that; it scared you off, made you keep your distance. It wasn't like in the movies where the camera made beauty seem like something that invited you in. In the real world, beauty was like a fence to keep you out, back you off.

But Katie, man, from that first day she'd come by with Bobby O'Donnell, and then he'd left her at the site while he and a few of his boys tore off across town to conduct some pressing business, left Katie behind like they'd forgot they ever had her—from that very first day, she was so basic and *normal;* she hung with Brendan as he applied flashing to the roof as if she was just another dude. She knew *his* name, and she said, "How come a guy as nice as you, Brendan, is working for Bobby O'Donnell?" Brendan. The word coming out of her mouth like she said it every day, Brendan up there with his knees on the edge of the roof feeling like he was going to swoon right off it. Swoon. No shit. That's what she did to him.

And tomorrow, soon as she called, they were gone. Gone together. Gone forever.

Brendan lay back on his bed and pictured the moon of her face floating above him. He knew he'd never sleep. He was too keyed up. But he didn't mind. He lay there, Katie floating and smiling, her eyes shining in the darkness behind his eyes.

AFTER WORK THAT NIGHT Jimmy Marcus had a beer with his brother-in-law, Kevin Savage, at the Warren Tap, the two of them sitting at the window and watching some kids play street hockey. There were six kids, and they were fighting the dark, their faces gone featureless with it. The Warren Tap was tucked away on a side street in the old stockyard district, and this made it great for hockey because there wasn't much traffic but shit for night games because none of the streetlights had worked in a decade.

Kevin was good company because he didn't talk much in general and neither did Jimmy, so they sat and sipped their beers and listened to the scuffle and scrape of rubber soles and wooden stick blades, the sudden metallic clang of the hard rubber ball banging off a hubcap.

At thirty-six, Jimmy Marcus had come to love the quiet of his Saturday nights. He had no use for loud, packed bars and drunken confessions. Thirteen years since he'd walked out of prison, and he owned a corner store, had a wife and three daughters at home, and believed he'd traded the wired-up boy he'd been for a man who appreciated an even pace to his life—a slowly sipped beer, a morning stroll, the sound of a baseball game on the radio.

He looked out onto the street. Four of the kids had given up and gone home, but two remained in the street, shrouded by the dark, scrabbling over that ball. Jimmy could barely make them out, but he could feel the fury of their energy in the slap of their sticks, the mad scramble of their feet.

It had to go somewhere, all that youthful uncoiling. When Jimmy was a kid—hell, until he was almost twenty-three—that energy had dictated his every action. And then . . . then you just learned how to stow it someplace, he guessed. You tucked it away.

His eldest daughter, Katie, was in the midst of that process now. Nineteen years old and so, so beautiful, all her hormones on red alert, surging. But lately he'd noticed an air of grace settling in his daughter. He wasn't sure where it had come from—some girls grew into womanhood gracefully, others remained girls their whole lives—but it was there in Katie all of a sudden, a peacefulness, a serenity even.

At the store this afternoon, as she was leaving, she'd kissed Jimmy's cheek and said, "Later, Daddy," and five minutes afterward Jimmy realized he could still feel her voice in his chest. It was her mother's voice, he realized, slightly lower and more confident than the voice he remembered his daughter having, and Jimmy found himself wondering when it had made its home in his daughter's vocal cords and why he hadn't noticed it until now.

Her mother's voice. Her mother, almost fourteen years dead now, and coming back to Jimmy through their daughter. Saying: She's a woman now, Jim. She's all grown up.

A woman. Wow. How'd that happen?

DAVE BOYLE hadn't even planned on going out that night.

Saturday night, sure, after a long week of work, but he'd reached an age where Saturday didn't feel much different than Tuesday, and drinking at a bar didn't seem all that much more enjoyable than drinking at home. Home, at least, you controlled the remote.

So he'd tell himself later, after it was all over and done, that Fate had played a hand. Fate had played a hand in Dave Boyle's life before—or at least luck, most of it bad—but it had never felt like a *guiding* hand before, more like a pissy, moody one. Fate sitting up in the clouds somewhere, someone saying to him, Bored today, Fate? Fate going, A bit. Kinda think I'll fuck with Dave Boyle, though, cheer myself right up. What're you gonna do?

So Dave knew Fate when he saw it.

Maybe that Saturday night, Fate was having a birthday or something, decided to finally give ol' Dave a break, let him release some steam without suffering the consequences, Fate saying, Take a swing at the world, Davey. I promise it won't swing back this time. As if Lucy, holding the football for Charlie Brown and just this once not being a bitch about it, allowed him to kick it clean. Because it hadn't been planned. It hadn't. Dave, alone late at night in the days afterward, would hold out his hands as if speaking to a jury and say that softly to the empty kitchen: You have to understand. It wasn't planned.

That night, he'd just come down the stairs after kissing his son, Michael, good night and was heading to the fridge for a beer when his wife, Celeste, reminded him that it was Girls' Night.

"Again?" Dave opened the fridge.

"It's been four weeks," Celeste said in that playful singsong of hers that gnawed at the ridges of Dave Boyle's spine sometimes.

"No kidding." Dave leaned against the dishwasher and cracked his beer. "What's tonight's selection?"

"Stepmom," Celeste said, eyes bright, hands clasped together.

Once a month, Celeste and three of her coworkers at Ozma's Hair Design got together at Dave and Celeste Boyle's apartment to read one another's tarot cards, drink a lot of wine, and cook something they'd never tried before. They capped off the evening by watching some chick movie that was usually about some driven but lonely career woman who found true love and big dick with some baggy-balled old cowhand, or else it was about two chicks who discovered the meaning of womanhood and the true depths of their friendship just before one of them caught some long-ass illness in the third act, died all beautiful and perfectly coifed on a bed the size of Peru.

Dave had three options on Girls' Night: he could sit in Michael's room and watch his son sleep, hide out in the back bedroom he shared with Celeste and thumb through the cable choices, or tip the hell on out the door and find someplace where he wouldn't have to listen to four women getting all sniffly because Baggy Balls decided he couldn't be tied down and rode back into the hills in pursuit of the simple life.

Dave usually chose Door #3.

And tonight was no different. He finished his beer and kissed Celeste, a small, milky curdle rippling through his stomach as she grabbed his ass and kissed him back hard, and then he walked out the door and down the stairs past Mr. McAllister's apartment and out through the front door into Saturday night in the Flats. He thought about walking down to Bucky's or over to the Tap, stood in front of the house for a few minutes debating, but then decided to drive instead. Maybe go up to the Point, take a gander at the college girls and yuppies who'd been flocking there in droves lately—so many elbowing into the Point, in fact, that a few had even begun to trickle down into the Flats.

They snapped up the brick three-deckers that suddenly weren't three-deckers anymore but Queen Annes. They encased them in scaffolding and gutted them, workers going in day and night until three months later, the L.L. Beans parked their Volvos out front, carried their Pottery Barn boxes inside. Jazz would creep out softly through their window screens, and they'd buy shit like port from Eagle Liquors, walk their little rat-dogs around the block, and have their tiny lawns sculpted. It was only those brick three-deckers so far, the ones up by Galvin and Twoomey Avenue, but if the Point was any kind of indicator, soon you'd see Saabs and gourmet grocery store bags by the dozen as far down as the Pen Channel at the base of the Flats.

Just last week, Mr. McAllister, Dave's landlord, had told Dave (idly, casually), "Housing values are going up. I mean, way, way up."

"So you sit on it," Dave said, looking back at the house where he'd had his apartment going on ten years, "and somewhere down the road you—"

"Somewhere down the road?" McAllister looked at him. "Dave, I could drown on the property taxes. I'm fixed income, for Christ's sake. I don't sell soon? Two, maybe three years, fucking IRS'll take it from me."

"Where would you go?" Dave thinking, Where would I go?

McAllister shrugged. "I dunno. Weymouth maybe. Got some friends in Leominster."

Saying it like he'd already made some calls, dropped in on a few open houses.

As Dave's Accord rolled into the Point, he tried to remember if he knew anyone his age or younger who lived up here anymore. He idled at a red light, saw two yups in matching cranberry crewnecks and khaki cargo shorts sitting on the pavement outside what used to be Primo's Pizza. It was called Café Society now, and the two yups, sexless and strong, spooned ice cream or frozen yogurt into their mouths, tanned legs stretched across the sidewalk and crossed at the ankles, gleaming mountain bikes leaning against the storefront window under a shiny wash of white neon.

Dave wondered where the hell he was going to live if the frontier mentality rolled the frontier right over him. On what he and Celeste made together, if the bars and pizza shops kept turning into cafés, they'd be lucky to qualify for a two-bedroom in the Parker Hill Projects. Get put on an eighteen-month waiting list so they could move into a place where stairwells smelled like piss, and rat corpses rotted their stench straight through moldy walls, and junkies and switchblade artists roamed the halls, waiting for your white ass to fall asleep.

Ever since a Parker Hill homey had tried to jack his car while he was in it with Michael, Dave kept a .22 under the seat. He'd never fired it, not even at a range, but he held it a lot, sighted down the barrel. He allowed himself the indulgence of wondering what those two matching yups would look like at the other end of the barrel, and he smiled.

But the light had turned green, and he was still stopped, and the horns erupted behind him, and the yuppies looked up and stared at his dented car to see what all the commotion was about in their new neighborhood.

Dave rolled through the intersection, suffocating on their sudden stares, their sudden, unreasonable stares.

THAT NIGHT Katie Marcus went out with her two best friends, Diane Cestra and Eve Pigeon, to celebrate Katie's last night in the Flats, last night, probably, in Buckingham. Celebrate like gypsies had just sprinkled them with gold dust, told them all their dreams would come true. Like they shared a winning scratch ticket and had all gotten negative pregnancy test results on the same day.

They slapped their packs of menthols down on a table in the back of Spires Pub and threw back kamikaze shots and Mich Lights and shrieked every time a good-looking guy shot one of them The Look. They'd eaten a killer meal at the East Coast Grill an hour before, then drove back into Buckingham and sparked up a joint in the parking lot before walking into the bar. Everything—old stories they'd heard each other tell a hundred times, Diane's recounting of the latest beating from her asshole boyfriend, Eve's sudden lipstick smear, two chubby guys waddling around the pool table—was hilarious.

Once the place got so jammed folks were standing three deep at the bar and it started taking twenty minutes to get a drink, they moved on toward Curley's Folly in the Point, smoking another joint in the car, Katie feeling the jagged shards of paranoia scrape the edges of her skull.

"That car's following us."

Eve looked at the lights in the rearview. "It ain't."

"It's been behind us since we left the bar."

"Friggin' Katie, man, that was, like, thirty seconds ago."

"Oh."

"Oh," Diane mimicked, then hiccuped a laugh, passed the joint back to Katie.

Eve deepened her voice. "It's quiet."

Katie saw where this was going. "Shut up."

"Too quiet," Diane agreed, and burst out laughing.

"Bitches," Katie said, trying for an edge of annoyance but catching the crest of a giggle-fit wave instead. She fell onto the backseat, losing it, the back of her head landing between the armrest and the seat, cheeks getting that pins-and-needles sensation they always got those rare times she smoked pot. The giggles subsided and she felt herself go all dreamy as she fixated on the pale dome light, thinking this was it, this was what you lived for, to giggle like a fool with your giggling-fool best friends on the night before you'd marry the man you loved. (In Vegas, okay. With a hangover, okay.) Still, this was the point. This was the dream.

FOUR BARS, three shots, and a couple of phone numbers on napkins later, Katie and Diane were so trashed they hopped up on the bar at McGills and danced to "Brown Eyed Girl" even though the jukebox was silent. Eve sang, "Slipping and a sliding," and Katie and Diane slipped and slid all along the waterfall with you, getting their hips into it, shaking their hair until it covered their faces. At McGills, the guys had thought it was a riot, but twenty minutes later at the Brown, they couldn't even get through the door.

Diane and Katie had Eve propped up between them at this point, and she was still singing (Gloria Gaynor's "I Will Survive" by this time), which was half the problem, and swaying like a metronome, which was the other half.

So they got the boot even before they could enter the Brown, which meant the only option left in terms of serving three legless East Bucky girls was the Last Drop, a clammy dump in the worst section of the Flats, a horror-show three-block stretch where the scaggiest hookers and johns did their mating dance and any car without an alarm lasted about a minute and a half.

Which is where they were when Roman Fallow showed up with his latest guppy of a girlfriend, Roman liking his women small and blond and big-eyed. Roman's appearance was good news for the bartenders because Roman tipped somewhere in the neighborhood of 50 percent. Bad news for Katie, though, because Roman was friends with Bobby O'Donnell.

Roman said, "You a tad hammered there, Katie?"

Katie smiled because Roman scared her. Roman scared just about everyone. A good-looking guy, and smart, he could be funny as hell when he felt like it, but man there was a hole in Roman, a complete lack of anything resembling real feeling that hung in his eyes like a vacancy sign.

"I'm a bit buzzed," she admitted.

That amused Roman. He gave her a short laugh, flashed his perfect teeth, and took a sip of Tanqueray. "A bit buzzed, huh? Yeah, okay, Katie. Let me ask you something," he said gently. "You think Bobby would like hearing you were making a fucking ass of yourself at McGills tonight? You think he'd like hearing that?"

"No."

"'Cause I didn't like hearing it, Katie. You see what I'm saying?"

"Right."

Roman cupped a hand behind his ear. "What's that?"

"Right."

Roman left his hand where it was, leaned into her. "I'm sorry. What?"

"I'll go home right now," Katie said.

Roman smiled. "You sure? I don't want to make you do anything you don't feel like."

"No, no. I've had enough."

"Sure, sure. Hey, can I settle your tab?"

"No, no. Thanks, Roman, we already paid cash."

Roman slung his arm around his bimbo. "Call you a cab?"

Katie almost slipped up and said she'd driven here, but she caught herself. "No, no. This time of night? We'll flag one down no problem."

"Yeah, you will. All right then, Katie, we'll be seeing you."

Eve and Diane were already at the door, had been, in fact, since they'd first seen Roman.

Out on the sidewalk, Diane said, "Jesus. You think he'll call Bobby?"

Katie shook her head, though she wasn't positive. "No. Roman doesn't deliver bad news. He just takes care of it." She put her hand over her face for a moment and in the darkness, she felt the alcohol turn to an itchy sludge in her blood and the weight of her aloneness. She'd always felt alone, ever since her mother had died, and her mother had died a long, long time ago.

In the parking lot, Eve threw up, some of it splashing against one of the rear tires of Katie's blue Toyota. When she was finished, Katie fished some mouthwash from her purse, handed the small bottle to Eve. Eve said, "You going to be okay to drive?"

Katie nodded. "What's it, fourteen blocks from here? I'll be fine."

As they pulled out of the parking lot, Katie said, "Just one more reason to leave. One more reason to get the hell out of this whole shitty neighborhood."

Diane piped up with a halfhearted "Yeah."

They rolled cautiously through the Flats, Katie keeping the needle at twenty-five, staying in the right lane, concentrating. They stayed on Dunboy for twelve blocks, then cut down Crescent, the streets darker, quieter. At the base of the Flats, they drove along Sydney Street, heading for Eve's house. During the drive, Diane had decided to crash on Eve's couch rather than go over to her boyfriend Matt's house and eat a ration of shit for showing up hammered, so she and Eve got out under the broken streetlight on Sydney Street. It had begun to rain, spitting against Katie's windshield, but Diane and Eve didn't seem to notice.

They both bent at the waist and looked back in through the open passenger window at Katie. The bitter drop the evening had taken in its last hour caused their faces to sag, their shoulders to droop, and Katie could feel their sadness on the side of her face as she looked through the windshield at the spitting drops. She could feel the rest of their lives weighing stilted and unhappy on top of them. Her best friends since kindergarten, and she might never see them again.

"You going to be okay?" Diane's voice had a high, bubbling pitch to it.

Katie turned her face toward them and smiled, giving it all she had even though the effort felt like it would rip her jaw in half. "Yeah. 'Course. I'll call you from Vegas. You'll come visit."

"Flights are cheap," Eve said.

"Real cheap."

"Real cheap," Diane agreed, her voice trailing off as she looked away down the chipped sidewalk.

"Okay," Katie said, the word popping from her mouth like a bright explosion. "I'm going to go before someone cries."

Eve and Diane stretched their hands in through the window and Katie took a lingering pull on each of them, and then they stepped back from the car. They waved. Katie waved back, and then she tooted the horn and drove off.

They stayed on the pavement, watching, long after Katie's taillights had sparked red and then disappeared as she took the sharp curve in the middle of Sydney Street. They felt there were other things to say. They could smell the rain and the tinfoil scent of the Penitentiary Channel rolling dark and silent on the other side of the park.

For the rest of her life, Diane would wish she'd stayed in that car. She would give birth to a son in less than a year and she'd tell him when he was young (before he became his father, before he became mean, before he drove drunk and ran over a woman waiting to cross the street in the Point) that she believed she was meant to stay in that car, and that by deciding to get out, on a whim, she felt she'd altered something, shaved the corner off an edge in time. She would carry that with her along with an overriding sense that her life was spent as a passive observer of other people's tragic impulses, impulses she never did enough to curb. She would say these things again to her son during visitation days at the prison, and he'd give her a long roll of his shoulders and shift in his seat and say, "Did you bring those smokes, Ma?"

Eve would marry an electrician and move to a ranch house in Braintree. Sometimes, late at night, she'd rest her palm on his big, kind chest and tell him about Katie, about that night, and he'd listen and stroke her hair and back, but he wouldn't say much because he knew there was nothing to say. Sometimes Eve just needed to say her friend's name, to hear it, to feel its heft on her tongue. They would have children. Eve would go to their soccer games, stand on the sidelines, and every now and then her lips would part and she'd say Katie's name, silently, for herself, on the damp April fields.

But that night they were just two drunken East Bucky girls, and Katie watched them fade in her rearview as she took the curve on Sydney and headed for home.

It was dead down here at night, most of the homes that overlooked the Pen Channel Park having been scorched in a fire four years before that left them gutted and black and boarded up. Katie just wanted to get home, crawl into bed, get up in the morning, and be long gone before Bobby or her father ever thought to look for her. She wanted to shed this place the way you'd shed clothes you'd been wearing during a thundershower. Wad it up in her fist and toss it aside, never look back at it.

And she remembered something she hadn't thought about in years. She remembered walking to the zoo with her mother when she was five years old. She remembered this for no particular reason except that the hanging tendrils of stale pot and booze in her brain must have bumped against the cell where the memory was stored. Her mother had held her hand as they walked down Columbia Road toward the zoo, and Katie could feel the bones in her mother's hand as small tremors snapped under the skin by her wrist. She looked up at her mother's thin face and gaunt eyes, her nose gone hawkish with weight loss, her chin a pinched nub. And Katie, five and curious and sad, said, "How come you're tired all the time?"

Her mother's hard, brittle face had crumbled like a dry sponge. She'd crouched down by Katie and placed both palms on her cheeks and stared at her with red eyes. Katie thought she was mad, but then her mother smiled, and the smile immediately curled downward and her chin went all jerky and she said, "Oh, baby," and pulled Katie to her. She tucked her chin into Katie's shoulder and said, "Oh, baby," again, and then Katie felt her tears in her hair.

She could feel them now, the soft drizzle of tears in her hair like the soft drizzle against her windshield, and she was trying to remember the color of her mother's eyes when she saw the body lying in the middle of the street. It lay like a sack just in front of her tires and she swerved hard to the right, feeling something bump under her rear left tire, thinking, Oh Jesus, oh God, no, tell me I didn't hit it, please, Jesus God no.

She slammed the Toyota into the curb on the right side of the street, and her foot came off the clutch, and the car lurched forward, sputtering, then died.

Someone called to her. "Hey, you okay?"

Katie saw him coming toward her, and she started to relax because he looked familiar and harmless until she noticed the gun in his hand.

AT THREE in the morning, Brendan Harris finally fell asleep.

He did so smiling, Katie floating above him, telling him she loved him, whispering his name, her soft breath like a kiss in his ear.

4

DON'T GET AROUND
MUCH ANYMORE

DAVE BOYLE had ended up in McGills that night, sitting with Stanley the Giant at the corner of the bar, watching the Sox play an away game. Pedro Martinez reigned on the mound, so the Sox were beating the holy piss out of the Angels, Pedro throwing so much ungodly heat the ball looked like a goddamn Advil by the time it crossed the plate. By the third inning, the Angel hitters looked scared; by the sixth, they looked like they just wanted to go home, start making dinner plans. When Garret Anderson blooped a dying sigh of a single into shallow right and ended Pedro's bid for a no-hitter, any excitement that had been left in the 8–0 game floated out past the bleachers, and Dave found himself paying more attention to the lights and the fans and Anaheim Stadium itself than to the actual game.

He watched the faces in the bleachers most—the disgust and defeated fatigue, the fans looking like they were taking the loss more personally than the guys in the dugout. And maybe they were. For some of them, Dave figured, this was the only game they'd attend this year. They'd brought the kids, the wife, walked out of their homes into the early California evening with coolers for the tailgate party and five thirty-dollar tickets so they could sit in the cheap seats and put twenty-five-dollar caps on their kids' heads, eat six-dollar rat burgers and $4.50 hot dogs, watered-down Pepsi and sticky ice cream bars that melted into the hairs of their wrists. They came to be elated and uplifted, Dave knew, raised up out of their lives by the rare spectacle of victory. That's why arenas and ballparks felt like cathedrals—buzzing with light and murmured prayers and forty thousand hearts all beating the drum of the same collective hope.

Win for me. Win for my kids. Win for my marriage so I can carry your winning back to the car with me and sit in the glow of it with my family as we drive back toward our otherwise winless lives.

Win for me. Win. Win. Win.

But when the team lost, that collective hope crumbled into shards and any illusion of unity you'd felt with your fellow parishioners went with it. Your team had failed you and served only to remind you that usually when you tried, you lost. When you hoped, hope died. And you sat there in the debris of cellophane wrappers and popcorn and soft, soggy drink cups, dumped back into the numb wreckage of your life, facing a long dark walk back through a long dark parking lot with hordes of drunk, angry strangers, a silent wife tallying up your latest failure, and three cranky kids. All so you could get in your car and drive back to your home, the very place from which this cathedral had promised to transport you.

Dave Boyle, former star shortstop for the glory-years baseball teams of Don Bosco Technical High School, '78 to '82, knew few things in this world were more moody than a fan. He knew what it was to need them, to hate them, to go down on your knees for them and beg for one more roar of approval, to hang your head when you'd broken their one shared, angry heart.

"You believe these chicks?" Stanley the Giant said, and Dave looked up to see two girls standing atop the bar all of a sudden, dancing as a third friend sang "Brown Eyed Girl" off-key, the two up on the bar shaking their asses and swaying their hips. The one on the right had fleshy skin and shiny gray "fuck me" eyes, Dave figuring she was in the peak of a tenuous prime, the kind of girl who'd probably be a great roll on the mattress for maybe another six months. Two years from now, though, she'd be gone hard to seed—you could see it in the chin—fat and flaccid and wearing a housedress, no way you'd be able to so much as imagine she'd been worthy of lust not all that long ago.

The other one, though . . .

Dave had known her since she was a little girl—Katie Marcus, Jimmy and poor, dead Marita's daughter, now the stepdaughter of his wife's cousin Annabeth, but looking all grown up, every inch of her firm and fresh and defying gravity. Watching her dance and thrust and swivel and laugh, her blond hair sweeping over her face like a veil, then flying back off again as she threw back her head and exposed a milky, arched throat, Dave felt a black, pining hope surge through him like a grease fire, and it didn't come from nowhere. It came from her. It was transmitted from her body to his, from the sudden recognition in her sweaty face when her eyes met his and she smiled and gave him a little finger wave that brushed straight through the bones in his chest and tingled against his heart.

He glanced at the guys in the bar, their faces dazed as they watched the two girls dance as if they were apparitions bestowed by God. Dave could see in their faces the same yearning he'd seen on the Angels' fans in the early innings, a sad yearning mixed with a pathetic acceptance that they were sure to go home unsatisfied. Left to stroking their own dicks in 3 A.M. bathrooms, wives and kids snoring upstairs.

Dave watched Katie shimmer above him and remembered what Maura Keaveny had looked like when she was naked beneath him, perspiration beading her brow, eyes loose and floating with booze and lust. Lust for him. Dave Boyle. Baseball star. Pride of the Flats for three short years. No one referring to him as that kid who'd been abducted when he was ten anymore. No, he was a local hero. Maura in his bed. Fate on his side.

Dave Boyle. Unaware, then, how short futures could be. How quick they could disappear, leave you with nothing but a long-ass present that held no surprises, no reason for hope, nothing but days that bled into one another with so little impact that another year was over and the calendar page in the kitchen was still stuck on March.

I will not dream anymore, you said. I will not set myself up for the pain. But then your team made the playoffs, or you saw a movie, or a billboard glowing dusky orange and advertising Aruba, or a girl who bore more than a passing resemblance to a woman you'd dated in high school—a woman you'd loved and lost—danced above you with shimmering eyes, and you said, fuck it, let's dream just one more time.

ONCE WHEN Rosemary Savage Samarco was on her deathbed (the fifth of ten), she'd told her daughter, Celeste Boyle: "Swear to Christ, the only pleasure I ever got in this life was snapping your father's balls like a wet sheet on a dry day."

Celeste had given her a distant smile and tried to turn away, but her mother's arthritic claw clamped over her wrist and squeezed straight through to the bone.

"You listen to me, Celeste. I'm dying, so I'm serious as shit. There's what you get—if you're *lucky*—in this life, and it ain't much in the first place. I'll be dead tomorrow and I want my daughter to understand: You get one thing. Hear me? One thing in the whole world that gives you pleasure. Mine was busting your bastard father's balls every chance I got." Her eyes gleamed and spittle dotted her lips. "Trust me, after a while? He loved it."

Celeste wiped her mother's forehead with a towel. She smiled down on her and said, "Momma," in a soft, cooing voice. She dabbed the spittle from her lips and stroked the inside of her hand, all the time thinking, I've got to get out of here. Out of this house, out of this neighborhood, out of this crazy place where people's brains rotted straight through from being too poor and too pissed off and too helpless to do anything about it for too fucking long.

Her mother kept living, though. She survived colitis, diabetic seizures, renal failure, two myocardial infarctions, cancerous malignancies in one breast and her colon. Her pancreas stopped working one day, just quit, then suddenly showed back up for work a week later, raring to go, and doctors repeatedly asked Celeste if they could study her mother's body after she died.

The first few times, Celeste had asked, "Which part?"

"All of it."

Rosemary Savage Samarco had a brother in the Flats she hated, two sisters living in Florida who wouldn't talk to her, and she'd busted her husband's balls so successfully he dove into an early grave to escape her.

Celeste was her only child after eight miscarriages. When she was little, Celeste used to imagine all those almost-sisters and almost-brothers floating around Limbo and think, You caught a break.

When Celeste had been a teenager, she'd been sure someone would come along to take her away from all this. She wasn't bad-looking. She wasn't bitter, had a good personality, knew how to laugh. She figured, all things considered, it should happen. Problem was, even though she met a few candidates, they weren't of sweep-her-off-her-feet caliber. The majority were from Buckingham, mostly Point or Flat punks here in East Bucky, a few from Rome Basin, and one guy from uptown she'd met while attending Blaine Hairstyling School, but he was gay, even though he hadn't figured it out yet.

Her mother's health insurance was for shit, and pretty soon Celeste found herself working simply to pay the minimum due on monstrous medical bills for monstrous diseases that weren't quite monstrous enough to put her mother out of her misery. Not that her mother didn't enjoy her misery. Every bout with disease was a fresh trump card to wield in what Dave called the Rosemary's Life Sucks Worse Than Yours Sweepstakes. They'd be watching the news, see some grieving mother weeping and wailing on the sidewalk after her house and two kids had gone up in a fire, and Rosemary would smack her gums and say, "You can always have more kids. Try living with colitis and a collapsed lung all in the same year."

Dave would smile tightly and go get another beer.

Rosemary, hearing the fridge open in the kitchen, would say to Celeste, "You're just his mistress, honey. His wife's name is Budweiser."

Celeste would say, "Momma, quit it."

Her mother would say, "What?"

It had been Dave who Celeste had ultimately settled—for?—on. He was good-looking and funny and very few things seemed to ruffle him. When they'd married, he'd had a good job, running the mail room at Raytheon, and even though that job had been lost to cutbacks, he eventually scored another on the loading docks of a downtown hotel (for about half his previous salary) and never complained about it. Dave, in fact, never complained about anything and almost never talked about his childhood before high school, which had only begun to seem odd to her in the year since her mother had died.

It had been a stroke that had finally done the job, Celeste coming home from the supermarket to find her mother dead in the tub, head cocked, lips curled hard up the right side of her face as if she'd bitten into something overly tart.

In the months after the funeral, Celeste would comfort herself with the knowledge that at least things would be easier now without her mother's constant reproach and cruel asides. But it hadn't quite worked out that way. Dave's job paid about the same as Celeste's and that was about a buck an hour more than McDonald's, and while the medical bills Rosemary had accrued during her life were thankfully not passed on to her daughter, the funeral and burial bills were. Celeste would look at the financial wreck of their lives—the bills they'd be paying off for years, the lack of money coming in, the tonnage going out, the new mountain of bills Michael and the advent of his schooling represented, and the destroyed credit—and feel like the rest of her life would be lived with a held breath. Neither she nor Dave had any college or any prospects for it, and while every time you turned on the news they were crowing about the low unemployment rate and national sense of job security, nobody mentioned that this affected mostly skilled labor and people willing to temp for no medical or dental and few career prospects.

Sometimes, Celeste found herself sitting on the toilet beside the tub where she'd found her mother. She'd sit in the dark. She'd sit there and try not to cry and wonder how her life had gotten here, and that's what she was doing at three in the morning, early Sunday, as a hard rain battered the windows, when Dave came in with blood all over him.

He seemed shocked to find her there. He jumped back when she stood up.

She said, "Honey, what happened?" and reached for him.

He jumped back again and his foot hit the doorjamb. "I got sliced."

"What?"

"I got sliced."

"Dave, Jesus Christ. What *happened*?"

He lifted the shirt and Celeste stared at a long sweeping gash along his rib cage that bubbled red.

"Sweetie, Jesus, you have to go to the hospital."

"No, no," he said. "Look, it's not that deep. It just bled like hell."

He was right. On a second look, she noticed it wasn't more than a tenth of an inch deep. But it was long. And it was bloody. Though not enough to account for all the blood on his shirt and neck.

"Who did this?"

"Some crackhead nigger psycho," he said, and peeled off the shirt, dumped it in the sink. "Honey, I fucked up."

"You what? How?"

He looked at her, eyes spinning. "The guy tried to mug me, right? So, so I swung on him. That's when he sliced me."

"You swung on a guy with a *knife,* Dave?"

He ran the faucet and tipped his head into the sink, gulped some water. "I don't know why. I freaked. I mean, I freaked seriously, babe. I fucked this guy up."

"You . . . ?"

"I mangled him, Celeste. I just went apeshit when I felt the knife in my side. You know? I knocked him down, got on top of him, and, baby, I went *off.*"

"So it was self-defense?"

He made a "sorta-kinda" gesture with his hand. "I don't think the court would see it that way, tell you the truth."

"I can't believe this. Honey"—she took his wrists in her hands—"tell me exactly what happened."

And for a quarter second, looking into his face, she felt nauseous. She felt something leering behind his eyes, something turned on and self-congratulatory.

It was the light, she decided, the cheap fluorescent directly above his head, because when his chin dipped toward his chest and he stroked her hands, the nausea went away and his face returned to normal—scared, but normal.

"I'm walking to my car," he said, and Celeste sat back on the closed toilet seat as he knelt in front of her, "and this guy comes up to me, asks me for a light. I say I don't smoke. Guy says neither does he."

"Neither does he."

Dave nodded. "So, my heart starts clocking a buck-fifty right then. 'Cause there's *no one* around but me and him. And that's when I see the knife and he says, 'Your wallet or your life, bitch. I'm leaving with one of 'em.' "

"That's what he said?"

Dave leaned back, cocked his head. "Why?"

"Nothing." Celeste thinking it just sounded funny for some reason, too clever maybe, like in the movies. But then everyone saw movies these days, more so now with cable, so maybe the mugger had learned his lines from a movie mugger, stayed up late at night saying them into a mirror until he thought he sounded like Wesley or Denzel.

"So . . . so then," Dave said, "I'm like, 'Come on, man. Just let me get in my car and go home,' which was *dumb* because now he wants my car keys, too. And I just, I dunno, honey, I get mad instead of scared. Whiskey-brave, maybe, I'm not sure, and I try to brush past him and that's when he slices me."

"I thought you said he swung on you."

"Celeste, can I tell the fucking story?"

She touched his cheek. "I'm sorry, baby."

He kissed her palm. "So, yeah, he sorta pushes me back against the car and takes a swing at me and I, like, *just* duck the punch and that's when Homeboy slices me, and I feel the knife cutting through my skin and I, I just flip. I crack him in the side of the head with my fist, and he ain't expecting it. He's like, 'Whoa, motherfucker,' and I swing again and hit like the side of his neck? And he drops. And the knife goes bouncing away, and I jump on him, and, and, and . . ."

Dave looked into the tub, his mouth still open, lips half puckered.

"What?" Celeste said, still trying to see the mugger swinging at Dave with one hand cocked into a fist, the other holding a knife at the ready. "What did you do?"

Dave turned back, looked at her knees. "I went fucking nuts on him, babe. I mighta killed him for all I know. I bashed his head off the parking lot and punched the shit out of his face, shattered his nose, you name it. I was so mad and so scared and all I could think about was you and Michael and how I might not have made the car alive, like I coulda died in some shitty parking lot just because some crackhead was too lazy to fucking work for a living." He looked in her eyes and said it again: "I mighta killed him, honey."

He looked so young. Eyes wide, face pale and sweaty, hair plastered to his head by perspiration and terror and—was that blood?—yes, blood.

AIDS, she thought for a moment. What if the guy had AIDS?

She thought: No. Deal with the right now. Deal with it.

Dave needed her. That was not the custom. And at that moment she realized why his never complaining had begun to bother her. When you complained to someone, you were, in a way, asking for help, asking for that person to fix what troubled you. But Dave had never needed her before, so he'd never complained, not after lost jobs, not while Rosemary had been alive. But now, kneeling before her, saying, desperately, that he may have killed a man, he was asking her to tell him it was all right.

And it was. Wasn't it? You tried to mug an honest citizen, tough shit if it didn't go the way you planned. Too bad you might have died. Celeste was thinking, I mean, sorry, but oops. You play, you pay.

She kissed her husband's forehead. "Baby," she whispered, "you hop in the shower. I'll take care of your clothes."

"Yeah?"

"Yeah."

"What are you going to do with them?"

She didn't have a clue. Burn them? Sure, but where? Not in the apartment. So that left the backyard. But it occurred to her pretty quickly that someone would notice her burning clothes in the backyard at 3 A.M. Or at any time, really.

"I'll wash them." She said it as the idea came to her. "I'll wash them good and then I'll put them in a trash bag and we'll bury that."

"Bury it?"

"Take it to the dump, then. Or, no, wait"—her thoughts going faster than her mouth now—"we'll hide the bag till Tuesday morning. Trash day, right?"

"Right . . ." He turned on the shower, looking at her, waiting, that gash along his side darkening, making her worry about AIDS again, or possibly hepatitis, the many ways another's blood can kill or poison.

"I know when they come. Seven-fifteen, on the dot, every week, except the first week in June when all the college kids take off, leave all that extra trash and then they're usually late, but . . ."

"Celeste. Honey. The point?"

"Oh, so when I hear the truck, I'll just run downstairs after them, like I forgot a bag, and toss it right in the back of the compactor thing. Right?" She smiled, though she didn't feel like it.

He put one hand under the shower spray, the rest of him still turned back toward her. "Okay. Look . . ."

"What?"

"You all right with this?"

"Yeah."

Hepatitis A, B, and C, she thought. Ebola. Hot zones.

His eyes went wide again. "I might have killed someone, honey. Jesus."

She wanted to go to him and touch him. She wanted to get out of the room. She wanted to caress his neck, tell him it would be okay. She wanted to run away until she could think this through.

She stayed where she was. "I'll wash the clothes."

"Okay," he said. "Yeah."

She found some plastic gloves under the sink, ones she used when cleaning the toilet, and she put them on and checked for any tears in the rubber. When she was satisfied there were none, she took his shirt from the sink and his jeans off the floor. The jeans were dark with blood, too, and left a smear on the white tile.

"How'd you get it on your jeans?"

"What?"

"The blood."

He looked at them hanging from her hand. He looked at the floor. "I was kneeling over him." He shrugged. "I dunno. I guess it splashed up, like on the shirt."

"Oh."

He met her eyes. "Yeah. Oh."

"So," she said.

"So."

"So, I'll wash these in the kitchen sink."

"Okay."

"Okay," she said, and backed out of the bathroom, left him standing there, one hand fluttering under the water, waiting for it to get hot.

In the kitchen, she dumped the clothes in the sink and ran the water, watched the blood and filmy chips of flesh and, oh Christ, pieces of brain, she was pretty sure, wash down the drain. It amazed her how much the human body could bleed. They said you had six pints in you, but to Celeste it always seemed like so much more. When she was in the fourth grade, she'd been running through a park with friends and she'd tripped. As she was trying to break her fall, she drove the center of her palm through a broken bottle that was pointing straight up out of the grass. She'd severed every major artery and vein in her hand, and it was only because she was so young that over the next decade they gradually repaired. But, still, she was twenty before sensation returned to all four fingertips. What she remembered most, however, was the blood. When she'd raised her hand from the grass, her elbow tingling as if she'd hit her funny bone, the blood had jetted straight up and out from her torn palm, and two of her friends had screamed. At home, she'd filled a sink with it while her mother called an ambulance. In the ambulance, they'd wrapped the hand in an Ace bandage as thick as her thigh, and the layers of fabric turned dark red in less than two minutes. At the hospital, she'd lain on a white gurney and watched as the wrinkles in the sheet formed small canyons that filled with red. And when the gurney had filled, her blood dripped onto the floor and eventually formed puddles until her mother screamed long enough and loud enough that one of the City ER residents decided Celeste should be bumped to the head of the line. All that blood from one hand.

And now, all this blood from one head. From Dave punching another human being's face, banging the skull off pavement. Hysterical, she was sure, from fear. She held her gloved hands under the water and checked them again for holes. None. She poured dishwashing liquid all over the T-shirt and scoured it with steel wool, then squeezed it out and went through the whole process again until the water that dripped from the shirt when she squeezed was no longer pink but clear. She did the same with the jeans, and by that time Dave was out of the shower and sitting at the kitchen table with a towel wrapped around his waist, smoking one of the long white cigarettes her mother had left behind in the cupboard and drinking a beer, watching her.

"Fucked up," he said softly.

She nodded.

"I mean, you know?" he whispered. "You go out, expecting one thing, a Saturday night, nice weather, and then . . ." He stood and came over by her, leaned against the oven, and watched her wring out the left leg of his jeans. "Why aren't you using the washing machine in the pantry?"

She looked over at him and noticed the cut along his side already going a puckered white after the shower. She felt a nervous need to giggle. She swallowed against it and said, "Evidence, sweetie."

"Evidence?"

"Well, I dunno for sure, but I figure blood and . . . other stuff have a better chance of sticking to the insides of a washing machine than to a sink drain."

He let out a low whistle. "Evidence."

"Evidence," she said, giving in to a grin now, feeling conspiratorial, dangerous, part of something big and worthwhile.

"Damn, babe," he said. "You're a genius."

She finished wringing out the jeans and shut off the water, took a small bow.

Four in the morning, and she was more awake than she'd been in years. She was Christmas-morning-when-you're-eight kind of awake. Her blood was caffeine.

Your whole life, you wished for something like this. You told yourself you didn't, but you did. To be involved in a drama. And not the drama of unpaid bills and minor, shrieking marital squabbles. No. This was real life, but bigger than real life. This was hyper-real. Her husband may have killed a bad man. And if that bad man really was dead, the police would want to find out who did it. And if the trail actually led here, to Dave, they'd need evidence.

She could see them sitting at the kitchen table, notebooks open, smelling of coffee and the previous night's taverns, asking her and Dave questions. They'd be polite, but scary. And she and Dave would be polite back and unruffled.

Because it all came down to evidence. And she'd just washed the evidence down the kitchen sink drain and out into the dark sewers. In the morning, she'd remove the drainpipe from under the sink and wash that, too, douse the insides with bleach and put it back in place. She'd put the shirt and jeans into a plastic trash bag and hide it until Tuesday morning and then toss it into the back of the garbage truck where it would be mashed and chewed and compacted with rotten eggs and spoiled chickens and stale bread. She'd do this and feel larger, better, than herself.

"It makes you feel alone," Dave said.

"What's that?"

"Hurting someone," he said softly.

"But you had to."

He nodded. His flesh was gray in the semidark of the kitchen. He looked younger still, as if fresh from his mother's belly and gasping. "I know. I do. But still, it makes you feel alone. It makes you feel . . ."

She touched his face and his Adam's apple bulged as he swallowed.

"Alien," he said.

5

ORANGE CURTAINS

SUNDAY MORNING AT SIX, four and a half hours before his daughter Nadine's First Communion, Jimmy Marcus got a call from Pete Gilibiowski down at the store telling him he was already in the weeds.

"The weeds?" Jimmy sat up in bed, looked over at the clock. "Friggin' Pete, it's six in the morning. You and Katie can't handle six, how you going to handle eight when the first church crowd comes in?"

"That's the thing, though, Jim. Katie ain't here."

"She ain't what?" Jimmy threw back the covers and got out of bed.

"She ain't here. Supposed to be at five-thirty, right? I got the doughnut guy honking his horn out back, and I got no coffee ready on account of—"

Jimmy said, "Uh-huh," and walked down the hallway toward Katie's room, feeling the cold drafts in the house on his feet, the early May mornings still carrying the raw bite of March afternoons.

"—a group of bar-hopping, drinking-in-the-park, methamphetamine-in-their-squashes construction workers come in here at five-forty and cleaned us out of Colombian *and* French roast. And the deli looks like shit. How much you paying those kids to work Saturday nights, Jim?"

63

Jimmy said, "Uh-huh," again and pushed open Katie's door after a quick knock. Her bed was empty and, worse, made, which meant she hadn't slept here last night.

" 'Cause you either got to give 'em raises or shitcan their worthless asses," Pete said. "I got an extra hour of prep work before I can even— How ya doing, Mrs. Carmody? Coffee's brewing now, hon, won't be a sec."

"I'm coming in," Jimmy said.

"Plus, I got all the Sunday papers still bundled up, circulars on top, look like crap—"

"I said I'm coming in."

"Oh. No shit, Jim? Thanks."

"Pete? Call Sal, see if he can make it in by eight-thirty, 'stead of ten."

"Yeah?"

Jimmy heard the sound of a hand standing on a car horn from Pete's end. "And Pete, Christ's sake, open the door for Yser's kid, will you? He ain't going to wait all day with those doughnuts."

Jimmy hung up and walked back to the bedroom. Annabeth was sitting up in bed, sheets off her body, yawning.

"The store?" she said, drawing the words out with another long yawn.

He nodded. "Katie no-showed."

"Today," Annabeth said. "Day of Nadine's First Communion, she no-shows for work. What if she no-shows at the church?"

"I'm sure she'll make it."

"I don't know, Jimmy. If she got so drunk last night, she blew off the store, you never know . . ."

Jimmy shrugged. There was no talking to Annabeth when it came to Katie. Annabeth had only two modes in terms of her stepdaughter— either irritated and frosty or elated that they were best friends. There was no in-between, and Jimmy knew—with some small amount of guilt—that most of the confusion stemmed from Annabeth coming into the picture when Katie was seven, just getting to know her father, and barely over the loss of her mother. Katie had been openly and honestly grateful for a female presence in the lonely apartment she'd shared with her father. But she'd also been wounded by her mother's death—if not irreparably, then at least profoundly, Jimmy knew—and anytime that loss would sneak up and slice through the walls of her heart over the years, she'd vent it mostly on Annabeth, who, as a real mother, never quite lived up to all the things Marita's ghost could have or would have been.

"Christ, Jimmy," Annabeth said as Jimmy pulled a sweatshirt over the T-shirt he'd slept in and went looking for his jeans, "you're not going in, are you?"

"Just for an hour." Jimmy found his jeans curled around the bedpost. "Two, tops. Sal was supposed to relieve Katie at ten anyway. Pete's putting a call in to him now, trying to get him in early."

"Sal's seventy-something years old."

"My point. He's going to be sleeping? Bladder probably woke him up at four, he's been watching AMC ever since."

"Shit." Annabeth pushed the sheets completely away from her and got out of bed. "Fucking Katie. She's going to screw this day up, too?"

Jimmy felt his neck get hot. "What other day has she screwed up lately?"

Annabeth showed him the back of her hand as she reached the bathroom. "You even know where she could be?"

"Diane or Eve's," Jimmy said, still back at that dismissive hand she'd raised over her shoulder. Annabeth—the love of his life, no question—man, she had no idea how cold she could be sometimes, no clue (and this was typical of the whole Savage family) just how corrosive an effect her negative moments or moods could have on other people. "Maybe a boyfriend's."

"Yeah? Who's she seeing these days?" Annabeth turned on the shower, stepped back to the sink to give it time to warm up.

"I figured you knew better than me."

Annabeth riffled the medicine cabinet for the toothpaste and shook her head. "She stopped seeing Little Caesar in November. That was good enough for me."

Jimmy, putting his shoes on, smiled. Annabeth always called Bobby O'Donnell "Little Caesar" unless she was calling him something far worse, and not just because he was a gangster-wannabe with a cold stare, but because he was short and fleshy like Edward G. Robinson. Those had been a tense several months, when Katie had begun seeing him last summer and the Savage brothers told Jimmy they'd clip the prick if it became necessary, Jimmy not sure if they were morally repulsed because such a scumbag was seeing their beloved stepniece, or because Bobby O'Donnell had become too much competition.

Katie had broken it off herself, though, and outside of a lot of 3 A.M. phone calls and one near-bloodfest around Christmas when Bobby and Roman Fallow showed up on the front porch, the breakup aftermath had passed pretty painlessly.

Annabeth's abhorrence of Bobby O'Donnell could amuse Jimmy because he half wondered sometimes if Annabeth hated Bobby not only because he looked like Edward G. and had slept with her stepdaughter, but also because he was a half-assed criminal as opposed to the pros she assumed her brothers were and knew, beyond a doubt, that her husband had been in the years before Marita died.

Marita had died fourteen years ago, while Jimmy served a two-year bid at the Deer Island House of Corrections in Winthrop. One Saturday during visitation hours, as five-year-old Katie squirmed in her lap, Marita told Jimmy a mole on her arm had been darkening lately, and she was going to visit a doctor at the community clinic. Just to be safe, she said. Four Saturdays later she was undergoing chemo. Six months after she'd told him about the mole, she was dead, Jimmy having been forced to watch his wife's body puree into chalk over a succession of Saturdays from the other side of a dark wood table scarred by cigarettes, sweat, come stains, and over a century's worth of convict bullshit and convict laments. The last month of her life Marita had been too sick to come, too weak to write, and Jimmy had to make do with phone calls during which she'd be exhausted or doped up or both. Usually both.

"You know what I dream about?" she slurred once. "All the time now?"

"What's that, baby?"

"Orange curtains. Big, thick orange curtains just . . ." She smacked her lips and Jimmy heard the sound of her gulping water. ". . . just flapping in the wind, hanging from these tall clotheslines, Jimmy. Just flapping. They never do anything else. Flap, flap, flap. Hundreds of 'em in this big, big field. Flapping away . . ."

He waited for more, but that was the extent of it, and he didn't want Marita to nod off in the middle of the conversation like she'd done several times before, so he said, "How's Katie?"

"Huh?"

"How's Katie doing, honey?"

"Your mom takes good care of us. She's sad."

"Who? My mom or Katie?"

"Both. Lookit, Jimmy? I gotta go. Nauseous. Tired."

"Okay, baby."

"Love you."

"Love you, too."

"Jimmy? We never owned any orange curtains. Right?"

"Right."

"Weird," she said, and then she hung up.

Last thing she ever said to him: Weird.

Yeah, it was weird. A mole that had been on your arm since you'd lain in a crib looking up at a cardboard mobile suddenly darkened, and twenty-four weeks later, almost two full years removed from the last time you'd lain in bed with your husband and curled your leg over his, you were dropped into a box and buried beneath the earth, your husband standing fifty yards away, flanked by armed guards, shackles clamped around his ankles and wrists.

Jimmy got out of prison two months after the funeral, stood in his kitchen in the same clothes he'd left it in, and smiled at his alien child. He might have remembered her first four years, but she didn't. She only remembered the last two, maybe some scattered fragments of the man he'd been in this house, before she was allowed to see him only on Saturdays from the other side of an old table in a dank, smelly place built on haunted Indian burial grounds, where winds whipped and walls dripped and the ceilings hung too low. Standing in his kitchen, watching her watch him, Jimmy had never felt more useless. He had never felt half as alone or frightened as when he squatted down by Katie and took her small hands in his and saw the two of them in his mind's eye as if he floated just above the room. And the floating him thought: Man, I feel bad for these two. Strangers in a shitty kitchen, sizing each other up, trying not to hate each other because she'd died and left them stuck together and incapable of knowing what the hell they were going to do next.

This daughter—this *creature,* living and breathing and partially formed in so many ways—was dependent on him now, whether either of them liked it or not.

"She's smiling down at us from heaven," Jimmy told Katie. "She's proud of us. Real proud."

Katie said, "Do you have to go back to that place again?"

"Nope. Never again."

"You going to go someplace else?"

Jimmy, at that moment, would gladly have done another six years in a shithole like Deer Island, or even someplace worse, rather than face twenty-four hours in his kitchen with this daughter-stranger, this scary unknown of a future, this cork—in no uncertain terms—on what remained of his life as a young man.

"No way," he said. "I'm sticking with you."

"I'm hungry."

And it hit Jimmy all the way—Oh, my God, I have to feed this girl whenever she's hungry. For the rest of our lives. Jesus Christ.

"Well, okay," he said, feeling the smile shake on his face. "We'll eat."

JIMMY GOT TO Cottage Market, the corner store he owned, by six-thirty and worked the cash register and the Lotto machine while Pete stocked the coffee counter with the doughnuts from Yser Gaswami's Dunkin' Donuts on Kilmer and the pastries, cannolis, and pigs-in-a-blanket delivered from Tony Buca's bakery. During lulls, Jimmy ran coffee from the brewing machines in back out to the oversize thermoses on the coffee counter and cut the twine on the Sunday *Globe*s, *Herald*s, and *New York Times*es. He placed the circulars and comics in the middle, then stacked them all neatly in front of the candy shelves below the cash counter.

"Sal say what time he'll be in?"

Pete said, "The best he could do was nine-thirty. His car shit the bed so he's going to have to T it. That's like two train lines and a bus transfer from here and he said he wasn't even dressed."

"Shit."

Around seven-fifteen, they handled a semirush of folks coming off the night shift—cops, mostly, from the D-9, some nurses from Saint Regina's, and a few working girls who serviced the illegal after-hours clubs down on the other side of Buckingham Avenue in the Flats and up in Rome Basin. All of them were weary but convivial and wired, too, emitting an aura of intense relief, as if they'd just walked off the same battlefield together, muddy, bloody, but erect and unmaimed.

During a five-minute recess before the early-mass crowd stormed the gates, Jimmy called Drew Pigeon and asked him if he'd seen Katie.

"I think she's here, yeah," Drew said.

"Yeah?" Jimmy heard the spike of hope in his voice and only then realized that he'd been more anxious than he'd allowed himself to admit.

"Think so," Drew said. "Lemme go check."

" 'Preciate it, Drew."

He listened to Drew's heavy feet echo away down a hardwood hall-way as he cashed two scratch tickets for Old Lady Harmon, trying not to blink away tears from the sharp assault of her old lady perfume. He heard Drew coming back toward the phone and felt a mild flutter in his chest as he handed Old Lady Harmon her fifteen bucks and waved bye to her.

"Jimmy?"

"Here, Drew."

"Sorry. It was Diane Cestra slept over. She's in there on the floor of Eve's bedroom, but no Katie."

The flutter in Jimmy's chest stopped hard, as if it had been pinched between tweezers.

"Hey, no problem."

"Eve said Katie dropped them off round one? Didn't say where she was going."

"Okay, man." Jimmy put a false brightness into his tone. "I'll track her down."

"She seeing anyone maybe?"

"Nineteen-year-old girls, Drew? Who could keep a tally?"

"That's the cold truth," Drew said with a yawn. "Eve, Jimmy? All the calls she gets from different guys, I'd swear she needs a roster by the phone to keep 'em straight."

Jimmy forced a chuckle. "Hey, thanks again, Drew."

"Anytime, Jimmy. Take care."

Jimmy hung up and looked down at the register keyboard as if it could tell him something. This wasn't the first time Katie had stayed out all night. Hell, it wasn't even the tenth. And it wasn't even the first time she'd blown off work, though in both cases, she usually called. Still, if she'd met a guy with movie-star looks and city-boy charm . . . Jimmy wasn't so far removed from nineteen himself that he couldn't remember what that was like. And while he'd never let Katie think he condoned it, he couldn't be so hypocritical in his heart as to condemn it.

The bell hanging from a ribbon tacked to the top of the door clanged and Jimmy looked up to see the first group of coiffed blue-hairs from the rosary-bead crowd charge into the store, yapping away about the raw morning, the priest's diction, the litter in the streets.

Pete stuck his head up from the deli counter and wiped his hands with the towel he'd been using to clean the prep table. He tossed a full box of surgical gloves up onto the counter and then came over behind the second cash register. He leaned in toward Jimmy and said, "Welcome to hell," and the second group of Holy Rollers followed fast on the heels of the first.

Jimmy hadn't worked a Sunday morning in nearly two years, and he'd forgotten what a zoo it could turn into. Pete was right. The blue-haired fanatics, who packed the seven o'clock mass at Saint Cecilia's while normal people slept, took their biblical shopping fury into Jimmy's store and decimated the pastry and doughnut trays, drained the coffee, stripped the dairy coolers to a shell, and reduced the newspaper stacks by half. They banged into display racks and stepped on the chip bags and plastic sleeves of peanuts that fell to their feet. They shouted out deli orders, Lotto orders, scratch ticket orders, and orders for Pall Malls and Chesterfields with a rabid indiscrimination as to their places in line. Then, as a sea of blue, white, and bald heads bobbed behind them, they dawdled at the counter to ask after Jimmy's and Pete's families while they fished for exact change down to the last lint-enfuzzed penny and took prolonged eons to lift their purchases off the counter and move out of the way for the raging clamor behind them.

Jimmy hadn't seen anything resembling this kind of chaos since the last time he'd attended an Irish wedding with an open bar, and when he finally glanced up at the clock at eight-forty-five as the last of them went out through the door to the street, he could feel the sweat drenching the T-shirt under his sweatshirt, soaking into his skin. He looked at the bomb that had exploded in the middle of his store and then over at Pete, and he felt a sudden flush of kinship and fraternity with him that made him think of the seven-fifteen crew of cops, nurses, and hookers, as if he and Pete had ascended to a new level of friendship just by surviving the eight o'clock Sunday blast of ravenous geriatrics.

Pete tossed him a tired grin. "Slows for about half an hour now. Mind if I step out back and grab a smoke?"

Jimmy laughed, feeling good now and swept by a sudden, odd pride at this little business he'd built into a neighborhood institution. "Fuck, Pete, smoke a whole pack."

He'd tidied the aisles, restocked dairy, and was replenishing the doughnut and pastry trays when the bell clanged, and he looked over to see Brendan Harris and his little brother, Silent Ray, walk past the counter and head for the small square of aisles where the breads and detergents and cookies and teas were stocked. Jimmy busied himself with the cellophane wraps over the pastries and doughnuts, and wished he hadn't given Pete the impression he could take a mini-vacation out back and that his ass would get back in here immediately.

He glanced over and noticed Brendan peering above the aisle tops at the cash registers, like he was either planning to stick the place up or hoping for a glimpse of someone. For one irrational second, Jimmy wondered if he'd have to fire Pete for dealing out of the store. But then he checked himself, remembered that Pete had looked him straight in the eyes and sworn he'd never jeopardize Jimmy's life's work by dealing pot in his place of business. Jimmy had known he was telling the truth because unless you were the Grand Wizard of All Liars, it was nearly impossible to lie to Jimmy when he looked in your eyes after asking you a direct question; he knew every tic and tell and eye movement, no matter how minor, that could give you away. Something he'd learned by watching his father make him drunken promises he never kept—you saw it enough, you recognized the animal every time it chose to resurface. So Jimmy remembered Pete looking him dead in the eyes and swearing he'd never deal out of this place, and Jimmy knew it was true.

So then who was Brendan looking for? Could he be stupid enough to

be considering a rip-off? Jimmy had known Brendan's father, Just Ray
Harris, so he knew a sizable chunk of dumb ran in the genes, but no one
was so dumb as to try to rob a store on the East Bucky Flats/Point line
with his thirteen-year-old mute brother in tow. Plus, if anyone got some
brains in the family, Jimmy would begrudgingly admit it was Brendan. A
shy kid, but good-looking as hell, and Jimmy had long ago learned the
difference between someone who was quiet because he didn't know the
meanings of many words and someone who just stayed inside himself,
watching, listening, taking it all in. Brendan had that quality; you sensed
he understood people a little too well, and that the knowledge made him
nervous.

He turned toward Jimmy and their eyes met, and the kid gave Jimmy
a nervous, friendly smile, putting too much into it, as if he were over-
compensating because there were other things on his mind.

Jimmy said, "Help you, Brendan?"

"Uh, no, Mr. Marcus, just picking up some, ah, some of that Irish tea
my mom likes."

"Barry's?"

"That's it, yeah."

"Next aisle over."

"Oh. Thanks."

Jimmy went back up behind the registers just as Pete came back in,
carrying that stale reek of a hastily puffed cigarette all over him.

"What time's Sal getting here again?" Jimmy said.

"Any time now, should be." Pete leaned back against the sliding cigarette rack below the scratch ticket rolls and sighed. "He's slow,
Jimmy."

"Sal?" Jimmy watched Brendan and Silent Ray communicate in sign
language, standing in the middle of the center aisle, Brendan clutching a
box of Barry's under his arm. "He's in his late seventies, man."

"I know *why* he's slow," Pete said. "I'm just saying. That was me and
him at eight o'clock, 'stead of me and you, Jim? Man, we'd still be in the
weeds."

"Which is why I put him on slow shifts. Anyway, it wasn't supposed
to be me and you or you and Sal on this morning. It was supposed to be
you and Katie."

Brendan and Silent Ray had reached the counter and Jimmy saw something catch in Brendan's face when he said his daughter's name.

Pete came off the cigarette rack and said, "That it, Brendan?"

"I . . . I . . . I . . ." Brendan stammered, then looked at his little brother. "Ahm, I think so. Let me check with Ray."

The hands went flying again, the two of them going so fast it would have been hard for Jimmy to keep up even if they were making sounds. Silent Ray's face, though, was as stone dead as his hands were electric and alive. He'd always been an eerie little kid, in Jimmy's opinion, more like the mother than the father, a blankness living in his face like an act of defiance. He'd mentioned it to Annabeth once and she'd accused him of being insensitive to the handicapped, but Jimmy didn't think that was it—something lived in Ray's dead face and silent mouth that you just wanted to beat out with a hammer.

They finished flinging their hands back and forth and Brendan bent over the candy rack and came back with a Coleman Chew-Chew bar, making Jimmy think about his father again, the stench of him that year he'd worked the candy plant.

"And a *Globe,* too," Brendan said.

"Sure thing, kid," Pete said, and rang it up.

"So's, ah, I thought Katie worked Sundays." Brendan handed Pete a ten-spot.

Pete raised his eyebrows as he punched the cash key and the door popped open against his belly. "You sweet on my man's daughter, Brendan?"

Brendan wouldn't look at Jimmy. "No, no, no." He laughed, and it died as soon as it left his mouth. "I was just wondering, you know, because usually I see her here."

"Her little sister's having her First Communion today," Jimmy said.

"Oh, Nadine?" Brendan looked at Jimmy, eyes too wide, smile too big.

"Nadine," Jimmy said, curious as to how the name had come to Brendan so fast. "Yeah."

"Well, tell her congrats from me and Ray."

"Sure, Brendan."

Brendan dropped his gaze to the counter and nodded several times as Pete bagged up the tea and candy bar. "So, yeah, okay, good seeing you guys. Come on, Ray."

Ray hadn't been looking at his brother when he spoke, but he moved anyway, and Jimmy remembered once again the thing that people usually forgot about Ray: he wasn't deaf, just mute, few people around the neighborhood or otherwise, Jimmy was sure, having encountered one like that before.

"Hey, Jimmy," Pete said when the brothers had gone, "I ask you something?"

"Shoot."

"Why you hate that kid so bad?"

Jimmy shrugged. "I don't know if it's hate, man. It's just . . . Come on, you don't find that mute little fucker just a little spooky?"

"Oh, *him*?" Pete said. "Yeah. He's a weird little shit, always staring like he sees something in your face he wants to pluck out. You know? But I wasn't talking about him. I was talking about Brendan. I mean, the kid seems nice enough. Shy but decent, you know? You notice how he uses sign language with his brother even though he don't have to? Kinda like he just wants the kid to feel he ain't alone. It's nice. But, Jimmy, man, you look at him like you're two steps from slicing off his nose, man, feeding it to him."

"No."

"Yeah."

"Really?"

"Straight up."

Jimmy looked out over the Lotto machine, past the dusty window onto Buckingham Avenue lying gray and damp under the morning sky. He felt Brendan Harris's shy goddamned smile in his blood, itching him.

"Jimmy? I was just playing with you. I didn't mean nothing by—"

"Here comes Sal," Jimmy said, and kept his eyes on the window, his head turned away from Pete as he watched the old man shuffle across the avenue toward them. "About fucking time, too."

6

BECAUSE IT'S
BROKEN

SEAN DEVINE'S SUNDAY—his first day back to work after a week's suspension—started when he was yanked from a dream, ripped out of it by the beep of an alarm clock followed by the seizure-realization, like a baby popping from the womb, that he'd never be allowed to go back in. He couldn't remember much of the specifics—just a few details, unconnected—and he had a sense that there hadn't been much of a narrative flow in the first place. Still, the raw texture of it had sunk like razor points into the back of his skull, left him feeling skittish all morning.

His wife, Lauren, had been in it, and he could still smell her flesh. She'd had messy hair the color of wet sand, darker and longer than in life, and wore a damp white bathing suit. She was very tan and a light dusting of sand had speckled her bare ankles and the tops of her feet. She'd smelled of the sea and the sun, and she'd sat in Sean's lap and kissed his nose, tickled his throat with long fingers. They were on the deck of a beach house, and Sean could hear the surf but couldn't see any ocean. Where the ocean should have been was a blank TV screen the width of a football field. When he looked in the center, Sean could only make out his own reflection, not Lauren's, as if he sat there holding air.

But it was flesh in his hands, warm flesh.

Next thing he remembered, he stood on the roof of the house, Lauren's flesh replaced by a smooth metal weather vane. He gripped it, and below him, at the base of the house, a huge hole yawned up at him, an upended sailboat beached at the bottom. Then he was naked on the bed with a woman he'd never seen before, feeling her, sensing in some dream logic that Lauren was in another room of the house, watching them on video, and a seagull crashed through the window, glass spitting onto the bed like ice cubes, and Sean, fully clothed again, stood over it.

The seagull gasped. The seagull said, "My neck hurts," and Sean woke up before he could say, "That's because it's broken."

He woke up with the dream draining thickly from the back of his brainpan, the lint and fuzz of it clinging to the undersides of his eyelids and the upper layer of his tongue. He kept his eyes closed as the alarm clock kept beeping, hoping that it was merely a new dream, that he was still sleeping, that the beeping only beeped in his mind.

Eventually, he opened his eyes, the feel of the unknown woman's hard body and the smell of the sea in Lauren's flesh still clinging to his brain tissue, and he realized it wasn't a dream, it wasn't a movie, it wasn't a sad, sad song.

It was these sheets, this bedroom, and this bed. It was the empty beer can on his windowsill, and this sun in his eyes and that alarm clock beep-beep-beeping on his bedside table. It was the faucet, dripping, he kept forgetting to fix. His life, all his.

He shut off the alarm, but didn't get out of bed right away. He didn't want to lift his head just yet because he didn't want to know if he had a hangover. If he had a hangover, the first day back to work would seem twice as long, and the first day back after a suspension, with all the shit he'd have to eat and all the jokes he'd have to hear at his expense, was going to seem pretty damn long in the first place.

He lay there and heard the beeping from the street, the beeping from the cokeheads next door who kept their TV loud from *Letterman* through *Sesame Street,* the beep of his ceiling fan, microwave, and smoke detectors, and the humming beep of the fridge. It beeped on the computers at work. It beeped on cell phones and PalmPilots and beeped from the kitchen and living room and beeped a constant beep-beep-beep on the street below and down at the station house and in the tenements of Faneuil Heights and the East Bucky Flats.

Everything beeped these days. Everything was fast and fluid and built to move. Everyone was getting along in this world, moving with it, growing up.

When the fuck did that start happening?

That's all he wanted to know, really. When had the pace picked up, left him staring at everyone's backs?

He closed his eyes.

When Lauren left.

That's when.

BRENDAN HARRIS LOOKED at the phone and willed it to ring. He looked at his watch. Two hours late. Not exactly a surprise, since time and Katie were never on what you'd call a first-name basis, but man, today of all days. Brendan just wanted to *go*. And where was she, if she wasn't at work? The plan had been that she'd call Brendan during her shift at Cottage Market, go to her half sister's First Communion, and then meet him afterward. But she hadn't gone into work. And she hadn't called.

He couldn't call her. That had been one of the big downsides of their being together ever since the first night they'd hooked up. Katie was usually one of three places—at Bobby O'Donnell's place in the early days of her and Brendan's relationship, in the apartment she'd grown up in on Buckingham Avenue with her father, stepmother, and two half sisters, or in the apartment above where a shitload of her crazy uncles lived, two of whom, Nick and Val, were legends of psychosis and really, really bad impulse control. And then there was her father, Jimmy Marcus, who hated Brendan deeply and for no logical reason that either Brendan or Katie could figure out. Still, Katie had been clear about it—over the years her father had made it his mandate: stay away from the Harrises; you ever bring one home, I disown you.

According to Katie, he was usually a rational guy, her father, but she told Brendan one night, tears dropping to his chest, "He's nuts when it comes to you. Nuts. He's drunk one night, right? I mean, hammered, and he starts going on about my mom, how much she loved me and every-thing, and then he says, he says, 'The fucking Harrises, Katie, they're scum.' "

Scum. The sound of the word caught in Brendan's chest like a pile of phlegm.

" 'You stay away from them. Only thing in life I demand of you, Katie. Please.' "

"So how'd it happen?" Brendan said. "You ending up with me?"

She'd rolled over in his arms and smiled sadly at him. "You don't know?"

Truth be told, Brendan didn't have a clue. Katie was Everything. A Goddess. Brendan was just, well, Brendan.

"No, I don't know."

"You're kind."

"I am?"

She nodded. "I see you with Ray or your mother and even everyday people on the street, and you're just so kind, Brendan."

"A lotta people are kind."

She shook her head. "A lot of people are nice. It's not the same thing."

And Brendan, thinking about it, had to admit that his whole life he'd never met anyone who didn't like him—not in a popularity contest type of way, but in a basic "That Harris kid's all right" type of way. He'd never had enemies, hadn't been in a fight since grade school, and couldn't remember the last time he'd heard a harsh word directed his way. Maybe it was because he *was* kind. And maybe, like Katie said, that was rare. Or maybe he just wasn't the type of guy who made people mad.

Well, except for Katie's father. That was a mystery. And there was no denying it for what it was: hate.

Just half an hour ago, Brendan had felt it in Mr. Marcus's corner store—that quiet, coiled hatred emanating from the man like a viral infection. He'd wilted under it. He'd stammered because of it. He couldn't look at Ray the whole way home because of how that hatred had made him feel—unwashed, his hair filled with nits, teeth covered in grime. And the fact that it made no sense—Brendan had never done any-thing to Mr. Marcus, hell, barely knew the man—didn't make it any easier. Brendan looked at Jimmy Marcus and saw a man looking back who wouldn't stop to piss on him if he was on fire.

Brendan couldn't call Katie at one of her two numbers and risk somebody on the other end having caller ID or star-69ing him, wondering what the hated Brendan Harris was doing calling their Katie. He'd almost done it a million times, but just the thought of Mr. Marcus or Bobby O'Donnell or one of those psycho Savage brothers answering the other end was enough to make him drop the phone from a sweaty hand back into the cradle.

Brendan didn't know who to fear more. Mr. Marcus was just a regular guy, owner of the corner store Brendan had been going to for half his life, but there was something about the guy—more than just his obvious hatred for Brendan—that could unsettle people, a capacity for something, Brendan didn't know what, but something, that made you lower your voice around the guy and try not to meet his eyes. Bobby O'Donnell was one of those guys nobody knew exactly what he did for a living but you'd cross a street to avoid him in either case, and as for the Savage brothers, they were a whole planetary system away from most people in terms of normal, acceptable behavior. The maddest, craziest, most dyed-in-the-wool, lunatic motherfuckers to ever come out of the Flats, the Savage brothers had thousand-yard stares and tempers so hair-trigger you could fill a notebook the size of the Old Testament with all the things that could set them off. Their father, a sick chucklehead in his own right, had, along with their thin, sainted mother, popped the brothers out one after another, eleven months apart, like they were running a midnight assembly line for loose cannons. The brothers grew up crammed and mangy and irate in a bedroom the size of a Japanese radio beside the el tracks that used to hover over the Flats, blotting out the sun, before they got torn down when Brendan was a kid. The floors in the apartment sloped hard to the east, and the trains hammered past the brothers' window twenty-one out of twenty-four hours each and every goddamned day, shaking the piece-of-shit three-decker so hard that most times the brothers fell out of bed and woke in the morning piled on top of one another, greeted the morning as irritable as waterfront rats, and pummeled the piss out of one another to clear the pile and start the day.

When they were kids, they had no individuality to the outside world.

They were just the Savages, a brood, a pack, a collection of limbs and armpits and knees and tangled hair that seemed to move in a cloud of dust like the Tasmanian Devil. You saw the cloud coming your way, you stepped aside, hoped they'd find someone else to fuck up before they reached you, or simply whirl on by, lost in the obsession of their own grimy psychoses.

Hell, until Brendan had started dating Katie on the sly, he wasn't positive just how many of them there actually were, and he'd grown up in the Flats. Katie laid it out for him, though: Nick was the oldest, gone from the neighborhood six years to serve ten minimum at Walpole; Val was the next and, according to Katie, the sweetest; then came Chuck, Kevin, Al (who usually got confused with Val), Gerard, just fresh from Walpole himself, and finally, Scott, the baby boy and mother's favorite when she'd been alive, who was also the only one with a college degree, and the only one who didn't live at home in the first- and third-floor apartments the brothers had commandeered after they'd successfully scared the previous tenants to another state.

"I know they have this rep," Katie said to Brendan, "but they're really nice guys. Well, except for Scott. He's kinda hard to warm up to."

Scott. The "normal" one.

Brendan looked at his watch again, then over at the clock by his bed. He looked at the phone.

He looked at his bed where just the other night he'd fallen asleep with his eyes on the back of Katie's neck, counting the fine blond hairs there, his arm draped over her hip so that his palm rested on her warm abdomen, the smell of her hair and perfume and a light sweat filling his nostrils.

He looked at the phone again.

Call, goddamnit. Call.

A COUPLE of kids found her car. They called it into 911 and the one who spoke into the phone sounded breathless, caught up in something beyond himself as the words spilled out:

"There's like this car with blood in it and, ah, the door's open, and, ah—"

The 911 operator broke in and said, "What's the location of the car?"

"In the Flats," the kid said. "By Pen Park. Me and my friend found it."

"Is there a street address?"

"Sydney Street," the kid expelled into the phone. "There's blood in there and the door's open."

"What's your name, son?"

"He wants to know her name," the kid said to his friend. "Called me 'son.' "

"Son?" the operator said. "I said your name. What's *your* name?"

"We're so fucking outta here, man," the kid said. "Good luck."

The kid hung up and the operator noted from his computer screen that the call had come in from a pay phone on the corner of Kilmer and Nauset in the East Bucky Flats, about half a mile from the Sydney Street entrance to Penitentiary Park. He relayed the information to Dispatch and Dispatch sent a unit out to Sydney Street.

One of the patrolmen called back and requested more units, a Crime Scene tech or two, and, oh yeah, maybe you want to send a couple Homicides down or somebody like that. Just an idea.

"Have you found a body, Thirty-three? Over."

"Ah, negative, Dispatch."

"Thirty-three, why the request for Homicide if there's no body? Over."

"Looks of this car, Dispatch? I kinda feel like we're going to find one around here sooner or later."

SEAN STARTED HIS first day back to work by parking on Crescent and walking around the blue sawhorses at the intersection with Sydney. The sawhorses were stamped with the label of the Boston Police Department, because they were first on-scene, but Sean guessed by what he'd heard on the scanners driving over here that this case would belong to State Police Homicide, his squad.

The car, as he understood it, had been found on Sydney Street, which was city jurisdiction, but the blood trail led into Penitentiary Park, which as part of reservation land fell under State jurisdiction. Sean walked down Crescent along the edge of the park, and the first thing he noticed was a Crime Scene Services van parked halfway down the block.

As he got closer, he saw his sergeant, Whitey Powers, standing a few feet away from a car with the driver's door ajar. Souza and Connolly, who'd been bumped up to Homicide only last week, searched the weeds outside the park entrance, coffee cups in hand, and two patrol units and the Crime Scene Services van were parked along the gravel shoulder, the CSS crew going over the car and shooting dirty looks at Souza and Connolly for trampling possible evidence and leaving the lids off their styrofoam cups.

"Hey, bad boy." Whitey Powers's eyebrows rose in surprise. "Someone call you already?"

"Yeah," Sean said. "I don't have a partner, though, Sarge. Adolph's out."

Whitey Powers nodded. "You get your hand slapped and that useless kraut takes a sudden medical." He put his arm around Sean. "You're with me, kid. The duration of your probation."

So that was how it was going to work, Whitey keeping watch on Sean until the department brass decided if he met their gold standard or not.

"Was looking like a quiet weekend, too," Whitey said as he turned Sean toward the car with the open door. "Whole county last night, Sean? Quieter than a dead cat. Had a stabbing in Parker Hill, 'nother in Bromley Heath, and some college kid took a beating from a beer bottle over in Allston. None of them fatal, though, and all of them City's. Hell, the Parker Hill vic, right? Walked into the ER at MGH on his own, big ol' steak knife sticking out of his collarbone, asked the admitting nurse where they kept a Coke machine 'round this bitch."

"She tell him?" Sean said.

Whitey smiled. He was one of State Homicide's brightest boys and had been forever, so he smiled a lot. He must have taken the call heading into his shift, though, because he wore sweatpants and his son's hockey jersey, a baseball hat riding backward on his head, iridescent blue flip-flops over bare feet, his gold badge hanging from a nylon cord over the jersey.

"Like the shirt," Sean said, and Whitey gave him another lazy grin as a bird broke overhead from the park and arced above them, letting loose a rattling caw that bit into Sean's spine.

"Man, half an hour ago? I was on my *sofa*."

"Watching cartoons?"

"Wrestling." Whitey pointed at the weeds and the park beyond. "I figure we'll find her over there somewhere. But, you know, we just started looking and Friel says we call it a Missing Persons till we find a body."

The bird swung over them again, a little lower, that sharp rattle of a caw finding the base of Sean's brain this time and nibbling.

"It's ours, though?" Sean said.

Whitey nodded. " 'Less the victim ran back out again, got snuffed somewhere down the block."

Sean glanced up. The bird had a big head and short legs tucked under a white chest that was striped gray in the center. Sean didn't recognize the species, but then he didn't hang out in nature all that much. "What is it?"

"A belted kingfisher," Whitey said.

"Bullshit."

He held up a hand. "Swear to God, man."

"Watched a lot of *Wild Kingdom* as a kid, didn't you?"

The bird let loose that hard rattle again and Sean wanted to shoot it.

Whitey said, "Want to look at the car?"

"You said 'her,' " Sean said as they ducked under yellow crime scene tape and headed for the car.

"CSS found the reg in the glove box. Car's owner is a Katherine Marcus."

"Shit," Sean said.

"Know her?"

"Might be the daughter of a guy I know."

"You guys close?"

Sean shook his head. "No, just to nod hello from around the neighborhood."

"Sure?" Whitey was asking if he wanted to pass on the case right here, right now.

"Yeah," Sean said. "Sure as shit."

They reached the car and Whitey pointed at the open driver's door as a CSS tech stepped back from it and stretched, arching her back, hands entwined and thrust toward the sky. "Just don't touch nothing, guys. Who's the point on this?"

Whitey said, "That'd be me. Park is State jurisdiction."

"But the car's on city property."

Whitey pointed at the weeds. "That blood spatter fell on state land."

"I dunno," the CSS tech said with a sigh.

"We got an ADA en route," Whitey said. "He can call it. Till then, it's State."

Sean took one look at the weeds leading up to the park and knew if they found a body, they'd find it in there. "What do we have?"

The tech yawned. "Door was ajar when we found it. Keys were in the ignition, headlights were on. Like on cue, the battery shit the bed about ten seconds after we got on the scene."

Sean noticed a bloodstain over the speaker on the driver's door. Some of it had dripped, black and crusty, over the speaker itself. He dropped to a squat and pivoted, saw another spot of black on top of the steering wheel. A third stain, longer and wider than the other two, clung to the edges of a bullet hole punched through the vinyl of the driver's seat back at shoulder level. Sean pivoted again so that he was looking past the door at the weeds to the left of the car, then he craned his head around to look at the outside of the driver's door, saw the fresh dent there.

He looked up at Whitey, and Whitey nodded. "Perp probably stood outside the car. The Marcus girl—if that's who was driving—slams him with the door. Cocksucker gets a round off, hits her, ah, I dunno, in the shoulder, maybe the biceps? The girl makes a run for it anyway." He pointed at some weeds freshly flattened by running feet. "They trample the weeds heading for the park. Her wound couldn't have been too bad, because we've only found a few blood spatters in the weeds."

Sean said, "We got units over in the park?"

"Two so far."

The CSS tech snorted. "They any smarter than those two?"

Sean and Whitey followed her gaze, saw that Connolly had accidentally dropped his coffee in the weeds, was standing over it, bitching out the cup.

"Hey," Whitey said, "they're new, cut 'em some slack."

"I gotta dust some more, guys."

Sean stepped back for the woman. "You find any ID besides the car reg?"

"Yup. Wallet under the seat, driver's license made out to Katherine Marcus. There was a backpack behind the passenger seat. Billy's checking the contents now."

Sean looked over the hood at the guy she'd indicated with a toss of her head. He was on his knees in front of the car, a dark blue backpack in front of him.

Whitey said, "How old did her license say she was?"

"Nineteen, Sergeant."

"Nineteen," Whitey said to Sean. "And you know the father? Fuck, man, he's in for a world of hurt, poor bastard probably has no idea."

Sean turned his head, watched as the lone rattling bird headed back for the channel, screeching, and a hard shaft of sun cut through the clouds. Sean felt the screech drive through his ear canal and into his brain, and he was pierced for a moment by the memory of that wild aloneness he'd seen in eleven-year-old Jimmy Marcus's face when they'd almost stolen that car. Sean could feel it now, standing by the weeds leading up to Penitentiary Park, as if the twenty-five years in between had passed as fast as a TV commercial, feel that beaten, pissed-off, begging aloneness that had lain in Jimmy Marcus like pulp hollowed from the core of a dying tree. To shake it, he thought of Lauren, the Lauren with long, sandy hair who'd marinated his dream this morning and smelled of the sea. He thought of that Lauren and wished he could just climb back into the tunnel of that dream and pull it over his head, disappear.

7

IN THE BLOOD

NADINE MARCUS, Jimmy and Annabeth's younger daughter, received the Blessed Sacrament of Holy Communion for the first time on Sunday morning at Saint Cecilia's in the East Bucky Flats. Her hands pressed together from the base of her palms to the tips of her fingers, white veil and white dress making her look like a baby bride or snow angel, she walked up the aisle in procession with forty other children, gliding, where the other kids stutter-stepped.

Or at least that's how it seemed to Jimmy, and while he might have been the first to admit that, yeah, he was biased in favor of his kids, he was also pretty sure he was right. Other kids these days spoke or yelled whenever they felt like it, cussed in front of their parents, demanded this and demanded that, showed absolutely no respect for adults, and had the slightly dazed, slightly feverish eyes of addicts who spent too much time in front of a TV, a computer screen, or both. They reminded Jimmy of silver pinballs—sluggish one moment, banging off everything in sight the next, clanging bells and careening from side to side. They asked for something, they usually got it. If they didn't, they asked louder. If the answer was still a tentative no, they screamed. And their parents—pussies one and all, as far as Jimmy was concerned—usually caved.

Jimmy and Annabeth doted on their girls. They worked hard to keep them happy and entertained and aware that they were loved. But there was a fine line between that and taking shit from them, and Jimmy made sure the girls all knew exactly where the line was.

Like these two little pricks now, coming up beside Jimmy's pew in the processional—two boys, shoving each other, laughing out loud, ignoring the shushes of the nuns, starting to play to the crowd, and some of the adults actually smiling back. Jesus. Back in Jimmy's time, the parents would have stepped out of the crowd, yanked the two off the ground by their hair, swatted their asses, and whispered promises for more into their ears before dropping them back down.

Jimmy, who'd hated his old man, knew the old ways sucked, too, no question, but, damn, there had to be an in-between solution somewhere that the majority of people seemed to be overlooking. A middle ground where a kid knew the parents loved him but were still the boss, rules existed for a reason, no really meant no, and just because you were cute didn't mean you were cool.

Of course, you could pass all that on, raise a good kid, and they still put you through misery. Like Katie today. Not only had she never showed up for work, but now it looked like she was blowing off her younger half sister's First Communion. What the hell was going through her mind? Nothing, probably, which was the issue.

Turning back to watch Nadine advance up the aisle, Jimmy was so proud he felt his anger (and, yeah, some worry, a minor but persistent niggle of it) at Katie subside a bit, though he knew it would come back. First Communion was an event in a Catholic child's life—a day to dress up and be adored and fawned over and taken to Chuck E. Cheese's afterward—and Jimmy believed in marking events in his children's lives, making them bright and memorable. Which was why Katie not showing up pissed him off so much. She was nineteen, okay, so the world of her younger half sisters probably couldn't compare to guys and clothes and sneaking into bars that had a lax ID policy. Jimmy understood this, so he usually gave Katie a wide berth, but skipping an event, particularly after all Jimmy had done when Katie was younger to mark the events in *her* life, was fucking lame.

He felt the anger rising again, knew as soon as he saw her, they'd have another of their "debates," as Annabeth called them, a frequent occurrence the last couple of years.

Whatever. Fuck it.

Because here came Nadine now, almost abreast with Jimmy's pew. Annabeth had made Nadine promise she wouldn't look at her father as she passed him and spoil the seriousness of the sacrament with something girlish and giddy, but Nadine stole a glance anyway—a small one, just enough to let Jimmy know she was risking the wrath of her mother to show love to her father. She didn't preen for her grandfather, Theo, and six uncles who filled the pew behind Jimmy, and Jimmy respected that: she was edging near the line, not over it. Her left eye snuck toward its corner, Jimmy tracking it through the veil, and he gave her a small three-finger wave from belt-buckle level and mouthed a huge, silent "Hi!"

Nadine's smile burst whiter than anything her veil or dress or shoes could match, and Jimmy felt it blow through his heart and his eyes and his knees. The women in his life—Annabeth, Katie, Nadine, and her sister Sara—could do that to him at the drop of a hat, buckle his knees with a smile or a glance, leave him weak.

Nadine dropped her eyes and clenched her small face to cover the smile, but Annabeth had caught it anyway. She dug an elbow into the space between Jimmy's ribs and his left hip. He turned to her, feeling his face going red, and said, "What?"

Annabeth tossed him a look that said his ass was slung when they got back home. Then she looked straight ahead, her lips tight, but jerking a bit at the corners. Jimmy knew all he'd have to say was "Problem?" in that innocent-boy voice of his and Annabeth would start cracking up in spite of herself, because something about a church just gave you a need to giggle, and that had always been one of Jimmy's big gifts: he could make the ladies laugh, no matter what.

He didn't look at Annabeth for a while after that, though, just followed the mass and then the sacramental rites as each child in turn took that wafer in cupped hands for the first time. He'd rolled up the program booklet, and it turned damp with heat in his palm as he drummed it against his thigh and watched Nadine lift the wafer from her palm and place it to her tongue, then bless herself, head down, and Annabeth leaned into him and whispered in his ear: "Our baby. My God, Jimmy, our *baby.*"

Jimmy put his arm around her, pulled her tight, wishing you could freeze moments in your life like snapshots, just stay in them, suspended, until you were ready to come out again, however many hours or days that might take. He turned his head and kissed Annabeth's cheek, and she leaned into him a little more, both of their eyes locked on their daughter, their floating angel of a baby girl.

THE GUY with the samurai sword stood at the edge of the park, his back to the Pen Channel, one foot raised up off the ground as he pivoted slowly with the other, the sword held at an odd angle behind the crown of his head. Sean, Whitey, Souza, and Connolly approached slowly, giving one another "What the fuck?" looks. The guy continued his slow pivot, oblivious to the four men approaching him in a loose line along the grass. He raised the sword over his head and began to bring it down in front of his chest. They were about twenty feet away now, the guy having pivoted 180 degrees so that his back was to them, and Sean saw Connolly put his hand to his right hip, unsnap the buckle of his holster, and leave the hand resting on the butt of his Glock.

Before this got any nuttier and someone got shot or the guy went all hara-kiri on them, Sean cleared his throat and said, "Excuse me, sir. Sir? Excuse me."

The guy's head cocked slightly as if he'd heard Sean, but he continued that deliberate pivot, revolving in increments toward them.

"Sir, we need you to lay your weapon on the grass."

The guy's foot dropped back to the ground and he turned to face them, his eyes widening and then clicking on each of them—one, two, three, four guns—and he held out the sword, either pointing it at them or trying to hand it to them, Sean couldn't tell which.

Connolly said, "The fuck—you deaf? On the ground."

Sean said, "Sssh," and stopped moving, ten feet from the guy now, thinking about the blood drops they'd found along the jogging path about sixty yards back, all four of them knowing what the drops meant, and then looking up to see Bruce Lee over here brandishing a sword the length of a small plane. Except Bruce Lee had been Asian and this guy was definitely white, youngish, maybe twenty-five, with curly black hair and shaven cheeks, white T-shirt tucked into gray sweats.

He was frozen now, and Sean was pretty sure it was fear that kept that sword pointed at them, the brain seizing up and unable to command the body.

"Sir," Sean said, sharp enough for the guy to look directly at him. "Do me a favor, okay? Put the sword down on the ground. Just open your fingers and let it drop."

"Who the hell are you guys?"

"We're police officers." Whitey Powers flashed his badge. "See? So, trust me here, sir, and drop that sword."

"Uh, sure," the guy said, and just like that it fell from his fingers, hit the grass with a damp thud.

Sean felt Connolly starting to move on his left, ready to rush the guy, and he put out his hand, kept the guy's eyes locked with his, and said, "What's your name?"

"Huh? Kent."

"Kent, how you doing? I'm State Trooper Devine. I need you to just take a couple of steps back from the weapon."

"The weapon?"

"The sword, Kent. Take a couple of steps back. What's your last name, Kent?"

"Brewer," he said, and backed up, his palms held up and out now like he was sure they were going to draw their Glocks all at once and unload.

Sean smiled and threw a nod at Whitey. "Hey, Kent, what was that you were doing out here? Looked like some kind of ballet to me." He shrugged. "With a sword, sure, but . . ."

Kent watched Whitey bend by the sword and pick it up gently by the hilt with a handkerchief.

"Kendo."

"What's that, Kent?"

"Kendo," Kent said. "It's a martial art. I take it Tuesdays and Thursdays and practice in the mornings. I was just practicing. That's all."

Connolly sighed.

Souza looked at Connolly. "You're dicking me, right?"

Whitey held out the sword blade for Sean to see. It was oiled and shiny and so clean it could have just come off the press.

"Look." Whitey slid the blade across his open palm. "I've had sharper *spoons*."

"It's never been sharpened," Kent said.

Sean felt that bird in his skull again, screeching. "Ah, Kent, how long you been here?"

Kent looked at the parking lot a hundred yards behind them. "Fifteen minutes? Tops. What's this about?" His voice was gaining confidence now, a shade of indignation. "It's not illegal to practice kendo in a public park, Officer, is it?"

"We're working on it, though," Whitey said. "And that's 'Sergeant,' Kent."

"You account for your whereabouts late last night, early this morning?" Sean asked.

Kent looked nervous again, racking his brain, holding in a breath. He closed his eyes for a moment, then let out the breath. "Yes, yes. I was, I was at a party last night with friends. I went home with my girlfriend. We got to sleep about three. I had coffee with her this morning and then I came here."

Sean pinched the top of his nose and nodded. "We're going to impound the sword, Kent, and we wouldn't mind if you dropped over to the barracks with one of the troopers, answered a few questions."

"The barracks?"

"The police station," Sean said. "We just got a different name for it."

"Why?"

"Kent, could you just agree to go with one of the troopers?"

"Uh, sure."

Sean looked at Whitey and Whitey grimaced. They knew Kent was too scared to be telling anything but the truth, and they knew the sword would come back from Forensics clean, but they had to play out every string and file a follow-up report till the paperwork looked like parade floats atop their desks.

"I'm getting my black belt," Kent said.

They turned back and looked at him. "Huh?"

"On Saturday," Kent said, his face bright under beads of perspiration. "Took me three years, but, ah, that's why I was down here this morning, making sure my form was tight."

"Uh-huh," Sean said.

"Hey, Kent?" Whitey said, and Kent smiled at him. "I mean, not for nothing, right, but who really gives a fuck?"

BY THE TIME Nadine and the other kids flowed out through the back of the church, Jimmy was feeling less pissed off at Katie, and more worried about her. For all the late nights and sneaking around with boys he didn't know, Katie wasn't one to let her half sisters down. They worshipped her, and she in turn doted on them—taking them to movies, Rollerblading, out for ice cream. Lately she'd been firing them up about next Sunday's parade, acting as if Buckingham Day was a nationally recognized holiday, up there with Saint Pat's and Christmas. She'd come home early Wednesday night and trooped the two girls upstairs to pick out what they were going to wear, making a mini-production out of it as she sat up on her bed and the girls came back and forth into the room modeling their outfits, asking her questions about their hair, their eyes, their manner of walking. Of course, the room the two girls shared turned into a cyclone of discarded clothing, but Jimmy didn't mind—Katie was helping the girls mark yet another event, using the tricks Jimmy had taught her to make even the most minor things seem major and singular.

So why would she blow off Nadine's First Communion?

Maybe she'd tied on one of legendary proportions. Or maybe she really had met that new guy with movie-star looks and attitude to spare. Maybe she'd just forgotten.

Jimmy left the pew and walked down the aisle with Annabeth and Sara, Annabeth squeezing his hand and reading the clench in his jaw, his distant gaze.

"I'm sure she's fine. Hung over, probably. But fine."

Jimmy smiled and nodded and squeezed back. Annabeth, with her psychic reads of him, her well-placed hand squeezes, her tender practicality, was Jimmy's foundation, plain and simple. She was his wife, mother, best friend, sister, lover, and priest. Without her, Jimmy knew beyond a doubt, he'd have ended up back in Deer Island or, worse, out in one of the maximum pens like Norfolk or Cedar Junction, doing hard time, his teeth rotting.

When he'd met Annabeth a year after his release, two to go on his probation, his relationship with Katie had just begun to jell, in increments. She had seemed to have gotten used to him being around all the time—wary, still, but warming—and Jimmy had gotten used to being permanently tired—tired from working ten hours a day and scuttling all over the city to pick up Katie or drop her off at his mother's, at school, at day care. He was tired and he was scared; those were the two constants in his life back then, and after a while he took it for granted they'd always be there. He'd wake up scared—scared Katie had managed to roll over wrong in her sleep at night and smother herself, scared the economy would continue cycling downward until he was out of a job, scared Katie would fall from the jungle gym at school during recess, scared she'd need something he couldn't provide, scared his life would continue as this constant grind of fear and love and exhaustion forever.

Jimmy carried that exhaustion into the church the day one of Annabeth's brothers, Val Savage, married Terese Hickey, both the bride and groom ugly, angry, and short. Jimmy pictured them having a litter as opposed to kids, raising a pack of indistinguishable, pug-nosed rage balls to bounce up and down Buckingham Avenue for years to come, igniting. Val had worked for Jimmy's crew back in the days when Jimmy had a crew, and he was grateful to Jimmy for taking a hard two-year fall and another three suspended on behalf of the whole crew when everyone knew Jimmy could have dimed them all out and skated. Val, tiny-limbed and tiny-brained, would have probably idolized Jimmy outright if Jimmy hadn't married a Puerto Rican chick, and one from outside the neighborhood, too.

After Marita died, the neighborhood whispers said, Well, there you go, don't you? That's what happens when you go against the way of things. That Katie, though, she'll be a real looker; half-breeds always are.

When Jimmy had gotten out of Deer Island, the offers rolled in. Jimmy was a pro, one of the best second-story guys to ever come out of a neighborhood that had a Hall of Fame roster's worth of second-story guys. And even when Jimmy said no, thanks, he was going straight, for the kid, you know, people nodded and smiled and knew he'd come back to it the first time things got tough and he had to choose between a car payment and Katie's Christmas present.

Didn't happen, though. Jimmy Marcus, B & E genius and a guy who'd run his own crew before he was old enough to legally drink, the man behind the Keldar Technics heist and a ton of other shit, stayed so straight it got to where people thought he was taunting them. Hell, rumor was Jimmy had even been discussing buying out Al DeMarco's corner store, letting the old man retire as owner-in-name with a chunk of the money Jimmy'd allegedly stashed away from the Keldar job. Jimmy as shopkeeper, wearing an apron—okay, sure, they said.

At Val and Terese's reception at the K of C on Dunboy, Jimmy asked Annabeth to dance, and folks there saw it right away—the curve of them as they leaned into the music, the tilt of their heads as they looked right at each other, bold as bulls, the way his palm lightly caressed the small of her back and she leaned back into it. They'd known each other as kids, someone said, though he'd been a few years ahead of her. Maybe it had always been there, waiting for the Puerto Rican to pack up, or God to pack up for her.

It had been a Rickie Lee Jones song they'd danced to, a few lines in the song that always got to Jimmy for some reason he didn't understand— "Well, good-bye, boys/Oh my buddy boys/Oh my sad-eyed Sinatras . . ." He lip-synced them to Annabeth as they swayed, feeling loose and at ease for the first time in years, lip-synced again at the chorus along with Rickie's mournful wisp of a voice, "So long, lone-ly ave-nue," smiling into Annabeth's crystal green eyes, and she'd smiled, too, in a soft, hidden way she had that cracked his heart, the two of them acting like this was their hundredth dance instead of their first.

They were the last ones to leave—sitting outside on the wide entrance porch, drinking light beers and smoking cigarettes and nodding to the other guests as they walked to their cars. They stayed out there until the summer night had chilled, and Jimmy slid his coat around her shoulders and told her about prison and Katie, and Marita's dreams of orange curtains, and she told him about growing up the only female Savage in a house full of maniac brothers, of her one winter dancing in New York before she figured out she wasn't good enough, of nursing school.

When the K of C management kicked them off the porch, they wandered over to the after-party in time for Val and Terese's first screaming match as a married couple. They clipped a six-pack from Val's fridge and left, walked off into the dark of Hurley's Drive-in and sat by the channel, listened to its sullen lapping. The drive-in had shut down four years before, and squat yellow diggers and dump trucks from Parks and Recreation and the D.O.T. convoyed onto the land every morning, turned the whole area along the Pen into an eruption of dirt and torn cement. Word was they were turning it into a park, but at that point it was just a mangled drive-in, the screen still looming white behind mountains of brown dirt and black-and-gray cakes of disgorged asphalt.

"They say it's in your blood," Annabeth said.

"What?"

"Stealing, crime." She shrugged. "You know."

Jimmy smiled at her around his beer bottle, took a sip.

"Is it?" she said.

"Maybe." It was his turn to shrug. "Lotta things are in my blood. Doesn't mean they have to come out."

"I'm not judging you. Believe me." Her face unreadable, even her voice, Jimmy wondering what she wanted to hear from him—that he was still in the life? That he was out? That he'd make her rich? That he'd never commit a crime again?

Annabeth had a calm, almost forgettable face from a distance, but when you got up close, you saw so many things in there that you didn't understand, a sense of a mind furiously at work, never sleeping.

"I mean, dancing's in your blood, right?"

"I dunno. I guess."

"But now that you've been told you can't do it anymore, you've stopped, right? It might hurt, but you've faced it."

"Okay . . ."

"Okay," he said, and slid a cigarette out of the pack that lay on the stone bench between them. "So, yeah, I was good at what I did. But I took a pinch and my wife died and that fucked my daughter up." He lit the cigarette and took a long exhale as he tried to put it exactly as he'd said it in his mind a hundred times. "I ain't fucking my daughter up again, Annabeth. You know? She can't go through another two years of me doing time. My mother? She ain't a well woman. She dies while I'm locked down? Then they take my daughter, make her a ward of the state, put her in some sort of Deer Island for tots. I couldn't take that shit. So that's it. In the blood, out of the blood, whatever the fuck, I'm staying straight."

Jimmy held her gaze as she studied his face. He could tell she was searching for flaws in his explanation, a whiff of bullshit, and he hoped he'd somehow managed to make the speech fly. He'd been working on it long enough, preparing for a moment like this. And, fact was, what he'd said was mostly true. He'd only left out that one thing he'd sworn to himself he'd never tell another soul, no matter who that soul was. So he looked in Annabeth's eyes and waited for her to make her decision, and tried to ignore images from that night by the Mystic River—the guy on his knees, saliva dripping down his chin, the screech of his begging—images that kept trying to push their way into his head like drill bits.

Annabeth took a cigarette. He lit it for her, and she said, "I used to have the worst crush on you. You know that?"

Jimmy kept his head steady, his gaze calm, even though the relief flooding through him was like a jet blast—he'd sold the half-truth. If things worked out with Annabeth, he'd never have to sell it again.

"No shit? You on me?"

She nodded. "When you'd come by the house to see Val? My God, I was, what, fourteen, fifteen? Jimmy, forget it. My skin would start to buzz just hearing your voice in the kitchen."

"Damn." He touched her arm. "It ain't buzzing now."

"Oh, sure it is, Jimmy. Sure it is."

And Jimmy felt the Mystic roll far away again, dissolve into the dirty depths of the Pen, gone from him, rolling off into the distance where it belonged.

BY THE TIME Sean got back to the jogging trail, the CSS woman was there. Whitey Powers radioed all units on-scene to do a sweep-and-detain of any vagrants in the park and squatted down beside Sean and the CSS woman.

"The blood heads that way," the CSS woman said, pointing deeper into the park. The jogging path went over a small wooden bridge and then curled off and down into a heavily wooded section of the park, circling around the old drive-in screen down at the far end. "There's more over there." She pointed with her pen, and Sean and Whitey looked back over their shoulders, saw smaller blood spatters in the grass on the other side of the joggers' path by the small wooden bridge, the leaves of a tall maple having protected the spatters from last night's rain. "I think she ran for that ravine."

Whitey's radio squawked and he put it to his lips. "Powers."

"Sergeant, we need you over by the garden."

"On my way."

Sean watched Whitey trot onto the jogging path and then head for the garden co-op around the next bend, the hem of his son's hockey shirt flapping around his waist.

Sean straightened from his squat and looked at the park, felt the sheer size of it, every bush, every knoll, all that water. He looked back at the small wooden bridge that led over a tiny ravine where the water was twice as dark and twice as polluted as the channel. Crusted with a permanent greasy film, it buzzed with mosquitoes in the summer. Sean noticed a spot of red in the thin, greening trees that sprouted along the bank of the ravine and he moved toward it, the CSS woman suddenly beside him, seeing it, too.

"What's your name?" Sean said.

"Karen," she said. "Karen Hughes."

Sean shook her hand, the two of them focused on that spot of red as they crossed the joggers' path, not even hearing Whitey Powers until he was almost on top of them, trotting, short of breath.

"We found a shoe," Whitey said.

"Where?"

Whitey pointed back down the joggers' path, past where it curved around the garden co-op. "In the garden. Woman's shoe. Size six."

"Don't touch it," Karen Hughes said.

"Duh," Whitey said, and got a look from her, Karen Hughes having one of those glacial looks that could shrink everything inside of you. "Excuse me. I meant—duh, *ma'am.*"

Sean turned back to the trees, and the spot of red was no longer a spot, it was a torn triangle of fabric, hanging from a thin branch about shoulder high. The three of them stood in front of it until Karen Hughes stepped back and snapped several photographs from four different angles, then dug in her bag for something.

It was nylon, Sean was pretty sure, probably from a jacket, and slick with blood.

Karen used a pair of tweezers to pull it from the branch and stared at it for a minute before dropping it into a plastic baggie.

Sean bent at the waist and craned his head, looked down into the ravine. Then he looked across to the other side, saw what could have been a heel print dug into the soft soil.

He nudged Whitey and pointed until Whitey saw it, too. Then Karen Hughes took a look and immediately snapped off a few shots from her department-issue Nikon. She straightened and crossed over the bridge, came down on the embankment, and took a few more photographs.

Whitey dropped into a squat and peered under the bridge. "I'd say she might have hid here for a bit. Killer shows up, she bolts to the other side and takes off running again."

Sean said, "Why's she keep going deeper into the park? I mean, her back's against the water here, Sarge. Why not cut back toward the entrance?"

"Could be she was disoriented. It's dark, she's got a bullet in her."

Whitey shrugged and used his radio to call Dispatch.

"This is Sergeant Powers. We're leaning toward a possible one-eighty-seven, Dispatch. We're going to need every available officer for a sweep of Pen Park. See if you can scare up some divers, maybe."

"Divers?"

"Affirmative. We need Detective Lieutenant Friel and someone from the DA on-scene ASAP."

"The detective lieutenant is en route. DA's office has been notified. Over?"

"Affirmative. Out, Dispatch."

Sean looked across at the heel mark in the soil, and he noticed some scratches to the left of it, the victim digging her fingers in as she'd scrambled up and over the embankment. "Feel like taking a guess what the fuck happened here last night, Sarge?"

"Ain't even going to try," Whitey said.

STANDING ATOP the church steps, Jimmy could just make out the Penitentiary Channel. It was a stripe of dull purple on the far side of the expressway overpass, the park that abutted it serving as the only evidence of green on this side of the channel. Jimmy spied the white sliver top of the drive-in movie screen in the center of the park peeking just above the overpass. It still stood, long after the state had grabbed the land for short money at the Chapter Eleven auction and turned it over to the Parks and Recreation Service. Parks and Recreation spent the next decade beautifying the place, ripping up the poles that supported the car speakers, leveling and greening the land, cutting bike paths and jogging paths along the water, erecting a fenced-in garden co-op, even building a boathouse and ramp for canoers who couldn't get very far before they were turned back at either end by the harbor locks. The screen stayed, though, ended up sprouting from the edge of a cul-de-sac they'd created by planting a stand of already-formed trees shipped in from Northern California. Summers, a local theater group performed Shakespeare in front of the screen, painting medieval backdrops on it and skipping back and forth across the stage with tinfoil swords, saying "Hark" and "Forsooth" and shit like that all the time. Jimmy had gone there with Annabeth and the girls two summers back, and Annabeth, Nadine, and Sara had all nodded off before the end of the first act. But Katie had stayed awake, leaning forward on the blanket, elbow on her knee, chin on the heel of her hand, so Jimmy had too.

They did *The Taming of the Shrew* that night, and Jimmy couldn't follow most of it—something about a guy slapping his fiancée into line until she became an acceptable servant wife, Jimmy failing to see the art in that but figuring he was losing a lot in the translation. Katie, though, was all over it. She laughed a bunch of times, went dead silent and rapt a few more, told Jimmy afterward it was "magic."

Jimmy didn't know what the hell she meant, and Katie couldn't explain it. She just said she'd felt it "transport" her, and for the next six months she kept talking about moving to Italy after graduation.

Jimmy, looking out at the edge of the East Bucky Flats from the church steps, thought: Italy. You bet.

"Daddy, Daddy!" Nadine broke away from a group of friends and ran toward Jimmy as he reached the bottom step, slammed into Jimmy's legs full-force, still saying it: "Daddy, Daddy."

Jimmy picked her up, got a sharp whiff of starch from her dress, and kissed her cheek. "Baby, baby."

With the same motion her mother used to push hair out of her eyes, Nadine used the backs of two fingers to push her veil out of her face. "This dress itches."

"It's itching me," Jimmy said, "and I'm not even wearing it."

"You'd look funny in a dress, Daddy."

"Not if it fit just so."

Nadine rolled her eyes and then scraped the underside of his chin with the stiff crown of her veil. "Does that tickle?"

Jimmy looked over Nadine's head at Annabeth and Sara, felt all three of them blow through his chest, fill him up, and turn him to dust at the same time.

A spray of bullets could hit his back right now, this second, and it would be okay. It would be all right. He was happy. Happy as you could get.

Well, almost. He scanned the crowd for Katie, hoping maybe she'd pulled up at the last moment. He saw a state police cruiser instead as it slammed around the corner of Buckingham Avenue, went wide into the left lane of Roseclair, rear tire slapping the median strip, the bleat-beep and sharp squawk of its siren slicing the morning air. Jimmy watched the driver floor it, heard the big engine rev as the cruiser shot down Roseclair toward the Pen Channel. A black unmarked followed a few seconds later, its sirens mute but no mistaking it for anything else, the driver cutting the hard ninety-degree turn onto Roseclair at forty miles an hour, engine humming.

And as Jimmy lowered Nadine back to the ground, he could feel it in his blood, a sudden, mean certainty, a sense of things falling miserably into place. He watched the two cop cars zip under the overpass and turn hard right onto the entrance road of Pen Park, and he felt Katie in his blood now along with that humming engine and slapping tires, the floating capillaries and cells.

Katie, he almost said aloud. Sweet Jesus. Katie.

8

OLD MACDONALD

CELESTE WOKE UP Sunday morning thinking about pipes—the network of them that coursed through homes and restaurants, movie multiplexes and shopping malls, and dropped in great skeletal sections from the tops of forty-story office buildings, floor by giant floor, plunging toward an even grander network of sewers and aqueducts that ran beneath cities and towns, connecting people more viably than language, with the sole purpose of flushing the things we'd consumed and rejected from our bodies, our lives, our dishes and crisper trays.

Where did it all go?

She supposed she'd considered the question before, in a vague sense, the way you wondered how a plane really stayed aloft without flapping its wings, but now she really wanted to know. She sat up in the empty bed, anxious and curious, heard the sounds of Dave and Michael playing Wiffle ball in the backyard three stories below. Where? she wondered.

It had to go somewhere. All those flushes, all that hand soap and shampoo and detergent and toilet paper and barroom vomit, all the coffee stains, bloodstains, and sweat stains, dirt from the cuffs of your pants and grime from the inside of your collar, the cold vegetables you scraped off the plate into the garbage disposal, cigarettes and urine and hard bristles of hair from legs, cheeks, groins, and chins—it all met up with hundreds of thousands of similar or identical entities every night and poured, she assumed, through dank corridors fleeced by vermin and out into vast catacombs where it commingled in rushing water that rushed off to . . . where?

They didn't dump it in the oceans anymore. Did they? They couldn't. She seemed to remember something about septic processing and the compacting of raw sewage, but she couldn't be sure that wasn't something she'd seen in a movie, and movies were so often full of shit. So if not the ocean, where? And if the ocean, why? There had to be some better way, right? But then she had an image of all those pipes again, all that waste, and she was left to wonder.

She heard the hollow plastic snap of the Wiffle-ball bat as it made contact with the ball. She heard Dave yell, "Whoa!" and Michael whoop and a dog bark once, the sound as crisp as the bat against the ball.

Celeste rolled over onto her back, realizing only at that moment that she was naked and had slept past ten. Neither circumstance had occurred much, if at all, since Michael could walk, and she felt a small wave of guilt roll through her chest, then die in the pit of her stomach as she remembered kissing the flesh around Dave's fresh scar in the kitchen at 4 A.M., on her knees, tasting the fear and adrenaline in his pores, any worries about AIDS or hepatitis conquered by this sudden need to taste him, to press herself as intimately as possible against him. She'd slid her bathrobe off her shoulders with her tongue still roaming along his skin, knelt there in a half-T-shirt and black underwear feeling the night slipping under the porch doorway and chilling her ankles and kneecaps. The fear had given Dave's flesh a half bitter, half sugary taste, and she ran her tongue up from the scar tissue to the base of his throat and cupped her hand between his thighs and felt him harden and heard his breathing grow shorter. She wanted this to last as long as possible, the taste of him, the power she suddenly possessed in her body, and she rose up and covered him. She slid her tongue over his and tightened her fingers in his hair and imagined she was sucking the pain of his parking lot encounter straight out of him and into her. She held his head and pressed her skin against his until he stripped off her shirt and sank his mouth over her breast, and she rocked herself against his groin and heard him moan. She wanted Dave to understand that this was what they were, this pressing of flesh, this enveloping of bodies and scent and need and love, yes, love, because she loved him as deeply as she ever had now that she knew she'd almost lost him.

His teeth pinched her breast, hurting, sucking too hard, and she pushed herself further into his mouth and welcomed the pain. She wouldn't have minded if he drew blood, because he was sucking at her, needing her, fingertips digging into her back, releasing the fear onto and into her. And she would take it all and spit it out for him, and they would both feel stronger than they'd ever felt before. She was sure of it.

When she'd first been dating Dave, their sex life had been characterized by a raw lack of boundaries; she'd come home to the apartment she shared with Rosemary covered in bruises and bite marks and scratches on her back, rubbed straight down to the bone with the kind of urgent exhaustion she imagined an addict felt between fixes. Since Michael's birth—well, actually, since Rosemary had moved in with them after cancer number one—Celeste and Dave had slipped into the type of predictable married-couple routine joked about nonstop on sitcoms, usually too weary or without enough privacy to do much more than a few perfunctory minutes of foreplay, a few oral, before moving on to the main event, which, over the years, seemed less like a main event and more like something to pass the time between the weather report and Leno.

But last night—last night had definitely been main event/title card sort of passion, leaving her, even now as she lay in the bed, bruised to the marrow with it.

It was when she heard Dave's voice from outside again, telling Michael to concentrate, concentrate, damn it, that she remembered what had been bothering her—before the pipes, before the memory of their crazy kitchen sex, maybe even before she'd crawled into bed this morning: Dave had lied to her.

She'd known in the bathroom when he'd first come home, but she'd decided to ignore it. Then, as she'd lain on the linoleum and raised her back and ass off the floor so he could enter her, she'd known it again. She watched his eyes, slightly glazed, as he inserted himself and pulled her calves over his hips, and she met his initial thrusts with the dawning certainty that his story didn't make sense.

For starters, who said things like, "Your wallet or your life, bitch. I'm leaving with one of them"? It was laughable. It was, as she had been sure in the bathroom, movie talk. And even if the mugger had prepared the line beforehand, no way he'd actually say it when the time came. No way. Celeste had been mugged once on the Common when she was in her late teens. The mugger, a high-yellow black man with flat, thin wrists and swimming brown eyes, had stepped up to her in the abandonment of a cold, late dusk, placed a switchblade to her hip, and let her see a glimpse of his winter eyes before he whispered, "Whatcha got?"

There had been nothing around them but trees stripped by December, the closest person a businessman hurrying home along Beacon on the other side of a wrought-iron fence, twenty yards away. The mugger had dug the knife a little harder into her jeans, not cutting, but applying pressure, and she smelled decay and chocolate on his breath. She'd handed over her wallet, trying to avoid his swimming brown eyes and the irrational feeling that he possessed more arms than he showed, and he'd slid her wallet into the pocket of his overcoat and said, "You lucky I'm short on time," and strolled off toward Park Street, no rush, no fear.

She'd heard similar stories from a lot of women. Men, at least in this city, rarely got mugged unless they were looking for it, but women, all the time. Always there was the threat of rape, either implied or intuited, and in all the stories she'd heard, she'd never come across a mugger with clever phrasing. They didn't have the time. They needed to be as succinct as possible. Get in and get out before someone screamed.

And then there was the issue of the punch thrown while the mugger held a knife in the other hand. If you assumed the knife hand was the favored hand, well, come on, who threw a punch with anything but their writing hand?

Yes, she believed Dave had been thrust into an awful situation where he'd been forced to succumb to a kill-or-be-killed mentality. Yes, she was sure he wasn't the type of guy to have gone looking for it. But . . . but, still, his story had flaws, gaps. It was like trying to explain lipstick on the inside of your shirt—you may very well have been faithful, but your explanation, no matter how ridiculous, had better add up.

She imagined the two detectives in their kitchen, asking them questions, and she felt sure Dave would crack. His story would fall apart under impersonal eyes and repeated questions. It would be like when she asked about his childhood. She'd heard the stories, of course; the Flats was nothing but a small town wrapped within a big city, and people whispered. So, she'd asked Dave once if something terrible had happened in his childhood, something he felt he couldn't share with anyone, letting him know that he could share it with her, his wife, pregnant with his baby at the time.

He'd looked at her as if confused. "Oh, you mean that thing?"

"What thing?"

"I'm playing with Jimmy and this kid, Sean Devine. Yeah, you know him. You cut his hair once or twice, right?"

Celeste remembered. He worked somewhere in law enforcement, but not with the city. He was tall, with curly hair and an amber voice that slid through you. He had that same effortless confidence Jimmy had—the kind that came to men who were either very good-looking or were rarely afflicted by doubt.

She couldn't picture Dave with these two men, even as boys.

"Okay," she'd said.

"So this car pulls up, I get in, and not long after, I escaped."

"Escaped."

He nodded. "Wasn't much to it, honey."

"But, Dave—"

He placed a finger to her lips. "That's sorta the end of it, okay?"

He was smiling, but Celeste could see a—what was it?—a kind of mild hysteria in his eyes.

"I mean—what?—I remember playing ball and kick-the-can," Dave said, "and going to the Looey-Dooey, trying to stay awake in class. I remember some birthday parties and shit. But, come on, it's a pretty boring time. Now, high school . . ."

She'd let it go, as she would when he lied about why he lost his job at American Messenger Service (Dave saying it was another budgetary cutback, but other guys from the neighborhood were walking in off the street in the weeks that followed and scooping up jobs left and right), or when he told her his mother died of a sudden heart attack when the whole neighborhood had heard the story of Dave coming home from senior year in high school to find her sitting by the oven, kitchen doors closed, towels pressed to the bottoms, gas filling the room. Dave, she'd come to believe, needed his lies, needed to rewrite his history and fashion it in such a way that it became something he could live with and tuck far away. And if it made him a better person—a loving, if occasionally distant, husband and attentive father—who was to judge?

But this lie, Celeste knew as she tossed on some jeans and one of Dave's shirts, could bury him. Bury *them,* now that she had joined in the conspiracy to obstruct justice by washing the clothes. If Dave didn't come clean with her, she couldn't help him. And when the police came (and they would; this wasn't TV; the dumbest, drunkest detective was smarter than either of them when it came to crime), they'd break Dave's story like an egg on the side of a pan.

DAVE'S RIGHT HAND was killing him. The knuckles had ballooned to twice their normal size and the bones closest to the wrist felt like they were ready to punch up through the skin. He could have forgiven himself, then, for floating meatballs to Michael, but he refused to. If the kid couldn't hit curves and knucklers from a Wiffle ball, he'd never be able to track a hardball coming twice as fast, hit it with a bat about ten times as heavy.

His son was small for seven, and far too trusting for this world. You could see it in the openness of his face, the glow of hope in the set of his blue eyes. Dave loved that in his son, but he hated it, too. He didn't know if he had the strength to take it away, but he knew that soon he'd have to, or the world would do it for him. That tender, breakable thing in his son was a Boyle curse, the same thing that made Dave, at thirty-five, repeatedly get mistaken for a college student, find himself getting carded at liquor stores outside the neighborhood. His hairline hadn't changed since he was Michael's age; no lines had ever creased his face; and his own blue eyes were vivid and innocent.

Dave watched Michael dig in as he'd been taught, adjust his cap, and cock the bat high above his shoulder. He swayed his knees a bit, flexing them, a habit Dave had been gradually working out of him, but one that kept coming back like a tic, and Dave released the ball fast, hoping to exploit the weakness, hiding the knuckler by releasing the ball before his arm was fully extended, the center of his palm screaming with the pinch of the grip.

Michael stopped flexing, though, as soon as Dave began his motion, quick as it was, and as the ball fluttered, then dropped over the plate, Michael swung low and teed off on it like he was holding a three-wood. Dave saw the flash of a hopeful smile on Michael's face mixed with a bit of amazement at his own prowess, and Dave almost let the ball go, but instead he slapped it back to the earth, felt something crumble in his chest as the smile disintegrated on his son's face.

"Hey, hey," Dave said, deciding to let his son feel the goodness of a sweet swing, "that was a great swing, Yaz."

Michael was still working on a scowl. "How come you could knock it down then?"

Dave picked the ball up off the grass. "I dunno. 'Cause I'm a lot taller than kids in Little League?"

Michael's smile was tentative, waiting to break again. "Yeah?"

"Lemme ask you—you know any second-graders who go five-ten?"

"No."

"And I had to jump for it."

"Yeah."

"Yeah. Keep a trip to a single, all five-ten of me."

Michael laughed now. It was Celeste's laugh, rippling. "Okay . . ."

"You were flexing, though."

"I know, I know."

"Once you dig in and set, buddy, you stop moving."

"But Nomar—"

"I know all about Nomar. And Derek Jeter, too. Your heroes, okay. But when you're pulling down ten million in the Show, you can fidget. Until then?"

Michael shrugged, kicked at the grass.

"Mike. Until then?"

Michael sighed. "Until then, I concentrate on the basics."

Dave smiled and tossed the ball above him, caught it without watching it fall. "It was a nice rip, though."

"Yeah?"

"Dude, that thing was heading for the Point. Heading *uptown.*"

"Heading *uptown,*" Michael said, and let ripple another of his mother's laughs.

"Who's heading uptown?"

They both turned to see Celeste standing on the back porch, hair tied back and barefoot, one of Dave's shirts hanging untucked over faded jeans.

"Hey, Ma."

"Hey, cutie. You going uptown with your father?"

Michael looked at Dave. It was their private joke suddenly, and he snickered. "Nah, Ma."

"Dave?"

"The ball he just hit, honey. The ball was going uptown."

"Ah. The *ball.*"

"Killed it, Ma. Dad knocked it down only cause he's so tall."

Dave could feel her watching him even when her eyes were on Michael. Watching and waiting and wanting to ask him something. He remembered her hoarse voice in his ear last night, as she rose off the kitchen floor to grab his neck and pull her lips to his ear and say, "I am you now. You are me."

Dave hadn't known what the hell she was talking about, but he liked the sound of it, and the hoarseness in her vocal cords had pushed him that much closer to climax.

Now, though, he had the feeling it was just one more attempt by Celeste to climb inside his head, poke around, and it pissed him off. Because once they got in there, they didn't like what they saw and they ran from it.

"So what's up, honey?"

"Oh, nothing." She wrapped her arms around herself, even though the day was warming up pretty fast. "Hey, Mike, did you eat?"

"Not yet."

Celeste frowned at Dave, like it was the crime of the century Michael hit a few balls before he got a sugar high from that crimson cereal he ate.

"Your bowl's full and milk's on the table."

"Good. I'm starving." Michael dropped the bat, and Dave felt a betrayal in the way he flipped the bat and hurried to the stairs. You were starving? And, what, I taped your mouth up so you couldn't tell me? Fuck.

Michael trotted past his mother and then hit the stairs leading up to the third floor like they'd disappear if he didn't reach the top fast enough.

"Skipping breakfast, Dave?"

"Sleeping till noon, Celeste?"

"It's ten-fifteen," Celeste said, and Dave could feel all the goodwill they'd pumped back into their marriage with last night's kitchen lunacy turn to smoke and drift off into the yards beyond theirs.

He forced himself to smile. You made the smile real enough, no one could get past it. "So what's doing, hon?"

Celeste came down into the yard, her bare feet a light brown on the grass. "What happened to the knife?"

"What?"

"The knife," she whispered, looking back over her shoulder at McAllister's bedroom window. "The one the mugger had. Where'd it go, Dave?"

Dave tossed the ball in the air, caught it behind his back. "It's gone."

"Gone?" She pursed her lips and looked down at the grass. "I mean, shit, Dave."

"Shit what, honey?"

"Gone where?"

"Gone."

"You're sure."

Dave was sure. He smiled, looked in her eyes. "Positive."

"Your blood's on it, though. Your DNA, Dave. Is it so 'gone' that it'll never be found?"

Dave didn't have an answer for that one, so he just stared at his wife until she changed the subject.

"You check the paper this morning?"

"Sure," he said.

"You see anything?"

"About what?"

Celeste hissed: "About *what*?"

"Oh . . . oh. Yeah." Dave shook his head. "No, there was nothing. No mention of it. 'Member, honey, it was late."

"It was late. Come on. Metro pages? They're always the last to go in, everyone waiting for the police blotters."

"You work for a newspaper, do you?"

"This isn't a joke, Dave."

"No, honey, it's not. I'm just saying there's nothing in the morning paper. That's all. Why? I don't know. We'll watch the noon news, see what's there."

Celeste looked back down at the grass, nodded to herself several times. "We going to see anything, Dave?"

Dave stepped back from her.

"I mean about some black guy found beat half to death in a parking lot outside . . . where was it?"

"The, ah, Last Drop."

"The—ah—Last Drop?"

"Yeah, Celeste."

"Oh, okay, Dave," she said. "Sure."

And she left him. She gave him her back and walked up the stairs to the porch, walked inside, and Dave listened to the soft footfalls of her bare feet as she climbed the staircase.

That's what they did. They left you. Maybe not physically all the time. But emotionally, mentally? They were never there when you needed them. It had been the same with his mother. That morning after the police had brought him home, his mother had cooked him breakfast, her back to him, humming "Old MacDonald," and occasionally turning to look back over her shoulder at him to toss him a nervous smile, as if he were a boarder she wasn't sure about.

She'd placed the plate of runny eggs and black bacon and under-cooked, soggy toast down in front of him and asked him if he wanted orange juice.

"Ma," he said, "who were those guys? Why did they—?"

"Davey," she said, "you want orange juice? I didn't hear."

"Sure. Look, Ma, I don't know why they took—"

"There you go." Placing the juice in front of him. "Eat your breakfast and I'm going to . . ." She waved her hands at the kitchen, no idea what the fuck she was going to do. "I'm going to . . . wash your clothes. Okay? And, then, Davey? We'll go see a movie. How's that sound?"

Dave looked at his mother, looked for something that was waiting for him to open his mouth and tell her, tell her about that car and the house in the woods, and the smell of the big one's aftershave. Instead he saw a bright, hard gaiety, the look she got sometimes as she was preparing to go out on Friday nights, trying to find just the right thing to wear, desperate with hope.

Dave put his head down and ate his eggs. He heard his mother leave the kitchen, humming "Old MacDonald" all the way down the hall.

Standing in the yard now, knuckles aching, he could hear it, too. Old MacDonald had a farm. And everything was hunky-dory on it. You farmed and tilled and reaped and sowed and everything was just fucking great. Everyone got along, even the chickens and the cows, and no one needed to talk about anything, because nothing bad ever happened, and nobody had any secrets because secrets were for bad people, people who didn't eat their eggs, people who climbed in cars that smelled of apples with strange men and disappeared for four days, only to come back home to find everyone they'd known had disappeared, too, been replaced with smiley-faced look-alikes who'd do just about anything but listen to you. Just about anything but that.

9

FROGMEN
IN THE PEN

THE FIRST THING Jimmy saw as he neared the Roseclair Street entrance to Pen Park was a K-9 van parked down on Sydney Street, its back doors open, two cops struggling with six German shepherds on long leather leashes. He'd walked up Roseclair from the church, trying hard not to trot, and reached a small crowd of onlookers by the overpass that stretched above Sydney. They stood at the base of the incline where Roseclair began its rise under the expressway and then over the Pen Channel, losing its name on the other side and becoming Valenz Boulevard as it left Buckingham and entered Shawmut.

Back where the crowd had gathered, you could stand at the top of a fifteen-foot retaining wall of poured concrete that served as Sydney's dead end and look down on the last street running north-south in the East Bucky Flats, a rusting guardrail pressed against your kneecaps. Just a few yards east of the overlook, the guardrail gave way to a purple limestone stairwell. As kids, they'd sometimes bring dates there, and sit in the shadows passing forty-ounce bottles of Miller back and forth and watching the images flicker across the white screen of Hurley's Drive-in. Sometimes, Dave Boyle would come with them, not because anyone particularly liked Dave, but because he'd seen just about every damn movie ever made, and sometimes, if they were stoned, they'd have Dave rattle off the lines as they watched the silent screen, Dave getting into it so much at times that he even changed his vocal inflections to fit the various characters. Then Dave suddenly got good at baseball, went off to Don Bosco to become a jock superstar, and they couldn't keep him around just for laughs anymore.

Jimmy had no clue why all this was flooding back to him suddenly, or why he stood frozen by the guardrail, eyes gaping down at Sydney, except that it had something to do with those dogs, the way they pranced nervously in place after they'd hopped from the van and pawed the asphalt. One of their handlers raised a walkie-talkie to his lips as a helicopter appeared in the sky over downtown and headed for them like a fat bee, growing fatter every time Jimmy blinked.

A baby of a cop stood blocking the purple stairwell and a bit farther up Roseclair, two cruisers and a few more boys in blue stood guard in front of the access road leading into the park.

The dogs never barked. Jimmy turned his head back as he realized that's what had been bugging him since he'd first seen them. Even though their twenty-four paws jittered back and forth on the asphalt, it was a tight, concentric jittering, like soldiers marching in place, and Jimmy felt a terrible efficiency in their black snouts and lean flanks, had an image of their eyes as hot coals.

The rest of Sydney looked like the waiting room to a riot. Cops filled the street and walked methodically through the weeds leading into the park. From up here, Jimmy had a partial view of the park itself, and he could see them in there, too, blue uniforms and earth-tone sport coats moving across the grass, peering off the edge into the Pen, calling out to one another.

Back down on Sydney, they gathered around something just on the far side of the K-9 van and several plainclothes detectives leaned against unmarked cars parked on the other side of the street, sipping coffee, but none of them bullshitting the way cops usually did, cracking each other up with war stories from recent shifts. Jimmy could feel pure tension—in the dogs, in the silent cops leaning against their cars, in the helicopter, no longer a bee now and roaring as it swept above Sydney, riding low, and disappeared in Pen Park on the other side of the imported trees and drive-in screen.

"Hey, Jimmy." Ed Deveau, opening a package of M&M's with his teeth, nudged Jimmy with his elbow.

"What up, Ed?"

Deveau shrugged. "That copter's the second one gone in. The first one kept doing passes over my house 'bout a half an hour ago, I says to the wife, 'Honey, we move to Watts, no one told me?' " He poured some M&M's into his mouth and shrugged again. "So, I come down to see what the fuss is about."

"What'd you hear?"

Deveau slid the flat of his hand over the air in front of them. "Nothing. They're locked up tighter than my mother's purse. But they're serious, Jimmy. I mean, shit, they got Sydney blocked off from every possible angle—cops and sawhorses on Crescent, Harborview, Sudan, Romsey, all the way down to Dunboy, what I hear. People live on the street can't get out, they're fucking pissed. I hear they got boats running up and down the Pen, and Boo Bear Durkin called, said he saw frogmen going in from his window." Deveau pointed. "I mean, look at that shit there."

Jimmy followed Deveau's finger and watched three cops pull a wino out of one of the scorched three-decker shells on the far side of Sydney, the wino not liking it much, struggling until one of the cops chucked him face first down the rest of the charred stairs, Jimmy still half-back at that word Ed had said: *frogmen*. They didn't send frogmen into a body of water if they were looking for something good, something alive.

"They ain't playing." Deveau whistled, then looked at Jimmy's clothes. "Why you all decked?"

"Nadine's First Communion." Jimmy watched a cop pick the wino up, say something into his ear before manhandling him to an olive sedan with the siren stuck cockeyed to the edge of the roof above the driver's door.

"Hey, congratulations," Deveau said.

Jimmy smiled his thanks.

"So, the hell you doing here then?"

Deveau looked back up Roseclair toward Saint Cecilia's, and Jimmy suddenly felt ridiculous. What the hell *was* he doing here in his silk tie and six-hundred-dollar suit, scuffing his shoes in the weeds that sprouted up from under the guardrail?

Katie, he remembered.

But that still seemed ridiculous. Katie'd blown off her half sister's First Communion to sleep off a drunk or listen to some more pillow talk from her latest guy. Shit. Why *would* she come to church if she wasn't dragged? Until Katie's own baptism, Jimmy himself hadn't been inside a church for a solid decade. And even after that, it hadn't been until he'd met Annabeth that he'd started going regular again. So what if he'd walked out of the church, seen the cruisers banging the turn onto Roseclair, and had felt a— what, premonition?—of dread? It had only been because he'd been worried about Katie—and pissed at her, too—and so she'd been on his mind as he watched some cops lead-foot it toward the Pen.

But now? Now he felt dumb. Dumb and overdressed and really fucking silly for telling Annabeth to take the girls to Chuck E. Cheese's, he'd meet her there, Annabeth looking into his face with a mix of exasperation, confusion, and anger held barely in check.

Jimmy turned to Deveau. "Just curious like everyone else, I guess." He clapped Deveau's shoulder. "Outta here, though, Ed," he said, and down on Sydney, one cop tossed a set of car keys to another and the second cop hopped in the K-9 van.

"Awright, Jimmy. You take care."

"You, too," Jimmy said slowly, still watching the street as the K-9 van backed up and stopped to shift gears and cut the wheels to the right, and Jimmy felt that mean certainty again.

You felt it in your soul, no place else. You felt the truth there sometimes—beyond logic—and you were usually right if it was a type of truth that was the exact kind you didn't want to face, weren't sure you could. That's what you tried to ignore, why you went to psychiatrists and spent too long in bars and numbed your brain in front of TV tubes—to hide from hard, ugly truths your soul recognized long before your mind caught up.

Jimmy felt that mean certainty drive nails through his shoes and plant him in place even though he wanted more than anything to run, run as fast as he ever had, do anything but stand there and watch that van pull out into the street. The nails found his chest, a fat, cold grouping of them as if shot from a cannon, and he wanted to shut his eyes but they were nailed, too, nailed wide open, as the van reached the middle of the street and Jimmy stared at the car it had been blocking, the car everyone was gathered around, dusting with brushes, photographing, peering inside, passing bagged items out to cops standing in the street and on the sidewalk.

Katie's car.

Not just the same model. Not one that looked like it. Her car. Right down to the dent on the right front bumper and the missing glass over the right headlight.

"Jesus, Jimmy. Jimmy? Jimmy! Look at me. You all right?"

Jimmy looked up at Ed Deveau, not sure how he'd ended up here, on his knees, the heels of his hands pressed to the ground, round Irish faces looking down at him.

"Jimmy?" Deveau offered him a hand. "You okay?"

Jimmy looked at the hand and had no idea how to answer that. Frogmen, he thought. In the Pen.

WHITEY FOUND SEAN in the woods a hundred yards past the ravine. They'd lost the blood trail and any evidence of footprints in the more open areas of the park, last night's rain having wiped clean anything that nature didn't cover.

"We got dogs sniffing something over by the old drive-in screen. You wanna take a walk over?"

Sean nodded, but then his walkie-talkie bleated.

"Trooper Devine."

"We got a guy out front here—"

"Which front?"

"The Sydney Street side, Trooper."

"Go ahead."

"Guy claims he's the father of the missing girl."

"The fuck's he doing on-scene?" Sean felt his face fill with blood, get hot and red.

"Slipped through, Trooper. What can I say?"

"Well, push him back. You got a psychologist on-scene yet?"

"En route."

Sean closed his eyes. Everyone was en route, like they were all sitting in the same fucking traffic jam.

"So, keep the father calm till the shrink's on-scene. You know the drill."

"Yeah, but he's asking for you, Trooper."

"Me."

"Said he knows you. Said someone told him you were here."

"No, no, no. Look—"

"He's got some guys with him."

"Guys?"

"Bunch of scary-looking dudes. Half of 'em are like semi-midget, and all of 'em look alike."

The Savage brothers. Shit.

"I'm on my way," Sean said.

ANY SECOND NOW, and Val Savage was going to get himself arrested. Chuck, too, maybe, the Savage blood—rarely down—up as all hell now, the brothers shouting at the cops, the cops looking like they'd be going knuckles-'n'-nightsticks any second.

Jimmy stood with Kevin Savage, one of the saner ones, a few yards from the crime scene tape where Val and Chuck were pointing with their fingers, saying, That's our niece in there, you dumb fucking prick pieces of shit.

Jimmy felt a controlled hysteria, a barely suppressed need to erupt that left him numb and just a little addled. Okay, so that was her car there, ten feet away. And, yes, no one had seen her since last night. And that *was* blood he'd glimpsed on the driver's seat back. So, yeah, it didn't look good. But there was a full battalion of cops searching in there now, and no body bags had come out yet. So there was that.

Jimmy watched an older cop light a cigarette and he wanted to pull it from his mouth, shove the burning coal deep into the veins of his nose, say, Get the fuck back in there and look for my daughter.

He counted back from ten, a trick he'd learned in Deer Island, counting slow, seeing the numbers appear, floating and gray in the darkness of his brain. Screaming would get him barred from the scene. Any outward show of grief or anxiety or the electric fear surging through his blood would result in the same thing. And then the Savages would go nuclear, and they'd all spend this day in a cell instead of on the street where his daughter was last seen.

"Val," he called.

Val Savage pulled his hand back over the crime scene tape and his finger out of the stony cop's face, looked back at Jimmy.

Jimmy shook his head. "Ease up."

Val charged back toward him. "They're fucking stonewalling us, Jim. They're holding us back."

"They're doing their job," Jimmy said.

"Their fucking *job,* Jim? All due respect, the doughnut shop's the other direction."

"You want to help me here?" Jimmy said as Chuck sidled up beside his brother, almost twice as tall, but half as dangerous, which was still more dangerous than most of the population.

"Sure," Chuck said. "Tell us what to do."

"Val?" Jimmy said.

"What?" Val's eyes spinning, fury pouring out of him like an odor.

"Do you want to help?"

"Yeah, yeah, yeah, I wanna help, Jimmy. Jesus fuck, you know?"

"I know," Jimmy said, hearing a rise in his voice that he tried to swallow against. "I fucking know, Val. That's my daughter in there. You hear what *I'm* saying?"

Kevin put his hand on Jimmy's shoulder and Val took a step back, looked down at his feet for a bit.

"Sorry, Jimmy. Awright, man? I'm just freaking. I mean, shit."

Jimmy got the calm back in his voice, forced his brain to work. "You and Kevin, Val? You go down the street to Drew Pigeon's house. You tell him what's going on."

"Drew Pigeon? Why?"

"I'm telling you why, Val. You talk to his daughter Eve and Diane Cestra, too, if she's still there. You ask them when they last saw Katie. What time, Val, exactly. You find out if they were drinking, if Katie had plans to meet anyone, and who she was dating. Can you do that, Val?" Jimmy asked, looking at Kevin, the one who'd hopefully keep Val in check.

Kevin nodded. "We got it, Jim."

"Val?"

Val looked over his shoulder at the weeds leading into the park, then back at Jimmy, his small head bobbing. "Yeah, yeah."

"These girls are friends. You don't have to get hard on them, but get those answers. Right?"

"Right," Kevin said, letting Jimmy know he'd keep it contained. He clapped his older brother's shoulder. "Come on, Val. Let's do it."

Jimmy watched them walk up Sydney, felt Chuck beside him, jumpy, ready to kill someone.

"How you holding up?"

"Shit," Chuck said, "I'm fine. You I'm worried about."

"Don't. I'm cool for now. Ain't no other choice, is there?"

Chuck didn't answer and Jimmy looked across Sydney, past his daughter's car, to see Sean Devine walking out of the park and into the weeds, eyes on Jimmy the whole way, Sean a tall guy and moving fast, but Jimmy could still see that thing in his face he'd always hated, the look of a guy the world had always worked for, Sean wearing it like a bigger badge than the one clipped to his belt, pissing people off with it even if he wasn't aware of it.

"Jimmy," Sean said, and shook his hand. "Hey, man."

"Hey, Sean. I heard you were in there."

"Since early this morning." Sean looked back over his shoulder, then around again to Jimmy. "I can't tell you anything right now, Jimmy."

"She in there?" Jimmy could hear the tremor in his own voice.

"I don't know, Jim. We haven't found her. I can tell you that much."

"So let us in," Chuck said. "We can help look. See it all the time on the news, ordinary citizens searching for missing kids and shit."

Sean kept his eyes on Jimmy, as if Chuck wasn't even there. "It's a little more than that, Jimmy. We can't have any nonpolice personnel in there until we've gone over every inch of the scene."

"And what's the scene?" Jimmy asked.

"The whole damn park at the moment. Look"—Sean patted Jimmy's shoulder—"I came out here to tell you guys there's nothing you can do right now. I'm sorry. I really am. But there it is. We know anything—the *first* thing, Jimmy? We'll tell you immediately. No bullshit."

Jimmy nodded and touched Sean's elbow. "I talk to you a sec?"

"Sure."

They left Chuck Savage on the curb and walked a few yards down the street. Sean squared himself, getting ready for whatever he thought Jimmy was going to say, all business, cop's eyes staring back at Jimmy, no mercy in them.

"That's my daughter's car," Jimmy said.

"I know. I—"

Jimmy held up a hand. "Sean? That's my daughter's car. It's got blood in it. She don't show up for work this morning, don't show up for her little sister's First Communion. No one's seen her since last night. Okay? That's my daughter we're talking about, Sean. You don't have kids, I don't expect you to understand all the way, but come on, man. My daughter."

Sean's cop's eyes stayed cop's eyes, Jimmy not even making a dent.

"What do you want me to say here, Jimmy? If you want to tell me who she was out with last night, I'll send some officers to talk to them. She had enemies, I'll go round them up. You want—"

"They brought fucking *dogs* in, Sean. Dogs, for my daughter. Dogs and frogmen."

"Yeah, they did. And we got half the fucking force in there, Jimmy. State *and* BPD. And two helicopters, and two boats, and we're going to find her. But you, there's nothing you can do, man. Not right now. Nothing. We clear?"

Jimmy looked back at Chuck standing on the curb, eyes on the weeds leading into the park, body tilting forward, ready to rip through his own skin.

"Why you got frogmen looking for my daughter, Sean?"

"We're covering all bases, Jimmy. We got a body of water, that's how we search it."

"Is she in the water?"

"All she is is *missing*, Jimmy. That's it."

Jimmy turned away from him for a moment, his mind not working too well, getting black and gummy. He wanted in that park. He wanted to walk down the joggers' path and see Katie walking toward him. He couldn't think. He needed in.

"You want a public relations nightmare on your hands?" Jimmy asked. "You want to have to bust me and every single one of the Savage brothers trying to get in there and look for our loved one?"

Jimmy knew the moment he stopped speaking that it was a weak threat, a grasp, and he hated that Sean knew it, too.

Sean nodded. "I don't want to. Believe me. But if I have to, Jimmy, yeah. I will, man." Sean flipped open a notepad. "Look, just tell me who she was with last night, what she was doing, and I'll—"

Jimmy was already walking away when Sean's walkie-talkie went off, loud and shrill. He turned back as Sean put it to his lips, said, "Go."

"We got something, Trooper."

"Say again."

Jimmy stepped up to Sean, heard the barely suppressed emotion in the voice of the guy on the other end of the walkie-talkie.

"I said we got something. Sergeant Powers said you need to get in here. Uh, ASAP, Trooper. Like right now."

"Your location?"

"The drive-in screen, Trooper. And, man, it's a fucking mess."

10

EVIDENCE

CELESTE WATCHED the twelve o'clock news on the small TV they kept up on the kitchen counter. She ironed as she watched, aware at one point that she could be mistaken for a 1950s housewife, doing menial chores and tending to the child while her husband went off to work carrying his metal lunchpail, returned home expecting a drink in his hand and dinner on the table. But it wasn't like that, really. Dave, for all his faults, pitched in when it came to housework. He was a duster and vacuumer and dishwasher, whereas Celeste took pleasure in laundry, in the sorting and folding and ironing, in the warm smell of fabric that had been cleansed and smoothed of wrinkles.

She used her mother's iron, an artifact from the early sixties. It was as heavy as a brick, hissed constantly, and released sudden bursts of steam without warning, but it was twice as capable as any of the newer ones that Celeste, lured by sales and claims of space-age technology, had tried over the years. Her mother's iron left creases you could split a loaf of French bread on and erased thick wrinkles in one smooth swoop that a newer one with a plastic shell would have had to ride over half a dozen times.

It could piss Celeste off sometimes to think about the way everything these days seemed built to crumble—VCRs, cars, computers, cordless phones—where the tools of her parents' time had been built to last. She and Dave still used her mother's iron and her blender, and kept her squat, black rotary phone by their bed. And yet, over their years together, they'd thrown out several purchases that had quit long before one would have assumed logical—TVs with blown picture tubes, a vacuum that poured blue smoke, a coffeemaker that produced liquid only slightly warmer than bathwater. These and other appliances had ended up discarded with the trash because it was almost cheaper to buy a new one than repair the old. Almost. So of course you spent the extra money on the next-generation model, which is what the manufacturers, she was sure, counted on. Sometimes Celeste found herself consciously trying to ignore a notion that it wasn't only the things in her life but her life, itself, that was not meant to have any weight or lasting impact, but was, in fact, programmed to break down at the first available opportunity so that its few usable parts could be recycled for someone else while the rest of her vanished.

So there she was ironing and thinking about her own disposability when, ten minutes into the news, the newscaster looked gravely into the camera and announced that police were looking for the assailant in a vicious assault outside one of the city's neighborhood bars. Celeste moved toward the TV to turn it up, and the newscaster said, "That story, plus Harvey on the weather when we return." Next thing, Celeste was watching a woman's manicured hands scrub a baking dish that looked like it had been submerged in warm caramel, a voice hawking the benefits of an all-new-and-improved dishwashing detergent, and Celeste wanted to scream. The news was like those disposable appliances somehow—built to tease and leer, to chuckle out of earshot at your gullibility in believing, yet again, that it would deliver on its promises.

She adjusted the volume and resisted the urge to rip the cheap knob off the piece-of-shit TV and went back to the ironing board. Dave had taken Michael out half an hour ago to shop for kneepads and a catcher's mask, saying he'd catch the news on the radio, Celeste not even bothering to look at him to see if he was lying. Michael, small and slim as he was, had proven himself a talented catcher—a "prodigy," his coach, Mr. Evans, had said, with a "ballistic missile" for an arm, a kid his age.

Celeste thought of kids she'd known growing up who'd played the position—big kids, usually, with flattened noses and missing front teeth—and she'd voiced her fears to Dave.

"These masks they make now, honey? They're like friggin' shark cages. Hit 'em with a truck, the truck breaks."

She'd taken a day to consider it and come back to Dave with her deal. Michael could play catcher or any other baseball position as long as he had the best equipment and, here was the clincher, never went out for organized football.

Dave, never a football player himself, agreed after only ten minutes of perfunctory argument.

So now they were out buying equipment so Michael could be a mirror of his old man, and Celeste stared at the TV, iron held stationary a few inches above a cotton shirt as a dog food commercial ended and the news returned.

"Last night in Allston," the newscaster said, and Celeste's heart sank, "a BC sophomore was assaulted by two men outside this popular nightspot. Sources say the victim, Carey Whitaker, was beaten with a beer bottle and is listed in critical condition at . . ."

She pretty much knew then, as small clumps of wet sand drizzled inside her chest, that she wasn't going to see anything on the assault or murder of a man outside the Last Drop. And once they turned to weather with a promise of sports to follow, she knew beyond any doubt.

By now, they would have found the man. If he'd died ("Honey, I may have killed a man"), the reporters would have picked up on it through sources at the precinct house, off the police blotter, or simply by monitoring the police radios.

So maybe Dave had overestimated the fury of his violence against the mugger. Maybe the mugger—or whoever it had been—had simply crawled off somewhere to lick his wounds after Dave left. Maybe those hadn't been pieces of brain she'd watched swirl down the drain last night. But all that blood? How could someone lose all that blood from his head and *survive,* never mind walk away?

Once she'd ironed the last pair of pants and put everything away in either Michael's closet or hers and Dave's, she returned to the kitchen and stood in the center of it, not sure what to do next. Golf played on the

TV now, the soft thwacks of the ball and the dry, muted cackles of applause temporarily calming something inside of her that had been itchy all morning. It went beyond her problems with Dave and the holes in his story, yet had something to do with that at the same time, something to do with last night and the sight of him coming through the bathroom door with blood on him, all that blood on his pants staining the tile, bubbling in his wound, turning pink as it swirled down the drain.

The drain. That was it. That's what she'd forgotten. Last night, she'd told Dave she would bleach out the inside of the drainpipe under the sink, eradicate the rest of the evidence. She went to it immediately, dropped to her knees on the kitchen floor and opened the cupboard underneath, stared in at the cleaning supplies and rags until she saw the lug wrench near the back. She reached back there, trying to ignore the phobia she had about reaching into the sink cupboard, an irrational feeling she always got that a rat lay waiting under the pile of rags, sniffing the air at the scent of her flesh, raising its snout from the rags now, whiskers twitching . . .

She snatched the lug wrench out, then rattled it through the rags and cans of cleanser just to be sure, quite aware that her fear was silly, but determined nonetheless, because, hey, that's why they called them phobias. She hated sticking her hand into low, dark places; Rosemary had been terrified of elevators; her father had hated heights; Dave broke out into cold sweats whenever he had to descend into the cellar.

She placed a bucket under the drainpipe to catch any excess runoff. She lay on her back and reached up, loosened the trap plug with the wrench, and then twisted with her hand until it came free and water came with it, splashing down into the plastic bucket. She worried for a moment that it would overfill the bucket, but soon the flow diminished to a dribble and she watched as a dark clump of hair and small kernels of corn followed the last of the water into the bucket. The slip nut closest to the rear wall of the cupboard was next, and that took a while, the nut refusing to budge and Celeste getting to the point where she was pushing off the base of the cupboard with her foot and pulling back on the lug wrench with so much force she feared either the wrench or her wrist would snap in half. And then the nut turned, just a fraction of an inch, with a loud metallic screech, and Celeste repositioned the lug wrench and pulled back again, the nut turning twice as much this time, though still fighting her.

A few minutes later she had the whole drainpipe on the kitchen floor in front of her. Her hair and shirt were damp with sweat, but she felt a sense of accomplishment that bordered on pure triumph, as if she'd fought something recalcitrant and indisputably male, muscle against muscle, and won. In the rag pile, she found a shirt Michael had grown out of, and she twisted it in her hands until she could thread it through the pipe. She worked it through the pipe several times until she was satisfied the pipe was clear of everything but old rust, and then she placed the shirt in a small plastic grocery bag. She took the pipe and a bottle of Clorox out onto the back porch and bleached the inside of the pipe, allowing the liquid to spill out the other end and into the dry, fuzzy soil of a potted plant that had died last summer and sat on the porch all winter waiting for them to throw it out.

When she was done, she refitted the pipe, finding it much easier going back on than it had been coming off, and reattached the trap plug. She found the plastic trash bag she'd put Dave's clothes into last night and added the bag with Michael's tattered shirt to it, poured the contents of the plastic bucket through a strainer over the toilet, wiped the strainer clean with a paper towel, and threw the towel in the bag with the rest of it.

So there it was: all the evidence.

Or at least all the evidence she could do anything about. If Dave had lied to her—about the knife, about leaving his fingerprints anywhere, about witnesses to his—crime? self-defense?—then she couldn't help him there. But she'd risen to the challenge here in her own home. She'd taken everything that had been thrown at her since he'd come home last night and she'd dealt with it. She'd conquered it. She felt giddy again, powerful, as vibrant and valid as she'd ever felt, and she knew with a sudden, refreshing certainty that she was still young and strong and she was most definitely not a disposable toaster or broken vacuum. She had lived through the deaths of both her parents and years of financial crises and her son's pneumonia scare when he was six months old and she hadn't grown weaker, as she'd thought, only wearier, yes, but that would change now that she'd remembered who she was. And she was—definitely—a woman who did not shrink from gauntlets, but stepped up to them, and said, Okay, bring it. Bring your worst. I will get back up. Every time. I will not shrivel and die. So watch out.

She picked the green trash bag up off the floor and twisted it in her hands until it resembled a scrawny old man's neck, then wrung it tight and tied it off in a knot at the top. She paused then, thinking it strange that it had reminded her of an old man's neck. Where had that come from? And she noticed that the TV had gone blank. One moment Tiger Woods was stalking the green, the next the screen was black.

Then a white line blipped up the screen, and Celeste knew that if this TV had blown a picture tube, too, it was going off the porch. Right now, fuck the consequences, it was going.

But the white line gave way to the newsroom studio, and the anchor-woman, looking rushed and harried, said, "We interrupt this broadcast to bring you a breaking story. Valerie Corapi is on the scene outside Penitentiary Park in East Buckingham, where police have launched a massive search for a missing woman. Valerie?"

Celeste watched as the studio shot gave way to a helicopter shot—a jerky overhead view of Sydney Street and Penitentiary Park and what looked like an invading army of police milling around outside. She saw dozens of small figures, black as ants from the distance, walking through the park, and police boats on the channel. She saw a line of the antlike figures moving steadily toward the grove of trees that surrounded the old drive-in screen.

The helicopter was buffeted by wind and the camera lens shifted, and for a moment Celeste was looking at the land on the other side of the channel, at Shawmut Boulevard and its stretch of industrial parks.

"This is the scene here in East Buckingham right now where police arrived early this morning and commenced a large-scale search for a missing woman that continues now into the early afternoon. Unconfirmed sources have told News Four that the woman's abandoned car showed signs of foul play. Now, this, Virginia, is—I don't know if you can see it yet . . ."

The helicopter camera turned away from the industrial parks on Shawmut in a nauseating one-eighty and pointed down at a dark blue car with its door open that sat on Sydney Street, looking somehow forlorn as police backed a tow truck up to it.

"Yes," the reporter said. "What you are looking at now is what I have been told is the missing woman's car. Police found it this morning and immediately launched this search. Now, Virginia, no one will confirm either the name of the missing woman or the reasons for this rather large—as I'm sure you can see—police presence. However, sources close to News Four have confirmed that the search seems to be focusing on the old drive-in screen, which, as you know, is the site of local theater in the summer. But this is not a fake drama playing out for us here today. This is real. Virginia?"

Celeste was trying to figure out what they'd just told her. She wasn't sure she'd learned anything except that police had, in fact, descended upon her neighborhood like they were taking it over.

The anchorwoman looked confused, too, as if she was being cued off camera in a language she didn't understand. She said, "We'll keep you posted on this . . . developing story as we learn more. Now we return you to your regularly scheduled program."

Celeste changed channels several times, but no other stations seemed to be covering the story yet, so she turned back to the golf and left the volume up.

Someone was missing in the Flats. A woman's car had been abandoned on Sydney. But police didn't launch this kind of massive operation—and it was massive; she'd noticed both state and city police cruisers down on Sydney—unless they had evidence of something more than just a missing woman to go on. There had to be something about that car that suggested violence. What had the reporter said?

Signs of foul play. That was it.

Blood, she was sure. It had to be blood. Evidence. And she looked down at the bag still twisted in her hand and thought:

Dave.

11

RED RAIN

JIMMY STOOD on the civilian side of the yellow tape, facing a ragged line of cops, as Sean walked away through the weeds and into the park, not looking back once.

"Mr. Marcus," this one cop, Jefferts, said, "get you some coffee or something?" The cop looked at Jimmy's forehead, Jimmy feeling a mild contempt and pity in the loose gaze and the way the cop used the side of his thumb to scratch his belly. Sean had introduced them, telling Jimmy this was Trooper Jefferts, a good man, and telling Jefferts that Jimmy was the father of the woman who, uh, owned the abandoned car. Get him anything he needs and hook him up with Talbot when she arrives, Jimmy figuring Talbot was either a shrink with a badge or some disheveled social worker with a mountain of student loans and a car that smelled of Burger King.

He ignored Jefferts's offer and walked back across the street to Chuck Savage.

"What's going on, Jim?"

Jimmy shook his head, pretty sure he'd puke all over himself and Chuck, too, if he tried to put what he was feeling into words.

"You got a cell phone?"

"Yeah, sure." Chuck scrambled his hands through his windbreaker. He put the phone in Jimmy's open hand, and Jimmy dialed 411, got a recorded voice asking him what city and state, and he hesitated a second before throwing his voice out into the phone line, had an image of his words traveling through miles and miles of copper cable before dropping down a vortex into the soul of some gargantuan computer with red lights for eyes.

"What listing?" the computer asked.

"Chuck E. Cheese's." Jimmy felt a sudden wave of bitter terror at saying such a ridiculous name on the open street near his daughter's empty car. He wanted to put the whole phone between his teeth and bite down, hear it crack.

Once he'd gotten the number and dialed, he had to wait as they paged Annabeth. Whoever had answered the phone hadn't put him on hold but merely placed the receiver down on a countertop, and Jimmy could hear the tinny echoes of his wife's name: "Will an Annabeth Marcus please contact the hostess stand? Annabeth Marcus." Jimmy could hear the peal of bells and eighty or ninety kids running around like maniacs and pulling one another's hair, shrieking, mingled with desperate adult voices trying to climb above the din, and then his wife's name was called again, echoing. Jimmy pictured her looking up at the sound, confused and frazzled, the whole Saint Cecilia's First Communion squad fighting for pizza slices around her.

Then he heard her voice, muffled and curious: "You called my name?"

For a moment, Jimmy wanted to hang up. What would he tell her? What was the point of calling her with no hard facts, only the fears of his own crazed imagination? Wouldn't it be better to leave her and the girls in the peace of ignorance for a little while longer?

But he knew there was already too much wounding going on today as it was, and Annabeth would be wounded if he left her unaware while he pulled out his hair on Sydney Street by Katie's car. She'd remember her bliss with the girls as unearned and, worse, as an assault, a false promise. And she'd hate Jimmy for it.

He heard her muffled voice again: "This one?" and then the scrape of her lifting the phone off the counter. "Hello?"

"Baby," Jimmy managed before he had to clear his throat.

"Jimmy?" A slight edge to her voice. "Where are you?"

"I'm . . . Look . . . I'm on Sydney Street."

"What's wrong?"

"They found her car, Annabeth."

"Whose car?"

"Katie's."

"They? The police? *They?*"

"Yeah. She's . . . missing. In Pen Park somewhere."

"Oh, Jesus God. No, right? No. No, Jimmy."

Jimmy felt it fill him now—that dread, that awful certainty, the horror of thoughts he'd kept clenched behind a shelf in his brain.

"We don't know anything yet. But her car's been here all night and the cops—"

"Jesus *Christ,* Jimmy."

"—are searching the park for her. Tons of them. So . . ."

"Where are you?"

"I'm on Sydney. Look—"

"On the fucking street? Why aren't you in there?"

"They won't let me in."

"They? Who the fuck are they? Is she their daughter?"

"No. Look, I—"

"You *get* in there. Jesus. She could be hurt. Lying in there somewhere, all cold and hurt."

"I know, but they—"

"I'm on my way."

"Okay."

"Get in there, Jimmy. I mean, God, what's wrong with you?"

She hung up.

Jimmy handed the phone back to Chuck, knowing that Annabeth was right. She was so completely right that it killed Jimmy to realize that he would regret his impotence of the last forty-five minutes for the rest of his life, never be able to think about it without cringing, trying to crawl away from it in his head. When had he become this thing—this man who'd say yes, sir, no, sir, right you are, sir, to fucking cops when his first-born daughter was missing? When had that happened? When had he stood at a counter and handed his dick over in exchange for feeling like, what, an upright citizen?

He turned to Chuck. "You still keep those bolt cutters under the spare in your trunk?"

Chuck got a look on his face like he'd been caught doing something. "Guy's gotta make a living, Jim."

"Where's your car?"

"Up the street, corner of Dawes."

Jimmy started walking and Chuck trotted up beside him. "We're going to cut our way in?"

Jimmy nodded and walked a little faster.

WHEN SEAN REACHED the part of the jogging path that circled around the fence of the co-op garden, he nodded at some of the cops working the flowers and soil for clues, could see a tight anticipation in most of their faces that told him they'd already heard by now. There was an air saturating the entire park that he'd felt at a few other crime scenes over the years, one that carried an edge of fatalism, a dank acceptance of someone else's doom.

They'd known coming into the park that she was dead, yet some infinitesimal piece of all of them, Sean knew, had held out for otherwise. It was what you did—you came on-scene knowing the truth, and then spent as much time as you could hoping you were wrong. Sean had worked one case last year where a couple had reported their baby missing. A ton of media showed up because the couple was white and respectable, but Sean and every other cop knew the couple's story was bullshit, knew the kid was dead even as they consoled the two assholes, cooed assurances to them that their baby was probably fine, ran down dumb-ass leads on suspicious ethnics seen in the area that morning, only to find the baby at dusk, stuffed in a vacuum cleaner bag and crammed in a crevice under the cellar stairs. Sean saw a rookie cry that day, the kid shaking as he leaned against his cruiser, but the rest of the cops looked irate yet unsurprised, as if they'd all spent the night dreaming the same shitty dream.

That's what you carried back home and into the bars and locker rooms of the precincts or barracks—an annoyed acceptance that people sucked, people were dumb and petty-bad, often murderously so, and when they opened their mouths they lied, always, and when they went missing for no discernibly good reason, they'd usually be found dead or way the hell worse off.

And often the worst thing wasn't the victims—they were dead, after all, and beyond any more pain. The worst thing was those who'd loved them and survived them. Often the walking dead from now on, shell-shocked, hearts ruptured, stumbling through the remainder of their lives without anything left inside of them but blood and organs, impervious to pain, having learned nothing except that the worst things did, in fact, sometimes happen.

Like Jimmy Marcus. Sean didn't know how the fuck he was going to look that guy in the eye and say, Yeah, she's dead. Your daughter's dead, Jimmy. Someone took her away for good. Jimmy, who'd already lost a wife. Shit. Hey, guess what, Jim—God said you owed another marker. He's come to collect. Hope that puts it in perspective, pal. Be seeing you.

Sean crossed the short plank bridge over the ravine and followed the path down into the circular grove of trees that stood facing the drive-in screen like a pagan audience. Everyone was down by the steps that led up to a door on the side of the screen. Sean could see Karen Hughes snapping away with her camera, Whitey Powers leaning against the door-jamb, looking in, taking notes, the assistant ME on his knees beside Karen Hughes, a goddamn platoon of uniformed troopers and BPD blues milling behind those three, Connolly and Souza studying something on the steps, and the big brass—Frank Krauser from BPD and Martin Friel from State, Sean's commanding officer—standing off a bit along the stage that stretched under the screen, talking to each other, heads close and tilted downward.

If the assistant ME said she'd died here in the park, it fell within State jurisdiction and made it Sean and Whitey's case. Sean's job to tell Jimmy. Sean's job to become intimate and obsessed with the victim's life. Sean's job to put the case down and give everyone an illusion, at least, of closure.

BPD, however, could ask for the case. It was within Friel's power to give it to them since the park was surrounded on all sides by City turf, and because the first attempt made on the victim's life had occurred within City jurisdiction. This would attract attention, Sean was sure. Homicide in a city park, the victim found near or in what was fast becoming a local and pop culture landmark. No motive readily apparent. No killer, either, unless he'd offed himself down there by Katie Marcus, which seemed doubtful or Sean would have heard. Huge media case, when you really thought about it, the whole city having been pretty much devoid of those the last couple of years. Shit, the press would fill the Pen with their drool.

Sean didn't want it, which, if prior experience was any kind of barometer, pretty much guaranteed he'd get it. He worked his way down a slope toward the base of the drive-in screen, his eyes on Krauser and Friel, trying to read the verdict in the smallest motions of their heads. If that was Katie Marcus in there—and Sean didn't have much doubt—the Flats would explode. Forget Jimmy—he'd probably be catatonic anyway. But the Savage brothers? Back at the Major Crimes Unit, they had files the size of doorstops on almost every one of those crazy fuckers. And that was just the State shit they'd pulled. Sean knew guys in the BPD said a Saturday night without at least one Savage in lockup was like a solar eclipse—other cops came down to have a look for themselves because they couldn't believe it.

On the stage below the screen, Krauser nodded once and Friel's head swiveled, looked around until he met Sean's eyes, and Sean knew this was his and Whitey's now. Sean saw a small amount of blood splattered on some leaves leading up to the base of the screen, saw some more on the steps leading up to the door.

Connolly and Souza looked up from the blood on the stairs, gave Sean grim nods, and went back to peering at the crevices where the steps met the risers. Karen Hughes came up off her haunches and Sean could hear the whir of her camera as she flicked a knob with her thumb and the film spooled to the end. She reached into her bag for a fresh roll and flicked open the back of the camera, Sean noticing that her ash blond hair had darkened at the temples and bangs. She glanced at him without expression and dropped the spent film in her bag, then reloaded.

Whitey was on his knees alongside the assistant ME, and Sean heard him say "What?" in a sharp whisper.

"Just what I said."

"You're sure now, yeah?"

"Not a hundred percent, but I'm leaning."

"Shit." Whitey looked back over his shoulder as Sean approached, and shook his head, jerked his thumb at the assistant ME.

Sean's view widened as he climbed up behind them and their shoulders dropped away and he was looking down into the doorway, down at the body scrunched in there, the space between the walls no more than three feet wide and the corpse sitting with her back against the wall on his left, her feet pushed up hard against the wall on his right, so that Sean's first impression was of a fetus seen through a sonogram screen. Her left foot was bare and muddy. What was left of the sock hung around her ankle, shriveled and torn. She wore a simple black shoe with a flat sole on her right foot, and it was caked in dried mud. Even after she'd lost the one shoe in the garden, she'd left the other one on. Her killer must have been breathing down her neck the whole way. And yet she'd come in here to hide. So for a moment she must have given him the slip, which meant something had slowed him down.

"Souza," he called.

"Yeah?"

"Get some uniforms to check the trail leading up here. Look in the bushes and shit for torn clothes, scraped-off skin, anything like that."

"We already got a guy doing casts on footprints."

"Yeah, but we need more. You on it?"

"I'm on it."

Sean looked down at the body again. She wore soft, dark pants and a navy blue blouse with a wide neck. Her jacket was red and torn and Sean figured it for a weekend outfit, too nice for everyday for a girl from the Flats. She'd been out somewhere, somewhere nice, maybe on a date.

And somehow she'd ended up stuffed in this narrow corridor, its mildewed walls the last thing she saw, probably the last thing she'd smelled.

It was as if she'd gone in here to escape a red rain, and the downpour remained in her hair and cheeks, stained her clothing in wet strings. Her knees were pressed close to her chest, and her right elbow was propped on her right knee, a clenched fist up by her ear so that again Sean was reminded of a child more than a woman, curled up and trying to keep some awful sound at bay. Stop it, just stop it, the body said. Stop it, please.

Whitey moved out of the way, and Sean squatted just outside the doorway. Even with all the blood on the body and pooled beneath it and the mildew clinging to the concrete around it, Sean could smell her perfume, just a hint of it, slightly sweet, slightly sensual, the lightest scent, which made him think of high school dates and dark cars, the panicky fumbling through fabric and the electric grazing of flesh. Underneath the red rain, Sean could see several dark bruises on her wrist and forearm and ankles, and he knew these were the places where she'd been hit with something.

"He beat her?" Sean said.

"Looks that way. The blood from the top of her head? That's from a split on the crown. Guy probably broke whatever he was hitting her with, he brought it down so hard."

Piled on the other side of her, filling this narrow corridor behind the screen, were wooden pallets and what looked like stage props—wooden schooners and cathedral tops, the bow of what looked like a Venetian gondola. She wouldn't have been able to move. Once she got in there, she was stuck. If whoever had been chasing her found her, then she'd die. And he'd found her.

He'd opened the door on her, and she'd curled tight into herself, trying to protect her body with nothing more substantial than her own limbs. Sean craned his head and peered around her clenched fist, looked into her face. It, too, was streaked with red, and her eyes were clenched as tight as her fist, trying to wish it all away, the eyelids locked by fear at first and now by rigor.

"That her?" Whitey Powers said.

"Huh?"

"Katherine Marcus," Whitey said. "That her?"

"Yeah," Sean said. She had a small scar curving underneath the right side of her chin, barely noticeable and faded with time, but you'd notice it on Katie when you'd see her around the neighborhood because the rest of her was so unblemished, her face a flawless record of her mother's dark, angular beauty combined with her father's more tousled good looks, his pale eyes and hair.

"Hundred percent positive?" the assistant ME asked.

"Ninety-nine," Sean said. "We'll have the father do a positive at the morgue. But, yeah, it's her."

"You see the back of her head?" Whitey leaned in and lifted the hair off her shoulders with a pen.

Sean peered back there, saw that a small piece of the lower skull was missing, the back of the neck gone dark with the blood.

"You telling me she was shot?" He looked at the ME.

The guy nodded. "That looks like a bullet wound to me."

Sean leaned back out of the smell of perfume and blood and mildewed concrete and sodden wood. He wished, for just a moment, that he could pull Katie Marcus's clenched fist down from her ear, as if by doing so those bruises he could see and the ones they were sure to find under her clothes would evaporate, and the red rain would ascend from her hair and body, and she would step back out of this tomb blinking sleep from her eyes, a bit groggy.

Off to his right, he heard the sounds of a commotion, several people yelling at once, the rustle of mad scrambling, and the K-9 dogs snarling and barking in a mad fury. When he looked over, he saw Jimmy Marcus and Chuck Savage burst through the trees at the far side of the grove, where the land turned green and manicured and sloped gracefully down toward the screen, the place where summer crowds spread their blankets and sat in the grass to watch a play.

At least eight uniforms and two plainclothes converged on Jimmy and Chuck, and Chuck went down right away, but Jimmy was fast and Jimmy was slippery. He slid straight through the line with a series of quick, seemingly illogical pivots that left his pursuers grasping air, and if he hadn't stumbled coming down the slope, he would have made the screen with no one to stop him but Krauser and Friel.

But he did stumble, his foot slipping out from under him on the damp grass, and his eyes locked with Sean's as he belly-flopped on the grass, his chin punching through the soil. A young trooper, all square head and high-school-tight-end body, landed on top of Jimmy like he was a sled, and the two of them slid another few feet down the slope. The cop pulled Jimmy's right arm behind his back and went for his cuffs.

Sean stepped out onto the stage and called: "Hey! Hey! It's the father. Just pull him back."

The young cop looked over, pissed and muddy.

"Just pull him back," Sean said. "The both of them."

He turned back toward the screen and that's when Jimmy called his name, his voice hoarse, as if the screams in his head had found his vocal cords and stripped them: "Sean!"

Sean stopped, caught Friel looking at him.

"Look at me, Sean!"

Sean turned back, saw Jimmy arching up under the young cop's weight, a dark smudge of soil on his chin, whiskers of grass hanging off it.

"You find her? Is it her?" Jimmy yelled. "Is it?"

Sean stayed motionless, holding Jimmy's eyes with his own, locking them until Jimmy's surging stare saw what Sean had just seen, saw that it was over now, the worst fear had been realized.

Jimmy began to scream and ropes of spit shot from his mouth. Another cop came down the slope to help the one on top of Jimmy, and Sean turned away. Jimmy's scream blew out into the air as a low, guttural thing, nothing sharp or high-pitched to it, an animal's first stage of reckoning with grief. Sean had heard the screams of a lot of victims' parents over the years. Always there was a plaintive character to them, a beseechment for God or reason to return, tell them it was all a dream. But Jimmy's scream had none of that, only love and rage, in equal quantity, shredding the birds from the trees and echoing into the Pen Channel.

Sean went back over and looked down at Katie Marcus. Connolly, the newest member of the unit, came up beside him, and they looked down for a while without saying anything, and Jimmy Marcus's scream grew more hoarse and ragged, as if he'd sucked in kernels of glass every time he took a breath.

Sean looked down at Katie with her fist clenched to the side of her head in the drench of the red rain, then over her body at the wooden props that had kept her from reaching the other side.

Off to their right, Jimmy continued to scream as they dragged him back up the slope, and a helicopter chopped the air over the grove as it made a hard pass, the engine droning as it turned to bank and come back, Sean figuring it was from one of the TV stations. It had a lighter sound than the police choppers.

Connolly, out of the side of his mouth, said, "You ever seen anything like this?"

Sean shrugged. It wouldn't matter much if he had. You got to the point where you stopped comparing.

"I mean, this is . . ." Connolly sputtered, trying to find the words, "this is some kind of . . ." He looked away from the body, off into the trees, with an air of wide-eyed uselessness, and seemed on the verge of trying to speak again.

Then his mouth closed, and after a while he quit trying to give it a name.

12

THE COLORS OF YOU

SEAN LEANED AGAINST the stage below the drive-in screen with his boss, Detective Lieutenant Martin Friel, and they watched Whitey Powers give direction to the coroner's van as it backed down the slope that led to the doorway where Katie Marcus's body had been found. Whitey walked backward, his hands raised and occasionally cutting left or right, his voice sniping the air with crisp whistles that shot through his lower teeth like puppy yelps. His eyes darted from the crime scene tape on either side of him to the van tires to the driver's nervous eyes in the side-view like he was auditioning for a job with a moving company, making sure those fat tires never strayed an inch or more from where he wanted them to go.

"A little more. Keep it straight. Little more, little more. That's it." When he had the van where he wanted it, he stepped aside and slapped the rear doors. "You're good."

Whitey opened the rear doors and pulled them wide so they blocked anyone's view of the space behind the screen, Sean thinking it never would have occurred to him to form protective wings around the doorway where Katie Marcus had died, and then reminding himself that

Whitey had a lot more time put in on crime scenes than he had, Whitey an old warhorse going back to a time when Sean was still trying to cop feels at high school dances and not pick at his acne.

The two coroner's assistants were both halfway out of their seats when Whitey called to them. "Ain't going to work that way, guys. You're gonna have to come out through the back."

They shut their doors and disappeared through the back of the van to retrieve the corpse, and Sean could feel a finality in their disappearance, a certainty that this was his to deal with now. The other cops and teams of techs and the reporters hovering in their copters overhead or on the other side of the crime scene barriers that surrounded the park would move on to something else, and he and Whitey would bear the lion's share of Katie Marcus's death alone, filing the reports, preparing the affidavits, working her death long after most of the people here had moved on to something else—traffic accidents, larcenies, suicides in rooms gone stale with recirculated air and overflowing ashtrays.

Martin Friel hoisted himself up onto the stage and sat there with his small legs dangling over the earth. He'd come here from the back nine at the George Wright and smelled of sunblock under his blue polo and khakis. He drummed his heels off the side of the stage, and Sean could feel a hint of moral annoyance in him.

"You've worked with Sergeant Powers before, right?"

"Yeah," Sean said.

"Any problems?"

"No." Sean watched Whitey take a uniformed trooper aside, point off to the stand of trees behind the drive-in screen. "I worked the Elizabeth Pitek homicide with him last year."

"Woman with the restraining order?" Friel said. "Ex-husband said something about paper?"

"Said, 'Paper rules her life, don't mean it rules mine.' "

"He got twenty, right?"

"Twenty solid, yeah." Sean wishing someone had gotten her a stronger piece of paper. Her kid growing up in a foster home, wondering what happened, who the fuck he belonged to now.

The trooper walked away from Whitey, grabbed a few more uniforms, and they headed off for the trees.

"Heard he drinks," Friel said, and pulled one leg up onto the stage with him, held the knee up against his chest.

"I've never seen it on the clock, sir," Sean said, wondering who was really on probation in Friel's eyes, him or Whitey. He watched Whitey bend and peer at a clump of grass near the van's rear tire, pull up the cuff of his sweatpants as if he were wearing a Brooks Brothers suit.

"Your partner's out on that bullshit disability claim, pulled something in his spine so he's recuperating on Jet Skis, parasailing in Florida, what I hear." Friel shrugged. "Powers requested you when you got back. Now you're back. We going to have any more incidents like the last one?"

Sean had been expecting to eat shit, particularly from Friel, so he kept his voice perfectly contrite. "No, sir. A momentary lapse of judgment."

"Several of them," Friel said.

"Yes, sir."

"Your personal life's a mess, Trooper, that's your problem. Don't let it bleed back into your job." Sean looked at Friel, caught a charged-electrode sheen in his eyes he'd seen before, a sheen that meant Friel was in a place where you couldn't argue with him.

Again Sean nodded, sucking it up.

Friel gave him a cold smile and watched a news copter arc in over the screen, flying lower than the agreed-upon distance, Friel getting a look on his face like he was going to be handing someone severance pay before sunset.

"You know the family, right?" Friel said, tracking the chopper. "You grew up here."

"I grew up in the Point."

"That's here."

"This is the Flats. Bit of a difference, sir."

Friel waved it away. "You grew up here. You were one of the first on-scene, and you know these people." He spread his hands. "I'm wrong?"

"About what?"

"Your ability to handle this." He gave Sean his summer-softball-coach smile. "You're one of my bright boys, right? Served your penance, ready to get back on the ball?"

"Yes, sir," Sean said. You bet, sir. Whatever it takes to keep this job, sir.

They looked over at the van as something thumped to the floor inside and the chassis dipped toward the wheels. The chassis bounced back up, and Friel said, "You notice they always drop them?"

They always did. Katie Marcus, zipped in the dark, plastic heat of a body bag now. Dumped inside that van, her hair matting to the plastic, organs softening.

"Trooper," Friel said, "you know what I like even less than ten-year-old black boys getting shot by bullshit gang-war crossfire?"

Sean knew the answer, but he didn't say anything.

"Nineteen-year-old white girls getting murdered in my parks. People don't say 'Oh, the vagaries of economics' then. They don't feel a wistful sense of the tragic. They feel pissed and they want somebody to be led onto the six o'clock in shackles." Friel nudged Sean. "I mean, right?"

"Right."

"That's what they want, because they're us and that's what we want." Friel grasped Sean's shoulder so he'd look at him.

"Yes, sir," Sean said, because Friel had that weird light in his eyes like he believed what he was saying the way some people believed in God or NASDAQ or the Internet-as-global-village. Friel was Born Again all the way, although what the Again had been Sean couldn't say, just that Friel had found something through his work that Sean could barely recognize, something that gave solace, maybe even belief, a certainty underfoot. Times, to be truthful, Sean thought his boss was an idiot, spouting bullshit platitudes about life and death and the ways to make it all right, cure the cancers and become one collective heart, if only everyone would listen.

Other times, though, Friel reminded Sean of his father, building his birdhouses in the basement where no birds ever flew, and Sean loved the *idea* of him.

Martin Friel had been Homicide Detective Lieutenant of Barracks Six going back a couple of presidents, and as far as Sean knew, no one had ever called him "Marty" or "buddy" or "old man." To look at him on the street, you would have guessed he was an accountant or maybe a claims adjuster for an insurance agency, something like that. He had a bland voice to go with his bland face, and nothing but a brown horseshoe remained of his hair. He was a small guy, particularly for a guy who'd worked his way up through the state trooper ranks, and you could lose him easily in a crowd because there was nothing distinctive to his walk. Loved the wife and two kids, forgot to remove the lift ticket from his parka during wintertime, active in his church, fiscally and socially conservative.

But what the bland voice and bland face couldn't begin to hint at was the mind—a dense, unquestioning combination of the practical and the moralistic. You committed a capital crime in Martin Friel's jurisdiction— and it was *his,* fuck you if you didn't get that—and he took it very, very personally.

"I want you sharp and I want you edgy," he'd said to Sean his first day in the Homicide Unit. "I don't want you overtly outraged, because outrage is emotion and emotion should never be overt. But I want you pretty fucking annoyed at all times—annoyed that the chairs here are too hard and all your friends from college are driving Audis. I want you annoyed that all perps are so dumb they think they can do their heinous shit in *our* jurisdiction. Annoyed enough, Devine, that you stay on the details of your cases so they don't get the ADAs blown out of court because of nebulous warrants and lack of probable cause. Annoyed enough to close every case clean and ram these nasty bastards into nasty cell blocks for the rest of their nasty fucking lives."

Around the barracks it was called "Friel's Spiel," and every new trooper to the unit got it on day one in exactly the same way. Like most of the things Friel said, you had no idea how much he believed and how much was just rah-rah-law-enforcement shtick. But you bought it. Or you washed out.

Sean had been in the State Police Homicide Unit two years, during which time he'd amassed the best clearance rate of anyone in Whitey Powers's squad, and Friel still looked at him sometimes like he wasn't sure about him. He was looking at him that way now, gauging something in him, deciding whether he was up to this: a girl killed in *his* park.

Whitey Powers ambled over to them, flipping through his report pad as he nodded at Friel. "Lieutenant."

"Sergeant Powers," Friel said. "Where are we so far?"

"Preliminary indications put time of death at roughly two-fifteen to two-thirty in the morning. No signs of sexual assault. Cause of death was

most likely the GSW to the back of the head, but we're not ruling out
blunt trauma from that bludgeoning she took. Shooter was most likely a
righty. We found the slug embedded in a pallet to the left of the victim's
body. Looks to be a thirty-eight Smith slug, but we'll know for sure once
Ballistics takes a look. Divers in the channel are looking for weapons
now. We're hoping the perp might have tossed the gun or at least what he
beat her with, which looks to have been a bat of some kind, maybe a
stick."

"A stick," Friel said.

"Two BPD officers on the house-to-houses along Sydney spoke with a
woman claims she heard a car hit something and stall out at one-forty-
five A.M., roughly a half an hour before T.O.D."

"What sort of physical evidence do we have?" Friel asked.

"Well, the rain kinda fucked us there, sir. We got some pretty shitty
footprint casts that may belong to the perp, definitely a couple belong to
the victim. We pulled about twenty-five separate latents off that door
behind the screen. Again, could be the victim's, the perp's, or just twenty-
five people who have nothing to do with this and come down here at
night to drink or take a breather during a jog. We got blood by the door
and inside—again, some of it might be the perp's, might not. A lot of it
definitely came from the victim. We got several distinct prints off the victim's car door. That's about it for physical right now."

Friel nodded. "Anything in particular I can report to the DA when he
calls me in ten or twenty minutes?"

Powers shrugged. "Tell him the rain fucked my crime scene, sir, and
we're doing the best we can."

Friel yawned into his fist. "Anything else I should know?"

Whitey looked back over his shoulder at the trail leading down to the
door behind the screen, the last ground Katie Marcus's feet had touched.

"The lack of footprints pisses me off."

"You mentioned the rain . . ."

Whitey nodded. "But *she* left a couple. I'm willing to bet the house
they were hers, anyway, because they were recent and she was digging her
heels some places and springing off the balls of her feet in others. We
found three, maybe four like that, and I'm pretty sure they belonged to
Katherine Marcus. But the perp? Nothing."

"Again," Sean said, "the rain."

"Accounts for why we found only three of hers, I'll grant you. But not *one* of this guy's far as we can see?" Whitey looked at Sean and then Friel and then he shrugged. "Whatever. Pisses me off is all."

Friel pushed himself off the stage and clapped some grit off his hands. "All right, guys: You have a six-man task force of detectives at your disposal. All your lab work has been bumped to the head of the line and given priority status. You'll have as many troopers as you need for the grunt work. So, Sergeant, tell me how you plan to utilize all this manpower we've gotten for you in our wisdom."

"I suppose we'll talk to the victim's father now and find out what he knows about her movements last night, who she was with, who might've had a beef with her. Then we'll talk to those people, reinterview this woman said she heard the car stall out on Sydney. We'll Q-and-A all the winos they pulled out of the park and off Sydney, hope the tech support teams give us solid latents or hair fibers to work with. Maybe his skin is under the Marcus girl's nails. Maybe his prints are on that door. Or maybe he was the boyfriend and they had a spat." Whitey gave another of his patented shrugs and kicked at some dirt. "That's about it."

Friel looked at Sean.

"We'll get the guy, sir."

Friel looked like he'd been expecting something better, but he nodded once and patted Sean's elbow before walking away from the stage and down into the bowl of seats where Lieutenant Krauser of the BPD stood talking with his boss, Captain Gillis of the D-6, everyone giving Sean and Whitey their best "Don't fuck up" stares.

" 'We'll get the guy'? " Whitey said. "Four years of college, that's the best line you can come up with?"

Sean's eyes met Friel's again for a moment and he gave him a nod that he hoped exuded competence and confidence. "It's in the manual," he said to Whitey. "Right after 'We'll nail the bastard' and before 'Praise the Lord.' You read it?"

Whitey shook his head. "Sick that day."

They turned as the coroner's assistant shut the back doors to the van and came around the driver's side.

"You got any theories?" Sean said.

"Ten years ago," Whitey said, "I'd be liking gang initiation rite. Now, though? Shit. Crime goes down, things get a lot less predictable. You?"

"Jealous boyfriend, but that's just by-the-numbers."

"Beats her with a *bat*? I'd say the boyfriend better have a history of anger-management problems."

"They always do."

The coroner's assistant opened the driver's door and looked over at Whitey and Sean. "Heard someone wanted to lead us out."

"That's us," Whitey said. "You pull ahead of us once we leave the park, but, hey, we're transporting next of kin, so don't leave her in the corridor when you get downtown. You know?"

The guy nodded and got in the van.

Whitey and Sean climbed in a cruiser and Whitey pulled it in front of the van. They headed down the slope between streams of yellow crime scene tape, and Sean watched the sun begin its descent through the trees, turning the Pen a rusty gold, adding a red glow to the treetops, Sean thinking if he were dead that's one of the things he'd probably miss most, the colors, the way they could come out of nowhere and surprise you, even though they could make you feel slightly sad, too, small, like you didn't belong here.

THE FIRST NIGHT Jimmy spent at Deer Island Correctional, he'd sat up all night, from nine to six, wondering if his cellmate would come for him.

The guy had been a New Hampshire biker named Woodrell Daniels who'd crossed into Massachusetts one night on a methamphetamine deal, stopped in a bar for several whiskey nightcaps, and ended up blinding a guy with a pool stick. Woodrell Daniels was a big meat slab of a man covered in tattoos and knife scars, and he'd looked at Jimmy and let loose this dry whisper of a chuckle that went through Jimmy's heart like a length of pipe.

"We'll see you later," Woodrell said at lights-out. "We'll see you later," he repeated, and let loose another of those whispery chuckles.

So Jimmy stayed up all night, listening for sudden creaks in the bunk above him, knowing he'd have to go for Woodrell's trachea if it came down to it, and wondering if he'd be capable of getting one good punch through Woodrell's massive arms. Hit the throat, he told himself. Hit the throat, hit the throat, hit the throat, oh Jesus, here he comes . . .

But it was just Woodrell rolling over in his sleep, creaking those springs, the weight of his body bulging down through the mattress until it hung over Jimmy like the belly of an elephant.

Jimmy heard the prison as a living creature that night. A breathing engine. He heard rats fighting and chewing and screeching with a mad, high-pitched desperation. He heard whispers and moans and the seesaw creak of bedsprings going up and down, up and down. Water dripped and men talked in their sleep and a guard's shoes echoed from a distant hall. At four, he heard a scream—just one—that died so fast it lived longer in echo and memory than it ever had in reality, and Jimmy, at that moment, considered taking the pillow out from behind his head and climbing up behind Woodrell Daniels and smothering him with it. But his hands were too slick and clammy and who knew if Woodrell was really sleeping or just faking it, and maybe Jimmy didn't have the physical strength in the first place to hold that pillow in place while the huge man's huge arms swung back at his head, scratched his face, gouged chunks of flesh from his wrists, shattered his ear cartilage with hammer fists.

It was the last hour that was the worst. A gray light rose through the thick, high windows and filled the place with metallic cold. Jimmy heard men wake and pad around their cells. He heard raspy, dry coughs. He had a sense that the machine was revving up, cold and eager to consume, the machine knowing it would die without violence, without the taste of human skin.

Woodrell jumped down onto the floor, the move so sudden Jimmy couldn't react. He closed his eyes to slits and deepened the rhythm of his breathing and waited for Woodrell to come close enough for him to hit his throat.

Woodrell Daniels didn't even look at him, though. He took a book from the shelf above the sink and opened it as he lowered himself to his knees, and then the man began to pray.

He prayed and read passages from Paul's letters and he prayed some more, and every now and then that whispery chuckle would escape from him but never interrupt the flow of words until Jimmy realized that the chuckling was some kind of uncontrollable emanation, like the sighs Jimmy's mother had let loose when he was younger. Woodrell probably didn't even notice that he made the sounds anymore.

By the time Woodrell turned and asked Jimmy if he'd consider accepting Christ as his personal savior, Jimmy knew the longest night of his life was over. He could see in Woodrell's face the light of the damned trying to navigate his way to salvation, and it was so apparent a glow that Jimmy couldn't understand how he'd failed to see it as soon as he'd met the man.

Jimmy couldn't believe his dumb, beautiful luck—he'd ended up in the lion's den, only his lion was a Christian, and Jimmy would accept Jesus, Bob Hope, Doris Day, or whoever the hell else Woodrell adored in his fevered Holy Roller mind as long as it meant this bulked-up freak would keep to his bed at night and sit beside Jimmy during meals.

"I was once lost," Woodrell Daniels said to Jimmy. "But now, praise the Lord, I am found."

Jimmy almost said it aloud: You got that fucking right, Woodrell.

Until today, Jimmy would judge all patience tests against that first night at Deer Island. He would tell himself that he could stand in place for as long as necessary—a day or two—to get what he wanted because nothing could rival that long first night with the living machine of a prison rumbling and gasping all around him as the rats screeched and bedsprings creaked and screams died as soon as they were born.

Until today.

Standing at the Roseclair Street entrance to Pen Park, Jimmy and Annabeth waited. They stood inside the first barrier the Staties had erected on the entrance road, but outside the second one. They were given cups of coffee and folding chairs to sit on, and the troopers were kind to them. But still, they had to wait, and when they asked for information, the troopers' faces turned a bit stony and a bit sad and they apologized but said they knew nothing more than anyone else on the outside of the park.

Kevin Savage had taken Nadine and Sara back to the house, but Annabeth had stayed. She sat with Jimmy in the lavender dress she'd worn to Nadine's First Communion, an event that already seemed as if it had hap-

pened weeks before, and she was silent and tight within the desperation of
her hope. Hope that what Jimmy had seen on Sean Devine's face was a mis-
interpretation. Hope that Katie's abandoned car and her all-day absence
and the cops in Pen Park were magically unrelated. Hope that what she
probably knew as truth was somehow, somehow, somehow a lie.

Jimmy said, "I get you another coffee?"

She gave him a raw, distant smile. "No. I'm okay."

"You're sure?"

"Yeah."

If you don't see the body, Jimmy knew, she's not really dead. That's
how he'd been rationalizing his own hope in the few hours since he and
Chuck Savage had been dragged away from the hill above the bowl.
Could be a girl who looked like her. Or it could be she was in a coma. Or
maybe she was crammed back in the space behind the screen and they
couldn't get her out. She was in pain, maybe deep pain, but alive. That
was the hope—a sliver of it the width of a baby hair—that flickered in the
lack of an absolute confirmation.

And even as he knew it was bullshit, some part of Jimmy couldn't let
it go.

"I mean, no one *said* anything to you," Annabeth had said early into
their vigil outside the park. "Right?"

"No one said anything." Jimmy stroked her hand, knowing that just
the fact that they'd been allowed within these police barriers was all the
confirmation they needed.

And yet that microbe of hope refused to die without a body to look
down at and say, "Yes, that's her. That's Katie. That's my daughter."

Jimmy watched the cops standing up by the wrought-iron arch that
curved over the entrance to the park. The arch was all that remained of
the penitentiary that had stood on these grounds before the park, before
the drive-in, before any of them standing here today had been born. The
town had sprung up around the Penitentiary, instead of the other way
around. The jailers had settled in the Point while the families of the con-
victs nestled down in the Flats. Incorporation into the city began when
the jailers got older, started running for office.

The walkie-talkie of the trooper closest to the arch squawked, and he
raised it to his lips.

Annabeth's hand tightened around Jimmy's with such force the bones in his hand ground against one another.

"This is Powers. We're coming out."

"Affirmative."

"Mr. and Mrs. Marcus out there?"

The trooper glanced at Jimmy and dropped his eyes. "Affirmative."

"Okay. Out."

Annabeth said, "Oh, Jesus, Jimmy. Oh, Jesus."

Jimmy heard a screech of tires and saw several cars and vans pull up outside the barrier on Roseclair. The vans had satellite dishes on their roofs and Jimmy watched as groups of reporters and cameramen jumped out onto the street, jostling one another, raising cameras, unspooling microphone cables.

"Get them *out* of here!" the trooper up by the arch screamed. "Now! Move 'em out."

The troopers by the front barrier converged on the reporters and the shouting started.

The trooper by the arch spoke into his walkie-talkie: "This is Dugay. Sergeant Powers?"

"Powers."

"We got a blockage out here. The press."

"Clear them."

"Working on it, Sergeant."

Up the entrance road about twenty yards past the arch, Jimmy could see a Statie cruiser round the bend and suddenly stop. He could see a guy behind the wheel, a walkie-talkie raised to his lips, Sean Devine sitting beside him. The edge of another car's grille stopped behind the cruiser, and Jimmy felt his mouth dry up.

"Get them back, Dugay. I don't care if you have to shoot their Columbine-fucker asses. You move those lice back."

"Affirmative."

Dugay and three other troopers jogged past Jimmy and Annabeth, Dugay shouting as he went, finger pointed: "You are violating a closed crime scene. Return to your vehicles immediately. You have no clearance for this area. Return to your vehicles now."

Annabeth said, "Oh shit," and Jimmy felt the blast of the helicopter before he heard it. He looked up as it flew overhead, then back over at the cruiser idling up the road. He could see the driver yelling into his walkie-talkie and then he heard the sirens, a cacophony of them, and suddenly navy-and-silver cruisers came tear-assing from every end of Roseclair, and the reporters started scrambling back into their vehicles and the helicopter banked sharply and cut back into the park.

"Jimmy," Annabeth said in the saddest voice Jimmy had ever heard come out of her. "Jimmy, please. Please."

"Please what, honey?" Jimmy held her. "What?"

"Oh, please, Jimmy. No. No."

It was the noise—the sirens and screeching tires and yelling voices and echoing rotor blades. The noise was Katie, dead, screaming in their ears, and Annabeth was crumpling under it in Jimmy's arms.

Dugay ran past them again and moved the sawhorses under the arch, and before Jimmy realized it had even moved, the cruiser was slamming to a stop beside him and a white van tore around it on the right and blew out onto Roseclair, took a hard left. Jimmy could see the words SUFFOLK COUNTY CORONER on the side of the van, and he felt all the joints in his body—his ankles, shoulders, knees, and hips—turn brittle and then liquefy.

"Jimmy."

Jimmy looked down at Sean Devine. Sean stared up at him through the open window of the passenger door.

"Jimmy, come on. Please. Get in."

Sean got out of the car and opened the rear door as the helicopter returned, higher this time, but still chopping the air close enough to Jimmy that he could feel it in his hair.

"Mrs. Marcus," Sean said. "Jimmy, man. Get in the car."

"Is she dead?" Annabeth said, and the words entered Jimmy and turned acidic.

"Please, Mrs. Marcus. If you could get in the car."

A phalanx of cruisers had formed a double escort line on Roseclair and their sirens raged.

Annabeth screamed over the noise, "Is my daughter—?"

Jimmy moved her because he couldn't hear that word again. He pulled her through the noise and they climbed in the back of the car and

Sean shut the door and climbed up front and the cop behind the wheel hit the gas and the sirens at the same time. They streaked across the entrance road and joined the escort cars and moved en masse out onto Roseclair, an army of vehicles with screaming engines and screaming sirens screaming through the wind toward the expressway, screaming and screaming.

SHE LAY on a metal table.

Her eyes were closed and she was missing a shoe.

Her skin was a black-purple, a shade Jimmy had never seen before.

He could smell her perfume, just a hint of it through the reek of formaldehyde that permeated this cold, cold room.

Sean put a hand against the small of Jimmy's back, and Jimmy spoke, barely feeling the words, certain that at this moment he was as dead as the body below him:

"Yeah, that's her," he said.

"That's Katie," he said.

"That's my daughter."

13

LIGHTS

"THERE'S A CAFETERIA upstairs," Sean said to Jimmy. "Why don't we go have some coffee?"

Jimmy remained standing over his daughter's body. A sheet covered it again, and Jimmy lifted the upper corner of the sheet and looked down at his daughter's face as if peering at her from the top of a well and wanting to dive in after her. "They got a cafeteria in the same building as a morgue?"

"Yeah. It's a big building."

"Seems weird," Jimmy said, his voice stripped of color. "You think when the pathologists go in there, everybody else sits on the other side of the room?"

Sean wondered if this was an early stage of shock. "I dunno, Jim."

"Mr. Marcus," Whitey said, "we were hoping to ask you a few questions. I know this is a hard time, but . . ."

Jimmy lowered the sheet back over his daughter's face, his lips moving, but no sounds leaving his mouth. He looked over at Whitey as if he were surprised to find him in the room, pen poised over his report pad. He turned his head, looked at Sean.

"You ever think," Jimmy said, "how the most minor decision can change the entire direction of your life?"

Sean held his eyes. "How so?"

Jimmy's face was pale and blank, the eyes turned up as if he were trying to remember where he'd left his car keys.

"I heard once that Hitler's mother almost aborted him but bailed at the last minute. I heard he left Vienna because he couldn't sell his paintings. He sells a painting, though, Sean? Or his mother actually aborts? The world's a way different place. You know? Or, like, say you miss your bus one morning, so you buy that second cup of coffee, buy a scratch ticket while you're at it. The scratch ticket hits. Suddenly you don't have to take the bus anymore. You drive to work in a Lincoln. But you get in a car crash and die. All because you missed your bus one day."

Sean looked at Whitey. Whitey shrugged.

"No," Jimmy said, "don't do that. Don't look at him like I'm crazy. I'm not crazy. I'm not in shock."

"Okay, Jim."

"I'm just saying there are threads, okay? Threads in our lives. You pull one, and everything else gets affected. Say it rained in Dallas and so Kennedy didn't ride in a convertible. Stalin stayed in the seminary. Say you and me, Sean, say we got in that car with Dave Boyle."

"What?" Whitey said. "What car?"

Sean held up a hand to him and said to Jimmy, "I'm losing you here."

"You are? If we got in that car, life would have been a very different thing. My first wife, Marita, Katie's mother? She was so beautiful. She was *regal*. You know the way some Latin women can be? Gorgeous. And she knew it. If a guy wanted to approach her, he better have some big fucking balls on him. And I did. I was King Shit at sixteen. I was fearless. And I *did* approach her, and I *did* ask her out. And a year later—Christ, I was seventeen, a fucking child—we got married and she was carrying Katie."

Jimmy walked around his daughter's body in slow, steady circles.

"Here's the thing, Sean—if we'd gotten in that car, been driven off to God knows where and had God knows what done to us by two ass-fucking freaks for four days when we were, what, eleven?—I don't think I'd have been so ballsy at sixteen. I think I would have been a basket case, you know, stoked on Ritalin or whatever. I know I *never* would have had what it took to ask out a woman as haughty-gorgeous as Marita. And so we never would have had Katie. And Katie, then, never would have been murdered. But she was. All because we didn't get in that car, Sean. You see what I'm saying?"

Jimmy looked at Sean like he was waiting for a confirmation, but a confirmation of what Sean didn't have a clue. He looked as if he needed to be absolved—absolved of not getting in that car as a boy, absolved of fathering a child who would be murdered.

Sometimes during a jog, Sean found himself back on Gannon Street, standing on the spot in the middle of the street where he and Jimmy and Dave Boyle had rolled around fighting, then looked up to see that car waiting for them. Sometimes Sean could still smell the odor of apples that had wafted from the car. And if he turned his head real quick, he could see Dave Boyle in the backseat of that car as it reached the corner, looking back at them, trapped and receding from view.

It had occurred to Sean once—on a bender about ten years before with some buddies, Sean and a bloodstream full of bourbon turning philosophical—that maybe they *had* gotten in that car. All three of them. And what they now thought of as their life was just a dream state. That all three of them were, in reality, still eleven-year-old boys trapped in some cellar, imagining what they'd become if they ever escaped and grew up.

The thing about that idea was that even though Sean would have expected it to be the first casualty of a night's drinking, it had remained lodged in his brain like a stone in the sole of his shoe.

And so occasionally he found himself on Gannon Street in front of his old house, catching glimpses of the receding Dave Boyle out of the corner of his eye, the odor of apples filling his nostrils, thinking, No. Come back.

He met Jimmy's plaintive glare. He wanted to say something. He wanted to tell him that he had also thought about what would have happened if they'd climbed in that car. That the thought of what could have been his life sometimes haunted him, hovered around approaching corners, rode the breeze like the echo of a name called from a window. He wanted to tell Jimmy that he occasionally sweated through his old dream, the one in which the street gripped his feet and slid him toward that open door. He wanted to tell him he hadn't truly known what to make of his life since that day, that he was a man who often felt light with his own weightlessness, the insubstantial nature of his character.

But they were in a morgue with Jimmy's daughter lying on a steel table in between them and Whitey's pen poised over paper, so all Sean said to the plea in Jimmy's face was: "Come on, Jim. Let's go get that coffee."

ANNABETH MARCUS, in Sean's opinion, was one tough god-damned woman. She sat in a cold, late-Sunday, municipal cafeteria with its warmed-over, cellophane-'n'-steam smell, seven stories above a morgue, talking about her stepdaughter with cold, municipal men, and Sean could tell it was killing her, yet she refused to crack. Her eyes were red, but Sean knew after a few minutes that she wouldn't weep. Not in front of them. No fucking way.

As they talked, she had to stop for breath a few times. Her throat would close up in midsentence, as if a fist wormed its way through her chest, pressing against her organs. She'd place a hand on her chest and open her mouth a little wider and wait until she'd gotten enough oxygen to continue.

"She came home from working at the store at four-thirty on Saturday."

"What store was that, Mrs. Marcus?"

She pointed at Jimmy. "My husband owns Cottage Market."

"On the corner of East Cottage and Bucky Ave.?" Whitey said. "Best damn coffee in the city."

Annabeth said, "She came in and hopped in the shower. She came out and we had dinner—wait, no, she didn't eat. She sat with us, talked to the girls, but she didn't eat. She said she was having dinner with Eve and Diane."

"The girls she went out with," Whitey said to Jimmy.

Jimmy nodded.

"So, she didn't eat . . ." Whitey said.

Annabeth said, "But she hung out with the girls, our girls, her sisters. And they talked about the parade next week and Nadine's First Communion. And then she was on the phone in her room for a bit, and then, about eight, she left."

"Do you know who she talked to on the phone?"

Annabeth shook her head.

"The phone in her room," Whitey said. "Private line?"

"Yes."

"Would you have any objections if we subpoenaed the phone company records to that line?"

Annabeth looked at Jimmy and Jimmy said, "No. No objections."

"So she left at eight. As far as you know to meet with her friends, Eve and Diane?"

"Yes."

"And you were still at the store at this time, Mr. Marcus?"

"Yeah. I did swing shift on Saturday. Twelve to eight."

Whitey flipped a page in his notebook and gave them both a small smile. "I know this is tough, but you're doing great."

Annabeth nodded and turned to her husband. "I called Kevin."

"Yeah? You talk to the girls?"

"I talked to Sara. I just told her we'd be home soon. I didn't tell her anything else."

"She ask about Katie?"

Annabeth nodded.

"What'd you tell her?"

"I just told her we'd be home soon," Annabeth said, and Sean heard a small crack in her voice on "soon."

She and Jimmy looked back at Whitey and he gave them another small, calming smile.

"I want to assure you—and this comes down all the way from the big office in City Hall—that this case is top priority. And we won't make mistakes. Trooper Devine here was assigned because he's a friend of the family and our boss knows that that'll make him work it that much harder. He's going to be with me every step of the way, and we will find the man responsible for harming your daughter."

Annabeth gave Sean a quizzical look. "Friend of the family? I don't know you."

Whitey scowled, thrown off his game.

Sean said, "Your husband and I were friends, Mrs. Marcus."

"Long time ago," Jimmy said.

"Our fathers worked together."

Annabeth nodded, still a bit confused.

Whitey said, "Mr. Marcus, you spent a good part of Saturday with your daughter at the store. Correct?"

"I did and I didn't," Jimmy said. "I was mostly in back. Katie worked the registers up front."

"But do you remember anything out of the ordinary? Was she acting odd? Tense? Fearful? Did she have a confrontation with a customer maybe?"

"Not while I was there. I'll give you the number of the guy who worked with her in the morning. Maybe something happened before I got in that he remembers."

"Appreciate that, sir. But while you were there?"

"She was herself. She was happy. Maybe a little . . ."

"What?"

"No, nothing."

"Sir, the littlest thing is something right now."

Annabeth leaned forward. "Jimmy?"

Jimmy gave them all an embarrassed grimace. "It's nothing. It was . . . I look up from my desk at one point and she's standing in the doorway. Just standing there, sipping a Coke through a straw, and looking at me."

"Looking at you."

"Yeah. And for a second, she looked like she did this one time when she was five and I was going to leave her in the car for just a sec while I ran into the drugstore. That time, right, she burst out crying because I'd just gotten back from prison and her mother had just died and I think, back then, she thought that every time you left her, even for a second, you weren't going to come back. So she'd get this look, right? I mean, whether she ended up crying or not, she'd get this look on her face like she was *preparing* herself to never see you again." Jimmy cleared his throat and let out a long sigh that widened his eyes. "Anyway, I hadn't seen that look in a few years, maybe seven or eight, but for a few seconds on Saturday, that's how she was looking at me."

"Like she was preparing herself to never see you again."

"Yeah." Jimmy watched Whitey write that in his report pad. "Hey, don't make too much of it. It was just a look."

"I'm not making anything out of it, Mr. Marcus, I promise. It's just info. That's what I do—I collect pieces of info until two or three pieces fit together. You say you were in prison?"

Annabeth said, "Jesus," very softly, and shook her head.

Jimmy leaned back in his chair. "Here we go."

"I'm just asking," Whitey said.

"You'd do the same if I'd said I worked at Sears fifteen years ago, right?" Jimmy chuckled. "I did time for a robbery. Two years at Deer Island. You write that in your notebook. That piece of information going to help you catch the guy who killed my daughter, Sergeant? I mean, I'm just asking."

Whitey shot a glance Sean's way.

Sean said, "Jim, no one means to offend anyone here. Let's just let it pass, get back to the point."

"The point," Jimmy said.

"Outside of that look Katie gave you," Sean said, "was there anything else out of the ordinary you can remember?"

Jimmy took his convict-in-the-yard stare off Whitey and drank some coffee. "No. Nothing. Wait—this kid, Brendan Harris— But, no, that was this morning."

"What about him?"

"He's just a kid from the neighborhood. He came in today and asked if Katie was around like he'd been expecting to see her. But they barely knew each other. It was just a little strange. It doesn't mean anything."

Whitey wrote the kid's name down anyway.

"Could she have been dating him maybe?" Sean said.

"No."

Annabeth said, "You never know, Jim . . ."

"I know," Jimmy said. "She wouldn't date that kid."

"No?" Sean said.

"No."

"Why you so sure?"

"Hey, Sean, what the fuck? You're going to grill me?"

"I'm not grilling you, Jim. I'm just asking how you could be so sure your daughter wasn't seeing this Brendan Harris kid."

Jimmy blew air out of his mouth and up at the ceiling. "A father knows. Okay?"

Sean decided to let it ride for now. He tossed it back to Whitey with a nod.

Whitey said, "Well, what about that? Who was she seeing?"

"No one at the moment," Annabeth said. "Far as we knew."

"How about ex-boyfriends? Anyone who might be holding a grudge? Guy she dumped or something?"

Annabeth and Jimmy looked at each other and Sean could feel it between them—a suspect.

"Bobby O'Donnell," Annabeth said eventually.

Whitey placed his pen on his report pad, stared across the table at them. "We talking about the same Bobby O'Donnell?"

Jimmy said, "I dunno. Coke dealer and pimp? About twenty-seven?"

"That's the guy," Whitey said. "We got him pegged for a lot of shit went down in your neighborhood the past two years."

"And yet you haven't charged him with anything."

"Well, first off, Mr. Marcus, I'm State Police. If this crime hadn't happened in Pen Park, I wouldn't even be here. East Bucky is, for the most part, under City jurisdiction, and I can't speak for the City cops."

Annabeth said, "I'll tell that to my friend Connie. Bobby and his friends blew up her flower shop."

"Why?" Sean asked.

"Because she wouldn't pay him," Annabeth said.

"Pay him to do what?"

"Not blow up her fucking flower shop," Annabeth said, and took another sip of coffee, Sean thinking it again—this woman was hard-core. Fuck with her at your peril.

"So your daughter," Whitey said, "was dating him."

Annabeth nodded. "Not for long. A few months, yeah, Jim? It ended back in November."

"How'd Bobby take it?" Whitey asked.

The Marcuses exchanged glances again, and then Jimmy said, "There was a beef one night. He came to the house with his guard dog, Roman Fallow."

"And?"

"And we made it clear they should leave."

"Who's we?"

Annabeth said, "Several of my brothers live in the apartment above us and the apartment below. They're protective of Katie."

"The Savages," Sean told Whitey.

Whitey placed his pen on the pad again and pressed his index and thumb tips against the skin at the corners of his eyes. "The Savage brothers."

"Yes. Why?"

"All due respect, ma'am, I'm a bit worried this could shape up into something ugly." Whitey kept his head down, kneading the back of his neck now. "I mean absolutely no offense here, but—"

"That's usually what someone says before they're about to say something offensive."

Whitey looked up at her with a surprised smile. "Your brothers, you must know, have some reputations themselves."

Annabeth met Whitey's smile with a hard one of her own. "I know what they are, Sergeant Powers. You don't have to dance around it."

"A friend of mine in Major Crimes told me a few months back that O'Donnell was making noise about moving into loan-sharking and heroin. Both of which, I'm told, are exclusively Savage territory."

"Not in the Flats."

"What's that, ma'am?"

"Not in the Flats," Jimmy said, his hand on his wife's. "Means they don't do that shit in their own neighborhood."

"Just someone else's," Whitey said, and let that lie on the table for a bit. "In either case, that would leave a vacuum in the Flats. Right? An exploitable vacuum. Which, if my info is correct, is what Bobby O'Donnell has been planning to exploit."

"And?" Jimmy said, rising up a bit in his seat.

"And?"

"And what does this have to do with my daughter, Sergeant?"

"Everything," Whitey said, his arms spreading wide. "Everything, Mr. Marcus, because all either side needed was one little excuse to go to war. And now they have it."

Jimmy shook his head, a bitter grin twitching at the edges of his mouth.

"Oh, you don't think so, Mr. Marcus?"

Jimmy raised his head. "I think my neighborhood, Sergeant, is going to disappear soon. And crime's going to go with it. And it won't be because of the Savages or the O'Donnells or you guys bucking up against them. It'll be because interest rates are low and property taxes are getting high and everyone wants to move back to the city because the restaurants in the suburbs suck. And these people moving in, they aren't the kind that need heroin or six bars per block or ten-dollar blow jobs. Their lives are fine. They like their jobs. They got futures and IRAs and nice German cars. So when they move in—and they're coming—crime and half the neighborhood will move out. So I wouldn't worry much about Bobby O'Donnell and my brothers-in-law going to war, Sergeant. War for what?"

"For the right now," Whitey said.

Jimmy said, "You honestly think O'Donnell killed my daughter?"

"I think the Savages might consider him a suspect. And I think someone needs to talk them out of that kind of thinking until we've had time to do our jobs."

Jimmy and Annabeth sat on the other side of the table, Sean trying to read their faces but getting nothing back.

"Jimmy," Sean said, "without distractions, we can close this case fast."

"Yeah?" Jimmy said. "I got your word on that, Sean?"

"You do. And close it clean, too, so nothing comes back on us in court."

"How long?"

"What?"

"How long would you say it'll take you to put her killer in jail?"

Whitey held up a hand. "Wait a second—are you bargaining with us, Mr. Marcus?"

"Bargaining?" Jimmy's face had that convict's deadness to it again.

"Yeah," Whitey said. "Because I'm perceiving—"

"You're *perceiving?*"

"—an aspect of threat to this conversation."

"Really?" All innocence now, but the eyes still dead.

"Like you're giving us a deadline," Whitey said.

"Trooper Devine pledged that he'd find my daughter's killer. I'm just asking in what sort of time frame he thinks this will happen."

"Trooper Devine," Whitey said, "is not in charge of this investigation.

I am. And we will depth-charge whoever did this, Mr. and Mrs. Marcus. What I don't need is anyone getting it in their head that our fear of a war between the Savage and O'Donnell crews can be used as some sort of leverage against us. I think that, I'll arrest them all on public nuisance charges and lose the paperwork until this is over."

A couple of janitors walked past them, trays in hand, the soggy food on top letting off a gray steam. Sean felt the air in the place grow staler, the night close in around them.

"So, okay," Jimmy said with a bright smile.

"Okay, what?"

"Find her killer. I won't stand in your way." He turned to his wife as he stood and offered her his hand. "Honey?"

Whitey said, "Mr. Marcus."

Jimmy looked down at him as his wife took his hand and stood.

"There'll be a trooper downstairs to drive you home," Whitey said, and reached into his wallet. "If you think of anything, give us a call."

Jimmy took Whitey's card and placed it in his back pocket.

Now that she was standing, Annabeth looked a lot less steady, like her legs were filled with liquid. She squeezed her husband's hand and her own whitened.

"Thank you," she whispered to Sean and Whitey.

Sean could see the ravages of the day finding her face and body now, beginning to drape her. The harsh light above them caught her face, and Sean could see what she'd look like when she was much older—a handsome woman, scarred by wisdom she'd never asked for.

Sean had no idea where the words came from. He wasn't even aware he was speaking until he heard the sound of his voice enter the cold cafeteria:

"We'll speak for her, Mrs. Marcus. If that's okay, we'll do that."

Annabeth's face crinkled momentarily, and then she sucked at the air and nodded several times, wavering slightly against her husband.

"Yes, Mr. Devine, that's okay. That's fine."

DRIVING BACK across the city, Whitey said, "What's this car business?"

Sean said, "What?"

"Marcus said you guys almost got in some car when you were kids."

"We . . ." Sean reached up by the dashboard and adjusted the side-view mirror until he could see the stream of headlights glowing behind them, fuzzy yellow dots bouncing slightly in the night, shimmying. "We, shit, well, there was this car. Me and Jimmy and a kid named Dave Boyle were playing out in front of my house. We were, like, eleven. And anyway, this car came up the street and took Dave away."

"An abduction?"

Sean nodded, keeping his eyes on those shimmying yellow lights. "Guys pretended to be cops. They convinced Dave to get in the car. Jimmy and me didn't. They had Dave four days. He managed to escape. Lives in the Flats now."

"They catch the guys?"

"One died, the other got busted about a year later, went the noose route in his cell."

"Man," Whitey said, "I wish there was an island, you know? Like in that old Steve McQueen movie where he was supposed to be French and everyone had an accent but him? He's just Steve McQueen with a French name. Jumps off the cliff at the end with the raft made of coconuts? You ever see that?"

"No."

"Good movie. But, like, if they had an island just for baby-rapers and chicken hawks? Just airlift food in a few times a week, fill the water with mines. No one gets off. First-time offenders, fuck you, you get life on the island. Sorry, fellas, just can't risk you getting out and poisoning someone else. 'Cause it's a transmittable disease, you know? You get it 'cause someone did it to you. And you go and pass it on. Like leprosy. I figure we put 'em all on this island, less chance they can pass it on. Each generation, we have fewer and fewer of them. A few hundred years, we turn the island into Club Med or something. Kids hear about these freaks the way they hear about ghosts now, as something we've, I dunno, *evolved* beyond."

Sean said, "Shit, Sarge, what're you, deep all of a sudden?"

Whitey grinned and turned onto the expressway ramp.

"Your buddy Marcus," he said. "Moment I laid eyes on him, I knew he'd done time. They never lose that tension, you know? In their shoulders mostly. Spend two years watching your own back, every second of every day, the tension's gotta settle somewhere."

"He just lost his daughter, man. Maybe that's what settled in his shoulders."

Whitey shook his head. "No. That's in his stomach right now. You see how he kept grimacing? That's the loss sitting in his stomach, turning it to acid. Seen it a million times. The shoulders, though, that's prison."

Sean turned from the rearview, watched the lights on the other side of the highway for a bit. They came in their direction like bullet eyes, streaked past them like hazy ribbons, blurring into one another. He felt the city girded all around them, with its high-rises and tenements and office towers and parking garages, arenas and nightclubs and churches, and he knew that if one of those lights went out, it wouldn't make any difference. And if a new light came on, no one would notice. And yet, they pulsed and glowed and shimmied and flared and stared at you, just like now—staring in at his and Whitey's own lights as they blipped past on the expressway, just one more set of red and yellow lights streaking along amid a current of red and yellow lights that blipped, blipped, blipped through an unremarkable Sunday dusk.

Toward where?

Toward the extinguished lights, dummy. Toward the shattered glass.

AFTER MIDNIGHT, once Annabeth and the girls had finally gone to sleep and Annabeth's cousin Celeste, who'd come by as soon as she'd heard, had started dozing on the couch, Jimmy went downstairs and sat on the front porch of the three-decker he shared with the Savage brothers.

He brought Sean's glove with him and he slipped it over his hand even though he couldn't get his thumb in there and the heel of the glove stopped in the middle of his palm. He sat looking out at the four lanes of Buckingham Avenue and tossed a ball into the webbing, the soft thwack of leather against leather calming something in him.

Jimmy had always liked sitting out here at night. The storefronts across the avenue were closed and mostly dark. At night, a hush fell over an area where commercial business was conducted during the day, and it was a hush unlike any other. The noise that normally ruled the daytime wasn't gone, it was merely sucked up, as if into a pair of lungs, and then held, waiting to be expelled. He trusted that hush, warmed to it, because it promised the return of the noise, even as it held it captive. Jimmy couldn't imagine living somewhere rural, where the hush *was* the noise, where silence was delicate and shattered upon touch.

But he did like this hush, this rumbling stillness. Up until now, the evening had seemed so noisy, so violent with voices and the weeping of his wife and daughters. Sean Devine had sent over two detectives, Brackett and Rosenthal, to search Katie's room with embarrassed eyes cast downward, whispering to Jimmy their apologies as they searched drawers and under the bed and mattress, Jimmy wishing they'd just speed it up, stop fucking talking to him. In the end, they didn't find anything unusual outside of seven hundred dollars in new bills in Katie's sock drawer. They'd shown it to Jimmy along with her bank book—stamped "Closed"—the final withdrawal having been made Friday afternoon.

Jimmy had no answer for them. It was a surprise to him. But given all the other surprises of the day, it had very little effect. It just added to the general numbness.

"We can kill him."

Val stepped out onto the porch and handed Jimmy a beer. He sat down beside him, his feet bare on the steps.

"O'Donnell?"

Val nodded. "I'd like to. You know, Jim?"

"You think he killed Katie."

Val nodded. "Or had someone else do it. Don't you? Her girlfriends sure thought so. They say Roman rolled up on them in a bar, threatened Katie."

"Threatened?"

"Well, gave her some shit anyway, like she was still O'Donnell's girl. Come *on,* Jimmy, it had to be Bobby."

Jimmy said, "I don't know that for sure yet."

"What'll you do when you do know?"

Jimmy put the baseball glove on the step below him and opened his beer. He took a long, slow drink from it. "I don't know that, either."

14

AIN'T EVER
GOING TO FEEL
THAT AGAIN

THEY WENT at it all night and into the morning—Sean, Whitey Powers, Souza and Connolly, two other members of the State Homicide Unit, Brackett and Rosenthal, plus a legion of troopers and CSS techs, photographers and medical examiners—everyone banging at the case like a steel box. They'd scraped every leaf in the park for evidence. They'd filled notebooks with diagrams and field reports. The troopers had conducted the house-to-house Q & A's of every house within walking distance of the park, filled a van with vagrants from the park and the burned-out shells on Sydney. They searched through the backpack they'd found in Katie Marcus's car and come up with the usual shit before finding a brochure for Las Vegas and a list of Vegas hotels on lined yellow paper.

Whitey showed the brochure to Sean and whistled. "What we in the biz call a clue. Let's go talk to the friends."

Eve Pigeon and Diane Cestra, maybe the last two decent people to see Katie Marcus alive according to her father, looked like they'd taken whacks to the back of their heads from the same shovel. Whitey and Sean worked them softly between the almost constant buckets of tears that streamed down their faces. The girls provided them with a timeline of Katie Marcus's actions on her last night alive and gave them the names of the bars they'd gone to along with approximate times of arrival and departure, but when it came to the personal stuff, both Sean and Whitey felt they were holding back, exchanging looks before they'd answer, getting vague where before they'd been definite:

"She dating anybody?"

"Nobody, like, regular."

"How about casually?"

"Well . . ."

"Yeah?"

"She didn't keep us real current on that kinda thing."

"Diane, Eve, come on. Your best friend since kindergarten, and she don't tell you who she's dating?"

"She was private like that."

"Yeah, private. That was Katie, sir."

Whitey tried another way in: "So there was nothing special about last night? Nothing out of the ordinary?"

"No."

"How about her planning to leave town?"

"What? No."

"No? Diane, she had a knapsack in the back of her car. It had brochures for Vegas in it. She was, what, carrying them around for someone else?"

"Maybe. I dunno."

Eve's father had piped in then: "Honey, you know something could help, you start talking. This is Katie getting, Jesus, murdered here."

Which had just brought on a fresh bucket of sobs, both girls going to hell then, beginning to wail and hug each other and shake, mouths wide and oval and slightly skewered in the pantomime of grief Sean had seen time and time again, the moment when, as Martin Friel called it, the levee broke and the permanence of the victim's absence truly hit home. Times like that, there was nothing you could do but watch or leave.

They watched and waited.

Eve Pigeon did look a bit like a bird, Sean thought. Her face was very sharp, her nose very thin. It nearly worked for her, though. She had a grace about her that gave her thinness an air of the almost-aristocratic. Sean guessed she was the kind of woman who looked better in formal clothing than casual, and she emanated a decency and intelligence that Sean figured would attract only serious men, weed out the scammers and Romeos.

Diane, on the other hand, oozed a defeated sensuality. Sean spotted a faded bruise just behind her right eye, and she struck him as denser than Eve, more given to emotion and possibly laughter, too. A fading hope hung in both her eyes like matching flaws, a neediness that Sean knew rarely attracted any other kind of man but the predatory kind. Sean figured she'd be at the center of a few 911 domestic disturbance calls over the coming years, and that by the time the cops reached her door, that dying hope would be long gone from her eyes.

"Eve," Whitey said gently when they'd finally stopped crying, "I need to know about Roman Fallow."

Eve nodded as if she'd been expecting the question, but she didn't say anything right away. She chewed the skin around her thumbnail and stared at some crumbs on the tabletop.

"That jerkoff hangs around Bobby O'Donnell?" her father said.

Whitey held up a hand to him, glanced over at Sean.

"Eve," Sean said, knowing Eve was the one they had to get to. She'd be harder to crack than Diane, but she'd yield more in the way of pertinent detail.

She looked at him.

"There won't be any reprisals, if that's what's worrying you. You tell us something about Roman Fallow or Bobby, and it stays with us. They'll never know it came from you."

Diane said, "What about when it goes to court? Huh? What about then?"

Whitey gave Sean a look that said: You're on your own.

Sean concentrated on Eve. "Unless you saw Roman or Bobby pull Katie from her car—"

"No."

"Then the DA wouldn't force either of you to testify in open court, Eve, no. He'd *ask* a lot probably, but he wouldn't force you."

Eve said, "You don't know them."

"Bobby and Roman? Sure I do. I put Bobby away for nine months when I was working narcotics cases." Sean reached out and laid his hand on the table about an inch from hers. "And he threatened me. But that's all he and Roman are—talk."

Eve gave Sean's hand a bitter half-smile with pursed lips. "Bull . . . shit," she said, dragging it out.

Her father said, "You don't talk like that in this house."

"Mr. Pigeon," Whitey said.

"No," Drew said. "My house, my rules. I won't have my daughter talking like she—"

"It was Bobby," Eve said, and Diane let out a small gasp, stared at her friend as if she'd lost her mind.

Sean saw Whitey's eyebrows arch.

"What was Bobby?" Sean said.

"Who Katie was dating. Bobby, not Roman."

"Jimmy know about this?" Drew asked his daughter.

Eve let go one of those sullen shrugs Sean had found endemic to kids her age, a slow twitch of the body that said it barely cared enough to make the effort.

"Eve," Drew said. "Did he?"

"He knew and he didn't," Eve said. She sighed and leaned her head back, stared up at the ceiling with those dark eyes. "Her parents thought it was over because for a while *she* thought it was over. The only one who didn't think it was over was Bobby. He wouldn't accept it. He kept coming back. One night he held her off a third-floor landing."

"You saw this?" Whitey said.

She shook her head. "Katie told me. He ran into her at a party six weeks, a month ago. He convinced her to come out in the hall to talk to him. 'Cept it was a third-floor apartment, you know?" Eve wiped her face with the back of her hand, even though by the looks of her, she was all cried out at the moment. "Katie told me she kept trying to explain to him that they were broken up, but Bobby wouldn't hear it, and finally he got so mad he grabbed her by the shoulders and lifted her over the railing. He held her over the stairway. Three stories down, the psycho. And he said if she broke up with him he'd break *her* up. She was his girl until he said otherwise and if she didn't like it, he'd drop her right fucking then."

"Jesus," Drew Pigeon said after a few moments' silence. "You *know* these people?"

Whitey said, "So, Eve, what did Roman say to her in the bar Saturday night?"

Eve didn't say anything for a bit.

Whitey said, "Why don't you tell us, Diane?"

Diane looked like she needed a drink. "We told Val. That was enough."

"Val?" Whitey said. "Val Savage?"

Diane said, "He was here this afternoon."

"And you told him what Roman said, but you won't tell us."

"He's her family," Diane said, and crossed her arms across her chest, gave them her best "fuck you, cop" face.

"I'll tell you," Eve said. "Jesus. He said he'd heard we were drunk and making asses of ourselves and he didn't like hearing that, and *Bobby* sure wouldn't like hearing it and maybe we should go home."

"So you left."

"You ever talk to Roman?" she said. "He's got a way of making his questions sound like threats."

"And that was it," Whitey said. "You didn't see him follow you out of the bar or anything?"

She shook her head.

They looked at Diane.

Diane shrugged. "We were pretty drunk."

"You had no more contact with him that night? Either of you?"

"Katie drove us to my house," Eve said. "She dropped us off. That's all we saw of her." She bit down on the last word, clenching her face like a fist as she tilted her head back again and looked up, sucking air.

Sean said, "Who was she planning to go to Vegas with? Bobby?"

Eve stared up at the ceiling for a while, her breath gone liquid. "Not Bobby," she said eventually.

"Who, Eve?" Sean said. "Who was she going to Vegas with?"

"Brendan."

"Brendan Harris?" Whitey said.

"Brendan Harris," she said. "Yeah."

Whitey and Sean looked at each other.

"Just Ray's kid?" Drew Pigeon said. "The one with the mute for a brother?"

Eve nodded and Drew turned to Sean and Whitey.

"Nice kid. Harmless."

Sean nodded. Harmless. Sure.

"You got an address?" Whitey asked.

NOBODY WAS HOME at Brendan Harris's address, so Sean called in, got two troopers to cover the place and call them when Harris returned.

They went to Mrs. Prior's house next, and sat through tea and stale coffee cakes and *Touched by an Angel* turned up so loud Sean could hear Della Reese in his head for an hour afterward screaming "Amen" and talking about redemption.

Mrs. Prior said she'd looked out her window around 1:30 A.M. the previous night, seen two kids playing in the street, little kids, out at a time like that, throwing cans at each other, fencing with hockey sticks, using foul language. She thought of saying something to them, but little old ladies had to be careful. Kids were crazy these days, shooting up schools, wearing those baggy clothes, using all that foul language. Besides, the kids eventually chased each other away and down the street and then they were someone else's problem, but the way they behaved today, I mean, is that any way to live?

"Officer Medeiros told us you heard a car around one-forty-five," Whitey said.

Mrs. Prior watched Della explain God's way to Roma Downey, Roma looking all solemn and dewy-eyed and filled to the brim with Jesus. Mrs. Prior nodded several times at the TV, then turned and looked back at Whitey and Sean.

"I heard a car hit something."

"Hit what?"

"The way people drive today, it's a blessing I don't have a license anymore. I'd be afraid to drive these streets. Everyone's just so mad."

"Yes, ma'am," Sean said. "Did it sound like a car hitting another car?"

"Oh, no."

"Hitting a person?" Whitey said.

"Good Lord, what would that sound like? I wouldn't even want to know."

"So it wasn't a really, really loud sound," Whitey said.

"Excuse me, dear?"

Whitey repeated himself, leaning in.

"No," Mrs. Prior said. "It was more like a car hitting a rock or a curb. And then it stalled and then someone said, 'Hi.' "

"Someone said, 'Hi'?"

"Hi." Mrs. Prior looked at Sean and nodded. "And then part of the car cracked."

Sean and Whitey looked at each other.

Whitey said, "Cracked?"

Mrs. Prior nodded her little blue head. "When my Leo was alive, he snapped the axle on our Plymouth? It made such a noise! Crack!" Her eyes grew bright. "Crack!" she said. "Crack!"

"And that's what you heard after someone said, 'Hi.' "

She nodded. "Hi and crack!"

"And then you looked out your window and saw what?"

"Oh, no, no," Mrs. Prior said. "I didn't look out my window. I was in my dressing gown by then. I'd been in bed. I wasn't looking out the window in my dressing gown. People could see."

"But fifteen minutes before, you'd—"

"Young man, I wasn't in my dressing gown fifteen minutes before. I'd just finished watching TV, a wonderful film with Glenn Ford. Oh, I wish I could remember the name."

"So you turned off the TV . . ."

"And I saw those motherless children in the street, and then I went upstairs and changed into my dressing gown, and then, young sir, I kept my shades drawn."

"The voice that said, 'Hi,' " Whitey said. "Was it male or female?"

"Female, I think," Mrs. Prior said. "It was a high voice. Not like either of yours," she said brightly. "You two have fine masculine voices. Your mothers must be proud."

Whitey said, "Oh, yes, ma'am. Like you wouldn't believe."

As they left the house, Sean said, "Crack!"

Whitey smiled. "She liked saying that, you know? Got some blood pumping in the old girl."

"You thinking snapped axle or gunshot?"

"Gunshot," Whitey said. "It's the 'Hi' that's throwing me."

"Would suggest she knew the shooter, she says hi to him."

"Would suggest. Wouldn't guarantee."

They worked the bars after that, coming away with nothing but boozy recollections of maybe seeing the girls in here, maybe not, and half-assed lists of possible patrons who'd been in at the approximate times.

By the time they got to McGills, Whitey was getting pissed.

"Two young chicks—and they were young, by the way, underage actually—hop up on this bar right here and dance, and you're telling me you don't recall that?"

The bartender was nodding halfway through Whitey's question. "Oh, those girls. Okay, okay. I remember them. Sure. They must have had great IDs, Detective, because we carded 'em."

"That's 'Sergeant,' " Whitey said. "You barely remembered they were here at first, but now you can remember carding them. You remember what time they left, maybe? Or is that selectively foggy?"

The bartender, a young guy with biceps so big they probably squeezed off the blood flow to his brain, said, "Left?"

"As in departed."

"I don't—"

"It was right before Crosby broke the clock," a guy on the stool said.

Sean glanced over at the guy—an old-timer with the *Herald* spread out on the bar between a bottle of Bud and a shot of whiskey, cigarette curling down into the ashtray.

"You were here," Sean said.

"I was here. Moron Crosby wants to drive home. His friends try to take his keys. Shithead throws them at them. He misses. Hits that clock."

Sean looked up at the clock over the doorway leading to the kitchen. The glass had spiderwebbed and the hands had stopped at 12:52.

"And they left before that?" Whitey asked the old-timer. "The girls?"

"About five minutes before," the guy said. "The keys hit the clock, I'm thinking, 'I'm glad those girls aren't here. They don't need to see that shit.' "

In the car, Whitey said, "You work up a timeline yet?"

Sean nodded, flipped through his notes. "They leave Curley's Folly at nine-thirty, do the Banshee, Dick Doyle's Pub, and Spire's in quick succession, end up at McGills around eleven-thirty, are inside the Last Drop at ten past one."

"And she's crashing her car about half an hour later."

Sean nodded.

"You see any familiar names on the bartender's list?"

Sean looked down at the list of Saturday night patrons the bartender at McGills had scribbled on a sheet of paper.

"Dave Boyle," he said aloud when he got to it.

"The same guy you were friends with as a kid?"

"Could be," Sean said.

"He might be a guy to talk to," Whitey said. "He thinks you're a friend, he won't treat us like cops, clam up for no good reason."

"Sure."

"We'll put him on tomorrow's to-do list."

THEY FOUND ROMAN FALLOW sipping a latte at Café Society in the Point. He sat with a woman who looked like a model—kneecaps as sharp as her cheekbones, eyes bulging slightly because the skin on her face was pulled so tight it looked like it had been glued to the bone, nice off-white summer dress with those spaghetti straps that made her look sexy and skeletal at the same time, Sean wondering how she pulled that off and deciding it must be the pearl glow of her perfect skin.

Roman wore a silk T-shirt tucked into pleated linen trousers, looking like he just stepped off a soundstage of one of those old RKO movies set in Havana or Key West. He sipped his latte and leafed through the paper with his girl, Roman reading the business section, his model thumbing through the style section.

Whitey pulled a chair over to them and said, "Hey, Roman, they sell men's clothes where you got that shirt?"

Roman kept his eyes on his paper, popped a piece of croissant in his mouth. "Sergeant Powers, how you doing? How's that Hyundai working out for you?"

Whitey chuckled as Sean sat down beside him. "Looking at you, Roman, you know, in this place, I'd swear you were just another yuppie, ready to get up in the morning and go do some day trading on your iMac."

"Got a PC, Sergeant." Roman closed his paper and looked at Whitey and Sean for the first time. "Oh, hi," he said to Sean. "I know you from somewhere."

"Sean Devine, State Police."

"Right, right," Roman said. "Sure, I remember now. Saw you in court once testifying against a friend of mine. Nice suit. They're stepping things up at Sears these days, huh? Getting hip."

Whitey glanced over at the model. "Get you a steak or something, honey?"

The model said, "What?"

"Maybe some glucose on an IV drip? My treat."

Roman said, "Don't do that. This is business, right? Keep it between us."

The model said, "Roman, I don't get it."

Roman smiled. "It's okay, Michaela. Just ignore us."

"Michaela," Whitey said. "Cool name."

Michaela kept her eyes on her newspaper.

"What brings you by, Sergeant?"

"The scones," Whitey said. "Love the scones in this place. And, oh yeah, you know a woman named Katherine Marcus, Roman?"

"Sure." Roman took a small sip of his latte and wiped his upper lip with his napkin, dropped it back on his lap. "She was found dead this afternoon, I heard."

"She was," Whitey said.

"Never good for the neighborhood rep when something like that happens."

Whitey crossed his arms, looked at Roman.

Roman chewed another piece of croissant and drank some more latte. He crossed his legs, dabbed at his mouth with the napkin, and held

Whitey's gaze for a bit, Sean thinking this was one of the things that had begun to bore him the most about his job—all these big-dick contests, everyone staring each other blind, nobody backing down.

"Yes, Sergeant," Roman said, "I knew Katherine Marcus. Is that what you came here to ask?"

Whitey shrugged.

"I knew her, and I saw her in a bar last night."

"And you exchanged words with her," Whitey said.

"I did," Roman said.

"What words?" Sean said.

Roman kept his eyes on Whitey, as if Sean didn't rate any more acknowledgment than he'd already given.

"She was dating a friend of mine. She was drunk. I told her she was making a fool of herself and she and her two friends should go home."

"Who's your friend?" Whitey said.

Roman smiled. "Come on, Sergeant. You know who it is."

"So say the words."

"Bobby O'Donnell," Roman said. "Happy? She was dating Bobby."

"Currently?"

"Excuse me?"

"Currently," Whitey repeated. "She was currently dating him? Or she had *once* dated him?"

"Currently," Roman said.

Whitey scribbled in his notebook. "Goes against the information we have, Roman."

"That so?"

"Yeah. We heard she dumped his doughy ass seven months back, but he wouldn't let go."

"You know women, Sergeant."

Whitey shook his head. "No, Roman, why don't you tell me?"

Roman closed his section of the paper. "She and Bobby went back and forth. One minute he was the love of her life, the next he was cooling his heels."

"Cooling his heels," Whitey said to Sean. "That sound like the Bobby O'Donnell you know?"

"Not at all," Sean said.

"Not at all," Whitey said to Roman.

Roman shrugged. "I'm telling you what I know. That's all."

"Fair enough." Whitey wrote in his notebook for a bit. "Roman, where'd you go last night after you left the Last Drop?"

"We went to a party at a friend's loft downtown."

"Oooh, a loft party," Whitey said. "Always wanted to go to one of those. Designer drugs, models, lots of white guys listening to rap, telling themselves how 'street' they are. By 'we,' Roman, you mean yourself and Ally McBeal over here?"

"Michaela," Roman said. "Yes. Michaela Davenport if you're writing it down."

"Oh, I'm writing it down," Whitey said. "Is that your real name, honey?"

"What?"

"Your real name," Whitey said, "is Michaela Davenport?"

"Yes." The model's eyes bulged a little more. "Why?"

"Your mother watch a lot of soaps before you were born?"

Michaela said, "Roman."

Roman held up a hand, looked at Whitey. "What I say about keeping this between us? Huh?"

"You taking offense, Roman? You going to go all Christopher Walken on me, try to come on strong? Is that the idea? Because, I mean, we could go on a drive till your alibi clears. We could do that. You got plans for tomorrow?"

Roman went back into that place Sean had seen most criminals go when a cop came down hard—a recession into self so total that you'd swear they'd stopped breathing, the eyes looking back at you, dark and disinterested and shrinking.

"No offense, Sergeant," Roman said, his voice a flat line. "I'll be happy to provide you with the names of everyone who saw me at the party. And I'm sure the bartender at the Last Drop, Todd Lane, will verify that I left the bar no earlier than two."

"Good boy," Whitey said. "Now what about your pal Bobby? Where can we find him?"

Roman allowed himself a broad smile. "You're going to love this."

"What's that, Roman?"

"If you're liking Bobby for Katherine Marcus's death, I mean, you're really going to love this."

Roman flicked his predator's glance in Sean's direction, and Sean felt the excitement he'd felt since Eve Pigeon had mentioned Roman and Bobby wither.

"Bobby, Bobby, Bobby." Roman sighed and winked at his girlfriend before turning back to Sean and Whitey. "Bobby was pulled over on a DUI Friday night." Roman took another sip of his latte, drawing it out. "He's been in jail all weekend, Sergeant." He wiggled his finger back and forth between the two of them. "Don't you guys check these things?"

SEAN WAS FEELING the day in his bones, sucking at the marrow, by the time the troopers radioed that Brendan Harris had returned to his apartment with his mother. Sean and Whitey got there at eleven, sat in the kitchen with Brendan and his mother, Esther, Sean thinking, They don't make apartments like this anymore, thank God. It was like something out of an old TV show—*The Honeymooners,* maybe—as if it could only be truly appreciated seen in black and white through a thirteen-inch picture tube that cackled with electricity and watery reception. It was a railroad apartment; the entrance doorway had been cut dead in the center so that you walked out of the stairwell and into a living room. Past the living room on the right was a small dining room that Esther Harris used as her bedroom, stacking her brushes and combs and assorted powders in the crumbling butler's pantry. Beyond that was the bedroom Brendan shared with his little brother, Raymond.

To the left of the living room was a short hallway with a lopsided bathroom branching off it on the right, and then the kitchen, tucked back there where the light reached for a total of maybe forty-five minutes in the late afternoon. The kitchen was done up in shades of faded green and greasy yellow, and Sean, Whitey, Brendan, and Esther sat at a small table with metal legs that were missing screws at the joints. The tabletop was covered in yellow-and-green floral Con-Tact paper that peeled up at the corners and had come away in chips the size of fingernails in the center.

Esther looked like she fit here. She was small and craggy and could have been forty, could have been fifty-five. She reeked of brown soap and cigarette smoke and her grim blue hair matched the grim blue veins in her forearms and hands. She wore a faded pink sweatshirt over jeans and fuzzy black slippers. She chain-smoked Parliaments and watched Sean and Whitey talk to her son as if she thought they couldn't be any less interesting if they tried but she didn't have anyplace better to be.

"When's the last time you saw Katie Marcus?" Whitey asked Brendan.

"Bobby killed her, didn't he?" Brendan said.

"Bobby O'Donnell?" Whitey said.

"Yeah." Brendan picked at the tabletop. He seemed to be in shock. His voice was monotonous, but he'd suddenly take these sharp breaths and the right side of his face would curl up as if he were being stabbed in the eye.

"Why would you say that?" Sean asked.

"She was afraid of him. She'd dated him, and she always said if he found out about us, he'd kill us both."

Sean glanced at the mother then, figuring he'd see some sort of reaction, but she just smoked, chugging out streams of it, wrapping the entire table in a gray cloud.

"Looks like Bobby has an alibi," Whitey said. "How about you, Brendan?"

"I didn't kill her," Brendan Harris said numbly. "I wouldn't hurt Katie. Never."

"So, again," Whitey said, "when's the last time you saw her?"

"Friday night."

"What time?"

"About, like, eight or so?"

" 'About, like, eight,' Brendan, or at eight?"

"I don't know." Brendan's face was twisted with an anxiousness Sean could feel jangling across the table between them. He clenched his hands together and rocked a bit in his chair. "Yeah, eight. We had a couple of slices at Hi-Fi, right? And then . . . then she had to go."

Whitey jotted *"Hi-Fi, 8p, Fri."* in his report pad. "She had to go where?"

"I dunno," Brendan said.

The mother crushed another cigarette into the pile she'd built in the ashtray, igniting one of the dead cigarettes so that a stream of smoke pirouetted up from the pile and snaked into Sean's right nostril. Esther Harris immediately fired up another butt, and Sean got a mental image of her lungs—knotty and black as ebony.

"Brendan, how old are you?"

"Nineteen."

"And when'd you graduate high school?"

"Graduate," Esther said.

"I, ah, got my GED last year," Brendan said.

"So, Brendan," Whitey said, "you have no idea where Katie went Friday night after she left you at Hi-Fi?"

"No," Brendan said, the word dying wet in his throat, his eyes beginning to grow red. "She'd dated Bobby and he was all psycho over her and then her father doesn't like me for some reason, so we had to keep the thing between us quiet. Sometimes she wouldn't tell me where she was going because it might be to meet Bobby, I guess, to try to convince him that they were over. I dunno. That night she just said she was going home."

"Jimmy Marcus doesn't like you?" Sean said. "Why?"

Brendan shrugged. "I have no idea. But he told Katie he never wanted her to see me."

The mother said, "What? That thief thinks he's better than this family?"

"He's not a thief," Brendan said.

"He *was* a thief," the mother said. "You don't know that, huh, GED? He was a scumbag burglar from way back. His daughter probably had the gene in her. She would've been just as bad. Count yourself lucky, son."

Sean and Whitey shot each other looks. Esther Harris was quite possibly the most miserable woman Sean had ever met. She was fucking evil.

Brendan Harris opened his mouth to say something to his mother, then closed it back up again.

Whitey said, "Katie had brochures for Las Vegas in her backpack. We hear she was planning to go there. With you, Brendan."

"We . . ." Brendan kept his head down. "We, yeah, we were going to Vegas. We were going to get married. Today." He raised his head and Sean watched the tears bubble in the red undercarriage of his eyes. Brendan wiped at them with the back of his hand before they could fall, and said, "I mean, that was the plan, right?"

"You were going to leave me?" Esther Harris said. "Just leave without a word?"

"Ma, I—"

"Like your father? That it? Leave me with your little brother never says a word? That's what you were going to do, Brendan?"

"Mrs. Harris," Sean said, "if we could just concentrate on the issue at hand. There'll be plenty of time for Brendan to explain later."

She threw a glance at Sean that he'd seen on a lot of hardened cons and nine-to-five sociopaths, a look that said he wasn't worth her attention right now, but if he continued to push it, she'd deal with him in a way that'd leave bruises.

She looked back at her son. "You'd do this to me? Huh?"

"Ma, look . . ."

"Look what? Look what, huh? What'd I do that was so bad? Huh? What did I do but raise you and feed you and buy you that saxophone for Christmas you never learned how to play? Thing's still in the closet, Brendan."

"Ma—"

"No, go get it. Show these men how good you play. Go get it."

Whitey looked at Sean like he couldn't believe this shit.

"Mrs. Harris," he said, "that won't be necessary."

She lit another cigarette, the match head jumping with her rage. "All I ever did was feed him," she said. "Buy him clothes. Raise him."

"Yes, ma'am," Whitey said as the front door opened and two kids came in with skateboards under their arms, both kids about twelve or so, maybe thirteen, one of them a dead ringer for Brendan—he had his good looks and dark hair, but there was something of the mother in his eyes, a spooky lack of focus.

"Hey," the other kid said as they came into the kitchen. Like Brendan's brother, he seemed small for his age, and he'd been cursed with a face both long and sunken, a mean old man's face on a kid's body, peeking out from under stringy hanks of blond hair.

Brendan Harris raised his hand. "Hey, Johnny. Sergeant Powers, Trooper Devine, this is my brother, Ray, and his friend, Johnny O'Shea."

"Hey, boys," Whitey said.

"Hey," Johnny O'Shea said.

Ray nodded at them.

"He don't speak," the mother said. "His father couldn't shut up, but his son don't speak. Oh, yeah, life's fucking fair."

Ray's hands signed something to Brendan, and Brendan said, "Yeah, they're here about Katie."

Johnny O'Shea said, "We went to go 'boarding in the park. They got it closed."

"It'll be open tomorrow," Whitey said.

"Tomorrow's supposed to rain," the kid said as if it were their fault he couldn't skateboard at eleven o'clock on a school night, Sean wondering when parents started letting kids get away with so much shit.

Whitey turned back to Brendan. "You think of any enemies she had? Anyone, besides Bobby O'Donnell, who might have been angry with her?"

Brendan shook his head. "She was nice, sir. She was just a nice, nice person. Everyone liked her. I don't know what to tell you."

The O'Shea kid said, "Can we, like, go now?"

Whitey cocked an eyebrow at him. "Someone say you couldn't?"

Johnny O'Shea and Ray Harris walked back out of the kitchen and they could hear them toss their skateboards to the floor of the living room, go back into Ray and Brendan's room, banging around into everything the way twelve-year-olds do.

Whitey asked Brendan, "Where were you between one-thirty and three this morning?"

"Asleep."

Whitey looked at the mother. "Can you confirm that?"

She shrugged. "Can't confirm he didn't climb out a window and down the fire escape. I can confirm he went into his room at ten o'clock and next I saw him was nine in the morning."

Whitey stretched in his chair. "All right, Brendan. We're going to have to ask you to take a polygraph. You think you're up for that?"

"Are you arresting me?"

"No. Just want you to take a polygraph."

Brendan shrugged. "Whatever. Sure."

"And here, take my card."

Brendan looked at the card. He kept his eyes on it when he said, "I loved her so much. I . . . I ain't ever going to feel that again. I mean, it don't happen twice, right?" He looked up at Whitey and Sean. His eyes were dry, but the pain in them was something Sean wanted to duck from.

"It don't happen once, most cases," Whitey said.

THEY DROPPED BRENDAN back at his place around one, the kid having aced the polygraph four times, and then Whitey dropped Sean back at his apartment, told him to get some sleep, they'd be up early. Sean walked into his empty apartment, heard the din of its silence, and felt the sludge of too much caffeine and fast food in his blood, riding his spinal column. He opened the fridge and took out a beer, sat on the counter to drink it, the noise and lights of the evening banging around inside his skull, making him wonder if he'd finally gotten too old for this, if he was just too tired of death and dumb motives and dumb perps, the soiled-wrapper feeling of it all.

Lately, though, he'd just been tired in general. Tired of people. Tired of books and TV and the nightly news and songs on the radio that sounded exactly like other songs on the radio he'd heard years before and hadn't liked much in the first place. He was tired of his clothes and tired of his hair and tired of other people's clothes and other people's hair. He was tired of wishing things made sense. Tired of office politics and who was screwing who, both figuratively and otherwise. He'd gotten to a point where he was pretty sure he'd heard everything anyone had to say on any given subject and so it seemed he spent his days listening to old recordings of things that hadn't seemed fresh the first time he'd heard them.

Maybe he was simply tired of life, of the absolute effort it took to get up every goddamned morning and walk out into the same fucking day with only slight variations in the weather and the food. Too tired to care about one dead girl because there'd be another after her. And another. And sending the killers off to jail—even if you got them life—didn't yield the appropriate level of satisfaction anymore, because they were just going home, to the place they'd been heading all their dumb, ridiculous lives, and the dead were still dead. And the robbed and the raped were still the robbed and the raped.

He wondered if this was what clinical depression felt like, a total numbness, a weary lack of hope.

Katie Marcus was dead, yes. A tragedy. He understood that intellectually, but he couldn't feel it. She was just another body, just another broken light.

And his marriage, too, what was that if not shattered glass? Jesus Christ, he loved her, but they were as opposite as two people could get and still be considered part of the same species. Lauren was into theater and books and films Sean couldn't understand whether they had subtitles or not. She was chatty and emotional and loved to string words together in dizzying tiers that climbed and climbed toward some tower of language that lost Sean somewhere on the third floor.

He'd first seen her onstage in college, playing the dumped girl in some adolescent farce, no one in the audience for one second believing that any man would discard a woman so radiant with energy, so on fire with *everything*—experience, appetite, curiosity. They'd made an odd couple even then—Sean quiet and practical and always reserved unless he was with her, and Lauren the only child of aging-hipster liberals who'd taken her all over the globe as they worked for the Peace Corps, filled her blood with a need to see and touch and investigate the best in people.

She fit in the theater world, first as a college actress, then as a director in local, black-box houses, and eventually as a stage manager of larger, traveling shows. It wasn't the travel, though, that overextended their marriage. Hell, Sean still wasn't sure what had done it, though he suspected it had something to do with him and his silences, the gradual dawn of contempt every cop grew into—a contempt for people, really, an inability to believe in higher motives and altruism.

Her friends, who had once seemed fascinating to him, began to seem childish, covered in a real-world retardant of artistic theory and impractical philosophies. Sean would be spending his nights out in the blue concrete arenas where people raped and stole and killed for no other reason but the itch to do so, and then he'd suffer through some weekend cocktail party in which ponytailed heads argued through the night (his wife included) over the motivations behind human sin. The motivation was easy—people were stupid. Chimps. But worse, because chimps didn't kill one another over scratch tickets.

She told him he was becoming hard, intractable, reductive in his thinking. And he didn't respond because there was nothing to argue. The question wasn't whether he'd become those things, but whether the becoming was a positive or a negative.

But still, they'd loved each other. In their own ways, they kept trying—Sean to break out of his shell and Lauren to break into it. Whatever that thing was between two people, that total, chemical need to attach to each other, they had it. Always.

Still, he probably should have seen the affair coming. Maybe he did. And maybe it wasn't the affair that truly bothered him, but the pregnancy that followed.

Shit. He sat down on his kitchen floor, in the absence of his wife, and put the heels of his hands to his forehead, and tried for the umpteenth time in the last year to see the wreck of his marriage clearly. But all he saw were the shards and shattered pieces of it, strewn across the rooms of his mind.

When the phone rang, he knew somehow—even before he lifted it off the kitchen counter and pressed "Talk"—that it was her.

"This is Sean."

On the other end of the line, he could hear the subdued rumble of a tractor-trailer idling and the soft whoosh of cars speeding past on an expressway. He could instantly picture it—a highway rest stop, the gas station up top, a bank of phones between the Roy Rogers and the McDonald's. Lauren standing there, listening.

"Lauren," he said. "I know it's you."

Someone passed by the pay phone jingling his keys.

"Lauren, just say something."

The tractor-trailer ground into first gear and the pitch of the engine changed as it rolled across the parking lot.

"How is she?" Sean said. He almost said, "How is my daughter?" but, then, he didn't know if she was his, only that she was Lauren's. So, he said again, "How is she?"

The truck shifted into second, the crush of its tires on gravel growing more distant as it headed for the mouth of the plaza and the road beyond.

"This hurts too much," Sean said. "Can't you just talk to me?"

He remembered what Whitey had said to Brendan Harris about love, how it doesn't happen even once to most people, and he could see his wife standing there, watching the truck depart, the phone pressed to her ear but not her mouth. She was a slim woman and tall, with hair the color of cherry wood. When she laughed, she covered her mouth with her fingers. In college, they'd run across campus in a rainstorm, and she kissed him for the first time under the library archway where they'd found shelter, and something had loosened in Sean's chest as her wet hand found the back of his neck, something that had been clenched and breathless since as long as he could remember. She told him that he had the most beautiful voice she'd ever heard, that it sounded like whiskey and wood smoke.

Since she'd left, the usual ritual was that he'd talk until she decided to hang up. She had never spoken, not once in all of the phone calls he'd received since she'd left him, calls from road stops and motels and dusty phone booths along the shoulders of barren roadways from here to the Tex-Mex border and back somewhere in between again. Yet even though it was usually just the hiss of a silent line in his ear, he always knew when it was her. He could feel her through the phone. Sometimes he could smell her.

The conversations—if you could call them that—could last as long as fifteen minutes depending on how much he said, but tonight Sean was exhausted in general and worn out from missing her, a woman who'd disappeared on him one morning when she was seven months pregnant, and fed up with his feelings for her being the only feelings he had left for anything.

"I can't do this tonight," he said. "I'm fucking weary and I'm in pain and you don't even care enough to let me hear your voice."

Standing in the kitchen, he gave her a hopeless thirty seconds to respond. He could hear the ding of a bell as someone pumped a tire with air.

"Bye, baby," he said, the words strangling on the phlegm in his throat, and then he hung up.

He stood very still for a moment, hearing the echo of the dinging air pump mix with the ringing silence that descended on the kitchen and thumped through his heart.

It would torture him, he was pretty sure. Maybe all night and into tomorrow. Maybe all week. He'd broken the ritual. He'd hung up on her. What if just as he'd been doing it, she had parted her lips to speak, to say his name?

Jesus.

The image of that got him walking toward the shower, if only so he could run away from it, from the thought of her standing by those pay phones, mouth opening, the words rising in her throat.

Sean, she might have been about to say, I'm coming home.

III

ANGELS

OF THE

SILENCES

15

A PERFECT GUY

MONDAY MORNING Celeste was in the kitchen with her cousin Annabeth as the house filled with mourners and Annabeth stood over the stovetop, cooking with a detached intensity, when Jimmy, fresh from the shower, stuck his head in to ask if he could help with anything.

When they were kids, Celeste and Annabeth had been more like sisters than first cousins. Annabeth had been the only girl in a family of boys, and Celeste had been the only child of parents who couldn't stand each other, so they'd spent a lot of time together, and in junior high had talked on the phone almost every night. That had changed, in almost imperceptible increments, over the years, as the estrangement between Celeste's mother and Annabeth's father had widened, moving from cordial to frosty to hostile. And somehow, without any single event to point to, that estrangement had wormed its way down from a brother and sister to their daughters, until Celeste and Annabeth saw each other on only the more formal occasions—weddings, after giving birth and at the subsequent christenings, occasionally on Christmas and Easter. It was the lack of a clear reason that got to Celeste most, and it stabbed her that a relationship that had once seemed unbreakable could slip apart so easily due to nothing more than time, family turmoil, and growth spurts.

Things had been better since her mother had died, though. Just last summer, she and Dave had gotten together with Annabeth and Jimmy for a casual cookout, and over the winter they'd gone out for dinner and drinks twice. Each time the conversation had come a little easier, and Celeste had felt ten years of bewildered isolation fall away and find a name: Rosemary.

Annabeth had been there for her when Rosemary died. She'd come to the house every morning and stayed until dark for three days. She'd baked and helped with the funeral arrangements and sat with Celeste while she'd wept for a mother who'd never shown much in the way of love, but had been her mother, nonetheless.

And now Celeste was going to be here for Annabeth, though the thought of someone as fearsomely self-contained as Annabeth needing support was alien for most, Celeste included.

But she stood by her cousin and let her cook and got her food from the fridge when she asked for it and fielded most of the phone calls.

And now here was Jimmy, less than twenty-four hours after he'd discovered his daughter was dead, asking his wife if she needed anything. His hair was still wet and barely combed, and his shirt was damp against his chest. He was barefoot, and pockets of grief and lack of sleep hung below his eyes, and all Celeste could think was, Jesus, Jimmy, what about *you*? Do you ever think about you?

All the other people who packed the house right now—filling the living room and the dining room, milling near the front of the hall, piling their coats on the beds in Nadine and Sara's room—were looking *to* Jimmy, as if it wouldn't occur to them to look out *for* him. As if he alone could explain this brutal joke to them, soothe the anguish in their brains, hold them up when the shock wore off and their bodies sagged under fresh waves of pain. The aura of command Jimmy possessed was of an effortless sort, and Celeste often wondered if he was aware of it, if he recognized it for the burden it must be, especially at a time like this.

"What's that?" Annabeth said, her eyes on the bacon crackling below her in a black pan.

"You need anything?" Jimmy asked. "I can work the stove a bit, you want."

Annabeth gave the stovetop a quick, weak smile and shook her head. "No, I'm fine."

Jimmy looked at Celeste as if to say: *Is* she?

Celeste nodded. "We've got things covered in here, Jim."

Jimmy looked back over at his wife, and Celeste could feel the tenderest of aches in the look. She could feel another teardrop piece of Jimmy's heart detach and free-fall down the inside of his chest. He leaned in and reached across the stove and wiped a bead of sweat from Annabeth's cheekbone with his index finger, and Annabeth said, "Don't."

"Look at me," Jimmy whispered.

Celeste felt like she should leave the kitchen, but she feared her moving would snap something between her cousin and Jimmy, something too fragile.

"I can't," Annabeth said. "Jimmy? If I look at you, I'll lose it, and I can't lose it with all these people here. Please?"

Jimmy leaned back from the stove. "Okay, honey. Okay."

Annabeth whispered, her head down, "I just don't want to lose it again."

"I understand."

For a moment, Celeste felt as if they stood naked before her, as if she were witness to something between a man and his wife that was as intimate as if she were watching them make love.

The door at the other end of the hall opened, and Annabeth's father, Theo Savage, entered the house, came down the hall with a case of beer on each shoulder. He was a huge man, a florid, jowly Kodiak of a human being with an odd dancer's grace as he squeezed down the narrow hall with the cases of beer on his boat-mast shoulders. Celeste was always a bit amazed to think that this mountain had sired so many stunted male offspring—Kevin and Chuck being the only sons who'd gotten some of his height and bulk, Annabeth the only child to inherit his physical grace.

"Behind you, Jim," Theo said, and Jimmy stepped out of the way as Theo spun delicately around him and moved into the kitchen. He brushed Celeste's cheek with his lips and a soft "How ya doing, honey?" then placed both cases on the kitchen table and wrapped his arms around his daughter's belly, pressed his chin to her shoulder.

"You holding up, sweetie?"

Annabeth said, "Trying, Dad."

He kissed the side of her neck—"My girl"—and then he turned to Jimmy. "You got some coolers, we can fill 'em up."

They filled the coolers on the floor by the pantry and Celeste went back to unwrapping all the food that had been brought over once friends and family had begun returning to the house early this morning. There was so much of it—Irish soda bread, pies, croissants, muffins, pastries, and three different plates of potato salad. Bags of rolls, platters of deli meat, Swedish meatballs in an oversize Crock-Pot, two cooked hams, and one massive turkey under crinkled tinfoil. There was no real reason for Annabeth to cook—they all knew that—but they all understood: she needed to. So she cooked bacon and sausage links and two heaping panfuls of scrambled eggs, and Celeste moved the food out to a table that had been pressed against the dining room wall. She wondered if all this food was an attempt to comfort the loved ones of the dead or if they somehow hoped to eat the grief, to gorge on it and wash it down with Cokes and alcohol, coffee and tea, until it filled and bloated everyone to the point of sleep. That's what you did at sadness gatherings—at wakes, at funerals, at memorial services and occasions like this: you ate and you drank and you talked until you couldn't eat or drink or talk anymore.

She saw Dave through the crowd in the living room. He sat beside Kevin Savage on a couch, the two of them talking, but neither of them looking particularly animated or comfortable, both of them leaning so far forward on the couch it was almost like a race to see who'd fall off first. Celeste felt a twinge of pity for her husband—for the minor, but everlasting, air of the foreign that seemed to hover around him sometimes, particularly in this crowd. They all knew him, after all. They all knew what had happened to him when he was a boy, and even if they could live with it and not judge him (and they probably could), Dave couldn't entirely, couldn't ease completely into a comfort zone around people who'd known him his whole life. Whenever he and Celeste went out with small groups of co-workers or friends from outside the neighborhood, Dave would be as laid-back and confident as they come, quick with the droll aside or quirky observation, as easygoing a person as you'd ever meet. (Her friends and their husbands from Ozma's Hair Design loved Dave.) But here, where he'd grown up and planted roots, he always looked like he was a half-sentence behind every conversation, a half-step out of beat with everyone else's stride, the last one to get a joke.

She tried to catch his eye and give him a smile, let him know that as long as she was in the apartment, he wasn't entirely isolated. But a knot of people found their way to the open archway that separated the dining room from the living room, and Celeste lost sight of him.

It was usually in a crowd when you most noticed how little you saw or spent quality time with the person you loved and lived with. She hadn't seen much of Dave period this week, outside of their Saturday night on the kitchen floor after he'd almost been mugged. And she'd seen barely any of him since yesterday when Theo Savage had called at six o'clock to say, "Hey, honey, we got some bad news. Katie's dead."

Celeste's initial reaction: "She is not, Uncle Theo."

"Sweetie, I'm dying here just telling you. But she is. Little girl was found murdered."

"Murdered."

"In Pen Park."

Celeste had looked over at the TV on the counter, at the lead story on the six o'clock news where they were still covering it live, a helicopter shot of police personnel forming a crowd by one end of the drive-in screen, the reporters still in the dark as to the name of the victim, but confirming that a young woman's body had been found.

Not Katie. No, no, no.

Celeste had told Theo she'd get over to Annabeth's right away, and that's where she'd been, except for a catnap back at her own place between three and six this morning, since the phone call.

And yet she still couldn't quite believe it. Even after all the crying she'd done with Annabeth and Nadine and Sara. Even after she'd held Annabeth on the living room floor as her cousin shook for five violent minutes of heaving spasms. Even after she'd found Jimmy standing in the dark of Katie's bedroom, his daughter's pillow held up to his face. He hadn't been weeping or talking to himself or making any noise whatso-ever. He merely stood with that pillow pressed to his face and breathed in the smell of his daughter's hair and cheeks, over and over. Inhale, exhale. Inhale, exhale . . .

Even after all that, it still hadn't sunk in entirely. Katie, she felt, would walk through that door any minute now, bounce into the kitchen and steal a piece of bacon from the plate on the stove. Katie couldn't be dead. She couldn't.

Maybe if only because there was that thing, that illogical thing clenched in the farthest crevice of Celeste's brain, that thing she'd felt upon seeing Katie's car on the news and thinking—again, illogically—blood = Dave.

And she felt Dave now on the other side of the crowd in the living room. She felt his isolation, and she knew that her husband was a good man. Flawed, but good. She loved him, and if she loved him he was good, and if he was good, then the blood on Katie's car had nothing to do with the blood she'd cleaned off Dave's clothes on Saturday night. And so Katie must still, somehow, be alive. Because all other alternatives were horrifying.

And illogical. Completely illogical, Celeste felt certain as she headed back toward the kitchen for more food.

She almost bumped into Jimmy and her uncle Theo as they lugged a cooler across the kitchen floor toward the dining room, Theo pivoting out of the way the last second and saying, "You gotta watch this one, Jimmy. She's hell on wheels."

Celeste smiled demurely, the way Uncle Theo expected women to smile, and swallowed against the sensation she got whenever Uncle Theo looked at her—a sensation she'd been experiencing since she was twelve years old—that his glances lingered just a little too long.

They manhandled the oversize cooler past her, and they looked like such an odd pair—Theo, ruddy and oversize in body and voice; Jimmy, quiet and fair and so stripped of body fat or any hint of excess, he always looked like he'd just come back from boot camp. They parted the crowd milling near the doorway as they pulled the cooler over by the table against the dining room wall, and Celeste noticed that the entire room turned to watch them place it under the table, as if the burden between them suddenly wasn't an oversize cooler of hard red plastic but the daughter Jimmy would bury this week, the daughter who had brought them all here to mingle and eat and see if they had the courage to say her name.

To watch them stock the coolers side by side and then work their way together through the crowds in the living room and dining room—Jimmy understandably subdued but pausing to thank each guest he met with an almost genteel warmth and double-palm handshake and Theo his usual blustery, force-of-nature self—several folks commented on how close they seemed to have become over the years, the way they moved through that room almost like a true father-and-son tandem.

You never would have thought it possible when Jimmy had first married Annabeth. Theo wasn't known for his friends back then. He was a boozer and a brawler, a man who'd supplemented his income as a taxi dispatcher by working nights as a bouncer at various buckets of blood and really liking the work. He was gregarious and quick to laugh, but there was always challenge in his jolly handshakes, threat in his chuckles.

Jimmy, on the other hand, had been quiet and serious since coming back from Deer Island. He was friendly, but in a reserved way, and at gatherings he tended to hang back in the shadows. He was the kind of guy, when he said something, you listened. It was just that he spoke so rarely, you were almost on edge wondering when, or if, anything would come out of his mouth.

Theo was enjoyable, if not particularly likable. Jimmy was likable, though not particularly enjoyable. The last thing anyone would have expected would be for these two to become friends. But here they were, Theo watching Jimmy's back like he might have to reach out at any moment and put his hand against it, keep Jimmy from hitting the back of his head against the floor, Jimmy occasionally pausing to say something into Theo's oversize prime rib of an ear before they moved on through the crowd. Best of pals, people said. That's what they look like, best of pals.

SINCE IT was closing in on noon—well, eleven, actually, but that was noon somewhere—most of the people dropping by the house now brought booze instead of coffee and meats instead of pastries. When the fridge filled, Jimmy and Theo Savage went searching for more coolers and ice upstairs in the third-floor Savage apartment—the one Val shared with Chuck, Kevin, and Nick's wife, Elaine, who dressed in black, either because she considered herself a widow until Nick came back from prison or, as some people said, because she just liked black.

Theo and Jimmy found two coolers in the pantry beside the dryer and several bags of ice in the freezer. They filled the coolers, tossed the plastic bags in the trash, and were cutting back through the kitchen when Theo said, "Hey, hold up a sec, eh, Jim."

Jimmy looked at his father-in-law.

Theo nodded at a chair. "Take a load off."

Jimmy did. He placed the cooler beside the chair and sat down, waited for Theo to get to the point. Theo Savage had raised seven kids in this very apartment, a small three-bedroom with sloping floors and noisy pipes. Theo once told Jimmy that he figured this meant he didn't have to apologize to anyone for anything for the rest of his life. "Seven kids," he'd said to Jimmy, "no more'n two years apart between any of 'em, all screaming their lungs out in that shitty apartment. People'd talk about the joys of childhood, right? I'd come home from work into all that noise and go, 'Fucking *show* me.' I didn't get no joy. Got a lot of headaches, though. Ton of those."

Jimmy knew from Annabeth that when her father came home to those headaches, he usually only stuck around long enough to eat his dinner and go back out again. And Theo had told Jimmy that he'd never lost much sleep when it came to child rearing. He'd had mostly boys, and boys were simple in Theo's opinion—you fed them, taught them how to fight and play ball, and they were pretty much good to go. Any coddling they needed, they'd get from their mother, come to the old man when they needed money for a car or someone to post bail. It was the daughters you spoiled, he told Jimmy.

"Is that what he called it?" Annabeth said when Jimmy mentioned it.

Jimmy wouldn't have cared what kind of parent Theo had been if Theo didn't take every opportunity to weigh in on Jimmy and Annabeth's deficiencies as parents, tell them with a smile that no offense, mind you, but he wouldn't let a kid get away with that.

Jimmy usually just nodded and said thanks and ignored him.

Now Jimmy could see that wise-old-man gleam in Theo's eyes as Theo sat down in the chair across from him and looked down at the floor. He gave a rueful smile to the clamor of feet and voices from the apartment below. "Seems like you only see your family and friends at weddings and wakes. Don't it, Jim?"

"Sure," Jimmy said, still trying to shake the feeling he'd had since four o'clock yesterday that his true self hovered above his body, treading air with slightly frantic strokes, trying to figure a way back in through his own skin before he got tired from all that flapping and sank like a stone to the black core of the earth.

Theo put his hands on his knees and looked at Jimmy until Jimmy raised his head and met his eyes. "How you handling this so far?"

Jimmy shrugged. "It hasn't totally sunk in yet."

"Gonna hurt like hell when it does, Jim."

"I imagine."

"Like hell. I can guarantee you that."

Jimmy shrugged again and felt an inkling of some kind of emotion—was it anger?—bubble up from the pit of his stomach. This was what he needed right now: a pep talk on pain from Theo Savage. Shit.

Theo leaned forward. "When my Janey died? Bless her soul, Jim, I was no good for six months. One day she was here, my beautiful wife, and the next day? Gone." He snapped his thick fingers. "God gained an angel that day, and I lost a saint. But my kids were all grown by then, thank Christ. I mean, I could *afford* to grieve for six months. I had that luxury. But you, though, you don't."

Theo leaned back in his chair and Jimmy felt that bubbling sensation again. Janey Savage had died ten years ago, and Theo had climbed into a bottle for a lot more than six months. More like two years. It was the same bottle he'd been renting for most of his life, he just took out a mortgage after Janey passed away. When she'd been alive, Theo had paid Janey about as much attention as week-old bread.

Jimmy tolerated Theo because he had to—he was his wife's father, after all. From the outside looking in, they probably seemed like friends. Maybe Theo thought they were. And age had mellowed Theo to the point that he openly loved his daughter and spoiled his grandkids. But it was one thing not to judge a guy for past sins. It was another thing to take advice from him.

"So, you see what I'm saying?" Theo said. "You make sure you don't let your grief become an *indulgence,* Jim, and, you know, pull you away from your domestic responsibilities."

"My domestic responsibilities," Jimmy said.

"Yeah. You know, you gotta take care of my daughter, those little girls. They got to be your priority now."

"Uh-huh," Jimmy said. "You figured that might slip my mind, Theo?"

"Ain't saying it *would,* Jim. Saying it *could.* That's all."

Jimmy studied Theo's left kneecap, pictured it exploding in a puff of red. "Theo."

"Yeah, Jim."

Jimmy saw the other kneecap blow up and shifted to the elbows. "You think we could have waited on this conversation?"

"No time like the present." Theo let loose his boom of a laugh, but there was a warning to it.

"Tomorrow, say." Jimmy's gaze left Theo's elbows and rose to his eyes. "I mean, tomorrow would have been all right. Wouldn't it, Theo?"

"What I say about the present, Jimmy?" Theo was getting annoyed. He was a big man with a violent temper and Jimmy knew that scared some people, that Theo could see the fear in faces on the street, that he'd grown accustomed to it and confused it with respect. "Hey, the way I look at it, there's no good time to have this conversation. Am I right? So I figured I'd just get it out of the way. ASAP, as it were."

"Oh, sure," Jimmy said. "Hey, like you said, no time like the present. Right?"

"Right. Good kid." Theo patted Jimmy's knee and stood up. "You'll get through this, Jimmy. You'll move on. You'll carry the pain, but you'll move on. 'Cause you're a man. I said to Annabeth—your wedding night?—I said, 'Honey, you got yourself a real old-school man there. The perfect guy, I said. A champ. A guy who—' "

"Like they put her in a bag," Jimmy said.

"What's that?" Theo looked down at him.

"That's what Katie looked like when I identified her in the morgue last night. Like someone had put her in a bag and beaten the bag with pipes."

"Yeah, well, don't let it—"

"Couldn't even tell what race she was, Theo. Coulda been black, coulda been Puerto Rican like her mother. Coulda been Arab. She didn't look white, though." Jimmy looked at his hands, clasped together between his knees, and noticed stains on the kitchen floor, a brown one by his left foot, mustard by the table leg. "Janey died in her sleep, Theo. All due respect and shit, but there you go. She went to bed, never woke up. Peaceful."

"You don't need to talk about Janey. All right?"

"My daughter, though? She was murdered. There's a bit of a difference."

For a moment, the kitchen was silent—buzzing with silence, really, the way only an empty apartment can when the one below is filled with people—and Jimmy wondered if Theo would be dumb enough to keep talking. Come on, Theo, say something stupid. I'm in that kind of mood, like I need to take this bubbling inside of me and push it on somebody.

Theo said, "Look, I understand," and Jimmy let loose a sigh through his nostrils. "I do. But, Jim, you don't have to get all—"

"What?" Jimmy said. "I don't have to get all *what*? Someone put a gun to my daughter's flesh and blew the back of her head out, and you want to make sure I got my—my what?—my grief priorities straight? Please, tell me. Do I got that part right? You want to stand here and play fucking grand *patriarch*?"

Theo looked down at his shoes and breathed heavily through his nostrils, both fists clenched and flexing. "I don't think I deserve that."

Jimmy stood and placed his chair back against the kitchen table. He lifted a cooler off the floor. He looked at the door. He said, "Can we go back down now, Theo?"

"Sure," Theo said. He left his chair where it was and lifted the other cooler off the floor. He said, "Okay, okay. Bad idea, me trying to talk to you this morning of all mornings. You're not ready yet. But—"

"Theo? Just leave it. Just don't talk. How about that? Okay?"

Jimmy hefted the cooler and started back downstairs. He wondered if maybe he'd hurt Theo's feelings, then decided he really didn't give a shit if he had. Fuck him. Right about now they'd be starting the autopsy on Katie. Jimmy could still smell her crib, but down in the medical examiner's office, they were laying out the scalpels and chest spreaders, powering up their bone saws.

LATER, AFTER it had thinned out a bit, Jimmy went out onto the back porch and sat under the flapping clothes that had been hanging from the lines stretched across the porch since Saturday afternoon. He sat there with the sun warming him and a pair of Nadine's denim overalls swaying back and forth through his hair. Annabeth and the girls had cried all last night, filled the apartment with their weeping, and Jimmy had figured he'd join them any second. But he hadn't. He had screamed on that slope when he saw the look in Sean Devine's eyes that told him his daughter was dead. Screamed himself hoarse. But outside of that, he hadn't been able to feel anything. So he sat on the porch now and willed the tears to come.

He tortured himself with snapshots of Katie as a baby, Katie on the other side of that scarred table at Deer Island, Katie crying herself to sleep in his arms six months after he'd gotten out of jail, asking him when her mommy was coming back. He saw little Katie squealing in the tub and eight-year-old Katie riding her bike back from school. He saw Katie smiling and Katie pouting and Katie scrunching her face up in anger and scrunching it up again in confusion as he helped her with long division at the kitchen table. He saw an older Katie sitting on the swing set out back with Diane and Eve, lazing away a summer day, the three of them gawky with preadolescence and braces and legs growing longer and faster than the rest of them could catch up with. He saw Katie lying on her stomach on her bed with Sara and Nadine crawling all over her. He saw her in her junior prom dress. He saw her sitting beside him in his Grand Marquis, chin trembling, as she pulled away from the curb the first day he'd taught her to drive. He saw her screaming and petulant and in his face through her teen years, and yet those images he often found more endearing than the cute, sunshiny ones.

He saw her and saw her and saw her and yet he couldn't cry.

It'll come, a calm voice whispered inside of him. You're just in shock.

But the shock's wearing off, he answered the voice in his head. Has been since Theo started fucking with me downstairs.

And once it wears off, you'll feel something.

I feel something already.

That's grief, the voice said. That's sorrow.

It's not grief. It's not sorrow. It's rage.

You'll feel some of that, too. But you'll get past it.

I don't want to get past it.

16

GOOD TO
SEE YOU, TOO

DAVE WAS WALKING Michael back from school when they turned the corner and saw Sean Devine and another guy leaning against the trunk of a black sedan parked in front of the Boyles' place. The black sedan had state government plates and enough antennae attached to the trunk to shoot transmissions to Venus, and Dave could tell just by looking at Sean's companion from fifteen yards away that, like Sean, the guy was a cop. He had that cop tilt to his chin, jutting up and out a bit, and a cop's way of leaning back on his heels and yet seeming set to lunge forward. And if that didn't give it away, the jarhead haircut on a guy in his mid-forties coupled with gold-rimmed aviator shades was definitely a tip-off.

Dave's hand tightened around Michael's, and his chest felt as if someone had dunked a knife in ice water and then placed the flat of the blade against his lungs. He almost stopped, his feet trying to plant themselves to the sidewalk, but something pushed him forward, and he hoped he looked normal, fluid. Sean's head swiveled in his direction, the eyes blithe and empty at first, then narrowing in recognition as they met Dave's.

Both men smiled at the same time, Dave giving it the full wattage and Sean's pretty wide, too, Dave surprised to see what might have been actual pleasure in Sean's face.

"Dave Boyle," Sean said, coming off the car with his hand extended, "what's it been?"

Dave shook the hand and got another small jolt of surprise when Sean clapped him on the shoulder.

"That time up the Tap," Dave said. "What, six years ago?"

"Yeah. About that. You're looking good, man."

"How you been, Sean?" And Dave could feel a warmth spread through him that his brain said he should run from.

But why? There were so few of them left from the old days anymore. And it wasn't just the old clichés—jail, drugs, or police forces—that had claimed them. The suburbs had taken just as many. Other states, too, the lure of fitting in with everyone else, becoming one big country of golf players and mall walkers and small-business owners with blond wives and big-screen TVs.

No, there weren't many of them left, and Dave felt a stirring of pride and happiness and odd sorrow as he gripped Sean's hand and remembered that day on the subway platform when Jimmy had jumped down on the tracks and Saturdays, in general, had felt like Anything Is Possible Days.

"I been good," Sean said, and it sounded like he meant it, though Dave could see something small crack in his smile. "And who's this?"

Sean bent down by Michael.

"This is my son," Dave said. "Michael."

"Hey, Michael. Pleased to meet you."

"Hi."

"I'm Sean, an old, old buddy of your dad."

Dave watched Sean's voice light something in Michael. Sean definitely had some kind of voice, like the guy who did the voice-overs for all the movie coming attractions, and Michael brightened at the sound of it, seeing a legend, perhaps, of his father and this tall, confident stranger as kids who'd played in these same streets and dreamed similar dreams to Michael's and those of his friends.

"Nice to meet you," Michael said.

"Pleasure, Michael." Sean shook Michael's hand and then rose up to face Dave. "Good-looking boy, Dave. How's Celeste?"

"Great, great." Dave tried to recall the name of the woman Sean had married and could remember only that he'd met her in college. Laura? Erin?

"Tell her I said hi, will you?"

"Sure. You still with the Staties?" Dave squinted as the sun broke from behind a cloud and bounced hard off the shiny black trunk of the government sedan.

"Yeah," Sean said. "Actually, this here is Sergeant Powers, Dave. My boss. State Police Homicide."

Dave shook Sergeant Powers's hand, that word hanging between them. Homicide.

"How you doing?"

"Good, Mr. Boyle. Yourself?"

"Okay."

"Dave," Sean said, "you got a minute, we'd love to ask you a couple quick questions."

"Uh, sure. What's up?"

"We maybe go inside, Mr. Boyle?" Sergeant Powers tilted his head in the direction of Dave's front door.

"Yeah, sure." Dave took Michael's hand again. "Follow me, guys."

Heading up the stairs past McAllister's place, Sean said, "I hear rents are rising even here."

"Even here," Dave said. "Trying to turn us into the Point, an antique shop on every fifth corner."

"The Point, yeah," Sean said with a dry chuckle. " 'Member my father's house? Cut it into condos."

"No shit?" Dave said. "That was a beautiful house."

" 'Course he sold it before the market got hot."

"And now it's *condos*?" Dave said, his voice loud in the narrow stair-well. He shook his head. "The yuppies who bought it probably get per unit what your old man sold the whole place for."

" 'Bout the size of it," Sean said. "What're you gonna do, right?"

"I dunno, man, but I almost think there's gotta be a way to stop them. Send them back to wherever they grow them *and* their goddamn cell phones. Friend of mine said the other day, Sean? He said, 'What this neighborhood needs is a good fucking crime wave.' " Dave laughed. "I mean, that'd send property values back to where they belong. Rents, too. Right?"

Sergeant Powers said, "Girls keep getting murdered in Pen Park, Mr. Boyle, you might get your wish."

"Oh, it's not *my* wish or nothing," Dave said.

Sergeant Powers said, "Sure."

"You said the f-word, Dad," Michael said.

"Sorry, Mike. Won't happen again." He winked over his shoulder at Sean as they opened the door to the apartment.

"Your wife home, Mr. Boyle?" Sergeant Powers said as they entered.

"Huh? No. No, she's not. Hey, Mike, you go do your homework now. Okay? We gotta get over to Uncle Jimmy and Aunt Annabeth's soon."

"Come on. I—"

"Mike," Dave said, and looked down at his son. "Just go upstairs. Me and the guys gotta talk."

Michael got that look of abandonment little kids got when they were brushed off from adult conversations, and he walked toward the stairs, his shoulders drooping and his feet dragging like he had blocks of ice tied to his ankles. He sighed his mother's sigh and then began to climb the stairs.

"Must be universal," Sergeant Powers said as he took a seat on the living room couch.

"What's that?"

"That shoulder thing he's doing. My kid used to do the same thing at his age when we'd send him up to bed."

Dave said, "Yeah?" and sat in the love seat on the other side of the coffee table.

For a minute or so, Dave looked at Sean and Sergeant Powers, and Sean and Sergeant Powers looked back, everyone's eyebrows raised and expectant.

"You heard about Katie Marcus," Sean said.

" 'Course," Dave said. "I was up the house this morning. Celeste is still there. I mean, Jesus Christ, Sean, you know? It's a fucking crime."

"You got that right," Sergeant Powers said.

"You get the guy?" Dave said. He rubbed his swollen right fist with his left palm, then noticed what he was doing. He leaned back and slid both hands in his pockets, trying to seem relaxed.

"We're working on it. Believe that, Mr. Boyle."

"How's Jimmy holding up?" Sean asked.

"Hard to tell." Dave looked at Sean, happy to tear his eyes away from Sergeant Powers, something in the man's face he didn't like, the way the guy peered at you like he could see your lies, every one of them as far back as the first one you ever told in your goddamned life.

"You know how Jimmy is," Dave said.

"Not really. Not anymore."

"Well, he still keeps it all in," Dave said. "No way to tell what's really going on up in that head of his."

Sean nodded. "The reason we came by, Dave . . ."

"I saw her," Dave said. "I don't know if you knew that."

He looked at Sean and Sean opened his hands, waiting.

"That night," Dave went on, "I guess it was the night she died, I saw her at McGills."

Sean and the cop exchanged glances, and then Sean leaned forward, fixed Dave in a friendly gaze. "Well, yeah, Dave, that's actually what brought us here. Your name showed up on a list of people were in McGills that night to the best of the bartender's recollection. We hear Katie put on quite a show."

Dave nodded. "She and a friend did some dancing on the bar."

The cop said, "They were pretty drunk, huh?"

"Yeah, but . . ."

"But what?"

"But it was a harmless kinda drunk. They were dancing, but they weren't stripping or nothing. They were just, I dunno, *nineteen.* You know?"

"Nineteen and getting served in a bar means the bar loses its liquor license for a while," Sergeant Powers said.

"You didn't?"

"What's that?"

"You never drank underage in a bar?"

Sergeant Powers smiled, and the smile got into Dave's skull the same way the man's eyes did, as if every inch of the guy was *peeping.*

"What time would you say you left McGills, Mr. Boyle?"

Dave shrugged. "Maybe one or so?"

Sergeant Powers wrote that down in a notebook perched atop his knee.

Dave looked at Sean.

Sean said, "Just crossing our *t*'s and dotting our *i*'s, Dave. You were hanging with Stanley Kemp, right? Stanley the Giant?"

"Yeah."

"How's he doing, by the way? Heard his kid caught some kind of cancer."

"Leukemia," Dave said. "Couple years back. He died. Four years old."

"Man," Sean said, "that just sucks. Shit. You never know. It's like one minute you're cruising on all cylinders, the next, you turn a corner, catch some weird disease in the chest, die five months later. This world, man."

"This world," Dave agreed. "Stan's all right, though, considering. Got a good job with Edison. Still shoots hoop in the Park League every Tuesday and Thursday night."

"Still a terror under the boards?" Sean chuckled.

Dave chuckled, too. "He do use those elbows of his."

"What time would you say the girls left the bar?" Sean said, his chuckle still trailing away.

"I dunno," Dave said. "The Sox game was winding down."

What was up with the way Sean slid that question in? He could have just asked it up front, but he'd tried to lull Dave with talk of Stanley the Giant. Hadn't he? Or maybe he'd just asked the question as it had occurred to him. Dave couldn't be certain either way. Was Dave a suspect? Was he actually a *suspect* in Katie's death?

"And that was a late game," Sean was saying. "In Califonia."

"Huh? Ten-thirty-five, yeah. So, I'd say the girls left maybe fifteen minutes before I did."

"So we'll say twelve-forty-five," the other cop said.

"Sounds about right."

"Any idea where the girls went?"

Dave shook his head. "Last I saw of them."

"Yeah?" Sergeant Powers's pen hovered over the pad on his knee.

Dave nodded. "Yeah."

Sergeant Powers scribbled in his pad, the pen scratching against the paper like a small claw.

"Dave, you remember a guy throwing his keys at another guy?"

"What?"

"A guy," Sean said, flipping through his own notebook, "name of, uh, Joe Crosby. His friends tried to take his car keys. He threw them at one of them. You know, all pissed off. You there for that?"

"No. Why?"

"Sounded like a funny story," Sean said. "Guy's trying not to give up his keys, he throws 'em anyway. Drunk's logic, right?"

"I guess."

"You didn't notice anything unusual that night?"

"How you mean?"

"Say someone in the bar maybe wasn't watching the girls in a real friendly manner? You've seen those guys—the ones look at young women with a kind of black hate, still pissed off they sat home the night of the prom and here it is fifteen years later and their lives still suck? Look at women like it's all their fault. You know those guys?"

"Met a few, sure."

"Any of those guys in the bar that night?"

"Not that I saw. I mean, I was watching the game mostly. I didn't even notice the girls, Sean, until they jumped up on the bar."

Sean nodded.

"Good game," Sergeant Powers said.

"Well," Dave said, "you had Pedro up there. Could have been a no-hitter, it wasn't for that bloop in the eighth."

"Got that right. Man earns his pay, don't he?"

"Best there is in the game today."

Sergeant Powers turned to Sean and they both stood at the same time.

"That's it?" Dave said.

"Yes, Mr. Boyle." He shook Dave's hand. "We appreciate your help, sir."

"No problem. Happy to."

"Oh, shit," Sergeant Powers said. "I forgot to ask: Where'd you go after you left McGills, sir?"

The word popped out of Dave's mouth before he could stop it: "Here."

"Home?"

"Yup." Dave kept his gaze steady, his voice firm.

Sergeant Powers flipped open his pad again. "Home by one-fifteen." He looked up at Dave as he wrote. "Sound right?"

"Roughly, sure."

"Okay then, Mr. Boyle. Thanks again."

Sergeant Powers made his way down the stairs, but Sean stopped at the door. "It was real good seeing you, Dave."

"You too," Dave said, trying to remember what it was he hadn't liked about Sean when they were kids. The answer wouldn't come, though.

"We should grab a beer sometime," Sean said. "Soon."

"I'd like that."

"Okay then. You take care, Dave."

They shook hands and Dave tried not to wince at the pressure on his swollen hand.

"You, too, Sean."

Sean walked down the stairs as Dave stood at the top on the landing. Sean waved once over his shoulder, and Dave waved back even though he knew Sean couldn't see it.

HE DECIDED to have a beer in the kitchen before heading back to Jimmy and Annabeth's. He hoped Michael wouldn't come running back down now that he'd heard Sean and the other cop leave, because Dave needed a few minutes' peace, a little time to get his head right. He wasn't entirely sure what had just transpired in the living room. Sean and the other cop had been asking him questions as if he were a witness or a suspect, and the lack of a firm tone to their questioning had left Dave uncertain as to the real reason they'd dropped by. And this uncertainty had left him with a bona fide motherfucker of a headache. Whenever Dave was unsure of a situation, whenever the ground seemed to be shifting and slick beneath his feet, his brain tended to split into two halves, as if cleaved by a carving knife. This gave him a headache and occasionally something worse.

Because sometimes Dave was not Dave. He was the Boy. The Boy Who'd Escaped from Wolves. But not merely that. The Boy Who'd

Escaped from Wolves and Grown Up. And that was a very different creature than simply Dave Boyle.

The Boy Who'd Escaped from Wolves and Grown Up was an animal
of the dusk that moved through wooded landscapes, silent and invisible.
It lived in a world that others never saw, never faced, never knew or
wanted to know existed—a world that ran like a dark current beside our
own, a world of crickets and fireflies, unseen except as a microsecond's
flare in the corner of your eye, already vanished by the time your head
turned toward it.

This is the world Dave lived in a lot of the time. Not as Dave, but as
the Boy. And the Boy had not grown up well. He'd gotten angrier, more
paranoid, capable of things that the real Dave could never so much as
imagine. Usually the Boy lived only in Dave's dream world, feral and
darting past stands of thick trees, giving up glimpses of himself only in
flashes. And as long as he stayed in the forest of Dave's dreams, he was
harmless.

Since childhood, though, Dave had suffered bouts of insomnia. They
could slip up on him after months and months of restful sleep, and suddenly he'd be back in that agitated, jangling world of the constantly waking and the never quite asleep. A few days of this, and Dave would begin
to see things out of the corner of his eye—mice mostly, zipping along
floorboards and across desks, sometimes black flies darting around corners and into other rooms. The air in front of his face would pop unex-
pectedly with minute balls of heat lightning. People would turn rubbery.
And the Boy would lift his leg over the threshold of the dream forest and
into the waking world. Usually, Dave could control him, but sometimes
the Boy scared him. The Boy yelled in his ears. The Boy had a way of
laughing at inappropriate times. The Boy threatened to leer up through
the mask that normally covered Dave's face and show himself to the people on the other side.

Dave hadn't slept much in three days. He'd been lying awake every
night watching his wife sleep, the Boy dancing through the sponge of his
brain tissue, bolts of lightning popping in the air before his eyes.

"I just need to get my head right," he whispered, and took a sip of
beer. I just need to get my head right and everything will turn out fine, he
told himself as he heard Michael descend the stairs. I just need to hold it

together long enough for everything to slow down and then I'll catch a nice long sleep and the Boy will go back to his forest, people will stop looking rubbery, the mice will go back in their holes, and the black flies will follow them.

WHEN DAVE got back to Jimmy and Annabeth's house with Michael, it was past four. The house had thinned out and there was a sense of things gone stale—the half trays of doughnuts and cakes, the air in the living room where people had been smoking all day, Katie's death. During the morning and early afternoon there'd been a quiet and communal air of both grief and love, but by the time Dave got back, it had turned into something colder, a kind of withdrawal maybe, the blood beginning to chafe with the restless scrape of chairs and the subdued good-byes called out from the hallway.

According to Celeste, Jimmy had spent most of the late afternoon on the back porch. He'd come into the house a few times to check on Annabeth and accept a few more condolences on their loss, but then he'd worked his way out to the back porch again, sat there under the clothes that hung from the line and had long since dried and stiffened. Dave asked Annabeth if he could do anything, get her anything, but she shook her head halfway through his offer, and Dave knew it had been silly to ask. If Annabeth had truly needed something, there were at least ten people, maybe fifteen, she'd turn to before Dave, and he tried to remind himself why he was here and not get irked by this. In general, Dave had found, he was not the kind of person people turned to when they were in need. It was as if he weren't even on this planet sometimes, and he knew, with a deep and resigned regret, that he'd be the kind of guy who would float through the rest of his life as someone who was rarely relied upon.

He took a sense of that ghostliness out onto the porch with him. He approached Jimmy from behind as Jimmy sat under the flapping clothes in an old beach chair, his head cocked slightly as he heard Dave approach.

"I bothering you, Jim?"

"Dave." Jimmy smiled as Dave came around the chair. "No, no, man. Have a seat."

Dave sat on a plastic milk crate in front of Jimmy. He could hear the apartment behind Jimmy as a hum of barely audible voices and clinking flatware, the hiss of life.

"I haven't had a chance to talk to you all day," Jimmy said. "How you doing?"

"How *you* doing?" Dave said. "Shit."

Jimmy stretched his arms above his head and yawned. "You know people keep asking me that? I guess it's to be expected." He lowered his hands and shrugged. "It seems to shift, hour to hour. Right now? I'm doing okay. Could change, though. Probably will." He shrugged again and looked at Dave. "What happened to your hand?"

Dave looked at it. He'd had all day to come up with an explanation, he'd just kept forgetting to. "This? I was helping a buddy move a couch into his place, slammed it against the doorjamb squeezing the couch up a staircase."

Jimmy tilted his head and looked at the knuckles, the bruised flesh between the fingers. "Uh, okay."

Dave could tell he wasn't sold, and he decided he'd need to come up with a better lie for the next person who asked.

"One of those stupid things," Dave said. "The ways you can manage to hurt yourself, right?"

Jimmy was looking into his face now, the hand forgotten, and Jimmy's features softening. He said, "It's good to see you, man."

Dave almost said, Really?

In the twenty-five years he'd known Jimmy, Dave could never remember a time he'd felt Jimmy was happy to see him. Sometimes, he'd felt Jimmy didn't *mind* seeing him, but that wasn't the same thing. Even after they'd rotated back into each other's lives when they'd married women who were first cousins, Jimmy had never once given an indication he could remember when he and Dave had been anything but the most casual of acquaintances. After a while, Dave had begun to accept Jimmy's version of their relationship as fact.

They had never been friends. They had never played stickball and kick-the-can and 76 on Rester Street. They had never spent a year of Saturdays hanging with Sean Devine, playing war in the gravel pits off Harvest, jumping roof to roof from the industrial garages near Pope Park, watching *Jaws* together at the Charles, huddled down in their seats and screaming. They had never practiced skids on their bikes together or argued over who would be Starsky, who would be Hutch, and who would get stuck being Kolchak from *The Night Stalker.* They had never cracked up their sleds during the same kamikaze run down Somerset Hill in the first days after the '75 blizzard. That car had never driven up Gannon Street, smelling of apples.

Yet here was Jimmy Marcus, the day after his daughter was found dead, saying it was good to see you, Dave, and Dave—as he had two hours before with Sean—could feel that it was.

"Good to see you, too, Jim."

"How are our girls holding up?" Jimmy said, and the playful smile almost reached his eyes.

"They're okay, I guess. Where are Nadine and Sara?"

"With Theo. Hey, man, thank Celeste for me, would you? She's been a godsend today."

"Jimmy, you don't have to thank anyone, man. Whatever we can do, me and Celeste are happy to."

"I know that." Jimmy reached across and squeezed Dave's forearm. "Thank you."

At that moment, Dave would have lifted a house for Jimmy, held it up to his chest until Jimmy told him where to put it down.

And he almost forgot why he'd come out here on the porch in the first place: He needed to tell Jimmy he'd seen Katie on Saturday night at McGills. He needed to get that information out or else he'd keep putting it off and by the time he finally did say something, Jimmy would wonder why he hadn't told him sooner. He needed to speak before Jimmy heard about it from someone else.

"Know who I saw today?"

"Who?" Jimmy said.

"Sean Devine," Dave said. " 'Member him?"

"Sure," Jimmy said. "I still got his glove."

"What?"

Jimmy waved it off with a shake of his hand. "He's a cop now. He's actually investigating Katie's . . . Well, he's working the case, I guess they call it."

"Yeah," Dave said. "He dropped by my place."

"He did?" Jimmy said. "Huh. What was he doing at your place, Dave?"

Dave tried to make it sound offhand, casual. "I was in McGills Saturday night. Katie was there. I showed up on a list of people who were in the place."

"Katie was there," Jimmy said, his eyes staring off the porch and growing small. "You saw Katie Saturday night, Dave? My Katie?"

"I mean, yeah, Jim, I was in the place and so was she. And then she left with her two friends and—"

"Diane and Eve?"

"Yeah, those girls she was always hanging with. They left and that was it."

"That was it," Jimmy said, staring far away.

"Well, I mean, as far as I saw of her. But, you know, I was on a list."

"You were on a list, right." Jimmy smiled, but not at Dave, at something he must have seen in that far-off gaze of his. "You talk to her at all that night?"

"Katie? No, Jim. I was watching the game with Stanley the Giant. I just nodded hello, you know. Next time I looked up, she was gone."

Jimmy sat silently for a bit, sucking up air through his nostrils and nodding to himself a few times. Eventually, he looked at Dave and smiled a broken smile.

"It's nice."

"What?" Dave said.

"Sitting out here. Just sitting. It's nice."

"Yeah?"

"Just to sit and look out at the neighborhood," Jimmy said. "You're on the go your whole life with work and kids and, shit, except when you're sleeping, you hardly have any time to slow down. Today, right? An out-of-the-ordinary day if ever there was one, but still I have to deal with *details.* I gotta call Pete and Sal and make sure they cover the store. I gotta make sure the girls are clean and dressed when they wake up. I gotta watch out for my wife, see she's holding up, you know?" He gave Dave a loopy smile and leaned forward, rocking a bit, his hands clenched into one big fist. "I gotta shake hands and accept condolences and find room in the fridge for all the food and beer and put up with my father-in-law, and then I got to call the medical examiner's office, find out when they'll be releasing my child's body because I need to make arrangements with Reed's Funeral Home and Father Vera at Saint Cecilia's, find a caterer for the wake and a hall for after the funeral and—"

"Jimmy," Dave said, "*we* can do some of that."

But Jimmy just kept going like Dave wasn't there.

"—I can't screw any of this up, can't screw up one fucking detail, or she dies all over again and all anyone remembers of her life ten years from now is that her funeral was fucked up, and I can't let that be what people remember—you know?—because Katie, man, one thing you could say about her since the time she was, like, *six* is that the girl was neat, she took care of her clothes, and so it's okay, it's almost nice, right, to come out here and just sit, just sit and look at the neighborhood and try and think of something about Katie that'll make me cry, because, Dave, I swear, it's starting to piss me off I haven't cried yet for her, my own daughter, and I can't fucking cry."

"Jim."

"Yeah?"

"You're crying now."

"No shit?"

"Feel your face, man."

Jimmy reached up and touched the tears on his cheekbones. He took his hand away and looked at the wet fingers for a bit.

"Damn," he said.

"You want me to leave you alone?"

"No, Dave. No. Sit here for a bit if that's cool."

"That's cool, Jim. That's cool."

17

A LITTLE LOOK

AN HOUR BEFORE their scheduled meeting at Martin Friel's office, Sean and Whitey stopped off at Whitey's place so he could change the shirt he'd spilled his lunch on.

Whitey lived with his son, Terrance, in a white brick apartment building just south of the city limits. The apartment had wall-to-wall beige carpeting and off-white walls and the same dead-air smell as motel rooms and hospital corridors. The TV was on when they came in, ESPN playing at low volume even though the apartment was empty, and the various parts of a Sega game system were spread out on the carpet in front of a hulking black slab of an entertainment center. There was a lumpy futon couch across from the entertainment center, and, Sean guessed, McDonald's wrappers in the wastebasket, a freezer stuffed with TV dinners.

"Where's Terry?" Sean said.

"Hockey, I think," Whitey said. "Could be baseball, though, this time a year, but hockey's his big thing. At it year-round."

Sean had met Terry once. At fourteen, he'd been gargantuan, a huge block of a kid, and Sean could only imagine his size two years later, the fear he must put in other kids as he came smoking down the ice, top speed.

Whitey had custody of Terry because his wife didn't want it. She'd left them both a few years back for a civil liability attorney with a crack problem that would eventually get the guy disbarred and sued for embezzlement. She stayed with the guy, though, or so Sean had heard, and she and Whitey had remained close. Sometimes, to hear him talk about her, you'd have to remind yourself they were divorced.

He did it now as he led Sean into the living room and looked down at the Sega system on the floor as he unbuttoned his shirt. "Suzanne says me and Terry got ourselves a real guy's fantasy pad going here. Rolls her eyes, you know, but I get the feeling she's a little jealous. Beer or something?"

Sean remembered what Friel had said about Whitey's drinking problem and imagined the look he'd get if he showed up for the meeting smelling like Altoids and Budweiser. Plus, knowing Whitey, it could be a test from him, too, everyone watching Sean these days.

"Take a water," he said. "Or a Coke."

"Good boy," Whitey said, smiling as if he really had been testing Sean but Sean seeing the need in the man's loose eyes, the way the tip of his tongue played against the corners of his mouth. "Two Cokes coming up."

Whitey came back out of the kitchen with the two sodas and handed one to Sean. He walked into a small bathroom just off the living room hallway, and Sean heard him strip off the shirt and run some water.

"This whole thing is looking more random," he called from the bathroom. "You getting that feeling?"

"A bit," Sean admitted.

"Fallow and O'Donnell's alibis look pretty solid."

"Don't mean they couldn't have hired it out," Sean said.

"I agree. You thinking that way, though?"

"Not really. Seems too messy for a hit."

"Don't rule it out, though."

"No, it don't."

"We'll need to take another run at the Harris kid, if only because he got no alibi, but, man, I don't see him for this. The kid's Jell-O, you know?"

"Motive, though," Sean said, "if, say, he had some building jealousy of O'Donnell, something like that."

Whitey came out of the bathroom, wiping his face with a towel, his white belly emblazoned with a red snake of scar tissue that cut a smile through the flesh from the lower edge of one side of his rib cage to the other.

"Yeah, but that kid?" He wandered back toward a rear bedroom.

Sean stepped into the hall. "I don't like him for it, either, but we gotta be sure."

"Well, the father, too, and her crazy fucking uncles, but I already got guys talking to the neighbors. I don't see it playing that way, either."

Sean leaned against the wall, sipped from his Coke. "If this was random, Sarge, I mean, shit . . ."

"Yeah, tell me about it." Whitey turned into the hallway, a fresh shirt over his shoulders. "The old lady, Prior," he said as he started buttoning, "she didn't hear a scream."

"Heard a gunshot."

"*We* say it was a gunshot. But, yeah, we're probably right. But she didn't hear a scream."

"Maybe the Marcus girl was too busy hitting the guy with her door and trying to run away."

"I'll give you that. But when she first saw him? He's coming toward her car?" Whitey passed Sean and turned into the kitchen.

Sean came off the wall and followed him. "Which means she probably knew him. That's why she said hi."

"Yeah." Whitey nodded. "And why else would she stop the car in the first place?"

"No," Sean said.

"No?" Whitey leaned against the counter, looked at Sean.

"No," Sean repeated. "That car was crashed, wheels turned into the curb."

"No skid marks, though."

Sean nodded. "She's driving maybe fifteen miles an hour and something causes her to swerve into the curb."

"What?"

"Fuck do I know? You're the boss."

Whitey smiled and drained his Coke in one long swallow. He opened the fridge for another. "What makes someone swerve without hitting the brakes?"

"Something in the road," Sean said.

Whitey lifted his fresh Coke in acknowledgment. "But there was nothing in the road by the time we got there."

"That was the next morning."

"So a brick, something like that?"

"Brick's too small, don't you think? That time a night?"

"A cinder block."

"Okay."

"*Something,* though," Whitey said.

"Something," Sean agreed.

"She swerves, hits the curb, her foot comes off the clutch, and the car kicks out."

"At which point, the perp appears."

"Who she *knows.* And then, what, he just walks up and caps her?"

"And she hits him with the door, and—"

"You ever been hit with a car door?" Whitey lifted his collar and slid his tie around it, started working on the knot.

"Missed out on the experience so far."

"It's like a punch. If you're standing real close, and a woman weighs one-ten pushes a shitty little Toyota door into you, it ain't going to do much but annoy you. Karen Hughes said the shooter was maybe six inches away when he fired his first round. Six inches."

Sean could see his point. "Okay. But maybe she falls back and kicks the door. That would do the job."

"Door's gotta be open, though. She can kick it all day if it's still closed and it ain't going to go nowhere. She had to open it, by hand, and shove off with her arm. So either the killer stepped *back* and caught the door when he wasn't expecting it, or . . ."

"He doesn't weigh much."

Whitey closed his collar back over the tie. "Which brings me back to the footprints."

"The fucking footprints," Sean said.

"Yes!" Whitey yelled. "The fucking footprints." He closed his top button, slid the knot up to his throat. "Sean, the doer's chasing this woman through a park. She's running full-out, he's gotta be charging after her like a raped ape. I mean, he's *booking* through that park. You telling me he's not going to dig in at least once?"

"It rained all night."

"But we found three of hers. Come on. Something's screwy about that."

Sean leaned his head back against the cupboard behind him, tried to picture it—Katie Marcus, arms pinwheeling as she came down the dark slope toward the drive-in screen, skin scratched by bushes, hair soaked with rain and sweat, blood dribbling down her arm and chest. And the killer, dark and faceless in Sean's mind, coming up over the rise a few seconds behind her, running, too, his ears pounding with bloodlust. A big man, though, in Sean's mind, a freak of nature. And smart in a way, too. Smart enough to put something in the middle of the street and get Katie Marcus to bang her front tires into that curb. Smart enough to pick a spot on Sydney where few people would be likely to hear or see anything. The fact that Old Lady Prior *had* heard something was an aberration, the one thing the killer couldn't have predicted, because even Sean had been surprised to learn anyone still lived on that scorched-out block. Otherwise, though, the guy had been smart.

"Smart enough to cover his tracks, you think?" Sean said.

"Huh?"

"The perp. Maybe he killed her and then went back and kicked mud into his own tracks."

"Possible, but how's he going to remember every place he stepped? He's in the dark. Even, let's say, he had a flashlight? That's still a lot of ground to cover, a lot of footprints to identify and make disappear."

"But the rain, man."

"Yeah." Whitey sighed. "I'll buy the rain theory if we end up looking at a guy weighs a hundred fifty or less. Otherwise . . ."

"Brendan Harris didn't look like he tipped the scales at much over that."

Whitey groaned. "You honestly think the kid has that in him?"

"No."

"Me, either. What about your pal, though? He's a slim guy."

"Who?"

"Boyle."

Sean came off the counter. "How'd we get to him?"

"We're getting to him now."

"No, wait a sec—"

Whitey held up a hand. "He says he left the bar around one? Bullshit. Those car keys stopped that fucking clock at *ten of.* Katherine Marcus left that bar at twelve-forty-five. That's solid, Sean. This guy's alibi's got a fifteen-minute gap that we know of. How do we know when he got home? I mean, really got home?"

Sean laughed. "Whitey, he's just a guy who was in the bar."

"The last place she went. The last place, Sean. You said it yourself."

"What'd I say?"

"We could be looking for a guy who stayed home on prom night."

"I was—"

"I'm not saying he did this, man. I'm not even in the ballpark of saying that. Yet. But there is something *wrong* about the guy. I mean, you heard that shit about this city needing a good fucking crime wave. He was serious about that shit."

Sean put his empty Coke on top of the kitchen counter. "You recycle?"

Whitey frowned. "No."

"Not even for a nickel a can?"

"Sean."

Sean tossed the can in the wastebasket. "You're telling me that you think a guy like Dave Boyle would kill his wife's—what?—second cousin because he's pissed about gentrification? That's the stupidest thing I ever heard."

"I busted a guy once killed his wife because she gave him shit about his cooking."

"But that's a marriage, man. That's shit building up between two people for years. You're talking about a guy saying, 'Damn, these rents are killing me. I should go kill a few people until they drop back to normal.' "

Whitey laughed.

"What?" Sean said.

"You put it that way," Whitey said. "Okay. It's dumb. Still, there's something about that guy. If he *didn't* have a hole in his alibi, I'd say okay.

If he *didn't* see the victim an hour before she died, I'd say okay. But he does have a hole, and he did see her, and there's something off about the guy. He says he went right home? I want his *wife* to confirm that. I want his first-floor neighbor to have heard him walking up the stairs at one-oh-five. You know? Then I'll forget about him. Did you notice his hand?"

Sean didn't say anything.

"His right hand was almost twice the size of his left. That guy got into something recently. I want to know what. Once I know it was just a beef down the bar, something like that, I'm good. I'll let it go."

Whitey drained his second Coke and tossed it in the wastebasket.

"Dave Boyle," Sean said. "You seriously want to take a look at Dave Boyle."

"A look," Whitey said. "Just a little look."

THEY MET in a third-floor conference room shared by Major Crimes and Homicide in the DA's office, Friel always preferring to hold his meetings here because it was cold and utilitarian, the chairs hard, the table black, the walls a cinder-block gray. It wasn't a room that gave itself to witty asides or rambling non sequiturs. No one hung around in this room; they did their business and they got back at it.

There were seven chairs in the room this afternoon, and every one was taken. Friel sat at the head of the table. To his right sat the deputy chief of the Suffolk County District Attorney's Homicide Unit, Maggie Mason, and to his left Sergeant Robert Burke, who ran Homicide's other squad. Whitey and Sean faced each other across the table, followed by Joe Souza, Chris Connolly, and the other two detectives from State Homicide, Payne Brackett and Shira Rosenthal. Everyone had stacks of field reports or copies of field reports on the table in front of them as well as crime scene photos, the medical examiner's reports, CSS reports, plus their own report pads and notebooks, a few napkins with names scribbled on them, and some crudely drawn crime scene diagrams.

Whitey and Sean went first, running down their interviews with Eve Pigeon and Diane Cestra, Mrs. Prior, Brendan Harris, Jimmy and Annabeth Marcus, Roman Fallow, and Dave Boyle, whom Whitey, to Sean's gratitude, referred to only as a "witness from the bar."

Brackett and Rosenthal went next, Brackett doing most of the talking but Rosenthal, Sean was sure if past history was any indicator, having done most of the legwork.

"Coworkers at her father's store all have solid alibis and no evident motive. To the man, they all stated that the victim, far as they knew, had no known enemies, no outstanding debt or narcotic dependency. Search of the victim's room yielded no controlled substances, seven hundred dollars in cash, and no diary. A review of the victim's bank records showed the victim's deposits were in statistical keeping with the amount of money she earned. No large deposits or withdrawals until the morning of Friday the fifth when she closed out the account. That money was recovered from the dresser drawer in her room and is in keeping with Sergeant Powers's discovery that she was planning to leave town on Sunday. Preliminary interviews with neighbors have yielded nothing to support any theories of family strife."

Brackett stacked his pages together against the table to indicate he was finished, and Friel turned to Souza and Connolly.

"We ran down the lists acquired from the bars the victim was seen in, her last night. We interviewed twenty-eight of the patrons so far out of a possible seventy-five, not counting the two Sergeant Powers and Trooper Devine took, ah, Fallow and this David Boyle. Troopers Hewlett, Darton, Woods, Cecchi, Murray, and Eastman took the remaining forty-five and we have preliminary reports from them."

"What's the word on Fallow and O'Donnell?" Friel said to Whitey.

"They're clean. Don't mean they couldn't have hired the job out, though."

Friel leaned back in his chair. "I've worked a lot of contract hits over the years, and this doesn't look like one."

"If it was a hit," Maggie Mason said, "why not just blast her there in the car?"

"Well, they *did*," Whitey said.

"I think she means more than once, Sergeant. Why not just unload?"

"Gun could have jammed," Sean said. And then to the narrowing eyes in the room, he said, "It's something we haven't considered. The gun jams, Katherine Marcus reacts. She knocks the guy down and takes off running."

That quieted the room for a bit, Friel thinking into the steeple he'd made of his index fingers. "It's possible," he said eventually. "Possible. But why beat her with a stick or a bat or whatever it was? That doesn't speak of a professional to me."

"I don't know that O'Donnell and Fallow run with that professional a crowd just yet," Whitey said. "They could have hired it out to some pipehead for a couple of rocks and a Bic."

"But you said that the old woman heard the Marcus girl greet her killer. Would she do that if a crack addict was approaching her car, all jacked up?"

Whitey gave what could have been a nod. "That's a point."

Maggie Mason leaned into the table. "We are going on the assumption that she knew her killer. Correct?"

Sean and Whitey looked at each other, then back at the head of the table, and nodded.

"So, not that East Bucky doesn't have its share of crack addicts, particularly in the Flats, but would a girl like Katherine Marcus have associated with them?"

"Another good point." Whitey sighed. "Yeah."

Friel said, "I wish for everyone's sake this *was* a hit. But the bludgeoning? That says rage to me. That says lack of control."

Whitey nodded. "But we can't rule it out entirely. All I'm saying."

"Agreed, Sergeant."

Friel looked back at Souza, who seemed a bit pissed by the digression. He cleared his throat and took his time looking back at his notes. "Anyway, we talked to this one guy—a Thomas Moldanado—who was drinking at the Last Drop, the last bar where Katherine Marcus went before she dropped off her friends. Seems they got one toilet in the whole place, and Moldanado said there was a line for it just as he noticed the three girls leaving. So he goes out back into the parking lot to take a piss, and he saw a guy sitting in a car, lights off. Moldanado said this was at one-thirty, on the dot. Said his watch was new and he checked to see if it glowed in the dark."

"Did it?"

"Apparently."

"The guy in the car, though," Robert Burke said, "could've been sleeping off a drunk."

"First point we made, Sergeant. Moldanado said that's what he thought at first, too, but, no, the guy was sitting upright, eyes open. Moldanado said he would have taken him for a cop, but the guy drove a small foreign car, like a Honda or a Subaru."

"A little banged up," Connolly said. "Dent in the front passenger quarter."

"Right," Souza said. "So then Moldanado figured he was a john. Said that area's popular at night for hookers. But if that was the case, what was the guy doing in a parking lot? Why not just cruise the avenue?"

Whitey said, "Okay, so—"

Souza held up a hand. "One sec, Sarge." He looked over at Connolly, his eyes bright and jumpy. "We took another look around the parking lot, and we found blood."

"Blood."

He nodded. "If you walked past it, you'd figure it for some guy was changing his oil in the lot. It was that thick, all pooled in mostly one place. We start looking around, we find a drop here, a drop there, all moving away from the spot. Find a few more drops on the walls and the floor of the alley behind the bar."

"Trooper," Friel said, "what the fuck are you telling us?"

"Someone else got hurt outside the Last Drop that night."

"How do you know it was the same night?" Whitey said.

"CSS confirmed. A night watchman parked his car in the lot that night, covered the blood, but also kept it from most of the heavy rain. Look, whoever the vic was, he's hurt bad. And the guy who attacked him? He's hurt, too. We found two types of blood in the lot. We're checking hospitals now, and cab companies, in case the victim hopped a ride. We found bloody hair fibers, skin, and some skull tissue. We're waiting on callbacks from six ERs. The rest have turned out negative, but I'm still betting we find a victim who walked into an ER *somewhere* with blunt head trauma on Saturday night, early Sunday morning."

Sean held up a hand. "The same night Katherine Marcus walks out of the Last Drop, you're telling us someone caved in someone's skull in the parking lot of the same bar?"

Souza smiled. "Yup."

Connolly picked up the ball. "CSS found dried blood, types A and B neg. A lot more A than B neg, so we figure the victim was A."

"Katherine Marcus's blood was type O," Whitey said.

Connolly nodded. "Hair fibers indicate the victim was male."

Friel said, "What's the operating theory here?"

"We don't have one. We just know that on the night Katherine Marcus was killed, someone else got his head handed to him in the parking lot of the last bar she went to."

Maggie Mason said, "There was a bar fight in the parking lot. So what?"

"None of the patrons at the bar remember any fights—in or out of the place. Between one-thirty and one-fifty, the only people to leave the bar were Katherine Marcus, her two friends, and this witness, Moldanado, who went right back in when his piss was finished. No one else entered. Moldanado sees someone staking out the parking lot at approximately one-thirty, guy he describes as 'regular-looking,' maybe mid-thirties, dark hair. Guy was gone when Moldanado exited the bar at one-fifty."

"At which point the Marcus girl was running through Pen Park."

Souza nodded. "We're not saying there's a clear connection. Maybe there's none at all. But it seems pretty coincidental."

"But again," Friel said, "what's your operating theory?"

Souza shrugged. "I don't know, sir. Let's say it *was* a hit. The guy in the parking lot, he's watching for the Marcus girl to leave. She does, he makes a phone call to the perp. The perp's waiting for her from that point on."

"And then what?" Sean said.

"Then what? He kills her."

"No, the guy in the car. The lookout. What's he doing? He just up and decides to beat some guy with a rock or something? Just for the hell of it?"

"Maybe someone came up on him."

"Doing *what*?" Whitey said. "Talking on his cell phone? Shit. We don't know if this has *anything* to do with the Marcus homicide."

"Sarge," Souza said, "you want we should just blow it off? Say, fuck it, there's nothing there?"

"Did I say that?"

"Well—"

"Did I say that?" Whitey repeated.

"No."

"No, I did not. Show some respect for your elders, Joseph, or we might send you back to working the crystal meth corridor around Springfield, hanging out with bikers and chicks who smell bad, eat lard straight from the can."

Souza checked himself with a slow exhalation. "I just think there's something to this. That's all."

"Not disagreeing, Trooper. Just saying you've got to bring us that something before we redirect manpower on what could turn out to be an isolated, unrelated incident. Also, the Last Drop's in BPD jurisdiction."

"We made contact," Souza said.

"They tell you it's their case?"

He nodded.

Whitey spread his hands. "There you go. Keep in touch with the detective in charge and keep us posted, but otherwise, leave it be for now."

Friel said, "Since we're on the subject of operating theories, Sergeant, what's yours?"

Whitey shrugged. "I got a couple, but that's all they are. Katherine Marcus died from the GSW to the back of her head. None of her other injuries, including the bullet wound to her left biceps, were considered life-threatening. Bludgeoning was committed by a wooden instrument with flat edges—some kind of stick or two-by-four. ME has conclusively stated that she was not sexually assaulted. From our own legwork, we know she was planning to elope with the Harris kid. Bobby O'Donnell was her ex-boyfriend. Problem was he hadn't accepted the 'ex' part yet. The father didn't like either O'Donnell or the Harris kid."

"Why not the Harris kid?"

"We don't know." Whitey glanced over at Sean and then back again. "We're working on it, though. So, best we can figure, she's planning to boogie on out of town in the morning. She has a pseudo-bachelorette party with her two friends, gets run out of a bar by Roman Fallow, and drives her friends home. It's starting to rain now and her wipers are for shit, the windshield dirty. She either misjudges where the curb is because she's drunk, nods off for a second at the wheel for the same reason, or swerves to avoid something in the road. Whatever the cause, she drives her car into the curb. Car stalls and someone approaches the car. According to our old lady witness, Katherine Marcus says, 'Hi.' That's when we think the perp fired his first shot. She manages to hit him with her car door— maybe his gun *did* jam, I dunno—and she takes off running into the park. She grew up there, maybe she thought she had a better chance of losing him there. Again, we can't even surmise why she chose to run for the park, except for it being a straight run in either direction on Sydney and not a lot in the way of neighbors to help her out for at least four blocks. If she'd stepped out into the open, the perp could have run her down with her own car or shot her pretty easily. So, she bolts for the park. She goes in a pretty consistent southeast pattern from that point on, cutting through the garden co-op, then attempting to hide in the ravine under the footbridge, then making a final beeline for the drive-in screen. She—"

"Her path consistently brought her deeper into the park," Maggie Mason said.

"Yes, ma'am."

"Why?"

"Why?"

"Yes, Sergeant." She removed her glasses and placed them on the table in front of her. "If I'm a woman being chased through a city park, whose terrain I'm familiar with, I may *begin* by leading my pursuer into it in the hopes he'll get lost or held up. But the moment I can, I'm going to start heading back out. Why didn't she cut north toward Roseclair, or double back toward Sydney? Why keep going deeper into the park?"

"Shock, maybe. And fear. Fear makes people forget how to think. Let's remember, too, her blood alcohol level was at point-oh-nine. She was drunk."

She shook her head. "I don't buy it. And here's something else—from your reports, am I to surmise that Miss Marcus was, in fact, faster than her pursuer?"

Whitey's mouth opened a bit, but he seemed to forget what he was going to say.

"Your report, Sergeant. It states that on at least two occasions, Miss Marcus seemed to choose hiding over running. She hid in the garden co-op. And she hid under the footbridge. That tells me two things—one, that she was faster than her pursuer, otherwise she wouldn't have had the time necessary to *attempt* to hide. And two, that she paradoxically felt that keeping ahead of her pursuer wasn't enough. You add that in with her lack of attempt to run back out of the park, and what does it tell you?"

No one had an answer for that.

Eventually, Friel said, "What does it tell you, Maggie?"

"It presents the possibility to me, anyway, that she felt surrounded."

For a minute, it seemed to Sean like the air in the room went static, popping with electrical currents.

"A gang or something?" Whitey said eventually.

"Or something," she said. "I don't know, Sergeant. I'm just going on your report. I can't for the life of me understand why this woman, who apparently was faster than her attacker, would elect not to just run right back out of the park unless she thought someone else was flanking her."

Whitey hung his head. "All due respect, ma'am, but there'd have been a hell of a lot more physical evidence on-scene in such a scenario."

"You yourself cite the rain in your report several times."

"Yes," Whitey said. "But if you got a gang of people—or hell, even two—chasing Katherine Marcus, we're going to see more than we did. At least a few more footprints. Something, ma'am."

Maggie Mason put her glasses back on and looked down at the report in her hand. Eventually, she said, "It's a theory, Sergeant. One that I think, on the basis of your own report, bears looking into."

Whitey kept his head down, though Sean could feel the contempt rising off his shoulders like sewer gas.

"What about it, Sergeant?" Friel said.

Whitey raised his head and gave them an exhausted smile. "I'll bear it in mind. I will. But gang activity in that neighborhood's at an all-time low. We pass on that, then we consider two guys as the perps, which brings us back to the possibility of a contract hit."

"Okay . . ."

"But if that's the case—and we all agreed at the outset here today that it was a long shot—then the second shooter would have emptied his piece the moment Katherine Marcus hit his partner with the door. The only way this makes sense is if it's one shooter and a panicked, drunken woman maybe growing faint with blood loss, not thinking clearly, and having a lot of bad luck."

"But you'll bear my theory in mind, of course," Maggie Mason said with a bitter smile, her eyes on the table.

"I will," Whitey said. "I'll take anything right about now. Honest to God. She knew her killer. Okay. Anyone with a reasonably logical motive, thus far, has been all but discounted. Every minute more that we work this case, it seems all that more likely the attack was random. The rain destroyed two-thirds of our physical evidence, the Marcus girl didn't have enemy-goddamned-one, no financial secrets, no drug dependency, nor was she a witness to any crimes on record. Her murder, as far as we can tell, benefited no one."

"Except O'Donnell," Burke said, "who didn't want her leaving town."

"Except him," Whitey agreed. "But his alibi's tight and it doesn't look like a hit. So who's that leave for enemies? No one."

"And yet she's dead," Friel said.

"And yet she's dead," Whitey said. "Which is why I'm thinking it's random. You take away money or love and hate as possible motives, you're not left with much. You're left with some dumb fucking stalker type who might have a Web site devoted to the victim or something stupid like that."

Friel raised his eyebrows.

Shira Rosenthal chimed in: "We're already checking that, sir. So far, nada."

"So you don't know what you're looking for," Friel said eventually.

"Sure," Whitey said. "A guy with a gun. Oh, yeah, and a stick."

18

WORDS
HE ONCE KNEW

AFTER HE'D LEFT DAVE on the porch, his face and eyes dry again, Jimmy took his second shower of the day. He could feel it in there with him, that need to weep. It welled up inside his chest like a balloon until he grew short of breath.

He'd gone into the shower because he wanted privacy in case it flooded out of him in gushes, as opposed to the few drops that had slid down his cheeks on the porch. He feared he might turn into a trembling puddle, end up weeping like he'd wept in the dark of his bedroom as a little boy, certain his being born had nearly killed his mother and that's why his father hated him.

In the shower, he felt it coming again—that old wave of sadness, the one that felt ancient and had been with him since he could remember, an awareness that tragedy loomed somewhere in his future, tragedy as heavy as limestone blocks. As if an angel had told him his future while he was still in the womb, and Jimmy had emerged from his mother with the angel's words planted somewhere in his mind, but faded from his lips.

Jimmy raised his eyes to the shower spray. He said without speaking:

I know in my soul I contributed to my child's death. I can feel it. But I don't know how.

And the calm voice said, You will.

Tell me.

No.

Fuck you.

I wasn't finished.

Oh.

The knowledge will come.

And damn me?

That's your choice.

Jimmy lowered his head and thought of Dave seeing Katie not long before she'd died. Katie alive and drunk and dancing. Dancing and happy.

It was this knowledge—that someone other than Jimmy possessed an image of Katie that postdated Jimmy's own—that had finally allowed him to weep in the first place.

The last time Jimmy had seen her, Katie had been walking out of the store at the end of her Saturday shift. It had been five past four, and Jimmy had been on the phone with his Frito-Lay vendor, placing orders and distracted, as Katie leaned in to kiss his cheek and said, "Later, Daddy."

"Later," he'd said, and watched her walk out of the back room.

But, no. That was bullshit. He hadn't watched her. He'd *heard* her walk out, but his eyes had been on the order sheet lying in front of him on the desk blotter.

So really, his final visual image of her had been of the side of her face as she'd pulled her lips from his cheek and said, "Later, Daddy."

Later, Daddy.

Jimmy realized it was the "later"—the later part of the evening, the later minutes of her life—that would stab him. If he'd been there, if he'd been able to share a little more time a little later into the evening with his daughter, maybe he'd be able to hold on to a more recent image of her.

But he wouldn't. Dave would. And Eve and Diane. And her killer.

If you had to die, Jimmy thought, if such things really are preordained, then I wish that somehow you could have died looking into my face. It would have hurt me to watch you die, Katie, but at least I would know that you felt a little less alone looking into my eyes.

I love you. I love you so much. I love you, in truth, more than I loved your mother, more than I love your sisters, more than I love Annabeth, so help me God. And I love them deeply, but I love you most because when I came back from prison and sat with you in the kitchen, we were the last two people on earth. Forgotten and unwanted. And we were both so afraid and confused and so utterly fucking forlorn. But we rose from that, didn't we? We built our lives into something good enough so that one day we weren't afraid, we weren't forlorn. And I couldn't have done that without you. I couldn't have. I'm not that strong.

You would have grown into a beautiful woman. A beautiful wife, maybe. A miracle of a mother. You were my friend, Katie. You saw my fear, and you didn't run. I love you more than life. And missing you will be my cancer. It will kill me.

And just for a moment, standing in the shower, Jimmy felt her palm on his back. That's what he'd forgotten of his final moment with her. She'd placed her hand on his back as she'd leaned in to kiss his cheek. She'd placed it flat against the spine, between the shoulder blades, and it had felt warm.

He stood in the shower with the touch of her hand lingering on his beaded flesh, and he felt the need to weep pass. He felt strong in his grief again. He felt loved by his daughter.

WHITEY AND SEAN found a parking space around the corner from Jimmy's place and walked back up onto Buckingham Avenue. The late afternoon was turning cool around them, the sky darkening toward navy, and Sean found himself wondering what Lauren was doing right now, if she was near a window, could see the same sky he saw at the same moment, feel a chill advancing.

Just before they reached the three-decker where Jimmy and his wife lived sandwiched between various Savage lunatics and their wives or girlfriends, they saw Dave Boyle leaning into the open passenger side of a Honda parked out front. Dave reached into the glove compartment and then snapped it shut, leaned back out of the car with a wallet in his hand. He noticed Sean and Whitey as he locked the car door, and he smiled at them.

"You two again."

"We're like the flu," Whitey said. "Always popping up."

Sean said, "How's it going, Dave?"

"Not much has changed in four hours. You dropping in on Jimmy?" They nodded.

"Did you have some kind of, what, break in the case?"

Sean shook his head. "Just dropping in to pay our respects, see how they're doing."

"They're okay right now. I think they're worn out, you know? Far as I can tell, Jimmy hasn't gone to bed since yesterday. Annabeth got a craving for cigarettes, so I offered to pick some up, forgot I'd left my wallet in the car." He held it up in his swollen hand, then slipped it into his pocket.

Whitey put his own hands in his pockets, rocked back on his heels, a tight smile on his face.

Sean said, "That looks painful."

"This?" Dave raised his hand again, considered it. "Ain't too bad, really."

Sean nodded, added his own tight smile to Whitey's, the two of them standing there, looking in at Dave.

"I was playing pool the other night?" Dave said. "You know the table they got at McGills, Sean. A good half of it is against the wall, you got to keep using that shitty short stick."

Sean said, "Sure."

"So the cue ball's lying just a hair off the rail, and the target ball's the other end of the table. I pull back my hand to shoot, like really hard, forgetting I'm against the wall? And bam! My hand goes through the fucking wall almost."

"Ouch," Sean said.

"You make it?" Whitey said.

"Huh?"

"The shot."

Dave frowned. "Scratched. 'Course I was no good for the rest of the game."

" 'Course not," Whitey said.

"Yeah," Dave said. "Sucked, 'cause I was in the zone until that happened."

Whitey nodded, looked over at Dave's car. "Hey, you have the same problem I had with mine?"

Dave looked back at his car. "Never had a problem with mine, no."

"Shit. The timing chain on my Accord went at sixty-five thousand on the nose. I find out the same thing happened to another buddy of mine. What it costs to fix ain't much less than the Blue Book, damn near totals the car. You know?"

Dave said, "Nope. Mine's been a dream." He looked over his shoulder, then back at them. "I'm going to go get those smokes. See you guys inside?"

"See you there," Sean said, and gave Dave a small wave before Dave stepped off the curb and crossed the avenue.

Whitey looked at the Honda. "Nice dent over the front quarter panel there."

Sean said, "Gee, Sarge, wasn't sure you'd noticed."

"And the pool stick story?" Whitey whistled. "What—he's holding the butt of the stick against his *palm*?"

"Got a problem, though," Sean said as they watched Dave enter Eagle Liquors.

"Yeah, what's that, Supercop?"

"If you make Dave for the guy Souza's witness saw in the parking lot of the Last Drop, then he was kicking someone else's head in when Katie Marcus was killed."

Whitey gave him a disappointed grimace. "You think so? I make him for a guy sitting in a parking lot when a girl who would die half an hour later left the bar. I make him for someone who *wasn't* home at one-fifteen like he said."

Through the glass storefront, they could see Dave at the counter, talking to the clerk.

Whitey said, "The blood CSS scraped off the ground in the parking lot could have been there for days. We got no proof anything ever happened there but a bar fight. Guys in the bar say it didn't happen that night? It could have happened the day before. It could have happened that afternoon. There's no causal connection between the blood in that parking lot and Dave Boyle sitting in his car at one-thirty. But there *is* one helluva causal connection between him in that car when Katie Marcus left the bar." He clapped Sean's shoulder. "Come on, let's go up."

Sean took a last look across the avenue as Dave handed cash to the clerk in the liquor store. He felt sorry for Dave. No matter what he may have done, Dave just elicited that in a person—pity, unrefined and a little bit ugly, sharp as shale.

CELESTE, sitting on Katie's bed, heard the policemen coming up the stairs, their heavy shoes tramping up the old risers just on the other side of the wall. Annabeth had sent her in here a few minutes ago to get a dress of Katie's that Jimmy could bring over to the funeral home, Annabeth apologizing for not being strong enough to go in the room herself. It was a blue dress with an off-the-shoulder cut to it, and Celeste remembered when Katie had worn it to Carla Eigen's wedding, a blue-and-yellow flower pinned to the side of her upswept hair just over the ear. She'd literally caused a few gasps that day, Celeste knowing she herself had never looked that good in her life, and Katie so completely unaware of just how dazzling her beauty was. The moment Annabeth had mentioned a blue dress, Celeste knew exactly which one she wanted.

So she'd come in here, where last night she'd seen Jimmy holding Katie's pillow to his face, breathing her in, and she'd opened the windows to clear the room of the musty scent of loss. She'd found the dress zipped up in a garment bag in the back of the closet, and she'd taken it out and sat on the bed for a moment. She could hear the sounds of the avenue below—the snap of car doors shutting, the stray, fading chatter of people walking along the sidewalks, the hiss of a bus as it opened its doors at the corner of Crescent—and she looked at a photograph of Katie and her father on Katie's nightstand. It had been taken a few years ago, Katie's smile tight around her braces as she sat on her father's shoulders. Jimmy held her ankles in his hands and looked into the camera with that wonderfully open smile he had, the one that could surprise you if only because so little about Jimmy seemed open, and the smile was one place where his reserve failed to reach.

She was picking the picture up off the nightstand when she heard Dave's voice from the pavement below: "You two again."

And she'd sat there, dying in increments, as she heard Dave and the policemen talk, and then heard what Sean Devine and his partner said after Dave had crossed the street to get Annabeth's cigarettes.

For ten or twelve horrible seconds, she almost vomited on Katie's blue dress. Her diaphragm lurched up and down and her throat constricted, and the contents of her stomach boiled. She bent in half, trying to hold it in, and a hoarse hacking noise escaped her lips several times, but she didn't throw up. And it passed.

She still felt nauseous, though. Nauseous and clammy, and her brain seemed to have caught fire. It burned, something raging in there, dimming the lights, filling her sinuses and the spaces immediately behind her eyes.

She lay back on the bed as Sean and his partner ascended the stairs, and she wished to be struck by lightning or have the ceiling cave in on her or to simply be lifted by some unknown force and tossed out the open window. All of these scenarios were preferable to the one she found herself facing now. But maybe he was merely protecting someone else, or maybe he had seen something he shouldn't have and he'd been threatened. Maybe the police questioning him meant only that they *considered* him a suspect. None of this meant, beyond a doubt, that her husband had murdered Katie Marcus.

His story about the mugger had always been a lie. She'd known that. She'd tried to hide from that knowledge several times over the last couple of days, to blot it out of her head the way a thick cloud blots out the sun. But she'd known, since the night he'd told her, that muggers don't punch with one hand when they can stab with the other, and they didn't use clever lines like "Your wallet or your life, bitch. I'm leaving with one of them." And they didn't get disarmed and beaten up by men like Dave who hadn't been in a fight since grade school.

If it had been Jimmy who'd come home with the same story, that would be another thing. Jimmy, slim as he was, looked like he could kill you. He looked like he knew how to fight and had simply matured past the point where violence was necessary in his life. But you could still smell danger coming from Jimmy, a capacity for destruction.

The scent Dave gave off was of another kind. It was of a man with secrets, grimy wheels turning in a sometimes grimy head, a fantasy life going on behind his too-still eyes that no one else could enter. She had been married to Dave for eight years, and she'd always thought his secret world would eventually open for her, but it hadn't. Dave lived up there in the world of his head far more than he lived down here in the world of everyone else, and maybe those two worlds had seeped into one another so that the darkness of Dave's head had spilled its darkness onto the streets of East Buckingham.

Could Dave have killed Katie?

He'd always liked her. Hadn't he?

And, honestly, could Dave—her *husband*—be capable of murder? Of chasing the daughter of his old friend into a dark park? Of beating her and hearing her scream and plead? Of firing a gun into the back of her head?

Why? Why would anyone do such a thing? And if you accepted that someone, in point of fact, *could,* was it a logical leap to assume Dave could be that person?

Yes, she told herself, he lived in a secret world. Yes, he'd probably never be whole because of the crimes committed against him when he was a child. Yes, he'd lied about the mugger, but maybe there was a reasonable explanation for that lie.

Like what?

Katie was murdered in Pen Park shortly after leaving the Last Drop. Dave had claimed to have fought off a mugger in the parking lot of the same bar. He had claimed he left the mugger there, unconscious, but no one had ever found the guy. The police *had* mentioned something about finding blood in the parking lot, though. So, maybe Dave had been telling the truth. Maybe.

And yet, she kept coming back to the timing of everything. Dave had told her he was at the Last Drop. Apparently, he'd lied about that to the police. Katie was murdered between two and three in the morning. Dave had walked back into the apartment at ten past three, covered in someone else's blood and with an unconvincing story as to how it had gotten there.

And that was the most glaring coincidence of all—Katie is murdered, Dave returns home covered in blood.

If she wasn't his wife, would she even question the conclusion?

Celeste bent forward again, trying to keep her insides in and block the voice in her head that kept saying the words in a hissing whisper:

Dave killed Katie. Jesus Christ. Dave killed Katie.

Oh, dear God. Dave killed Katie, and I want to die.

"SO YOU'VE DISCOUNTED Bobby and Roman as suspects?" Jimmy said.

Sean shook his head. "Not completely. It doesn't rule out the possibility that they hired someone."

Annabeth said, "But I can see it in your face, you don't think that's likely."

"No, Mrs. Marcus, we don't."

Jimmy said, "So who do you suspect? Anyone?"

Whitey and Sean looked at each other, and then Dave came into the kitchen, unwrapping the cellophane from a pack of cigarettes, and handed them to Annabeth. "Here you go, Anna."

"Thank you." She looked at Jimmy with a minor embarrassment in her face. "I just got the urge."

He smiled softly and patted her hand. "Honey, whatever you need right now is fine. It's cool."

She turned to Whitey and Sean as she lit up. "I quit ten years ago."

"Me, too," Sean said. "Can I bum one?"

Annabeth laughed, the cigarette jerking between her lips, and Jimmy thought it may have been the first beautiful sound he'd heard in twenty-four hours. He saw the grin on Sean's face as he took a cigarette from his wife, and he wanted to thank him for making her smile.

"You're a bad boy, Trooper Devine." Annabeth lit his cigarette.

Sean took a puff. "I've heard that before."

"Heard it last week from the commander," Whitey said, "if I remember right."

Annabeth said, "Really?" and fixed Sean in the warmth of her interest, Annabeth being one of those rare people who could invest as much effort in her listening as in her talking.

Sean's grin widened as Dave took a seat, and Jimmy could feel the air in the kitchen grow lighter.

"I'm just coming off a suspension," Sean admitted. "Yesterday was my first day back."

"What did you do?" Jimmy said, leaning into the table.

Sean said, "That's confidential."

"Sergeant Powers?" Annabeth said.

"Well, Trooper Devine here—"

Sean looked over at him. "I got stories about you, too."

Whitey said, "Good point. Sorry, Mrs. Marcus."

"Oh, come *on*."

"No way. Sorry."

"Sean," Jimmy said, and when Sean looked over at him, Jimmy tried to convey through his eyes that *this* was good, this was what they needed right now. A respite. A conversation that had nothing to do with homicide or funeral homes or loss.

Sean's face softened until for a moment it looked like the face he'd had as an eleven-year-old, and he nodded.

He turned back to Annabeth and said, "I buried a guy in phantom tickets."

"You *what*?" Annabeth leaned forward, cigarette held up by her ear, eyes wide.

Sean leaned his head back, took a drag from his cigarette, and blew it out at the ceiling. "There was this guy I didn't like, never mind why. Anyway, once a month or so, I'd enter his license plate into the RMV database as a parking offender. I'd mix it up—one month it was parking at an expired meter, the next it was parking in a commercial zone, et cetera, et cetera. Anyway, the guy goes into the system, but he doesn't know it."

"Because he never got a ticket," Annabeth said.

"Exactly. And every twenty-one days he gets hit another five bucks for failure to pay, and then the fines keep racking up until one day he gets a summons to court."

Whitey said, "And finds out he owes the Commonwealth about twelve hundred dollars."

"Eleven hundred," Sean said. "But yeah. He says he never got the tickets, but the court didn't believe him. They hear that all the time. So the guy's screwed. He's in the computer, after all, and computers don't lie."

Dave said, "This is great. You do this a lot?"

"No!" Sean said, and Annabeth and Jimmy laughed. "No, I do not, David."

"Calling you 'David' now," Jimmy said. "Watch out."

"I did it this *one* time to this *one* guy."

"So, how'd you get caught?"

"Guy's aunt worked in the RMV," Whitey said. "You believe that?"

"No," Annabeth said.

Sean nodded. "Who knew? The guy paid the fines, but then he put his aunt on it and she traced it back to my barracks, and since I had a previous history with the gentleman in question, it was easy for the commander to add motive to opportunity and narrow down the suspects, so I got bagged."

"Exactly how much shit," Jimmy said, "did you have to eat over this?"

"Bags of it," Sean admitted, and this time all four of them laughed. "Big, huge, trash-can-size bags." Sean caught the glee in Jimmy's eyes and started laughing himself.

Whitey said, "Poor old Devine ain't had the best year."

"You're lucky no one in the press got to this," Annabeth said.

"Oh, we take care of our own," Whitey said. "We may have kicked his ass, but all the lady at the RMV had was the barracks the tickets emanated from, not the badge number. What'd we blame—clerical error?"

"Computer glitch," Sean said. "Commander made me pay full restitution, blah, blah, blah, suspended me a week without pay and put me on three months' probation. Could've been a lot worse, though."

"Could've demoted him," Whitey said.

"Why didn't they?" Jimmy said.

Sean stubbed out his cigarette and held out his arms. "Because I'm Supercop. Don't you read the papers, Jim?"

Whitey said, "What Ego-head here is trying to tell you is that he's put down some pretty serious cases in the last few months. Has the highest 'solved' rate in my unit. We got to wait till his average goes down before we can dump him."

"That road-rage thing," Dave said. "I saw your name once in the paper."

"*Dave* reads," Sean said to Jimmy.

"Not books on shooting pool, though," Whitey said with a smile. "How's that hand feeling?"

Jimmy looked over at Dave, caught his eyes just as Dave dropped them, Jimmy getting a strong sense the big cop was fucking with Dave, pushing him. Jimmy had experienced enough of that back in the day to know its tone, and he realized it was Dave's hand the cop was razzing him about. So what had he meant about shooting pool?

Dave opened his mouth to speak, but then his face was stricken by something over Sean's shoulder. Jimmy followed his gaze and every inch of him stiffened.

Sean turned his head and saw Celeste Boyle holding a dark blue dress, the hanger up by her shoulder so that the dress hovered beside her as if covering a body no one could see.

Celeste saw the look on Jimmy's face and said, "I'll take it over to the funeral home, Jim. Really."

Jimmy looked like he'd forgotten how to move.

Annabeth said, "You don't have to do that."

"I want to," Celeste said with a weird, desperate laugh. "Really. I'd like to. It'll get me out for a few minutes. I'd be happy to, Anna."

"You're sure?" Jimmy said, his voice coming out of him with a small croak.

"Yeah, yeah," Celeste said.

Sean couldn't remember the last time he'd seen a person so desperate to leave a room. He came out of his chair toward her, hand extended.

"We met a few times. I'm Sean Devine."

"Oh, right." Celeste's hand was slick with sweat as it slid into Sean's.

"You cut my hair once," Sean said.

"I know, I know. I remember."

"Well . . ." Sean said.

"Well."

"Don't want to keep you."

Celeste let out that desperate laugh again. "No, no. So it was good seeing you. I gotta go."

"Bye."

"Bye."

Dave said, "Bye, honey," but Celeste was already moving down the hallway and heading for the front door like she'd smelled a gas leak.

Sean said, "Shit," and looked back over his shoulder at Whitey.

Whitey said, "What?"

"I left my report pad in the cruiser."

Whitey said, "Oh, better go get it then."

As Sean went down the hall, he heard Dave say, "What, he can't borrow a page from yours?"

He didn't get to hear whatever bullshit Whitey slung, because he moved out through the doorway and down the stairs, came out onto the front porch as Celeste reached the driver's side of the car. She got her key in the lock and opened the door, then reached in and unlocked the back door. She opened it and slid the dress carefully onto the backseat. When she closed the door, she looked over the roof and saw Sean coming down the stairs, and Sean could see pure terror in her face, the look of someone who expected to get hit by a bus. Now.

He could be subtle or direct, and one look at her face told him direct was the only hope he had. Get her while she was unbalanced for whatever reason.

"Celeste," he said, "I just wanted to ask you a quick question."

"Me?"

He nodded as he reached the car and leaned into it, put his hands on the roof. "What time did Dave come home on Saturday night?"

"What?"

He repeated the question, holding her with his eyes.

"Why would you be interested in Dave's Saturday night?" she said.

"It's a little thing, Celeste. We asked Dave some questions today because he was in McGills the same time Katie was. Some of Dave's answers didn't add up and it's bothering my partner. Me, I just figure Dave had had a few that night and can't remember exact details, but my partner, he's a pain in the ass. So, I just need to know what time he came back, exactly, so I can get my partner off my back and we can concentrate on finding Katie's killer."

"You think Dave did it?"

Sean leaned back from the car, cocked his head at her. "I didn't say anything like that, Celeste. Hell, why would I even *think* that?"

"Well, I don't know."

"But *you* said it."

Celeste said, "What? What are we talking about? I'm confused."

Sean smiled as comfortingly as he could. "The sooner I know what time Dave came home, the sooner I can get my partner to move on to other things besides holes in your husband's story."

For a moment, she looked like she might hurl herself backward into traffic. She looked that abandoned, that confused, and Sean felt the same raw pity for her that he often felt for her husband.

"Celeste," he said, knowing Whitey would give him an F on his probationary report if he heard what he was about to say, "I don't think Dave did anything. I swear to God. But my partner does, and he's the ranking officer. He decides which avenues the investigation explores. You tell me what time Dave got home, we'll be done here. And Dave will never have to worry about us again."

Celeste said, "But you saw this car."

"What?"

"I heard you talking earlier. Someone saw this car parked outside the Last Drop the night Katie was killed. Your partner thinks Dave killed Katie."

Shit. Sean couldn't fucking believe this.

"My partner wants to take a closer look at Dave. It's not the same thing. We don't have a suspect, Celeste. Okay? We don't. What we have are holes in Dave's story. We close those holes, it's over and done. No worries."

He was mugged, Celeste wanted to say. *He came home with blood all over him but only because someone tried to mug him. He didn't do it. Even if I think he might have, another part of me knows that Dave is not that kind of guy. I make love to him. I married him. And I wouldn't marry a killer, you fucking cop.*

She tried to remember the way in which she'd planned to be calm when the police arrived asking questions. That night, as she'd washed his clothes of blood, she was sure that she'd had a plan for how to deal with this. But she hadn't known Katie was dead at that point and that the cops would be questioning her about Dave's involvement in her death. How could she have predicted that? And this cop, he was so smooth and cocky and charming. He wasn't the potbellied, hungover, grizzled type she'd expected. He was an old friend of Dave's. Dave had told her that this man, Sean Devine, had been on the street with him and Jimmy Marcus when Dave had been abducted. And he'd grown up into this tall, smart, handsome guy with a voice you could listen to all night and eyes that seemed to peel you away in layers.

Jesus Christ. How was she supposed to deal with this? She needed time. She needed time to think and be by herself and look at the situation rationally. She didn't need a dead girl's dress staring back up at her from the backseat and a cop on the other side of the car staring at her with venomous, bedroom eyes.

She said, "I was asleep."

"Huh?"

"I was asleep," she said. "Saturday night, when Dave got home. I was already in bed."

The cop nodded. He leaned into the car again, patted his hands on the roof. He seemed satisfied. He seemed as if all his questions had been answered. She remembered that his hair had been very thick and had almost toffee-colored streaks up by the crown amid the light brown. She remembered thinking he'd never have to worry about going bald.

"Celeste," he said in that smoky, amber voice of his, "I think you're scared."

Celeste felt like her heart was clenched in a dirty hand.

"I think you're scared and I think you know something. I want you to understand that I'm on your side. I'm on Dave's side, too. But I'm on your side more because, like I said, you're scared."

"I'm not scared," she managed, and opened the driver's door.

"Yes, you are," Sean said, and stepped back from the car as she got in it and drove off down the avenue.

19

WHO THEY'D
PLANNED TO BE

WHEN SEAN got back up to the apartment, he found Jimmy in the hallway, talking on a cordless phone.

Jimmy said, "Yeah, I'll remember the photographs. Thank you," and hung up. He looked at Sean. "Reed's Funeral Home," he said. "They picked up her body from the medical examiner's office, said I can come down with her effects." He shrugged. "You know, finalize the service details, that sort of thing."

Sean nodded.

"You get your report pad?"

Sean patted his pocket. "Right here."

Jimmy tapped the cordless against his thigh several times. "So, I guess I better get down to Reed's."

"You look like you could use some sleep, man."

"No, I'm all right."

"Okay."

As Sean went to pass him, Jimmy said, "I was wondering if I could ask you a favor."

Sean stopped. "Sure."

"Dave'll probably be leaving soon to take Michael home. I don't know what your schedule's like, but I was kind of hoping maybe you'd keep Annabeth company for a bit. Just so she's not alone, you know? Celeste will probably be back, so it won't be long. I mean, Val and his brothers took the girls out to a movie, so there's no one in the house, and I know Annabeth doesn't want to come down to the funeral home yet, so I just, I dunno, I figured . . ."

Sean said, "I don't think it'll be a problem. I gotta check with my sarge, but our official shift was over a couple hours ago. Let me talk to him. Okay?"

"I appreciate it."

"Sure." Sean started walking back toward the kitchen and then he stopped, looked back at Jimmy. "Actually, Jim, I need to ask you something."

"Go ahead," Jimmy said, getting that wary con's look of his.

Sean came back down the hallway. "We got a couple of reports that you had a problem with that kid you mentioned this morning, that Brendan Harris."

Jimmy shrugged. "Not problems, really. I just don't care for the kid."

"Why?"

"I don't know." Jimmy put the cordless in his front pocket. "Some people just rub you wrong. You know?"

Sean stepped in close, put a hand on Jimmy's shoulder. "He was dating Katie, Jim. They were planning to elope."

"Bullshit," Jimmy said, his eyes on the floor.

"We found brochures for Vegas in her backpack, Jim. We made a few calls and found reservations under both their names with TWA. Brendan Harris confirmed it."

Jimmy shrugged off Sean's hand. "He kill my daughter?"

"No."

"You're a hundred percent positive."

"Close to it. He passed a poly with flying colors, man. Plus, the boy don't strike me as the type. He seemed like he really loved your daughter."

"Fuck," Jimmy said.

Sean leaned against the wall and waited, giving Jimmy time to take it all in.

"Elope?" Jimmy said after a while.

"Yeah. Jim, according to Brendan Harris and both of Katie's girl-friends, you were dead set against them ever dating. What I don't under-stand is why. Kid didn't strike me as a problem kid. You know? Maybe a bit dim, I dunno. But he seemed decent, nice really. I'm confused."

"You're confused?" Jimmy chuckled. "I just found out my daugh-ter—who is, you know, dead—was planning to elope, Sean."

"I know," Sean said, lowering his voice to nearly a whisper in hopes Jimmy would follow suit, the man about as agitated as Sean had seen him since yesterday afternoon by the drive-in screen. "I'm just curious, man—why were you so adamant that your daughter never see the kid?"

Jimmy leaned against the wall beside Sean and took a few long breaths, let them out slow. "I knew his father. They called him 'Just Ray.' "

"What, he was a judge?"

Jimmy shook his head. "There were so many guys named Ray around at the time—you know, Crazy Ray Bucheck and Psycho Ray Dorian and Ray the Woodchuck Lane—that Ray Harris got stuck with 'Just Ray' because all the cool nicknames had been taken." He shrugged. "Anyway, I never liked the guy much and then he cut out on his wife when she was pregnant with that mute kid she's got now and Brendan only six, so I dunno, I just thought, 'The acorn don't fall far from the tree' and shit, and I didn't want him seeing my daughter."

Sean nodded, though he didn't buy it. Something about the way Jimmy had said he'd never liked the guy much—there was a small hitch in his voice, and Sean had heard enough bullshit stories in his time to rec-ognize one no matter how logical it may have sounded.

"That's it, huh?" Sean said. "That's the only reason?"

"That's it," Jimmy said, and pushed himself off the wall, started back up the hallway.

"I THINK IT'S a good idea," Whitey said as he stood outside the house with Sean. "Stick close to the family for a bit, see if you can pick up any more. What'd you say to Boyle's wife, by the way?"

"I told her she looked scared."

"She vouch for his alibi?"

Sean shook his head. "Said she was asleep."

"But you think she was afraid?"

Sean looked back up at the windows fronting the street. He gestured to Whitey and tilted his head up the street, and Whitey followed him to the corner.

"She heard us talking about the car."

"Fuck," Whitey said. "She tells the husband, he might skip."

"And go where? He's an only child, mother deceased, low income, and he ain't got much in the way of friends. Ain't like he's going to blow the country, try living in Uruguay."

"Doesn't mean he's not a flight risk."

"Sarge," Sean said, "we got *nothing* to charge him with."

Whitey took a step back, looked at Sean in the glow of the street lamp above them. "You going native on me, Supercop?"

"I just don't see him for this, man. Lack of motive, for one."

"His alibi's shit, Devine. His stories are so full of holes, they were a boat, they'd be sitting on the ocean floor. You said the wife was scared. Not annoyed. Scared."

"Okay, yeah. She was definitely holding something back."

"So, you think she really was asleep when he came home?"

Sean saw Dave when they were little kids, getting in that car, weeping. He saw him dark and far away in the backseat as the car turned the corner. He wanted to bang his head against the wall behind him and knock the images right the fuck out.

"No. I think she knows when he came home. And now that she overheard us, she knows he was at the Last Drop that night. So, maybe, she had all these things in her head about that night that didn't jibe, and now she's putting all the pieces together."

"And those pieces are scaring the shit out of her?"

"Maybe. I dunno." Sean kicked at a piece of loose stone at the base of a building. "I feel like . . ."

"What?"

"I feel like we got all these parts banging around near each other, but they don't fit. I feel like we're missing something."

"You really don't think Boyle did it?"

"I'm not ruling him out. I'm not. I'd buy him for it, if for one second I could imagine a motive."

Whitey stepped back and lifted his heel, rested it against the light pole. He looked at Sean the way Sean had seen him look at a witness he wasn't sure would hold up in court.

"Okay," he said, "lack of motive's bothering me, too. But not much, Sean. Not much. I think there's something out there that could tie him to this. Otherwise, why the fuck's he lying to us?"

"Come on," Sean said. "That's the job. People lie to us for no other reason but to see what it feels like. That block surrounding the Last Drop? There's some serious street trade there at night—you got regular hookers, transvestites, friggin' kids all working that circuit. Maybe Dave was just getting a hummer in his car, doesn't want the wife to find out. Maybe he has a lady on the side. Who knows? But nothing, so far, connects him to within a mile of murdering Katherine Marcus."

"Nothing but a bunch of his lies and my feeling the guy's dirty."

"Your feeling," Sean said.

"Sean," Whitey said, and started ticking off points on his fingers, "the guy lied to us about when he left McGills. He lied to us about when he got home. He was parked outside the Last Drop when the victim left. He was at *two* of the same bars as she was, yet he's trying to cover that up. He's got a badly bruised fist and a bullshit story about how it got that way. He knew the victim, which as we've already agreed, our suspect did, too. He fits the profile—to a fucking T—of your average thrill killer; he's white, mid-thirties, marginally employed, and, guessing by what you told me yesterday, he was sexually abused as a kid. You kidding me? On paper, this guy should be in jail already."

"You just said it yourself, though—he's a past victim of sexual abuse, and yet Katherine Marcus wasn't sexually assaulted. That don't make sense, Sarge."

"Maybe he just whacked off over her."

"There was no semen at the scene."

"It rained."

"Not where her body was found. In the random thrill kill, sexual emission is part of the equation, like, ninety-nine-point-nine percent of the time. Where is it in this case?"

Whitey lowered his head and drummed the sides of the light pole with his palms. "You were friends with the victim's father *and* a potential suspect when you were—"

"Oh, come *on.*"

"—kids. That compromises you. Don't tell me it don't. You're a fucking liability here."

"I'm a—?" Sean lowered his voice and brought his hand back down from his chest. "Look," he said, "I'm just in disagreement with you over the profile of the suspect. I'm not saying that if we zero in on Dave Boyle for more than just a few inconsistencies, I won't be right there with you to bust him. You know I will be. But if you go to the DA right now with what you got, what's he going to do?"

Whitey's palms drummed a little harder against the pole.

"Really," Sean said. "What's he going to do?"

Whitey raised his arms above his head and let out a shuddering yawn. He met Sean's eyes and gave him a weary frown. "Point taken. But"—he held up a finger—"*but,* you clubhouse fucking lawyer, you, I'm going to find the stick she was beat with, or the gun, or some bloody clothes. I don't know what exactly, but I'm going to find something. And when I find it, I'm going to drop your friend."

"He ain't my friend," Sean said. "Turns out you're right? I'll have my cuffs off my hip faster than yours."

Whitey came off the pole and stepped up to Sean. "Don't compromise yourself on this, Devine. You do that, you'll compromise me, and I'll bury you. I'm talking a transfer to the goddamn Berkshires, pulling radar-gun details from a fucking snowmobile."

Sean ran both hands up his face and through his hair, trying to rub the weariness out of him. "Ballistics should be back by now," he said.

Whitey stepped back from him. "Yeah, that's where I'm going. Lab work on the prints should be in the computer, too. I'm going to run them, hope we get lucky. You got your cell?"

Sean patted his pocket. "Yeah."

"I'll call you later." Whitey turned away from Sean and headed down Crescent for the cruiser, Sean feeling washed in the man's disappointment, that probationary period suddenly seeming a lot more real than it had this morning.

He headed back up Buckingham toward Jimmy's as Dave walked down the front steps with Michael.

"Heading home?"

Dave stopped. "Yeah. I can't believe Celeste never came back with the car."

"I'm sure she's fine," Sean said.

"Oh, yeah," Dave said. "I just gotta walk is all."

Sean laughed. "What's it, five blocks?"

Dave smiled. "Almost six, man, you look at it close."

"Better get going," Sean said, "while there's still a little light left. Take it easy, Mike."

"Bye," Michael said.

"Take care," Dave said, and they left Sean by the stairs, Dave's steps just a bit spongy from the beers he'd been knocking back in Jimmy's place, Sean thinking, If you did do it, Dave, you better cut that shit out right away. You're going to need every brain cell you got if Whitey and I come gunning for you. Every goddamn one.

THE PEN CHANNEL was silver at this time of night, the sun set but some light still left in the sky. The treetops in the park had turned black, though, and the drive-in screen was just a hard shadow from over here. Celeste sat in her car on the Shawmut side, looking down at the channel and the park and then East Bucky rising like landfill behind it. The Flats was almost completely obscured by the park except for stray steeples and the taller rooftops. The homes in the Point, though, rose above the Flats and looked down on it all from paved and rolling hills.

Celeste couldn't even remember driving over here. She'd dropped off the dress with one of Bruce Reed's sons, the kid decked out in funereal black, but his cheeks so clean-shaven and his eyes so young that he looked more like he was heading out for the prom. She'd left the funeral home and the next thing she knew she was pulling into the back of the long-closed Isaak Ironworks, driving past the empty shells of hangar-sized buildings and pulling to the end of the lot, her bumper touching the rotted pilings and her eyes following the sluggish current of the Pen as it lapped toward the harbor locks.

Ever since she'd overheard the two policemen talking about Dave's car—*their* car, the one she sat in right now—she'd felt drunk. But not a good drunk, all loose and easy with a soft buzz. No, she felt like she'd been drinking the cheap stuff all night, had come home and passed out, then woken up, still fuzzy-brained and thick-tongued, but rancid with the poison now, dull and dense and incapable of concentration.

"You're scared," the cop had said, cutting to the core of her so completely that her only response was pure, belligerent denial. "No, I'm not." As if she were a child. No, I'm not. Yes, you are. No, I'm not. Yes, you are. I know you are, but what am I? Nah-nah-nah-nah-nah.

She was scared. She was terrified. She felt turned to pudding by the fear.

She'd talk to him, she told herself. He was still Dave, after all. A good father. A man who'd never raised a hand to her or shown a propensity for violence in all the years she'd known him. Never so much as kicked a door or punched a wall. She was sure she could still talk to him.

She'd say, Dave, whose blood did I wash off your clothes?

Dave, she'd say, what really happened Saturday night?

You can tell me. I'm your wife. You can say anything.

That's what she'd do. She'd talk to him. She had no reason to fear him. He was Dave. She loved him and he loved her and all of this would somehow work out. She was sure of it.

And yet she stayed there, on the far side of the Pen, dwarfed by an abandoned ironworks that had recently been purchased by a developer who supposedly planned to turn it into a parking lot if the stadium deal went through on the other side of the river. She stared across at the park where Katie Marcus had been murdered. She waited for someone to tell her how to move again.

JIMMY SAT WITH Bruce Reed's son Ambrose in his father's office, going over the details, wishing he was dealing with Bruce himself instead of this kid who looked straight out of college. You could see him playing Frisbee a lot easier than hoisting a casket, and Jimmy couldn't imagine those smooth, unlined hands down in the embalming room, touching the dead.

He'd given Ambrose Katie's date of birth and social security number, the kid filling it in with a gold pen on a form attached to a clipboard, and then saying in a velvet voice that was a younger version of his father's, "Good, good. Now, Mr. Marcus, will this be a traditional Catholic ceremony? A wake, a mass?"

"Yeah."

"I'd suggest we hold the wake on Wednesday, then."

Jimmy nodded. "The church has already been reserved for Thursday morning at nine."

"Nine o'clock," the boy said, and wrote that down. "Have you thought of a time for the wake?"

Jimmy said, "We'll do two. One between three and five. The other seven to nine."

"Seven to nine," the boy repeated as he wrote it down. "I see you brought photographs. Good, good."

Jimmy looked at the stack of framed photos on his lap: Katie at her graduation. Katie and her sisters on the beach. Katie and him at the opening of Cottage Market when she was eight. Katie with Eve and Diane. Katie, Annabeth, Jimmy, Nadine, and Sara at Six Flags. Katie's sixteenth birthday.

He put the stack on the chair beside him, felt a minor burning in his throat that went away when he swallowed.

"Have you thought about flowers?" Ambrose Reed said.

"I placed an order with Knopfler's this afternoon," he said.

"And the notice?"

Jimmy met the kid's eyes for the first time. "The notice?"

"Yes," the kid said, and looked down at his clipboard. "How the notice should read in the paper. We can take care of it if you'll just give me the basic information on how you'd like it to read. If you'd prefer donations in lieu of flowers, things like that."

Jimmy turned away from the kid's comforting eyes and looked down at the floor. Below them, somewhere in the basement of this white Victorian, Katie lay in the embalming room. She'd be naked before Bruce Reed and this boy and his two brothers as they went to work on her, cleaning her, touching her up, preserving her. Their cool, manicured hands would run over her body. They'd lift parts of it. They'd take her chin between thumb and index finger and turn it. They'd run combs through her hair.

He thought of his child naked and exposed with the color drained from her flesh as she waited to be touched one last time by these strangers—with care, possibly, but a callous care, a clinical one. And then satin cushions would be propped behind her head in the casket, and she'd be wheeled into the viewing room with a doll's frozen face and her favorite blue dress. She'd be peered at and prayed over and commented on and grieved, and then, ultimately, she'd be entombed. She would descend into a hole dug by men who hadn't known her either, and Jimmy could hear the dirt thudding distantly as if he were on the inside of the coffin with her.

And she would lie in the dark with the earth packed above her for six feet until it gave way to grass and open air she'd never see or feel or smell or sense. She would lie there for a thousand years, unable to hear the footfalls of the people who came to visit her headstone, unable to hear anything of the world she'd left because all that dirt was packed in between.

I'm going to kill him, Katie. Somehow, I'm going to find him before the police do, and I'm going to kill him. I'm going to put him in a hole a lot worse than the one you're going into. I'm going to leave them nothing to embalm. Nothing to mourn. I'm going to make him vanish as if he'd never lived, as if his name and everything he was, or thinks he is right now, was just a dream that passed through someone's mind in a blip and was forgotten before they woke up.

I'm going to find the man who put you on that table downstairs, and I'm going to erase him. And *his* loved ones—if he has any—will feel more anguish than yours do, Katie. Because they'll never have the certainty of knowing what happened to him.

And don't you worry whether I'm up to it, baby. Daddy's up to it. You never knew this, but Daddy's killed before. Daddy's done what needed to be done. And he can do it again.

He turned back to Bruce's son, who was still new enough at this to be unnerved by long pauses.

Jimmy said, "I'd like it to read 'Marcus, Katherine Juanita, dearly beloved daughter of James and Marita, deceased, stepdaughter of Annabeth, and sister to Sara and Nadine . . .'"

———

SEAN SAT on the back porch with Annabeth Marcus as she took tiny sips from a glass of white wine and smoked her cigarettes no more than halfway before she'd extinguish them, her face lit by the exposed bulb above them. It was a strong face, never pretty probably, but always striking. She was not unused to being stared at, Sean guessed, and yet she was probably oblivious as to why she was worth the trouble. She reminded Sean a bit of Jimmy's mother but without the air of resignation and defeat, and she reminded Sean of his own mother in her complete and effortless self-possession, reminded him of Jimmy, actually, in that way, as well. He could see Annabeth Marcus as being a fun woman, but never a frivolous one.

"So," she said to Sean as he lit a cigarette for her, "what are you doing with your evening after you're released from comforting me?"

"I'm not—"

She waved it away. "I appreciate it. So what're you doing?"

"Going to see my mother."

"Really?"

He nodded. "It's her birthday. Go celebrate it with her and the old man."

"Uh-huh," she said. "And how long have you been divorced?"

"It shows?"

"You wear it like a suit."

"Ah. Separated, actually, for a bit over a year."

"She live here?"

"Not anymore. She travels."

"You said that with acid. 'Travels.' "

"Did I?" He shrugged.

She held up a hand. "I hate to keep doing this to you—getting my mind off Katie at your expense. So you don't have to answer any of my questions. I'm just nosy, and you're an interesting guy."

He smiled. "No, I'm not. I'm actually very boring, Mrs. Marcus. You take away my job, and I disappear."

"Annabeth," she said. "Call me that, would you?"

"Sure."

"I find it hard to believe, Trooper Devine, that you're boring. You know what's odd, though?"

"What's that?"

She turned in her chair and looked at him. "You don't strike me as the kind of guy who'd give someone phantom tickets."

"Why's that?"

"It seems childish," she said. "You don't seem like a childish man."

Sean shrugged. In his experience, everyone was childish at one time or another. It's what you reverted to, particularly when the shit piled up.

In more than a year, he'd never spoken to anyone about Lauren—not his parents, his few stray friends, not even the police psychologist the commander had made a brief and pointed mention of once Lauren's moving out had become common knowledge around the barracks. But here was Annabeth, a stranger who'd suffered a loss, and he could feel her probing for his loss, needing to see it or share it or something along those lines, needing to know, Sean figured, that she wasn't being singled out.

"My wife's a stage manager," he said quietly. "For road shows, you know? *Lord of the Dance* toured the country last year—my wife stage-managed. That sort of thing. She's doing one now—*Annie Get Your Gun*, maybe. I'm not sure, to tell you the truth. Whatever they're recycling this year. We were a weird couple. I mean, our jobs, right, how further apart can you get?"

"But you loved her," Annabeth said.

He nodded. "Yeah. Still do." He took a breath, leaning back in his chair and sucking it down. "So the guy I gave the tickets to, he was . . ." Sean's mouth went dry and he shook his head, had the sudden urge to just get the hell off this porch and out of this house.

"He was a rival?" Annabeth said, her voice delicate.

Sean took a cigarette from the pack and lit one, nodding. "That's a nice word for it. Yeah, we'll say that. A rival. And my wife and I, we were going through some shit for a while. Neither of us was around much, and so on. And this, uh, rival—he moved in on her."

"And you reacted badly," Annabeth said. A statement, not a question.

Sean rolled his eyes in her direction. "You know anyone who reacts well?"

Annabeth gave him a hard look, one that seemed to suggest that sarcasm was below him, or maybe just something she wasn't a fan of in general.

"You still love her, though."

"Sure. Hell, I think she still loves me." He stubbed out his cigarette. "She calls me all the time. Calls me and doesn't talk."

"Wait, she—"

"I know," he said.

"—calls you up and doesn't say a word?"

"Yup. Been going on for about eight months now."

Annabeth laughed. "No offense, but that's the weirdest thing I've heard in a while."

"No argument." He watched a fly dart in and away from the bare lightbulb. "One of these days, I figure, she's gotta talk. That's what I'm holding out for."

He heard his half-assed chuckle die in the night and the echo of it embarrassed him. So they sat in silence for a bit, smoking, listening to the buzz of the fly as it made its crazy darts toward the light.

"What's her name?" Annabeth asked. "This whole time, you've never once said her name."

"Lauren," he said. "Her name's Lauren."

Her name hung in the air for a bit like the loose strand of a cobweb.

"And you loved her since you were kids?"

"Freshman year of college," he said. "Yeah, I guess we were kids."

He could remember a November rainstorm, the two of them kissing for the first time in a doorway, the feel of goose bumps on her flesh, both of them shaking.

"Maybe that's the problem," Annabeth said.

Sean looked at her. "That we're not kids anymore?"

"One of you, at least," she said.

Sean didn't ask which one.

"Jimmy told me you said Katie was planning to elope with Brendan Harris."

Sean nodded.

"Well, that's just it, isn't it?"

He turned in his chair. "What?"

She blew a stream of smoke up at the empty clotheslines. "These silly dreams you have when you're young. I mean, what, Katie and Brendan Harris were going to make a life in *Las Vegas*? How long would that little Eden have lasted? Maybe they'd be on their second trailer park, second kid, but it would hit them sooner or later—life isn't happily ever after and golden sunsets and shit like that. It's work. The person you love is rarely worthy of how big your love is. Because *no one* is worthy of that and maybe no one deserves the burden of it, either. You'll be let down. You'll be disappointed and have your trust broken and have a lot of real sucky days. You lose more than you win. You hate the person you love as much as you love him. But, shit, you roll up your sleeves and work—at everything—because that's what growing older is."

"Annabeth," Sean said, "anyone ever tell you that you're a hard woman?"

She turned her head to him, her eyes closed, a dreamy smile on her face. "All the time."

BRENDAN HARRIS went into his room that night and faced the suitcase under his bed. He'd packed it tightly with shorts and Hawaiian shirts, one sportcoat and two pairs of jeans, but no sweaters or wool pants. He'd packed what he'd expected they wore in Las Vegas, no winter clothes, because he and Katie had agreed that they never wanted to face another windchill or thermal-sock sale at Kmart or windshield crusted with ice. So when he opened the suitcase, what stared back up at him was a bright array of pastels and floral patterns, an explosion of summer.

This was who they'd planned to be. Tanned and loose, their bodies not weighted down by boots or coats or someone else's expectations. They would have drank drinks with goofy names from daiquiri glasses and spent afternoons in the hotel swimming pool and their skin would have smelled of sunblock and chlorine. They would have made love in a room iced by the air conditioner, yet warmed where the sun cut through the blinds, and when the night cooled everything off, they would have dressed in the better of their clothes and walked the Strip. He could see the two of them doing that as if from far away, looking down from several stories at the two lovers as they strolled through the neon wash, and those lights swept the black tar with watery reds and yellows and blues. And there they were—Brendan and Katie—walking lazily down the middle of the wide boulevard, dwarfed by the buildings, the chatter-and-ching of the casinos rattling out through the doors.

Which one you want to go to tonight, honey?

You pick.

No, you pick.

No, come on, you pick.

Okay. How about that one?

Looks good.

That one it is, then.

I love you, Brendan.

I love you, too, Katie.

And they would have walked up the carpeted stairs between the white columns and into the clamor of the smoky, clanging palace. They would have done this as man and wife, starting their lives together, still kids really, and East Buckingham would have been a million miles behind them and receding a million more with every step they took.

That's what it would have been like.

Brendan sat down on the floor. He just needed to sit for a second. Just a second or two. He sat and pulled the soles of his high-tops together and gripped his ankles like a little boy. He rocked a bit, dropping his chin to his chest and closing his eyes, and he felt the pain soften for an instant. He felt a calm in the dark and in his rocking.

And then it passed, and the horror of Katie's removal from the earth—the total lack of her—swam back through his blood and he felt pulverized by it.

There was a gun in the house. It had belonged to his father, and his mother had left it behind the removable ceiling slat above the butler's pantry where his father had always kept it. You could sit on the counter of the butler's pantry and reach under the lip of the curved wooden cornice, and touch the three slats there until you felt the weight of the gun. Then all you had to do was push up, reach in, and curl your fingers around it. It had been there since Brendan could remember, and one of his first memories was of stumbling out of the bathroom late one night and watching as his father withdrew his hand from underneath the cornice. Brendan had even taken the gun out and showed it to his friend Jerry Diventa when they were thirteen, Jerry looking at it with wide eyes and saying, "Put it back, put it back." It was covered in dust and quite possibly had never been fired, but Brendan knew it was just a matter of cleaning it.

He could take the gun out tonight. He could walk down to Café Society, where Roman Fallow hung out, or over to Atlantic Auto Glass, which Bobby O'Donnell owned and where, according to Katie, he conducted most of his business from the back office. He could go to either of those places—or better yet, both—and point his father's gun in each of their faces and pull the fucking trigger, over and over and over, until it clicked on an empty chamber and Roman and Bobby never killed another woman again.

He could do that. Couldn't he? They did it in the movies. Bruce Willis, man, if someone killed the woman he loved, he wouldn't be sitting on the floor, holding his ankles, rocking like a Sped case. He'd be loading up. Right?

Brendan pictured Bobby's fleshy face in his sights, the man begging. No, please, Brendan! No, please!

And Brendan saying something cool like, "Please *this,* motherfucker. Please this all the way to hell."

He started crying then, still rocking, still holding his ankles, because he knew that he wasn't Bruce Willis, and Bobby O'Donnell was a real person, not something out of a movie, and the gun would need cleaning, serious cleaning, and he didn't even know if it had bullets because he wasn't even sure how to open the thing, and when you got right down to it, wouldn't his hand shake? Wouldn't it shake and jump the way his fist used to when he was a kid and knew there was no way out, he *was* going to get into a fight? Life wasn't a fucking movie, man, it was . . . fucking life. It didn't play out like it did where the good guy had to win in two hours so you knew he *would* win. Brendan didn't know much about himself in the hero sense; he was nineteen and he'd never been challenged in that way. But he wasn't sure he could walk into a guy's place of business—that is if the doors weren't locked and there weren't all these other guys hanging around—and shoot the guy in the face. He just wasn't sure.

But he missed her. He missed her so badly, and the pain of her not being around—and not ever going to be around again—made his teeth ache until he felt he had to do *something*, anything, if only so he'd stop feeling like this for one fucking second of this newly miserable life.

Okay, he decided. Okay. I'll clean the gun tomorrow. I'll just clean it and make sure it has bullets. I'll do that much. I'll clean the gun.

Ray came into the room then, still wearing his Rollerblades, using his new hockey stick as a walking staff as he seesawed on wobbly ankles over to his bed. Brendan stood up quick, wiped the tears from his cheeks.

Ray took off his Rollerblades, watching his brother, and then he signed, "You okay?"

Brendan said, "No."

Ray signed, "Anything I can do?"

Brendan said, "It's all right, Ray. No, you can't. But don't worry about it."

"Ma says you are better off."

Brendan said, "What?"

Ray repeated it.

"Yeah?" Brendan said. "How's she figure?"

Ray's hands went flying. "If you left, Ma would have bummed."

"She'd have gotten over it."

"Maybe, maybe not."

Brendan looked at his brother sitting on the bed, staring up into his face.

"Don't piss me off now, Ray. Okay?" He leaned in close, thinking about that gun. "I loved her."

Ray gazed back, his face as empty as a rubber mask.

"You know what that's like, Ray?"

Ray shook his head.

"It's like knowing all the answers on a test the minute you sit down at your desk. It's like knowing everything's going to be okay for the rest of your life. You're going to ace. You're going to be fine. You'll walk around forever, feeling relieved, because you *won*." He turned away from his brother. "That's what it's like."

Ray tapped the bedpost so he'd look at him, and then he signed, "You will feel it again."

Brendan dropped to his knees and shoved his face into Ray's. "No, I won't. Fucking get that? No."

Ray pulled his feet up onto the bed and backed up, and Brendan felt ashamed, but still angry, because that was the thing about those who were mute—they could make you feel stupid for talking. Everything Ray said came out succinctly, just as he'd intended. He didn't know what it was like to fumble for words or trip over them because his speech was going faster than his brain.

Brendan wanted to spill, he wanted the words to come out of his mouth in a gush of passionate, fucked-up, not entirely sensible, but completely honest testament to Katie and what she'd meant to him and how it had felt to press his nose against her neck in *this bed* and hook one of his fingers around one of hers and wipe ice cream off her chin and sit beside her in a car and watch her eyes dart as she came to intersections and hear her talk and sleep and snore and . . .

He wanted to go on for hours. He wanted someone to listen to him and to understand that speech wasn't just about communicating ideas or opinions. Sometimes, it was about trying to convey whole human lives. And while you knew even before you opened your mouth that you'd fail, somehow the trying was what mattered. The trying was all you had.

Ray, though, no way he could grasp that. Words for Ray were flicks of the fingers, deft droppings and raisings and sweepings of the hand. Words were not wasted with Ray. Communication was not relative to him. You said exactly what you meant, and then you were done with it. To unload his grief and overemote in front of his blank-faced brother would have merely shamed Brendan. It wouldn't have helped.

He looked down at his scared little brother, backed up on the bed and staring at him with bug eyes, and he held out his hand.

"I'm sorry," he said, and heard his voice crack. "I'm sorry, Ray. Okay? I didn't mean to blast you."

Ray took the hand and stood.

"So, it's okay?" he signed, his eyes on Brendan as if he was ready to dive out the window at the next outburst.

"It's okay," Brendan signed back. "I guess it's all right."

20

WHEN SHE
COMES HOME

SEAN'S PARENTS LIVED in Wingate Estates, a gated community of two-bedroom stucco town houses thirty miles south of the city. Every twenty units formed a section, and each section had its own pool and a recreational center where they held dances on Saturday nights. A small, par-three golf course stretched around the outer edge of the complex like a fallen slice of crescent moon, and from late spring until early autumn the air hummed with the buzz of cart engines.

Sean's father didn't play golf. He'd long ago decided it was a rich man's game and to take it up would represent some form of betrayal to his blue-collar roots. Sean's mother had tried it for a while, though, and then gave it up because she'd believed her companions secretly laughed at her form, her slight brogue, and her clothing.

So they lived here quietly and, for the most part, friendless, though Sean knew his father had struck up an acquaintanceship with a small Irish plug of a guy named Riley who'd also lived in one of the city's neighborhoods before coming to Wingate. Riley, who had no use for golf either, would occasionally join Sean's father for drinks at the Ground Round on the other side of Route 28. And Sean's mother, a natural, if reflexive, caretaker, often tended to older neighbors with infirmities. She'd drive them to the drugstore to fill prescriptions or to the doctor's so new prescriptions could take up residence in the medicine cabinet beside the older ones. His mother, pushing seventy, felt young and vibrant on these drives, and given that most of the people she helped were widowed, she felt, too, that her and her husband's continued health was a blessing donated from above.

"They're alone," she'd said to Sean once regarding her sickly friends, "and even if the doctors won't tell them, that's what they're dying from."

Often when he pulled past the guard kiosk and drove up the main road, striped every ten yards with yellow speed bumps that rattled his axles, Sean could almost see the ghost streets and ghost neighborhoods and ghost lives the Wingate residents had left behind, as if cold-water flats and dull white iceboxes, wrought-iron fire escapes and shrieking children floated through the present landscape of eggshell stucco and spiky lawns like a morning mist just beyond the limits of his peripheral vision. An irrational guilt would settle in him, the guilt of a son who'd packed his parents away in a retirement home. Irrational, because Wingate Estates wasn't technically a community for people over sixty (though Sean had frankly never seen a resident under that age), and his parents had moved here completely of their own volition, packing up their decades-long complaints about the city and its noise and crime and traffic jams to come here, where, as his father put it, "You can walk at night without looking over your shoulder."

Still, Sean felt as if he'd failed them, as if they'd expected he would have tried harder to keep them near. Sean saw this place and he saw death, or at least a depot en route, and it wasn't just that he hated to think of his parents here—biding their time until the day someone needed to drive *them* to the doctors—he hated to think of himself here or someplace like it. Yet he knew there was little chance he'd end up anyplace else. And, as it stood now, without kids or a wife to care. He was thirty-six, a little more than halfway toward a Wingate duplex already, with the second half likely to pass at a far more furious clip than the first had.

His mother blew out the candles on her cake at the small dinette table that perched in the alcove between the tiny kitchen and the more spacious living room, and they ate quietly, then sipped their tea to the click of the clock on the wall above them and the hum of the climate-control system vents.

When they were finished, his father stood. "I'll clear the plates."

"No, I'll get them."

"You sit down."

"No, let me."

"Sit, birthday girl."

His mother sat back with a small smile, and Sean's father stacked the plates and took them around the corner into the kitchen.

"Careful with the crumbs," his mother said.

"I'm careful."

"If you don't wash them all the way down the drain, we'll get ants again."

"We had one ant. One."

"We had more," she said to Sean.

"Six months ago," his father said over the running water.

"And mice."

"We've never had mice."

"Mrs. Feingold did. Two of them. She had to get traps."

"We don't have mice."

"That's because I make sure you don't leave crumbs in the sink."

"Jesus," Sean's father said.

Sean's mother sipped her tea and looked over the cup at Sean.

"I clipped an article for Lauren," she said when she'd placed the cup back on the saucer. "I've got it here someplace."

Sean's mother was always clipping articles from the paper and giving them to him when he'd visit. Or else, she'd mail them in stacks of nine or ten, Sean opening the envelope to see them folded neatly together like a reminder of how long it had been since his last visit. The articles varied in topic, but they were all of the household-tip or self-help variety—methods to prevent lint fires in your dryer; how to successfully avoid freezer burn every time; the pros and cons of a living will; how to avoid pickpockets while on vacation; health tips for men in high-stress jobs ("Walk Your Heart to the Century Mark!"). They were his mother's way of sending him love, Sean knew, the equivalent of buttoning his coat and fixing his scarf before he left for school on a January morning, and Sean still smiled when he thought of the clipping that had arrived two days before Lauren left— "Leap into in Vitro!"—his parents never grasping that Sean and Lauren's childlessness was a choice, if anything, one steeped in their shared (though never discussed) fear that they'd be terrible parents.

When she finally had gotten pregnant, they'd kept it from his parents while they tried to figure out if she'd have the baby, their marriage crumbling around them, Sean discovering the affair she'd had with an actor, of all things, starting to ask her, "Whose kid is it, Lauren?" And Lauren coming back with, "Take a paternity test, you're so worried."

They'd backed out of dinners with his parents, made excuses for not being home when they made the drive into the city, and Sean felt his mind breaking apart under the fear that the child wasn't his and the other fear, too—that he wouldn't want it, even if it was.

Since Lauren had left, Sean's mother would only refer to her absence as "taking some sorting-out time," and all the clippings were now for her, not him, as if one day they'd overflow in a drawer to the point that he and Lauren would have to get back together if only so they could close the drawer again.

"You talk to her recently?" Sean's father asked from the kitchen, his face hidden behind the mint-green wall between them.

"Lauren?"

"Uh-huh."

"Well, who else?" his mother said brightly as she rummaged through a drawer in the sideboard.

"She calls. She doesn't say anything."

"Maybe she's just making small talk because she—"

"No. I mean, Dad, she doesn't speak. At all."

"Nothing?"

"Zip."

"Then how do you know it's her?"

"I just know."

"But *how*?"

"Jesus," Sean said. "I can hear her breathing. Okay?"

"How odd," his mother said. "Do *you* talk though, Sean?"

"Sometimes. Less and less."

"Well, at least you're communicating somehow," his mother said, and placed the latest clipping down in front of him. "You tell her I thought she'd find this interesting." She sat down and smoothed a wrinkle in the tablecloth with the outer edges of both palms. "When she comes home again," she said, peering at the wrinkle as it dissolved under her hands.

"When she comes home," she repeated, her voice a light wisp, like the voice of a nun, certain of the essential order in all things.

"DAVE BOYLE," Sean said to his father an hour later as they sat at one of the tall bar tables in the Ground Round. "That time he disappeared from in front of our house."

His father frowned and then concentrated on pouring the rest of a Killian's into his frosted mug. As the foam neared the top of the mug and the beer slowed to a trickle of fat drops, his father said, "What—you couldn't look it up in old newspapers?"

"Well—"

"Why ask me? Shit. It was on TV."

"Not when his kidnapper was found," Sean said, hoping that would suffice, that his father wouldn't press him on why Sean had come to him because Sean didn't have a complete answer yet.

It had something to do with needing his father to place *him* in the context of the event, maybe help him see himself back there in a way newspapers or old case files couldn't. And maybe it was about hoping to talk to his father about something more than just the daily news, the Red Sox's need for a lefty in the bullpen.

It seemed to Sean—sometimes—that he and his father may have once talked about more than just incidental things (just as it seemed that he and Lauren had), but for the life of him, Sean couldn't remember what those things may have been. In the fog that was his remembrance of being young, he feared he'd invented intimacies and moments of clear communication between his father and him that, while they'd achieved a mythic stature over the years, had never happened.

His father was a man of silences and half-sentences that trailed off into nothing, and Sean had spent most of his life interpreting those silences, filling in the blanks left in the wake of those ellipses, creating a concept of what his father *meant* to say. And lately Sean wondered if he, himself, ever finished sentences as he thought he did, or if he, too, was a creature of silences, silences he'd seen in Lauren, too, and had never done enough about until her silence was the only piece of her he had left. That, and the air hiss on the phone when she called.

"Why you want to go back there?" his father said eventually.

"You know that Jimmy Marcus's daughter was murdered?"

His father looked at him. "That girl in Pen Park?"

Sean nodded.

"I saw the name," his father said, "figured it might be a relative, but his daughter?"

"Yeah."

"He's your age. He has a nineteen-year-old daughter?"

"Jimmy had her when he was, I dunno, seventeen or so, a couple years before he got sent up to Deer Island."

"Aww Jesus," his father said. "That poor son of a bitch. His old man still in prison?"

Sean said, "He died, Dad."

Sean could see that the answer hurt his father, rocked him back to the kitchen on Gannon Street, he and Jimmy's father working on those soft Saturday afternoon beer buzzes as their sons played in the backyard, the thunder of their laughter exploding into the air.

"Shit," his father said. "He die on the outside at least?"

Sean considered lying, but he was already shaking his head. "Inside. Walpole. Cirrhosis."

"When?"

"Not long after you moved. Six years ago, maybe seven."

His father's mouth widened around a silent "seven." He sipped his beer and the liver spots on the back of his hands seemed more pronounced in the yellow light hanging above them. "It's so easy to lose track. To lose time."

"I'm sorry, Dad."

His father grimaced. It was his only response to sympathy or compliments. "Why? You didn't do it. Hell, Tim did himself in when he killed Sonny Todd."

"Over a pool game. Right?"

His father shrugged. "They were both drunk. Who knows anymore? They were drunk and they both had big mouths and bad tempers. Tim's temper was just a lot worse than Sonny Todd's." His father sipped some more beer. "So, what's Dave Boyle's disappearance have to do with—what was her name, was it Katherine? Katherine Marcus?"

"Yeah."

"So what does the one have to do with the other?"

"I'm not saying they do."

"You're not saying they don't."

Sean smiled in spite of himself. Give him a hardened gangbanger in the box any day, some guy trying to lawyer up who knew the system better than most judges, because Sean would crack him. But take one of these old-timers, these hard-as-nails, mistrustful bastards from his father's generation—working stiffs with a lot of pride and no respect for any state or municipal office—and you could bang at them all night, and if they didn't want to tell you anything, you'd still be there in the morning with nothing but the same unanswered questions.

"Hey, Dad, let's not worry about any connections just yet."

"Why not?"

Sean held up a hand. "Okay? Just humor me."

"Oh, sure, it's what's keeping me alive, the chance I might get to humor my own son."

Sean felt his hand tighten around the handle of his glass mug. "I looked up the case file on Dave's abduction. The investigating officer is dead. No one else remembers the case, and it's still listed as unsolved."

"So?"

"So, I remember you coming into my room maybe a year after Dave came home and saying, 'It's over. They got the guys.' "

His father shrugged. "They got one of them."

"So, why didn't—?"

"In Albany," his father said. "I saw the picture in the paper. The guy had confessed to a couple molestations in New York and claimed he'd done a few more in Massachusetts and Vermont. The guy hung himself in his cell before he could get to the particulars. But I recognized the guy's face from the sketch the cop drew in our kitchen."

"You're sure?"

He nodded. "Hundred percent. The investigating detective—his name was, ah—"

"Flynn," Sean said.

His father nodded. "Mike Flynn. Right. I'd kept in contact with him, you know, a bit. So I called him after I saw the picture in the paper, and he said, yeah, it was the same guy. Dave had confirmed it."

"Which one?"

"Huh?"

"Which guy?"

"Oh. The, ah, how'd you describe him? 'The greasy one who looked sleepy.' "

Sean's child's words seemed strange coming out of his father's mouth and across the table at him. "The passenger."

"Yeah."

"And his partner?" Sean said.

His father shook his head. "Died in a car crash. Or so the other one said. That's as far as I know, but I wouldn't put too much stock in what I know. Hell, you had to tell me Tim Marcus was dead."

Sean drained what remained in his mug, pointed at his father's empty glass. "Another?"

His father considered the glass for a bit. "What the hell. Sure."

When Sean came back from the bar with fresh beers, his father was watching *Jeopardy!* run silently on one of the TV screens above the bar. As Sean sat down, his father said, "Who is Robert Oppenheimer?" to the TV.

"Without the volume," Sean said, "how do you know if you got it right?"

"Because I do," his father said, and poured his beer into his mug, frowning at the stupidity of Sean's question. "You guys do that a lot. I'll never understand it."

"Do what? What guys?"

His father gestured at him with the beer mug. "Guys your age. You ask a lot of questions without thinking the answer might be obvious if you just gave it some friggin' thought."

"Oh," Sean said. "Okay."

"Like this Dave Boyle stuff," his father said. "What does it matter what happened twenty-five years ago to Dave? You know what happened. He disappeared for four days with two child molesters. What happened was exactly what you'd think would happen. But here you come dredging it back up again because . . ." His father took a drink. "Hell, I don't know why."

His father gave him a befuddled smile and Sean matched it with his own.

"Hey, Dad."

"Yeah."

"You telling me that nothing ever happened in your past that you don't think about, turn over in your head a lot?"

His father sighed. "That's not the point."

"Sure, it is."

"No, it isn't. Bad shit happens to everyone, Sean. Everyone. You ain't special. But your whole generation, you're scab pickers. You just can't leave well enough alone. You have evidence linking Dave to Katherine Marcus's death?"

Sean laughed. The old man had come around his flank, pushing Sean's buttons with the "your generation" slurs while all the time what he wanted to know was if Dave was involved in Katie's death.

"Let's say there are a couple of circumstantial things which make Dave look like someone we'd like to keep an eye on."

"You call that an answer?"

"You call that a question?"

His father's terrific smile broke across his face then and erased a good fifteen years from his face, Sean remembering how that smile could spread through the whole house when he was young, lighting everything up.

"So you were bugging me about Dave because you're wondering if what those guys did to him could turn him into a guy who'd kill a young girl."

Sean shrugged. "Something like that."

His father gave that some thought as he stirred the peanuts in the bowl between them and sipped some more beer. "I don't think so."

Sean chuckled. "You know him that well, do you?"

"No. I just remember him as a kid. He didn't have that kind of thing in him."

"Lot of nice kids grow up to be adults who do shit you wouldn't believe."

His father cocked an eyebrow at him. "You trying to tell me about human nature?"

Sean shook his head. "Just police work."

His father leaned back in his chair, considered Sean with the tug of a smile playing at the corners of his mouth. "Come on. Enlighten me."

Sean felt his face redden a bit. "Hey, no, I'm just—"

"Please."

Sean felt foolish. It was amazing how fast his father could do that, make him feel as if what would pass as a normal set of observations with most of the people Sean knew was, in his father's eyes, the boy Sean trying to act grown up and merely succeeding at sounding pompous instead.

"Give me a little credit. I think I know a bit about people and crime. It's, you know, my job."

"So you think Dave could have butchered a nineteen-year-old girl, Sean? Dave, who you used to play with in the backyard. That kid?"

"I think anyone's capable of anything."

"So, I could have done it." His father put a hand to his chest. "Or your mother."

"No."

"Better check our alibis."

"I didn't say that. Jesus."

"Sure you did. You said anyone was capable of anything."

"Within reason."

"Oh," his father said loudly. "Well, I didn't hear that part."

He was doing it again—wrapping Sean up in knots, playing him like Sean played suspects in the box. No wonder Sean was so good at interrogation. He'd learned from a master.

They sat in silence for a bit, and eventually his father said, "Hey, maybe you're right."

Sean looked at him, waited for the punch line.

"Maybe Dave could have done what you think. I dunno. I'm just remembering the kid. I don't know the man."

Sean tried to see himself through his father's eyes then. He wondered if that's what his father saw—the kid, not the man—when he looked at his son. Probably hard to do otherwise.

He remembered the way his uncles used to talk about his father, the youngest brother in a family of twelve who'd emigrated from Ireland when his father was five. The "old Bill," they'd say, referring to the Bill Devine who'd existed before Sean was born. The "scrapper." Only now could Sean hear their voices and feel the hint of patronization an older generation feels for a younger, most of Sean's uncles having a good twelve or fifteen years on their baby brother.

They were all dead now. All eleven of his father's brothers and sisters. And here was the baby of the family, closing in on seventy-five, and holed up here in the suburbs by a golf course he'd never use. The last one left, and yet still the youngest, always the youngest, squaring off at all times against even the whiff of condescension from anyone, particularly his son. Blocking out the whole world, if he had to, before he'd endure that, or even the perception of it. Because all those who'd had the right to behave that way toward him had long since passed from the earth.

His father glanced at Sean's beer and tossed some singles onto the table for a tip.

"You about done?" he said.

THEY WALKED BACK across Route 28 and up the entrance road with its yellow speed bumps and sprinkler spray.

"You know what your mother likes?" his father said.

"What?"

"When you write to her. You know, a card every now and then for no good reason. She says you send funny cards and she likes the way you write. She keeps them in the bedroom in a drawer. Has ones going back to when you were in college."

"Okay."

"Every now and then, you know? Drop one in the mail."

"Sure."

They reached Sean's car and his father looked up at the dark windows of his duplex.

"She gone to bed?" Sean asked.

His father nodded. "She's driving Mrs. Coughlin to physical therapy in the morning." His father reached out abruptly and shook Sean's hand. "Good seeing you."

"You, too."

"She coming back?"

Sean didn't have to ask who "she" was.

"I dunno. I really don't."

His father looked at him under the pale yellow street lamp above them, and for a moment, Sean could see that it pierced something in him, knowing his son was hurting, knowing he'd been abandoned, damaged, and that that did something permanent to you, spooned something out of you that you'd never get back.

"Well," his father said, "you look good. Like you're taking care of yourself. You drinking too much, anything like that?"

Sean shook his head. "I just work a lot."

"Work's good," his father said.

"Yeah," Sean said, and felt something bitter and abandoned rise up in his throat.

"So . . ."

"So."

His father clapped a hand on his shoulder. "So, okay then. Don't forget to call your mother Sunday," he said, and left Sean by the car, walked toward his front door with the stride of a man twenty years younger.

"Take care," Sean said, and his father raised his hand in confirmation.

Sean used the remote to unlock the car, and he was reaching for the door handle when he heard his father say, "Hey."

"Yeah?" He looked back and saw his father standing by the front door, his upper half dissolved in a soft darkness.

"You were right not to get in that car that day. Remember that."

Sean leaned against his car, his palms on the roof, and tried to make out his father's face in the dark.

"We should have protected Dave, though."

"You were kids," his father said. "You couldn't have known. And even if you could have, Sean . . ."

Sean let that sink in. He drummed his hands on the roof and peered into the dark for his father's eyes. "That's what I tell myself."

"Well?"

He shrugged. "I still think we *should* have known. Somehow. Don't you think?"

For a good minute, neither of them said anything, and Sean could hear crickets amid the hiss of the lawn sprinklers.

"Good night, Sean," his father said through the hiss.

" 'Night," Sean said, and waited until his father had gone inside before he climbed into his car and headed home.

21

GOBLINS

DAVE WAS SITTING in the living room when Celeste came home. He sat on the corner of the cracked leather couch with two columns of empty beer cans rising up beside the arm of the chair and a fresh one in his hand, the remote control resting on his thigh. He watched a movie where everyone, it seemed, was screaming.

Celeste took her coat off in the hall and watched the light flicker off Dave's face, heard the screams grow louder and more panicked, intermingled with Hollywood sound effects of tables shattering and what could only be the squishing of body parts.

"What are you watching?" she said.

"Some vampire movie," Dave said, his eyes on the screen as he raised the Bud to his lips. "The head vampire's killing everyone at this party the vampire slayers were having. They work for the Vatican."

"Who?"

"The vampire slayers. Oooh, shit," Dave said, "he just tore that guy's head clean off."

Celeste stepped into the living room, looked at the screen as a guy in black flew across the room and grabbed a terrified woman by the face and snapped her neck.

"Jesus, Dave."

"No, it's cool, 'cause now James Woods is pissed."

"Who's James Woods?"

"The lead vampire slayer. He's a bad-ass."

She saw him now—James Woods in a leather jacket and tight jeans as he picked up some sort of crossbow and started to point it at the vampire. But the vampire was too quick. He swatted James Woods all the way across the room like he was a moth, and then another guy came running into the room, firing an automatic pistol at the vampire. It didn't seem to do much good, but then they were suddenly running past the vampire, as if he'd forgotten where they were.

"Is that a Baldwin brother?" Celeste said. She sat on the arm of the couch, up by where it met the back, and leaned her head against the wall.

"I think so, yeah."

"Which one?"

"I don't know. I lose track."

She watched them run across a motel room strewn with more corpses than Celeste would have thought could fit in such a small space, and her husband said, "Man, the Vatican's going to have to train a whole new team of slayers."

"Why's the Vatican care about vampires again?"

Dave smiled and looked up at her with his boyish face and beautiful eyes. "They're a big problem, honey. Notorious chalice thieves."

"Chalice thieves?" she said, and felt an urge to reach down and run her hand through his hair, the whole horrible day dropping away in this silly discussion. "I didn't know that."

"Oh, yeah. Big problem," Dave said, and drained his beer as James Woods and the Baldwin brother and some drugged-up-looking girl raced down an empty road in a pickup truck, the vampire flying after them now. "Where you been?"

"I dropped off the dress at Reed's."

"Hours ago," Dave said.

"And then I just felt like I needed to sit somewhere and think. You know?"

"Think," Dave said. "Sure." He got up off the couch and walked into the kitchen, opened the fridge. "You want one?"

She didn't, really, but she said, "Yeah, okay."

Dave came back into the room and handed her the beer. She could often tell what kind of mood he was in by whether he'd opened the can for her. The can had been opened, but she wasn't sure if this was good or bad. She was having trouble gauging him.

"So, what'd you think about?" He popped the tab on his own can and it was an even louder sound than the screeching tires on the TV as the pickup truck flipped over.

"Oh, you know."

"Not really, Celeste, no."

"Things," she said, and took a sip of the beer. "The day, Katie being dead, poor Jimmy and Annabeth, those things."

"Those things," Dave said. "You know what I was thinking about as I was walking back home with Michael, Celeste? I was thinking how embarrassing it must have been for him to hear his mother just drove off and didn't tell anyone where she was going or when she was coming back. I was thinking about that a lot."

"I just told you, Dave."

"Told me what?" He looked up at her and smiled again, but it wasn't boyish this time. "Told me what, Celeste?"

"I just felt like thinking. I'm sorry I didn't call. But it's been a tough couple of days. I'm not myself."

"Nobody's themselves."

"What?"

"Like this movie?" he said. "They don't know who the real people are and who the vampires are. I've seen parts of this before, right, and that Baldwin brother there? He's going to fall in love with that blond girl, even though he knows she's been bitten. So she's going to turn into a vampire, but he don't care, right? Because he loves her. Yet she's a bloodsucker. She's going to suck his blood and turn *him* into the walking dead. I mean, that's the whole thing about vampirism, Celeste—there's something attractive about it. Even if you know it'll kill you and damn your soul for an eternity and you'll have to spend all your time biting people in the neck, and hiding out from the sun and, you know, Vatican hit squads. Maybe one day you wake up and forget what it was to be human. Maybe that happens, and then it's okay. You've been poisoned, but the poison ain't all that bad once you learn how to live with it." He propped his feet up on the coffee table, took a long drink from the can. "That's my opinion anyway."

Celeste remained very still, sitting up on the arm of the couch and looking down at her husband. "Dave, what the fuck are you talking about?"

"Vampires, sweetie. Werewolves."

"Werewolves? You're not making any sense."

"I'm not? You think I killed Katie, Celeste. That's the kinda sense we're making these days."

"I don't . . . Where did you come up with that?"

He picked at the beer tab with his fingernail. "You could barely look at me in Jimmy's kitchen before you left. You're holding her dress up like she's still inside of it, and you couldn't even look at me. I start thinking about it. I think, why would my own wife seem repulsed by me? And then it hits me—Sean. He said something to you, didn't he? Him and that creepy fucking partner of his asked you questions."

"No."

"No? Bullshit."

She didn't like how calm he was. She could chalk some of that up to the beer, Dave having always been something of a mellow drunk, but there was an ugly air to his calm now, a sense of something coiled too tightly.

"David—"

"Oh, it's 'David.' "

"—I don't think anything. I'm just confused."

He tilted his head and looked back up at her. "Well, let's talk it out then, honey. That's the key to any good relationship—solid communication."

She had $147 in her checking account and a five-hundred-dollar limit on her Visa, with about two-fifty already spent. Even if she could get Michael out of here, they wouldn't get far. Two or three nights in a motel somewhere, and Dave would find them. He'd never been a stupid man. He could track them, she was sure.

The bag. She could hand over the trash bag to Sean Devine and he could find blood in the fabric of Dave's clothes, she was sure. She'd heard all about the advances they'd been making in DNA technology. They'd find Katie's blood on the clothes and arrest Dave.

"Come on," Dave said. "Let's talk, honey. Let's hash this out. I'm serious. I want to, what's it, *allay* your fears."

"I'm not afraid."

"You look it."

"I'm not."

"Okay." He brought his heels off the coffee table. "So tell me what's, uh, *bothering* you, honey?"

"You're drunk."

He nodded. "I am. Don't mean I can't have a conversation, though."

On the TV, the vampire was decapitating someone again, a priest this time.

Celeste said, "Sean didn't ask me any questions. I overheard them talking when you went to get Annabeth's cigarettes. I don't know what you told them earlier, Dave, but they don't believe your story. They know you were at the Last Drop around last call."

"What else?"

"Someone saw our car in the parking lot around the time Katie left. And they don't believe your story about how you bruised your hand."

Dave held the hand out in front of him, flexed it. "That it?"

"That's all I heard."

"And that made you think what?"

She almost touched him again. For a moment, the threat seemed to have left his body and been replaced by defeat. She could see it in his shoulders and in his back and she wanted to reach out and touch him, but she held back.

"Dave, just tell them about the mugger."

"The mugger."

"Yeah. So maybe you'd have to go to court. What's the big deal? It's a lot better than having a murder pinned on you."

Now's the time, she thought. Say you didn't do it. Say you never saw Katie leave the Last Drop. Say it, Dave.

Instead he said, "I see how your mind's working. I do. I come home with blood on me the same time Katie's murdered. I must have killed her."

It popped out of Celeste: "Well?"

Dave put down his beer then and started laughing. His feet came back up off the floor and he fell into the couch cushions and he laughed and laughed. He laughed like he was having a seizure of them, every gasp for breath turning into another giggling peal. He laughed so hard that tears sprang from his eyes, and his entire upper body shook. "I . . . I . . . I . . . I . . ." He couldn't get it out. The laughter was too strong. It rolled over him and out of him again and the tears came hard now, pouring down his cheeks and into his open mouth, bubbling on his lips.

It was official: Celeste had never been more terrified in her life.

"Ha-ha-ha-Henry," he said, the laughter finally trailing off into chuckles.

"What?"

"Henry," he said. "Henry and George, Celeste. Those were their names. Isn't that fucking hilarious? And George, lemme tell ya, he *was* curious. Henry, though, Henry was just flat-out mean."

"What are you talking about?"

"Henry and George," he said brightly. "I'm talking about Henry and George. They took me for a ride. A four-day ride. And they buried me in a cellar with this old ratty sleeping bag on a stone floor, and, man, Celeste, did they have their fucking fun. No one came to help old Dave then. No one burst in to rescue Dave. Dave had to pretend it was happening to someone else. He had to get so fucking strong in his mind that he could *split* it in two. That's what Dave did. Hell, Dave died. The kid who came out of that cellar, I don't know who the fuck he was—well, he's me, actually—but he's sure as shit not Dave. Dave's dead."

Celeste couldn't speak. In eight years, Dave had never talked about what everyone knew had happened to him. He'd told her he'd been playing with Sean and Jimmy and he'd been abducted and he'd escaped and that was all he was ever going to say. She'd never heard the names of the men. She'd never heard about the sleeping bag. She'd never heard any of this. It was as if, right at this moment, they were awakening from a dream life of their marriage and confronting against their wills all the rationalizations, half-lies, submerged wants, and hidden selves they'd built it on.

Watching it crumble under the wrecking-ball truth that they'd never known each other, they'd merely hoped they would someday.

"The thing is, right?" Dave said. "The thing is, it's like I was saying about the vampires, Celeste. It's the same thing. The same goddamned thing."

"What's the same thing?" she whispered.

"It doesn't come out. Once it's in you, it stays." He was looking at the coffee table again and she could feel him fading away on her.

She touched his arm. "Dave, what doesn't come out? What's the same thing?"

Dave looked at her hand like he was going to sink his teeth into it with a snarl, rip it off at the wrist. "I can't trust my mind anymore, Celeste. I'm warning you. I can't trust my mind."

She removed her hand, and it tingled where it had touched his flesh.

Dave stood up, wavering. He cocked his head and looked at her as if not sure who she was and how she'd gotten there on the edge of his couch. He looked over at the TV as James Woods fired that crossbow into someone's chest, and Dave whispered, "Blow 'em all away, Slayer. Blow 'em all away."

He turned back to Celeste, gave her a drunken grin. "I'm going to go out."

"Okay," she said.

"I'm going to go out and think."

"Yeah," Celeste said. "Sure."

"If I can just get my head around this, I think it'll be all okay. I just need to get my head around it."

Celeste didn't ask what "it" was.

"So, okay then," he said, and walked to the front door. He opened the door and had crossed the threshold when she saw his hand curl around the wood and he leaned his head back in.

Just his head, tilted and staring at her, when he said, "Oh, I took care of the trash, by the way."

"What?"

"The trash bag," he said. "Where you put my clothes and stuff? I took it out earlier and threw it away."

"Oh," she said, and felt the need to vomit again.

"So, I'll be seeing you."

"Yeah," she said as he ducked his head back out onto the landing. "I'll see you."

She listened to his footfalls until they reached the bottom landing. She heard the front door creak open and Dave step out onto the porch and descend the steps. She went over the stairs leading up to Michael's room and she could hear him sleeping up there, his breathing deep. Then she went into the bathroom and threw up.

HE COULDN'T FIND where Celeste had parked the car. Sometimes, particularly during snowstorms, you might drive eight blocks before you found a parking space, so Celeste could have buried the car as far away as the Point for all Dave knew, even though he noticed some empty spaces not far from the house. It was probably just as well. He was too hammered to drive in all likelihood. Maybe a good long walk would help him clear his head.

He walked up Crescent to Buckingham Avenue and took a left, wondering what the hell had been going through his head that he'd tried to explain things to Celeste. Christ, he'd even said those names—Henry and George. He'd mentioned werewolves, for crying out loud. Shit.

And now it was confirmed—the police suspected him. They'd be watching. No more thinking of Sean as an old long-lost friend. They were past that, and Dave could now remember what he hadn't liked about Sean when they were kids: the sense of entitlement, the sense that he was always sure he was right, like most kids who were lucky enough—and that's all it was, luck—to have both parents and a nice house and the newest clothes and athletic equipment.

Fuck Sean. And those eyes of his. And that voice. And the way you could see the women in the kitchen all but drop their panties when he came in the room. Fuck him and his good looks. Fuck him and his morally superior attitude and his funny/cool stories and his cop's swagger and his name in the paper.

Dave wasn't stupid, either. He'd be up to the challenge once he got his head straight. He just needed to get his head straight. If that meant taking it off and screwing it back on tight, then he'd figure out a way to do even that.

The biggest problem right now was that the Boy Who'd Escaped from Wolves and Grown Up was showing his face too much. Dave had hoped that what he'd done Saturday night would settle that, shut the fucker up, send him back deep into the forest of Dave's mind. He'd wanted blood that night, the Boy, he'd wanted to cause some fucking pain. So Dave had obliged.

At first it had just been minor, a few punches, a kick. But then it had gotten out of control, Dave feeling the rage welling up inside of him as the Boy took over. And the Boy was one mean customer. The Boy wasn't satisfied until he saw pieces of brain.

But then, once it was over, the Boy receded. He went away and left Dave to clean up the mess. And Dave had done that. He'd done a damn good job of it. (Maybe not as good as he'd hoped, sure, but still pretty good.) And he'd done it—specifically—so the Boy would stay gone for a while.

But the Boy was a prick. Here was the Boy again, knocking on the door, telling Dave he was coming out, ready or not. We got things to do, Dave.

The avenue looked a little blurry before him, sliding from side to side as he walked, but Dave knew they were nearing the Last Drop. They were nearing the two-block shithole of freaks and prostitutes, everyone gladly selling what Dave had had torn from him.

Torn from me, the Boy said. You grew up. Don't try to carry my cross.

The worst were the kids. They were like goblins. They darted out from doorways or the shells of cars and offered you blow jobs. They offered you fucks for twenty bucks. They'd do anything.

The youngest, the one Dave had seen Saturday night, couldn't have been older than eleven. He had circles of grime around his eyes and white, white skin, and a big bushel of matted red hair on his head, which had only underscored the goblin effect. He should have been home watching sitcoms but he was out here on the street, offering blow jobs to freaks.

Dave had seen him from across the street as he'd walked out of the Last Drop and stood by his car. The kid stood against a street pole, smoking a cigarette, and when he locked eyes with Dave, Dave felt it. The stirring. The desire to melt. To take the red-haired kid's hand and find a quiet place together. It would be so easy, so relaxing, so fucking welcome to just give in. Give in to what he'd been feeling for the last decade at least.

Yes, the Boy said. Do it.

But (and this is where Dave's brain always split in half) he knew deep in his soul that this would be the worst sin of all. He knew it would be crossing a line—no matter how inviting—from which he could never come back. He knew that if he crossed that line, he'd never be able to feel whole, that he might just as well have stayed in that basement with Henry and George for the rest of his life. He would tell himself this in times of temptation, passing school bus stops and playgrounds, public swimming pools in the summer. He would tell himself that he was not going to become Henry and George. He was better than that. He was raising a son. He loved his wife. He would be strong. This was what he told himself more and more every year.

But that wasn't helping Saturday night. Saturday night, the urge was as strong as he'd ever felt it. The red-haired kid leaning against the light pole seemed to know this. He smiled around his cigarette at Dave, and Dave felt tugged toward the curb. He felt as if he stood barefoot on a slope made of satin.

And then a car had pulled up across the street, and after some talk, the kid had climbed in after giving Dave a pitying glance over the hood. Dave had watched the car, a two-toned, midnight-blue-and-white Cadillac, pull across the avenue and come toward him into the rear of the Last Drop's parking lot. Dave climbed into his car, and the Cadillac pulled back by the overgrown trees that spilled over the sagging fence. The driver shut off the lights but left the engine running, and the Boy had whispered in his ear: Henry and George, Henry and George, Henry and George . . .

Tonight, before he could reach the Last Drop, Dave turned around even though the Boy was screaming in his ears. The Boy was screaming, I am you, I am you, I am you.

And Dave wanted to stop and cry. He wanted to put his hand out against the nearest building and weep, because he knew the Boy was right. The Boy Who'd Escaped from Wolves and Grown Up had become a Wolf himself. He'd become Dave.

Dave the Wolf.

It must have happened recently, because Dave couldn't remember any body-racking instance in which he'd felt his soul shift and evaporate to make way for this new entity. But it had happened. Probably while he slept.

But he couldn't stop. This section of avenue was too dangerous, too likely to be populated by junkies who'd see Dave, drunk as he was, as an easy mark. There, right now, across the street, he could see a car trolling along slowly, watching him, waiting for him to give off the scent of the victim.

He sucked in a big breath and straightened his walk, concentrated on looking confident and aloof. He put a bit of rise into his shoulders, gave his eyes a "fuck you" glare and started heading back the way he'd come, back toward home, his head not any clearer, really, what with the Boy still screaming in his ears, but Dave decided to ignore him. He could do that. He was strong. He was Dave the Wolf.

And the volume of the Boy's voice did lessen. It became more conversational as Dave walked back through the Flats.

I am you, the Boy said in the tone of a friend. I am you.

CELESTE CAME OUT of the house with Michael half-asleep on her shoulder and discovered that Dave had taken the car. She'd parked it half a block up, surprised to get the space this late on a weekday night, but now there was a blue Jeep in its place.

That hadn't figured into her plans. She'd seen herself placing Michael in the passenger seat and their bags in the backseat and driving the three miles to the Econo Lodge along the expressway.

"Shit," she said aloud, and resisted the urge to scream.

"Mommy?" Michael mumbled.

"It's okay, Mike."

And maybe it was, because she looked back up to see a cab turning off Perthshire onto Buckingham Avenue. Celeste raised the hand that held Michael's bag, and the cab pulled over right in front of her, Celeste thinking she could spare the six bucks for a ride to the Econo Lodge. She could spare a hundred if it got her out of here right now, far enough away to think things through without having to watch for the turn of a door-knob and the return of a man who may have already decided she was a vampire, worthy only of a stake through her heart followed by a swift beheading, just to be sure.

"Where you going?" the cabbie said as Celeste put her bags on the seat and slid in beside them with Michael on her shoulder.

Anywhere, she wanted to say. Anywhere but here.

IV

GENTRIFICATION

22

THE HUNTING FISH

"YOU TOWED his car?" Sean said.

"His car was towed," Whitey said. "Not the same thing."

As they pulled out of the morning rush-hour traffic and down onto the East Buckingham exit ramp, Sean said, "For what kind of cause?"

"It was abandoned," Whitey said, whistling lightly through his teeth as he turned onto Roseclair.

"Where?" Sean said. "In front of the man's house?"

"Oh, no," Whitey said. "The car was found down in Rome Basin along the parkway. Lucky for us the parkway's State jurisdiction, ain't it? Appears someone jacked it, took it for a joyride, then abandoned it. These things happen, you know?"

Sean had woken up this morning from a dream in which he'd held his daughter and spoken her name, even though he didn't know it and couldn't remember what he'd said in the dream, so he was still a little foggy.

"We found blood," Whitey said.

"Where?"

"The front seat of Boyle's car."

"How much?"

Whitey held his thumb and index finger a hair's width apart. "A bit. Found some more in the trunk."

"In the trunk," Sean said.

"A lot more actually."

"So?"

"So, it's at the lab."

"No," Sean said. "I meant so what if you found blood in the trunk? Katie Marcus never got in anyone's trunk."

"That's a fly in the ointment, sure."

"Sarge, your search of the car's going to be tossed out."

"No."

"No?"

"The car was stolen and abandoned in State jurisdiction. Purely for insurance purposes and, I might add, in the best interest of the owner—"

"You did a physical search and filed a report."

"Ah, you're quick, boy."

They pulled up in front of Dave Boyle's house and Whitey raised the gearshift on the driver's column into park. He killed the engine. "I got enough to bring him in for a chat. That's all I want right now."

Sean nodded, knowing there was no point in arguing with the man. Whitey got to be a sergeant in the Homicide Unit by the dog-to-a-bone tenacity he had regarding his hunches. You didn't talk him out of his hunches, you rode them out.

"What about the ballistics?" Sean said.

"That's a weird one, too," Whitey said as they sat looking at Dave's house, Whitey making no move to leave just yet. "The gun was a thirty-eight Smith like we figured. Part of a lot stolen from a gun dealer in New Hampshire in 'eighty-one. The same gun that killed Katherine Marcus was involved in a liquor store holdup in 'eighty-two. Right here in Buckingham."

"The Flats?"

Whitey shook his head. "Up in Rome Basin, place called Looney Liquors. It was a two-man job, both guys wearing rubber masks. They came in through the back after the owner had shut the front doors, and the first guy into the store fired a warning shot that went through a bottle of rye and embedded in the wall. Rest of the robbery went smooth-'n'-styling, but the bullet was recovered. Ballistics matched it to the same gun as the one killed the Marcus girl."

"So that would tend to point in another direction, don't you think?" Sean said. "Nineteen-eighty-two, Dave was, like, seventeen and starting out at Raytheon. I don't think he was pulling any liquor store jobs."

"Don't mean the *gun* didn't eventually end up in his hands. Shit, kid, you know the way they get passed around." Whitey didn't sound as sure of himself as he had last night, but he said, "Let's go get him," and pushed open his door.

Sean got out of the passenger side and they walked up to Dave's place, Whitey thumbing the cuffs on his hip like he was hoping he'd get an excuse to use them.

JIMMY PARKED his car and carried a cardboard tray of coffee cups and a bag of doughnuts across the cracked tar parking lot toward the Mystic River. The cars slammed across the metal extension spans of the Tobin Bridge above him, and Katie knelt by the water's edge with Just Ray Harris, both of them peering into the river. Dave Boyle was there, too, his bruised hand ballooned to the size of a boxing glove. Dave sat in a sagging lawn chair beside Celeste and Annabeth. Celeste had some kind of zipper contraption covering her mouth and Annabeth smoked two cigarettes at once. All three of them wore black sunglasses and didn't look at Jimmy. They stared up at the underside of the bridge, and gave off an air that said they'd prefer to be left alone in their lawn chairs, thank you very much.

Jimmy put the coffee and doughnuts down beside Katie and knelt between her and Just Ray. He looked down at the water and saw his reflection, saw Katie's and Just Ray's, too, as they turned toward him, Ray with a big red fish clamped between his teeth, the fish still flopping.

Katie said, "I dropped my dress in the river."

Jimmy said, "I can't see it."

The fish plopped out of Just Ray's mouth and landed in the water, lay there on top of the surface flopping away.

Katie said, "He'll get it. He's a hunting fish."

"Tasted just like chicken," Ray said.

Jimmy felt Katie's warm hand on his back, and then he felt Ray's on the back of his neck, and Katie said, "Why don't you go get it, Dad?"

And they pushed him over the edge and Jimmy saw the black water and the flopping fish rise up to meet him and he knew he was going to drown. He opened his mouth to scream and the fish jumped up inside there, cutting off his oxygen, and the water felt like black paint when his face plunged into it.

He opened his eyes and turned his head, saw the clock reading seven-sixteen, and he couldn't remember coming to bed. He must have, though, because here he was, Annabeth sleeping beside him, Jimmy waking up to a brand-new day with an appointment to pick out a headstone in a little over an hour, and Just Ray Harris and the Mystic River knocking at his door.

THE KEY to any successful interrogation was to get as much time as possible before the suspect demanded a lawyer. The hard cases—the dealers and gangbangers and bikers and mobbed-up guys—usually asked for a "mouth" right off the bat. You could fuck with them a little bit, try to rattle them before the lawyer showed up, but for the most part, you were going to have to rely on physical evidence to make your case. Rarely had Sean taken a hard guy into the box and come out with much of use.

When you were dealing with regular citizens or first-time felons, on the other hand, most of your cases were dunked during Q & A's. The "road rage" case, Sean's career topper so far, had been made like that. Out in Middlesex, guy's driving home one night, the right front tire of his SUV came off at eighty miles an hour. Just came off, rolled across the highway. The SUV flipped over nine or ten times, and the guy, Edwin Hurka, was dead on-scene.

Turned out the lug nuts on both his front tires were loose. So they were looking at involuntary manslaughter at best because prevailing opinion was that it was probably just some hungover mechanic's error, and Sean and his partner, Adolph, found out that the victim did have his tires replaced just a few weeks before. But Sean had also found a piece of paper in the victim's glove compartment that bothered him. It was a license plate, hastily scrawled, and when Sean ran it through the RMV computer, he'd come up with the name Alan Barnes. He'd dropped by Barnes's house and asked the guy who answered the door if he was Alan Barnes. The guy, nervous as hell, said, Yeah, why? And Sean, feeling it through his whole body, said, "I'd like to talk to you about some lug nuts."

Barnes broke right there in his doorway, told Sean he'd just meant to fuck the guy's car up a little, give him a scare, the two of them having gotten into it a week before in the merge lane heading into the airport tunnel, Barnes so pissed by the end of it that he hung back, skipped his appointment, and followed Edwin Hurka home, waited till the guy had shut off all the lights in his house before he went to work with his tire iron.

People were stupid. They killed each other over the dumbest things and then they hung around hoping to get caught, walked into court pleading not guilty after giving some cop a four-page, signed confession. It was knowing how stupid they really were that was a cop's best weapon. Let them talk. Always. Let them explain. Let them unload their guilt as you plied them with coffee and the tape recorder reels spun.

And when they asked for a lawyer—and the average citizen almost always *asked*—you frowned and asked if they were sure that's what they wanted and let a very unfriendly vibe fill the room until they decided that they'd really like all three of you to be friends, so maybe they'd talk a bit more before they brought that lawyer down here and spoiled the mood.

Dave didn't ask for a lawyer, though. Not once. He sat in the chair that buckled when you leaned too far back in it, and he looked hungover and annoyed and pissed at Sean, in particular, but he didn't look scared and he didn't look nervous, and Sean could tell it was beginning to get to Whitey.

"Look, Mr. Boyle," Whitey said, "we know you left McGills before you said you did. We know you showed up a half-hour later in the parking lot of the Last Drop around the same time the Marcus girl left. And we sure as shit know you didn't get that swollen hand by banging it off a wall making a pool shot."

Dave groaned. He said, "How about a Sprite, something like that?"

"In a minute," Whitey said for the fourth time in the half an hour they'd been in here. "Tell us what really happened that night, Mr. Boyle."

"I already did."

"You lied."

Dave shrugged. "Your opinion."

"No," Whitey said. "Fact. You lied about leaving McGills. The fuck-ing clock was stopped, Mr. Boyle, five minutes *before* you claim to have left."

"Five whole minutes?"

"You think this is funny?"

Dave leaned back a bit in the chair and Sean waited to hear the tell-tale crack it emitted before it would buckle, but it didn't, Dave pushing it to the edge, but not going any further.

"No, Sergeant, I don't think it's funny. I'm tired. I'm hungover. And my car was not only stolen but now you're telling me you won't release it to me. You say I left McGills five minutes before I said I did?"

"At least."

"Fine. I'll give you that. Maybe I did. I don't look at my watch as much as you guys apparently do. So if you say I left McGills at ten of one instead of five of one, I say, okay. Maybe I did. Oops. But that's it. I went home right after that. I didn't go to any other bar."

"You *were* seen in the parking lot of—"

"No," Dave said. "A Honda with a dented quarter panel was seen. Right? You know how many Hondas there are in this city? Come on, man."

"How many with dents, though, Mr. Boyle, in the same place as yours?"

Dave shrugged. "A bunch, I bet."

Whitey looked at Sean and Sean could feel that they were losing. Dave was right—they could probably find twenty Hondas with dented quarter panels on the passenger side. Twenty, easy. And if Dave could throw that at them, then his lawyer would come up with a lot more.

Whitey came around the back of Dave's chair and said, "Tell us how the blood got in your car."

"What blood?"

"The blood we found in your front seat. Let's start there."

Dave said, "How about that Sprite, Sean?"

Sean said, "Sure."

Dave smiled. "I get it. You're a good cop. How about a meatball sub while you're at it?"

Sean, half out of his chair, sat back down. "Ain't your bitch, Dave. Looks like you'll have to wait awhile."

"You're somebody's bitch, though. Aren't you, Sean?" There was a crazy leer in his eyes when he said it, a preening cockiness, and Sean started thinking maybe Whitey was right. Sean wondered if his father, seeing this Dave Boyle, would have the same opinion of him as he'd had last night.

Sean said, "The blood on your front seat, Dave. Answer the sergeant."

Dave looked back up at Whitey. "We got a chain-link fence in our backyard. You know the kind, with the links curling inward at the top? I was doing yard work the other day. My landlord's old. I do it, he keeps the rent reasonable. So I'm cutting away these bamboo-looking things he's got back there—"

Whitey sighed, but Dave didn't seem to notice.

"—and I slip. I got this electric hedge trimmer in my hand, and I don't want to drop it, so when I slip, I fall into the chain-link fence and I slice myself against it." He patted his rib cage. "Right here. It wasn't bad, but it bled like hell. Like ten minutes later? I gotta go pick up my son at Little League practice. It was probably still bleeding, I got into the seat. That's the best I can figure it."

Whitey said, "So that was your blood in the front seat?"

"Like I said—best I can figure it."

"And what blood type are you?"

"B negative."

Whitey gave him a broad grin as he came back around the chair, perched on the edge of the table. "Funny. That's the exact type we found in the front seat."

Dave held up his hands. "Well, there you go."

Whitey mimicked Dave's hands. "Not quite. Care to explain the blood in the trunk? That blood wasn't B negative."

"I don't know anything about any blood in my trunk."

Whitey chuckled. "No idea how a good half pint of blood got in the trunk of your car?"

"No, I don't," Dave said.

Whitey leaned in, patted Dave's shoulder. "I don't mind telling you,

Mr. Boyle, that this is not the avenue you want to take. You claim in court that you don't know how someone else's blood got in your car, how's that going to look?"

"Fine, I suppose."

"How do you figure?"

Dave leaned back again and Whitey's hand fell from his shoulder. "You filled out the report, Sergeant."

"What report?" Whitey said.

Sean saw it coming and thought, Oh, shit, he's got us.

"The stolen car report," Dave said.

"So?"

"So," Dave said, "the car wasn't in my possession last night. I don't know what the car thieves used it for, but maybe you want to find out, because it sounds like they were up to no good."

For a long thirty seconds, Whitey sat completely still, and Sean could feel it dawning on him—he'd gotten too smart and he'd fucked himself. Just about anything they found in that car would be thrown out in court because Dave's lawyer could claim the car thieves had put it there.

"The blood was old, Mr. Boyle. Older than a few hours."

"Yeah?" Dave said. "You can prove that? I mean, conclusively, Sergeant? You're sure it didn't just dry fast? I mean, it wasn't a humid night last night."

"We can prove it," Whitey said, but Sean could hear the doubt in his voice, so he was pretty sure Dave could hear it, too.

Whitey got up off the table and turned his back to Dave. He put his fingers over his mouth and drummed them against his upper lip as he walked the length of the table down toward Sean's end, his eyes on the floor.

"Things looking any better on that Sprite?" Dave said.

"WE'RE BRINGING DOWN the kid Souza talked to, the one who saw the car. Tommy, ah—"

"Moldanado," Sean said.

"Yeah." Whitey nodded, his voice a little thin, his face a fist of distraction, the look of a guy who'd had a chair pulled out from under him, found his ass hitting the floor, wondering how he got there. "We'll, ah, put Boyle in a lineup, see if this Moldanado picks him out."

"It's something," Sean said.

Whitey leaned against the corridor wall as a secretary passed them, her perfume the same kind Lauren used, Sean thinking maybe he'd call *her* on her cell, see how she was doing today, see if she'd talk now that he'd made the first move.

Whitey said, "He's *too* cool in there. Guy's first time in the box and he's not even sweating?"

Sean said, "Sarge, it's not looking good, you know?"

"No shit."

"No, I mean, even if we didn't get blown out on the car, it's not the Marcus girl's blood. There's nothing to tie him to this."

Whitey looked back at the door to the interrogation room. "I can break him."

"He kicked our asses in there," Sean said.

"I'm not even warmed up."

Sean could see it in his face, though, the doubt, the first crumbling of the primary hunch. Whitey was stubborn and mean, too, if he thought he was right, but the man was too smart to ever flame out on a hunch that kept running into substantiation problems.

"Look," Sean said, "let's let him sweat a bit in there."

"He ain't sweating."

"He might start, we leave him alone to think."

Whitey looked back at the door like he wanted to burn it down. "Maybe."

"I think it's the gun," Sean said. "We bust this open on that gun."

Whitey chewed the inside of his mouth and eventually nodded. "It'd be nice to know more about the gun. You want to take that?"

"Same guy still own the liquor store?"

Whitey said, "I don't know. The case file was from 'eighty-two, but the owner then was a Lowell Looney."

Sean smiled at the name. "Has a ring to it, don't it?"

Whitey said, "Why don't you take a ride over? I'll watch fuckhead in there through the glass, see if he starts singing songs about dead girls in the park."

LOWELL LOONEY was about eighty years old and looked like he could beat Sean in a hundred-yard dash. He wore an orange T-shirt from Porter's Gym over blue sweats with white piping and spanking-new Reeboks, and he moved around like he'd jump for the highest bottle behind the counter if you asked him to.

"Right there," he said to Sean, pointing at a row of half-pint bottles behind the counter. "Went in through a bottle and stuck right in that wall there."

Sean said, "Scary, huh?"

The old man shrugged. "Scarier than a glass of milk, maybe. Not as scary as some nights around here, though. Some wacko kid put a shotgun in my face ten years ago, had that crazed-dog look in his eyes, kept blinking at the sweat? That was scary, son. The guys who put the bullet in the wall, though, they were pros. Pros I can deal with. They just want the money, they ain't pissed at the world."

"So these two guys . . . ?"

"Come in the back," Lowell Looney said, zipping down to the other end of the counter where a black curtain hung over the storeroom. "There's a door back there leads to the loading dock. I had a kid working part-time for me back then who'd dump the trash, smoke himself a little weed while he was out there. Half the time he'd forget to lock the door when he come back in. Either he was in on it or they watched him enough times to know he was brain-dead. That night, they came in through the unlocked door, fired off the warning round to keep me from reaching for my own gun, and took what they came for."

"How much they hit you for?"

"Six grand."

Sean said, "That's a chunk of change."

"Thursdays," Lowell said, "I used to cash checks. I don't anymore, but back then I was stupid. 'Course, if the thieves had been a little brighter, they would have hit me in the morning before a lot of those checks were cashed." He shrugged. "I said they were pros, just not the smartest pros around, I guess."

"This kid who left the door open," Sean said.

"Marvin Ellis," Lowell said. "Hell, maybe he was involved. I fired him the next day. Thing is, the only reason they would have fired that shot was because they knew I kept a piece under the counter. And it wasn't like that was common knowledge, so it was either Marvin who told 'em, or one of them two used to work here."

"And you told the police that at the time?"

"Oh, sure." The old guy waved his hand at the memory. "They went through my old records, questioned everyone who used to work for me. So they said, anyway. They never arrested no one. You say the same gun was used in another crime?"

"Yeah," Sean said. "Mr. Looney—"

"Lowell, for Christ's sake, please."

"Lowell," Sean said, "you still got those employment records?"

DAVE STARED at the mirrored glass in the interrogation room knowing that Sean's partner, and maybe Sean, too, stared back at him.

Good.

How's it going? I'm enjoying this Sprite myself. What's it they put in the stuff? Limon. That's right. I'm enjoying my limon, Sergeant. Mmm-mmm good. Yes siree. Can't wait to get me another can of this.

Dave stared straight into the center of the mirror from the other side of the long table and he felt great. True, he didn't know where Celeste had gone with Michael, and a dread came with the ignorance that polluted his brain far more than the fifteen or so beers he'd downed last night. But she'd come back. He seemed to remember he might have scared her last night. He definitely hadn't made much sense, going on about vampires and things that went in you not being able to come back out, so maybe she'd gotten a little spooked.

Couldn't say he blamed her. It was really his fault allowing the Boy to take over like that and show his ugly, feral face.

But outside of Celeste and Michael being gone, he felt strong. He felt none of the indecision he'd felt over the last few days. Hell, he'd even managed to sleep six hours last night. He woke feeling stale and woolen-mouthed, his skull weighted down by granite, yet somehow clear.

He knew who he was. And he knew he'd done right. And killing someone (and Dave couldn't blame it on the Boy anymore; it was him, Dave—he'd done the killing) had empowered him now that he'd gotten his head around it. He'd heard somewhere of ancient cultures that used to eat the hearts of the people they murdered. They ate the hearts, and the dead were subsumed into them. It gave them power, the power of two, the spirit of two. Dave felt that way. No, he hadn't eaten anyone's heart. He wasn't that fucked in the head. But he had felt the glory of the predator. He had murdered. And he had done right. And he had stilled the monster inside of him, the freak who longed to touch a young boy's hand and melt into his embrace.

That freak was fucking gone now, man. Gone down to hell with Dave's victim. In killing someone, he'd killed that weak part of himself, that freak who had lain in him since he was eleven years old, standing in his window, looking down at the party they were throwing on Rester Street in honor of his return. He'd felt so weak, so exposed at that party. He'd felt people were secretly laughing at him, parents smiling at him with the fakest smiles, and he could see behind their public faces that they privately pitied him and feared him and hated him, and he'd had to leave the party just to escape that hate because it made him feel like a puddle of piss.

But now another's hate would make him strong, because *now* he had another secret that was better than his old, sorry secret, the one that most people seemed to guess anyway. Now, he had a secret that made him tall, not small.

Come close, he'd feel like saying to people now, I've got a secret. Closer, and I'll whisper it in your ear:

I've killed someone.

Dave locked his eyes on the fat cop behind the mirror:

I've killed someone. And you can't prove it.

Who's weak now?

SEAN FOUND WHITEY in the office on the other side of the two-way mirror overlooking Interview Room C. Whitey stood there, one foot planted on the seat of a torn leather chair, looking in at Dave and sipping coffee.

"You do the lineup?"

"Not yet," Whitey said.

Sean came up beside him. Dave was looking directly back at them, seemed almost to be locking eyes with Whitey as if he could see him. And, even weirder, Dave was smiling. It was a small smile, but it was there.

Sean said, "Feeling bad, huh?"

Whitey looked over at him. "I've felt better."

Sean nodded.

Whitey pointed his coffee cup at him. "You've got something. I can tell, prick. Give it up."

Sean wanted to draw it out a little longer, drive Whitey a little nuts with the waiting, but in the end he didn't have the heart.

"I got someone interesting who used to work at Looney Liquors."

Whitey placed his coffee cup on the table behind him and took his foot off the chair. "Who?"

"Ray Harris."

"Ray . . . ?"

Sean felt his grin break wide across his face. "Brendan Harris's father, Sarge. And he's got a rap sheet."

23

LITTLE VINCE

WHITEY SAT UP on the empty desk across from Sean's own with the probation report open in his hand. "Raymond Matthew Harris—born September the sixth, 1955. Grew up on Twelve Mayhew Street in the East Bucky Flats. Mother, Delores, a housewife. Father, Seamus, a laborer who left the family in 1967. Predictable shit follows as the father is arrested on petty larceny in Bridgeport, Connecticut, 1973. Bunch of DUIs and D and D's follow. Father dies of a coronary in Bridgeport, 1979. Same year, Raymond marries Esther Scannell—that lucky *bastard*—and takes a job working for the MBTA as a subway car operator. First child, Brendan Seamus, born 1981. Late the same year, Raymond indicted in a scam to embezzle twenty thousand dollars in subway tokens. Charges ultimately dismissed, but Raymond is fired for cause from the MBTA. Works odd jobs after that—day laborer on a home improvement crew, stock clerk at Looney Liquors, bartender, forklift operator. Lost the forklift operator job over the disappearance of some petty cash. Again, charges filed, then dropped, Raymond gets fired. Questioned in the 1982 robbery of Looney Liquors, released on lack of evidence. Questioned in the robbery, same year, of Blanchard

Liquors in Middlesex County; once again, released on lack of evidence."

"Beginning to become known, though," Sean said.

"He's getting popular," Whitey agreed. "A known associate, one Edmund Reese, fingers Raymond in the 1983 heist of a rare comic book collection from a dealer in—"

"Fucking comic books?" Sean laughed. "You go, Raymond."

"A hundred fifty thousand dollars' worth of comic books," Whitey said.

"Oh, excuse me."

"Raymond returns said literature unharmed and is given four months, a year suspended, two months time served. Comes out of prison apparently with a wee bit of a chemical dependency problem."

"My, my."

"Cocaine, of course, this being the eighties, and that's where the rap sheet grows. Somehow Raymond's smart enough to keep whatever it is he's doing to pay for the cocaine under the radar, but not so smart he doesn't get picked up in his attempts to *procure* said narcotic. Violates his parole, does a year solid inside."

"Where he learns the error of his ways."

"Apparently not. Picked up by a joint Major Crime Unit/FBI sting for trafficking stolen goods across state lines. You're going to love this. Guess what Raymond stole. Think 1984 now."

"No hints?"

"Go with your first instinct."

"Cameras."

Whitey shot him a look. "Fucking cameras. Go get me some coffee, you're not a cop anymore."

"What then?"

"Trivial Pursuit," Whitey said. "Never saw that one coming, did you?"

"Comic books and Trivial Pursuit. Our boy's got style."

"He's got a shitload of grief, too. He stole the truck in Rhode Island, drove it into Massachusetts."

"Hence the federal interstate rap."

"Hence," Whitey said, shooting Sean another look. "They've got his balls, basically, but he does no time."

Sean sat up a bit, took his feet off his desk. "He rolled on someone?"

"Looks that way," Whitey said. "After that, nothing else on the rap sheet. Raymond's probie notes that Raymond is dutiful in appearing for his appointments until he's released from probation in late 'eighty-six. His employment records?" Whitey looked over the file at Sean.

Sean said, "Oh, I can talk now?" He opened his own file. "Employment records, IRS records, social security payments—everything comes to a dead halt in August of 1987. Poof, he disappears."

"You check nationally?"

"The request is being processed as we speak, good sir."

"What are our possibilities?"

Sean propped the soles of his shoes up on his desk again and leaned back in his chair. "One, he's dead. Two, he's in Witness Protection. Three, he went deep, deep, deep underground and just popped back into the neighborhood to pick up his gun and shoot his son's nineteen-year-old girlfriend."

Whitey tossed his file down onto the empty desk. "We don't even know if it's his gun. We don't know shit. What are we doing here, Devine?"

"We're getting up for the dance, Sarge. Come on. Don't gas out on me this early. We got a guy who was a prime suspect in a robbery eighteen years ago during which the murder weapon was used. Guy's son *dated* the victim. Guy has a rap sheet. I want to look at him and I want to look at the son. You know, the one with no alibi."

"Who passed a poly and who you and I agreed didn't have the stuff necessary to do this."

"Maybe we were wrong."

Whitey rubbed his eyes with the heels of his hands. "Man, I'm sick of being wrong."

"So you're saying you were wrong about Boyle?"

Whitey's hands remained over his eyes as he shook his head. "Ain't saying that at all. I still think the guy's a piece of shit, but whether I can tie him to Katherine Marcus's death is another matter." He lowered his hands, the puffy flesh under his eyes ringed red now. "But this Raymond Harris angle doesn't look too promising, either. Okay, we take another run at the son. Fine. And we try to track down the father. But then *what*?"

"We tie somebody to that gun," Sean said.

"Gun could be in the fucking ocean by now. I know that's what I'd do with it."

Sean tipped his head toward him. "You would've done that after you held up a liquor store eighteen years ago, though, too."

"True."

"Our guy didn't. Which means . . ."

"He ain't as bright as me," Whitey said.

"Or me."

"Jury's still out there."

Sean stretched in his chair, locking his fingers and raising his arms above his head, pushing toward the ceiling until he could feel the muscles stretch. He let loose a shudder of a yawn, and brought his head and hands back down. "Whitey," he said, trying to hold back as long as possible on the question he'd known he'd have to ask all morning.

"What's up?"

"Anything in your file on known associates?"

Whitey lifted the file off the desk and flipped it open, turned the first few pages over. " 'Known criminal associates,' " he read, " 'Reginald (aka Reggie Duke) Neil, Patrick Moraghan, Kevin "Whackjob" Sirracci, Nicholas Savage'—hmm—'Anthony Waxman . . . ' " He looked up at Sean, and Sean knew it was there. " 'James Marcus,' " Whitey said, " 'aka "Jimmy Flats," reputed leader of a criminal crew sometimes called the Rester Street Boys.' " Whitey closed the file.

Sean said, "And the hits just keep on coming, don't they?"

THE HEADSTONE Jimmy picked was simple and white. The salesman spoke in a low, respectful voice, as if he'd rather be anyplace but here, and yet he kept trying to nudge Jimmy toward more expensive stones, ones with angels and cherubs or roses engraved in the marble. "Maybe a Celtic cross," the salesman said, "a choice that's quite popular with . . ."

Jimmy waited for him to say "your people," but the salesman caught himself and finished with ". . . an awful lot of people these days."

Jimmy would have forked over the money for a mausoleum if he thought it would make Katie happy, but he knew his daughter had never been a fan of ostentation or overadornment. She'd worn simple clothes and simple jewelry, no gold, and she'd rarely used makeup unless it was a special occasion. Katie had liked things clean, with just a subtle hint of style, and that's why Jimmy chose the white and ordered the engraving in the calligraphic script, the salesman warning him that the latter choice would double the engraver's cost, and Jimmy turning his head to look down at the little vulture, backing him up a few feet as he said, "Cash or check?"

Jimmy had asked Val to drive him over, and when he left the office, he got back in the passenger seat of Val's Mitsubishi 3000 GT, Jimmy wondering for probably the tenth time how a guy in his mid-thirties could drive a car like this and not think he looked anything but silly.

"Where to next, Jim?"

"Let's get some coffee."

Val usually had some sort of bullshit rap music blaring from his speakers, the bass throbbing behind tinted windows as some middle-class black kid or white-trash wannabe sang about bitches and hos and whipping out his gat and made what Jimmy assumed were topical references to all these MTV pussies Jimmy would never have known of if he hadn't overheard Katie using their names on the phone with her girlfriends. Val kept his stereo off this morning, though, and Jimmy was grateful. Jimmy hated rap and not because it was black and from the ghetto—hell, that's where P-Funk and soul and a lotta kick-ass blues had come from—but because he couldn't for the life of him see any talent in it. You strung a bunch of limericks together of the "Man from Nantucket" variety, had a DJ scratch a few records back and forth, and threw out your chest as you spoke into a microphone. Oh, yeah, it was raw, it was street, it was the truth, motherfucker. So was pissing your name in the snow and vomiting. He'd heard some moron music critic on the radio say once that sampling was an "art form" and Jimmy, who didn't know much about art, wanted to reach through the speaker and bitch-slap the obviously white, obviously overeducated, obviously dickless pinhead. If sampling was an art form, then most of the thieves Jimmy had known growing up were artists, too. Probably be news to them.

Maybe he was just getting old. He knew it was always a first sign that your generation had passed the torch of relevancy if it couldn't understand the music of the younger one. Still, deep in his heart, he was pretty sure that wasn't it. Rap just sucked, plain and simple, and Val listening to it was a lot like Val driving this car, trying to hold on to something that had never been all that worthwhile in the first place.

They stopped at a Dunkin' Donuts and tossed their lids in the trash on the way out the door, sipped their coffee leaning against the spoiler attached to the trunk of the sports car.

Val said, "We went out last night, asked around like you said."

Jimmy tapped his fist into Val's. "Thanks, man."

Val tapped back. "It ain't just 'cause you did two years for me, Jim. Ain't just 'cause I miss your brain running things, either. Katie was my niece, man."

"I know."

"Maybe not by birth or nothing, but I loved her."

Jimmy nodded. "You guys were the best uncles any kid could have had."

"No shit?"

"No shit."

Val sipped some coffee and went silent for a bit. "Well, all right, here's the deal: looks like the cops were right about O'Donnell and Farrow. O'Donnell was in county lockup. Farrow was at a party and we personally talked to, like, nine guys who vouched for him."

"All solid?"

"Half, at least," Val said. "We also sniffed around and there's been no contracts floating along the street for a while. And, Jim, it's been a year and a half since the last time I can even remember a hired hit, so we'd a heard. You know?"

Jimmy nodded and drank some coffee.

"Now the cops have been all over this," Val said. "They're smothering the bars, the street trade around the Last Drop, everything. Every hooker I've talked to has already been questioned. Every bartender. Every single soul who was in McGills or the Last Drop that night. I mean, the law *descended,* Jim. So it's out there. Everyone's trying to remember something."

"You talk to anybody who did?"

Val held up two fingers as he took another drink. "One guy—you know Tommy Moldanado?"

Jimmy shook his head.

"Grew up in the Basin, paints houses. Anyway, he claims he saw someone staking out the parking lot of the Last Drop just before Katie left. He said the guy definitely wasn't no cop. Drove a foreign car with a dented front quarter, passenger side."

"Okay."

"Other weird thing was, I talk to Sandy Greene. 'Member her from the Looey?"

Jimmy could see her sitting in the classroom, brown pigtails, crooked teeth, always chewed her pencils until they snapped in her mouth and she had to spit out the lead.

"Yeah. What's she doing these days?"

"Hooking," Val said. "And she looks rough, man. Our age, right? And my mother looked better in her *coffin.* Anyway, she's like the oldest pro out there on that circuit near the Last Drop. She says she sort of adopted this kid. Runaway kid, works the trade."

"Kid?"

"Like eleven-, twelve-year-old boy."

"Ah, Jesus."

"Hey, that's life. Anyway, this kid, she thinks his real name is Vincent. Everyone called him 'Little Vince' except Sandy. She said he preferred 'Vincent.' And Vincent's a lot older than twelve, you know? Vincent's a pro. She says he'll fuck you up you try anything with him, keeps a razor blade tucked under his Swatch band, that sorta thing. There six nights a week. Until this Saturday, that is."

"What happened to him on Saturday?"

"No one knows. But he vanished. Sandy said he sometimes crashed at her place. She gets back there Sunday morning and his shit is gone. He blew town."

"So, he blew town. Good for him. Maybe he got out of the life."

"That's what I said. Sandy said, No, this kid was *into* it. She said he

was going to make one very scary adult, you know? But for now, he's a
kid, and he dug the work. She said if he blew town, only one thing could
have caused it and that was fear. Sandy thinks he saw something, something that terrified him, and she said that something would have to be
pretty bad, because little Vince don't scare easy."

"You got feelers out?"

"Yeah. It's hard, though. The kiddie trade ain't, like, organized. You
know? They're just living on the street, picking up a couple of bucks
however they can, blowing town whenever they feel like it. But I got people looking. We find this Vincent kid, I figure maybe he knows something about the guy sitting in the parking lot of the Last Drop, maybe he
saw the, you know, Katie's death."

"*If* it had anything to do with this guy in the car."

"Moldanado said the guy gave off a bad vibe. Something about him,
he said, even though it was dark, he couldn't see the guy good, he just
said a vibe came from that car."

A vibe, Jimmy thought. Oh, yeah, that's helpful.

"And this was just before Katie left?"

"Just before, yeah. The police, right, they sealed off the parking lot
Monday morning, had a whole team down there, scraping the asphalt."

Jimmy nodded. "So something went down in that parking lot."

"Yeah. That's what I don't get. Katie was taken off on Sydney, man.
That's like ten blocks away."

Jimmy drained his coffee cup. "What if she went back?"

"Huh?"

"To the Last Drop. I know what the prevailing theory is—she
dropped Eve and Diane, drove up Sydney, and that's when it happened.
But what if she drove back to the Last Drop first? She drove back, she
runs into the guy. He abducts her, forces her to drive back to Pen Park,
and *then* it goes down like the cops think?"

Val tossed his empty coffee cup back and forth between his hands.
"That's possible. But what brought her back to the Last Drop?"

"I don't know." They walked to the trash barrel and dumped their
cups, and Jimmy said, "What about Just Ray's kid, you find anything out
there?"

"Asked around in general about him. The kid's a mouse by all accounts. No trouble to anyone. If he wasn't so good-looking, I'm not sure anyone would even remember meeting him. Eve and Diane both said he loved her, Jim. Loved her like once-in-a-lifetime kinda love. I'll take a run at him, you want."

"Let's hold off for the time being," Jimmy said. "Watch and wait when it comes to him. Try to track down that Vincent kid."

"Yeah, okay."

Jimmy opened the passenger door, saw Val looking at him over the roof, Val holding something back, chewing it.

"What?"

Val blinked in the sunlight, smiled. "Huh?"

"You want to spit something. What is it?"

Val lowered his chin out of the sun, spread his arms on the roof. "I heard something this morning. Just before we left."

"Yeah?"

"Yeah," Val said, and looked off into the doughnut shop for a moment. "I heard those two cops were by Dave Boyle's again. You know, Sean from the Point and his partner, the fat one?"

Jimmy said, "Dave was in McGills that night, yeah. They probably just forgot to ask him something, had to come back."

Val's gaze left the doughnut shop and his eyes met Jimmy's. "They took him with them when they left, Jim. You know what I mean? Put him in the *back*seat."

MARSHALL BURDEN CAME into the Homicide Unit during lunch hour and called to Whitey as he pushed through the small gate attached to the reception desk. "You the guys looking for me?"

Whitey said, "That's us. Come on over."

Marshall Burden was a year short of his thirty and he looked it. He had the milky-wet eyes of a man who'd seen more of the world and more of himself than anyone wanted to, and he carried his tall, flabby frame like he'd rather move backward than forward, as if the limbs were at war with the brain and the brain just wanted out of the whole deal. He'd run the property room for the last seven years, but before that he'd been one of the aces of the whole State Police Department, groomed for a colonel's slot, working his way up from Narcotics to Homicide to Major Crimes without a bump in the road until one day, the story went, he just woke up scared. It was a disease that usually afflicted the guys who worked undercover and sometimes the highway troopers who suddenly couldn't pull over one more car, so sure were they that the driver had a gun in his hand and nothing left to lose. But Marshall Burden caught it somehow, too, started becoming the last guy through the door and dragging his ass to calls, freezing in stairwells as everyone else kept climbing.

He took a seat beside Sean's desk, giving off an air of spoiled fruit, and thumbed through the *Sporting News* page-a-day calendar Sean kept there, the pages going back to March.

"Devine, right?" he said without looking up.

"Yeah," Sean said. "Good to meet you. We studied some of your work in the Academy, man."

Marshall shrugged as if the memory of his old self embarrassed him. He thumbed through a few more pages. "So what's up, guys? I gotta get back in half an hour."

Whitey wheeled his chair over by Marshall Burden. "You worked a task force with the Feebs in the early eighties, right?"

Burden nodded.

"You took down a small-timer named Raymond Harris, stole a truck-load of Trivial Pursuit from a rest stop in Cranston, Rhode Island."

Burden smiled at one of the Yogi Berra quotes in the calendar. "Yeah. Trucker went to take a piss, didn't know he was staked out. The Harris guy jacked the truck and drove away, but the trucker called in, put it on the wire right away, we pulled the thing over in Needham."

"But Harris walked," Sean said.

Burden looked up at him for the first time, Sean seeing the fear and self-hatred in those milky eyes and hoping he never caught what Burden had.

"He didn't walk," Burden said. "He rolled. He rolled on the guy who'd hired him for the trucking job, guy name a Stillson, I think. Yeah, Meyer Stillson."

Sean had heard about Burden's memory—supposedly photographic—but to see the guy reach back eighteen years and pluck names out of the fog like he'd been talking about them yesterday was humbling and depressing at the same time. Guy could have run the whole show, for Christ's sake.

"So he rolled and that was it?" Whitey said.

Burden frowned. "Harris had a record. He wasn't walking just because he gave us his boss's name. No, BPD's Anti-Gang Unit stepped in to get info on another case, and he rolled again."

"On who?"

"Guy ran the Rester Street Boys, Jimmy Marcus."

Whitey looked over at Sean, one eyebrow cocked.

"This was after the counting room robbery, right?" Sean said.

"What counting room robbery?" Whitey asked.

"It's what Jimmy did time for," Sean said.

Burden nodded. "Him and another guy took off the MBTA counting room on a Friday night. In and out in two minutes. They knew what time the guards changed shifts. They knew exactly when they bagged up the cash. They had two guys out on the street who stalled the Brinks truck as it came to make the pickup. They were slick as hell and they knew too much not to have had a guy on the inside, or at least someone who'd worked for the T at some point in the previous year or two."

"Ray Harris," Whitey said.

"Yup. He gave us Stillson and he gave the BPD the Rester Street Boys."

"All of 'em?"

Burden shook his head. "No, just Marcus, but he was the brains. Cut off the head, the body dies, you know? BPD picked him up coming out of a storage warehouse the morning of the Saint Pat's parade. That was the day they planned to split up the take, so Marcus had a suitcase full of money in his hand."

"But wait," Sean said, "did Ray Harris testify in open court?"

"No. Marcus cut a deal long before it went to court. He dummied up on who he'd been working with and he took the fall. All the shit everyone *knew* he'd been behind they couldn't prove. Kid was like nineteen or something. Twenty? He'd been running that crew since he was seventeen and he'd never even been arrested. DA cut the deal for two inside, three suspended, because he knew there was a good chance they wouldn't even be able to convict in open court. Heard the Anti-Gang guys were pissed, but whatta you going to do?"

"So Jimmy Marcus never knew Ray Harris ratted him out?"

Burden looked up from the calendar again, fixed his swimming eyes on Sean with a vague contempt. "In a three-year span, Marcus pulled off something like sixteen major heists. Once, right, he hit twelve different jewelers in the Jeweler's Exchange building on Washington Street. Even now, no one knows how the fuck he did it. He had to circumvent close to twenty different alarms—alarms running off phone lines, satellites, *cellular,* which was a completely new technology back then. He was eighteen. You believe that shit? Eighteen years old and he's breaking alarm codes that pros in their forties couldn't crack. The Keldar Technics job? He and his guys went in through the roof, jammed the fire department frequencies, and then they set off the sprinkler system. Best anyone could figure at the time, they were hanging suspended up at the ceiling until the sprinkler system shorted out the motion detectors. The guy was a fucking genius. If he went to work for NASA instead of himself? We'd be taking the wife and kids on vacation to Pluto. You think a guy this smart wouldn't have figured out who fingered him? Ray Harris vanished from the face of the earth two months after Marcus rotated back into the free world. What does that tell you?"

Sean said, "It tells me you think Jimmy Marcus murdered Ray Harris."

"Or he had that midget prick, Val Savage, do it. Look, call Ed Folan at the D-7. He's a captain there now, but he used to work the Anti-Gang Unit. He can tell you all about Marcus and Ray Harris. Every cop who worked East Bucky in the eighties will tell you the same thing. If Jimmy Marcus didn't kill Ray Harris, I'm the next Jewish pope." He pushed the calendar away with his finger and stood up, hitched his pants. "I gotta go eat. You take her easy, fellas."

He walked back through the squad room, his head swiveling as he took it all in, maybe the desk he used to sit at, the board where his cases used to be listed beside everyone else's, the person he had been in this room before that person went AWOL, ended up in the property room praying for the day when he could punch that clock for the last time, go someplace where no one remembered who he could have been.

Whitey turned to Sean. "Pope Marshall the Lost?"

THE LONGER HE SAT in the rickety chair in that cold room, the more Dave realized that what he'd thought was a hangover this morning had merely been the continuation of last night's drunk. The true hangover began to set in around noon, crawling through him like tight packs of termites, taking over his bloodstream and then his circulation, squeezing his heart and picking at his brain. His mouth dried up and sweat turned his hair damp, and he could smell himself suddenly as the alcohol began to leak through his pores. His legs and arms filled with mud. His chest ached. And a wash of the downs cascaded through his skull and settled behind his eyes.

He didn't feel brave anymore. He didn't feel strong. The clarity that just two hours ago had seemed as permanent as a scar left his body and took off out of the room and down the road, only to be replaced by a dread far worse than any he'd ever experienced. He felt certain he was going to die soon and die badly. Maybe he'd stroke out right here in this chair, slam the back of his head off the floor as his body shook with convulsions and his eyes leaked blood and he swallowed his tongue so deeply no one could pull it back out. Maybe a coronary, his heart already banging against the walls of his chest like a rat in a steel box. Maybe once they let him out of here, if they ever did, he'd step out on the street, hear a horn right beside him, and be flat on his back as the thick treads of a bus tire rolled up his cheekbone and kept rolling.

Where was Celeste? Did she even know he'd been picked up and taken down here? Did she even care? And what about Michael? Did he miss his father? The worst thing about being dead was that Celeste and Michael would move on. Oh, it might hurt them for a small amount of time, but they would endure and start new lives because that's what people did every day. It was only in movies that people pined for the dead, their lives freezing up like broken clocks. In real life, your death was mundane, a forgettable event to everyone but you.

Dave sometimes wondered if the dead looked down on the ones they'd left behind and wept to see how easily their loved ones were getting along without them. Like Stanley the Giant's kid, Eugene. Was he up there in the ether somewhere with his little bald head and white hospital johnny, looking down at his dad laughing in a bar, thinking, Hey, Dad, what about me? You remember me? I lived.

Michael would get a new dad, and maybe he'd be in college and he'd tell a girl about the father who'd taught him baseball, the one he barely remembered. It happened so long ago, he'd say. So long ago.

And Celeste was certainly attractive enough to get another man. She'd have to. Loneliness, she'd tell her friends. It just got to me. And he's a nice guy. He's good with Michael. And her friends would betray Dave's memory in a flash. They'd say, Good for you, honey. It's healthy. You have to get back on that bike and move ahead with your life.

And Dave would be up there with Eugene, the two of them looking down, calling out their love in voices none of the living could hear.

Jesus. Dave wanted to huddle in the corner and hug himself. He was falling apart. He knew if those cops came back in now, he'd crack. He'd tell them anything they wanted to know if they'd just show him a little warmth and get him another Sprite.

And then the door to the interrogation room opened up on Dave and his dread and his need for human warmth, and the trooper who entered in full uniform was young and looked strong and had those trooper eyes, the kind that managed to be impersonal and imperious at the same time.

"Mr. Boyle, if you could come with me now."

Dave stood up and went to the door, his hands trembling slightly as the alcohol continued to fight its way out of him.

"Where?" he asked.

"You'll be stepping into a lineup, Mr. Boyle. Someone wants to take a look at you."

TOMMY MOLDANADO wore jeans and a green T-shirt speckled with paint. There were specks of paint in his curly brown hair and teardrops of it on his tan work boots and chips of it on the frames of his thick glasses.

It was the glasses that worried Sean. Any witness who walked into court wearing glasses might as well have put a target sign on his chest for the defense attorney. And the juries, forget about it. Experts all in regard to eyeglasses and the law thanks to *Matlock* and *The Practice,* they watched the bespectacled take the stand the same way they watched drug dealers, blacks without ties, and jailhouse rats who'd cut a deal with the DA.

Moldanado pressed his nose up against the viewing room glass and looked in at the five men in the lineup. "I can't really tell with them looking head-on. Can they turn to the left?"

Whitey flicked the switch on the dais in front of him and spoke into the microphone. "All subjects turn to the left."

The five men shifted left.

Moldanado put his palms against the glass and squinted. "Number Two. It could be Number Two. Could you get him to step closer?"

"Number Two?" Sean said.

Moldanado looked back over his shoulder at him and nodded.

The second guy in the lineup was a narc named Scott Paisner, who normally worked Norfolk County.

"Number Two," Whitey said with a sigh. "Take two steps forward."

Scott Paisner was short, bearded, and round with a rapidly receding hairline. He looked about as much like Dave Boyle as Whitey did. He turned face-front and stepped up to the glass, and Moldanado said, "Yeah, yeah. That's the guy I saw."

"You sure?"

"Ninety-five percent," he said. "It was night, you know? There are no lights in that parking lot and, hey, I was buzzed. But otherwise I'm almost positive that's the guy I saw."

"You didn't mention a beard in your statement," Sean said.

"No, but I think now that, yeah, the guy had a beard maybe."

Whitey said, "No one else in that lineup looks like the guy?"

"Shit, no," he said. "They ain't even close. What're they—cops?"

Whitey lowered his head to the dais and whispered, "Why do I even do this fucking job?"

Moldanado looked at Sean. "What? What?"

Sean opened the door behind him. "Thanks for coming down, Mr. Moldanado. We'll be in touch."

"I did good, though, right? I mean, I helped."

"Sure," Whitey said. "We'll FedEx that merit badge to you."

Sean gave Moldanado a smile and a nod and shut the door on him as soon as he crossed the threshold.

"No witness," Sean said.

"Uh, no shit."

"The physical evidence from the car won't hold up in court."

"I'm aware of that."

Sean watched Dave put a hand over his eyes and squint into the light. He looked like he hadn't slept in a month.

"Sarge. Come on."

Whitey turned from the microphone and looked at him. He was starting to look exhausted, too, the whites of his eyes gone pink.

"Fuck it," he said. "Kick him loose."

24

A BANISHED TRIBE

CELESTE SAT by the window of Nate & Nancy's Coffee Shop on Buckingham Avenue across from Jimmy Marcus's house as Jimmy and Val Savage parked Val's car half a block up and started walking back down toward the house.

If she were going to do this, actually do it, she had to get out of her chair now and approach them. She stood, her legs trembling, and her hand hit the underside of the table. She looked down at it. Trembling, too, and the skin scraped along the lower half of the thumb bone. She raised it to her lips and then turned toward the door. She still wasn't sure she could do this, say the words that she'd prepared in the motel room this morning. She'd decided to tell Jimmy only what she knew—the physical details of Dave's behavior since early Sunday morning without any conclusions as to what they meant—and allow him to make his own judgments. Without the clothes Dave had worn home that night, it didn't make much sense to go to the police. She told herself this. She told herself this because she wasn't sure the police could protect her. She had to live in this neighborhood, after all, and the only thing that could protect you from something dangerous in the neighborhood was the neighborhood itself. And if she told Jimmy, then not only he, but the Savages as well, could form a kind of moat around her that Dave would never dare cross.

She went through the door as Jimmy and Val neared their front steps. She raised her sore hand. She called Jimmy's name as she stepped into the avenue, looking like a crazy woman, she was sure—hair wild, eyes puffy and black with fear.

"Hey, Jimmy! Val!"

They turned as they reached the bottom step and looked over at her. Jimmy gave her a small, bewildered smile, and she noticed again what an open, lovely thing his smile was. It was unforced and strong and genuine. It said, I'm your friend, Celeste. How can I help?

She reached the curb and Val kissed her cheek. "Hey, cuz."

"Hey, Val."

Jimmy gave her a light peck, too, and it seemed to enter her flesh and tremble at the base of her throat.

He said, "Annabeth was trying you this morning. Couldn't get you at home or work."

Celeste nodded. "I've been, ah . . ." She looked away from Val's stunted, curious face as it peered into her own. "Jimmy, could I talk to you a sec?"

Jimmy said, "Sure," the bewildered smile returning. He turned to Val. "We'll talk about those things later, right?"

"You bet. See you soon, cuz."

"Thanks, Val."

Val went inside and Jimmy sat down on the third step, made a space for Celeste beside him. She sat and cradled her bruised hand in her lap and tried to find the words. Jimmy watched her for a bit, waiting, and then he seemed to sense that she was all bottled up, incapable of speaking her mind.

In a light voice, he said, "You know what I was remembering the other day?"

Celeste shook her head.

"I was standing up by those old stairs above Sydney. 'Member the ones where we'd all go and watch the drive-in movies, smoke some bones?"

Celeste smiled. "You were dating—"

"Oh, don't say it."

"—Jessica Lutzen and her bodacious bod, and I was seeing Duckie Cooper."

"The Duckster," Jimmy said. "Hell ever happened to him?"

"I heard he joined the marines, caught some weird skin disease overseas, lives in California."

"Huh." Jimmy tilted his chin up, his gaze gone back half his lifetime, and Celeste could suddenly see him doing the exact same thing eighteen years earlier when his hair was a little blonder and he was a whole lot crazier, Jimmy the kind of guy who'd climb telephone poles in thunderstorms, all the girls watching, praying he didn't fall. And yet even at the craziest times, there was this stillness, these sudden pauses of self-reflection, this sense one got from him, even when he was a boy, that he carefully considered everything with the exception of his own skin.

He turned and lightly slapped her knee with the back of his hand. "So what's up, dude? You look, uh . . ."

"You can say it."

"What? No, you look, well, a little tired is all." He leaned back on the step and sighed. "Hell, I guess we all do, right?"

"I spent last night at a motel. With Michael."

Jimmy stared straight ahead. "Okay."

"I dunno, Jim. I may have left Dave for good."

She noticed a change in his face, a setting of the jawbone, and she suddenly had the feeling Jimmy knew what she was going to say.

"You left Dave." His voice was a monotone now, his gaze on the avenue.

"Yeah. He's been acting, well . . . He's been acting nuts lately. He's not himself. He's starting to frighten me."

Jimmy turned to her then and the smile on his face was so icy she almost slapped it with her hand. In his eyes, she could see the boy who'd climbed those telephone poles in the rain.

"Why don't you start from the beginning?" he said. "When Dave started acting different."

She said, "What do you know, Jimmy?"

"Know?"

"You know something. You're not surprised."

The ugly smile faded and Jimmy leaned forward, his hands entwined in his lap. "I know he was taken in by the police this morning. I know he's got a foreign car with a dent in the front passenger quarter. I know he told me one story about how he fucked up his hand and he told the police another. And I know he saw Katie the night she died, but he didn't tell me that until after the police had questioned him about it." He unlocked his hands and spread them. "I don't know what all this means exactly, but it's beginning to bug me, yeah."

Celeste felt a momentary wash of pity for her husband as she pictured him in some police interrogation room, perhaps handcuffed to a table, a harsh light in his pale face. Then she saw the Dave who'd craned his head around the door last night and looked at her, tilted and crazed, and fear overrode pity.

She took a deep breath, let it out. "At three in the morning on Sunday, Dave came back to our apartment covered in someone else's blood."

It was out there now. The words had left her mouth and entered the atmosphere. They formed a wall in front of her and Jimmy and then that wall sprouted a ceiling and another wall behind them and they were suddenly cloistered within a tiny cell created by a single sentence. The noises along the avenue died and the breeze vanished, and all Celeste could smell was Jimmy's cologne and the bright May sun baked into the steps at their feet.

When he spoke, Jimmy sounded like someone's hand clenched his throat. "What did he say happened?"

She told him. She told him everything, up to and including last night's vampire madness. She told him, and she saw that every word out of her mouth became just one more word he wanted to hide from. They burned him. They entered his skin like darts. His mouth and eyes curled back from them, and the skin tightened on his face until she could see the skeleton underneath, and her body temperature dropped at an image of him lying in a coffin with long, pointed fingernails and a crumbling jaw, flowing moss for hair.

And when the tears began to fall silently down his cheeks, she resisted the urge to press his face to her neck, to feel those tears leak into her blouse and down her back.

She kept talking because she knew if she stopped, she'd stop for good, and she couldn't stop because she had to tell someone why she'd left, why she'd run from a man she'd sworn to stand by in good times and bad, a man who'd fathered her child, and told her jokes, and caressed her hand, and provided his chest for her to fall asleep on. A man who'd never complained and who'd never hit her, and who'd been a wonderful father and a good husband. She needed to tell someone how confused she was when that man seemed to vanish as if the mask that had been his face fell to the floor and a leering monstrosity peeked back at her.

She finished up by saying, "I still don't know what he did, Jimmy. I still don't know whose blood that was. I don't. Not conclusively. I just don't. But I'm so, so scared."

Jimmy turned on the step so that his upper half was propped against the wrought-iron banister. The tears had dried into his skin, and his mouth formed a small oval of shock. He stared back at Celeste with a gaze that seemed to go through her and down the avenue and fixate on something blocks away that no one else could see.

Celeste said, "Jimmy," but he waved her away and closed his eyes tight. He lowered his head and sucked oxygen into his mouth.

The cell around them evaporated, and Celeste nodded at Joan Hamilton as she walked by and gave them both a sympathetic and yet vaguely suspicious glance before clicking her shoes up the sidewalk. The sounds of the avenue returned with its beeps and door creakings, its distant calling of names.

When Celeste looked back at Jimmy, she was fixed in his gaze. His eyes were clear, his mouth closed, and he'd pulled his knees up by his chest. He rested his arms on them and she could feel a fierce and belligerent intelligence coming from him, his mind beginning to work far faster and with more originality than most people would muster in a lifetime.

"The clothes he wore are gone," he said.

She nodded. "I checked. Yeah."

He placed his chin on his knees. "How scared are you? Honestly."

Celeste cleared her throat. "Last night, Jimmy, I thought he was going to bite me. And then just keep biting."

Jimmy tilted his face so that his left cheek rested on his knees now, and he closed his eyes. "Celeste," he whispered.

"Yes?"

"Do you think Dave killed Katie?"

Celeste felt the answer rumble up through her body like last night's vomit. She felt its hot feet pound across her heart.

"Yes," she said.

Jimmy's eyes snapped open.

Celeste said, "Jimmy? God help me."

SEAN LOOKED ACROSS his desk at Brendan Harris. The kid looked confused and tired and scared, just the way Sean wanted him. He'd sent two troopers over to pick him up at his house and bring him back down here, and then he'd let Brendan sit on the other side of his desk while he scrolled down his computer screen and studied all the data he'd amassed on the kid's father, taking his time about it, ignoring Brendan, letting him sit there and fidget.

He looked back at the screen now, tapped the scroll-down key with his pencil simply for effect, and said, "Tell me about your father, Brendan."

"What?"

"Your father. Raymond senior. You remember him?"

"Barely. I was, like, six when he bailed on us."

"So you don't remember the guy."

Brendan shrugged. "I remember little things. He used to come in the house singing when he was drunk. He took me to Canobie Lake Park once and bought me cotton candy and I ate half of it and puked all over the teacup ride. He wasn't around a lot, I remember that. Why?"

Sean's eyes were back on the screen. "What else you remember?"

"I dunno. He smelled like Schlitz and Dentyne. He . . ."

Sean could hear a smile in Brendan's voice and he looked up, caught it sliding softly across his face. "He what, Brendan?"

Brendan shifted in his chair, his gaze fixed on something that wasn't in the squad room, wasn't even in the current time zone. "He used to carry all this change, you know? It weighed down his pockets, and he made noise when he walked. When I was a kid, I'd sit in the living room at the front of the house. It was a different place than where we live now. It was nice. And I'd sit there around five o'clock and keep my eyes closed until I heard him and his coins coming up the street. Then I'd bolt out of the house to see him, and if I could guess how much he had in one pocket—if I was even close, you know?—he'd give it to me." Brendan's smile widened and he shook his head. "The man had a lot of change."

"What about a gun?" Sean said. "Your father have a gun?"

The smile froze and Brendan's eyes narrowed at Sean like he didn't understand the language. "What?"

"Did your father have a gun?"

"No."

Sean nodded and said, "You seem pretty sure for someone who was only six when he left."

Connolly entered the squad room carrying a cardboard box. He walked over to Sean and placed the box on Whitey's desk.

"What is it?" Sean said.

"A bunch of stuff," Connolly said, peering inside. "CSS reports, ballistics, fingerprint analysis, the 911 tape, a bunch of stuff."

"You already said that. What's up on the fingerprints?"

"No matches to anyone in the computer."

"You ran it through the national database?"

Connolly said, "*And* Interpol. Zip. There's one real flawless latent we pulled off the door. It's a thumb. If it's the doer, he's short."

"Short," Sean said.

"Yup. Short. Could be anyone's, though. We pulled six clean ones, not a match on any of 'em."

"You listen to the 911?"

"No. Should I?"

"Connolly, you should familiarize yourself with everything and anything that has to do with the case, man."

Connolly nodded. "You gonna listen to it?"

Sean said, "That's what we got you for." He turned back to Brendan Harris. "About your father's gun."

Brendan said, "My father didn't have a gun."

"Really?"

"Yeah."

"Oh," Sean said, "then I guess we were misinformed. By the way, Brendan, you talk to your father much?"

Brendan shook his head. "Never. He said he was going out for a drink, and he took off, left my mother and me behind, and her pregnant, too."

Sean nodded as if he could feel his pain. "But your mother never filed a missing persons report."

"That's 'cause he wasn't missing," Brendan said, some fight coming into his eyes. "He told my mother he didn't love her. He told her she was always harping on him. Two days later, he leaves."

"She never tried to find him? Nothing like that?"

"No. He sends money, so fuck it."

Sean took his pencil away from the keyboard and laid it flat on his desk. He looked at Brendan Harris, trying to read the kid, getting nothing back but a whiff of depression and residual anger.

"He sends money?"

Brendan nodded. "Once a month like clockwork."

"From where?"

"Huh?"

"The envelopes the money comes in. Where are they sent from?"

"New York."

"Always?"

"Yeah."

"Is it cash?"

"Yeah. Five hundred a month mostly. More at Christmas."

Sean said, "Does he ever write a note?"

"No."

"So how do you know it's him?"

"Who else would send us money every month? He's guilty. My ma says he was always that way—he'd do shitty things, think that just because he felt bad about them it absolved him. You know?"

Sean said, "I want to see one of the envelopes the money came in."

"My mother throws 'em away."

Sean said, "Shit," and swiveled the computer screen out of his line of vision. Everything about the case was bugging him—Dave Boyle as a suspect, Jimmy Marcus's being the father of the victim, the victim herself having been killed with her boyfriend's father's gun. And then he thought of something else that bugged him, though not in any way pertinent to the case.

"Brendan," he said, "if your father abandoned the family while your mother was pregnant, why'd she name the baby after him?"

Brendan's gaze drifted off into the squad room. "My mom ain't entirely *there*. You know? She tries and all, but . . ."

"Okay . . ."

"She says she named him Ray to remind herself."

"Of what?"

"Men." He shrugged. "How if you give 'em half a chance, they'll fuck you over just to prove they can."

"But when your brother turned out mute, how'd that make her feel?"

"Pissed," Brendan said, and a tiny smile played on his lips. "Kinda proved her point, though. Least in her mind." He touched the paperclip tray on the edge of Sean's desk, and the tiny smile vanished.

"Why you asking me if my father had a gun?"

Sean was suddenly tired of games and being polite and cautious. "You know why, kid."

"No," Brendan said. "I don't."

Sean leaned across the desk, barely resisting an inexplicable desire to keep going, to lunge at Brendan Harris and squeeze his throat in his hand. "The gun that killed your girlfriend, Brendan, was the same gun your father used in a robbery eighteen years ago. You want to tell me about that?"

"My father didn't have a gun," he said, but Sean could see something beginning to go to work in the kid's brain.

"No? Bullshit." He slapped the desk hard enough to jerk the kid in his chair. "You say you loved Katie Marcus? Let me tell you what I love, Brendan. I love my clearance rate. I love my ability to put down cases in seventy-two hours. Now you are fucking lying to me."

"No, I'm not."

"Yes, you are, kid. You know your father was a thief?"

"He was a subway—"

"He was a fucking thief. He worked with Jimmy Marcus. Who was also a fucking thief. And now Jimmy's daughter is killed with your father's gun?"

"My father didn't have a gun."

"Fuck you!" Sean bellowed, and Connolly shot up in his chair, looked over at them. "You want to bullshit someone, kid? Bullshit your cell."

Sean took his keys from his belt and tossed them over his head at Connolly.

"Lock this maggot up."

Brendan stood. "I didn't do anything."

Sean watched Connolly step up behind the kid, tensing on the balls of his feet.

"You got no alibi, Brendan, and you had a prior relationship with the victim, and she was shot with your father's gun. Until I got better, I'll take you. Have a rest, think about the statements you just made to me."

"You can't lock me up." Brendan looked behind him at Connolly. "You can't."

Connolly looked back at Sean, wide-eyed, because the kid was right. Technically, they couldn't lock him up unless they charged him. And they had nothing to charge him with, really. It was against the law in this state to charge anyone with suspicion.

But Brendan didn't know any of that, and Sean gave Connolly a look that said: Welcome to Homicide, new boy.

Sean said, "You don't tell me something right now, kid, I'm doing it."

Brendan opened his mouth, and Sean saw a dark knowledge pass through him like an electric eel. Then his mouth closed, and he shook his head.

"Suspicion of capital murder," Sean said to Connolly. "Jail his ass."

DAVE GOT BACK to his empty apartment in the mid-afternoon and went straight to the fridge for a beer. He hadn't eaten anything and his stomach felt hollow and bubbling with air. Not the best conditions under which to throw back a beer, but Dave needed one. He needed to soften the edge in his head and take the crimps out of his neck, ease the wild-rat banging of his heart.

The first one went down easy as he walked around the empty apartment. Celeste could have come home while he was gone and then went off to work, and he thought of calling Ozma's to see if she was in there now, cutting heads and chatting with the ladies, flirting with Paolo, the gay guy who worked the same shifts as she did and flirted in that loose but not entirely harmless way gay men did. Or maybe he'd go down to Michael's school, give him a big wave and a hug, then walk him back toward home, stop for chocolate milk on the way.

But Michael wasn't in school and Celeste wasn't at work. Dave somehow knew that they were hiding from him, so he finished his second beer sitting at the kitchen table, feeling it work its way into his body, calming everything, turning the air in front of him a tad silver and a tad swirly.

He should have told her. Right from the start, he should have told his wife what had really happened. He should have had faith in her. Not many wives stood by has-been high school ballplayers who'd been molested as children and couldn't hold down a decent job. But Celeste had. Just the thought of her over the sink the other night, washing those clothes, saying she was taking care of the evidence, babe—Jesus, she was something. How could Dave have lost sight of that? How did you get to the point where you'd been around someone for so long that you couldn't even see them?

Dave got the third and last beer out of the fridge and walked around the apartment some more, his body filling with love for his wife and love for his son. He wanted to curl up against his wife's naked body as she stroked his hair and tell her how much he'd missed her in that interrogation room with its cracked chair and its cold. Earlier, he'd thought he'd wanted human warmth, but the truth was he'd just wanted Celeste's warmth. He wanted to wrap her body around his and make her smile and kiss her eyelids and caress her back and smother himself with her.

It's not too late, he'd tell her when she came home. My brain's just been miswired recently, all jumbled up. This beer in my hand ain't helping matters, I suppose, but I need it until I have you again. And then I'll quit. I'll quit drinking and I'll take computer classes or something, get a good white-collar job. The National Guard offers tuition reimbursement, and I can do that. I can do one weekend a month and a few weeks in the summer for my family. For my family, I can do that standing on my head. It'll help me get back into shape, lose the beer weight, clear my mind. And when I get that white-collar job, I'll move us out of here, out of this whole neighborhood with its steadily rising rents and stadium deals and gentrification. Why fight it? They'll push us out sooner or later. Push us out and make a Crate & Barrel world for themselves, discuss their summer homes at the cafés and in the aisles of the whole-food markets.

We'll go someplace good, though, he'd tell Celeste. We'll go someplace clean where we can raise our son. We'll start fresh. And I'll tell you what happened, Celeste. It's not pretty, but it's not as bad as you think. I'll tell you that I have some scary, perverse things in my head and maybe

I need to see someone about them. I have wants that disgust me, but I'm trying, honey. I'm trying to be a good man. I'm trying to bury the Boy. Or at the very least, teach him something about compassion.

Maybe that's what the guy in the Cadillac had been looking for—a little compassion. But the Boy Who'd Escaped from Wolves wasn't about any fucking compassion Saturday night. He'd had that gun in his hand and he'd hit the guy in the Cadillac through his open window, Dave hearing bone crack as the red-haired kid scrambled up and out through the passenger door, stood there with his mouth agape as Dave hit the guy again and again. He'd reached in and pulled him out through the door by his hair, and the guy hadn't been as helpless as he'd pretended. He'd been playing possum, and Dave only saw the knife as it sliced through his shirt and into his flesh. It was a switchblade, feebly swung, but sharp enough to cut Dave before he rammed his knee into the guy's wrist, pinned his arm against the car door. When the knife fell to the pavement, Dave kicked it under the car.

The red-haired kid looked scared, but excited too, and Dave, enraged beyond reason now, brought the butt of the gun down on top of the guy's head so hard, he cracked the handle. The guy rolled onto his stomach, and Dave hopped on his back, feeling the wolf, hating this man, this freak, this fucking degenerate child molester, getting a good grip on the bastard's hair and pulling his head up and then ramming it down into the pavement. Just ramming it, over and over again, pulverizing this guy, this Henry, this George, this, oh Jesus, this Dave, this Dave.

Die, you motherfucker. Die, die, die.

The red-haired kid ran off then, Dave turning his head and realizing the words were coming out of his mouth. "Die, die, die, die, die." Dave watched the kid run off through the parking lot and he scrambled after him, his hands dripping with the guy's blood. He wanted to tell the red-haired kid that he'd done this for him. He'd saved him. And he would protect him forever if that's what he wanted.

He stood in the alley behind the bar, out of breath, knowing the kid was long gone. He looked up at the night sky. He said, "Why?"

Why put me here? Why give me this life? Why give me this disease, a disease that I despise, in particular, more than any other? Why scramble my brain with moments of beauty and tenderness and intermittent love for my child and my wife—glimpses, really, of a life that could have been mine if that car hadn't rolled down Gannon Street and taken me to that basement? Why?

Answer me, please. Oh, please, please, answer me.

But, of course, there was nothing. Nothing but silence and the drip of gutters and the light rain turning stronger.

He walked back out of the alley a few minutes later and found the man lying beside his car.

Wow, Dave thought. I killed him.

But then the guy rolled over onto his side, gasping like a fish. He had blond hair and a pillow for a belly on an otherwise slim frame. Dave tried to remember what his face had looked like before he'd plunged his hand through the open window and hit him with the gun. He remembered only that his lips had seemed too red and too wide.

The guy's face was gone now, though. It looked like it had been pressed against a jet engine, and Dave felt a wave of nausea as he watched this bloody thing suck at the air, heaving.

The guy didn't seem to be aware of Dave standing over him. He rolled onto his knees and started crawling. He crawled toward the trees behind the car. He crawled up the small embankment and put his hands on the chain-link fence that separated the parking lot from the scrap metal company on the other side. Dave took off the flannel shirt he was wearing over his T-shirt. He wrapped it around the gun as he walked toward the faceless creature.

The faceless creature reached up another rung in the fence, and then his energy left him. He fell back down and tilted to his right, ended up sitting against the fence, his legs splayed, his faceless face watching Dave come.

"No," he whispered. "No."

But Dave could tell he didn't mean it. He was as exhausted with who he'd become as Dave was.

The Boy knelt in front of the guy and placed the wrapped-up ball of flannel shirt against his torso, just above the abdomen, Dave floating above them now, watching.

"Please," the guy croaked.

"Sssh," Dave said, and the Boy pulled the trigger.

The faceless creature's body jerked hard enough to kick Dave in the armpit, and then the air left it with the whistle of a kettle.

And the Boy said, Good.

It was only once he'd manhandled the guy into the Honda's trunk that Dave realized he should have used the guy's Cadillac. He'd already rolled up its windows and shut off the engine and then wiped down the front seat and everything he'd touched with the flannel shirt. But what was the point of riding around in his Honda with the guy in the trunk, trying to find a place to dump him, when the answer was right in front of him?

So Dave backed his car in beside the Caddy, his eyes on the side door of the bar, no one having come out for a while. He popped his trunk, then popped the Caddy's trunk, and pulled the body from one car to the other. He shut the two trunks and wrapped the switchblade and his gun in the flannel shirt, tossed it on the Honda's front seat, and got the hell out of there.

He threw the shirt and knife and the gun off the Roseclair Street Bridge and into the Penitentiary Channel, realizing only later that as he'd been doing that, Katie Marcus was probably in the process of dying herself in the park below. And then he'd driven home, certain that any minute someone would find the car and the body in the trunk.

He'd driven by the Last Drop late Sunday, and there was a car parked beside the Caddy, the lot otherwise empty. But he recognized the other car as belonging to Reggie Damone, one of the bartenders. The Caddy looked innocent, forgotten. Later that same day, he'd gone back, and felt like he was having a heart attack when he saw an empty slot where the Caddy used to be. He realized he couldn't ask about it, even casually, like, "Hey, Reggie, you guys tow if a car's in your lot too long?" and then he realized whatever had happened to it, there was nothing to connect it to him anymore.

Nothing but the red-haired kid.

But as time had passed, it occurred to him that even though the kid had been scared, he'd been pleased, too, excited. He was on Dave's side. He wasn't anything to worry about.

And now the cops had nothing. They didn't have a witness. They didn't have the evidence from Dave's car, not the kind they could use in court anyway. So Dave could relax. He could talk to Celeste and come clean and let the chips fall where they may, offer himself up to his wife and hope she'd accept him as flawed but trying to change. As a good man who'd done a bad thing for a good reason. As a man who was trying his damnedest to slay the vampire in his soul.

I will quit driving by parks and public swimming pools, Dave told himself as he drained his third beer. He held up the empty can. I will quit this, too.

But not today. Today he was already three beers in and, what the hell, Celeste didn't look like she'd be coming home soon. Maybe tomorrow. That'd be good. Give them both some space, time to heal and repair. She'd come home to a new man, an improved Dave with no more secrets.

"Because secrets are poison," he said aloud in the kitchen where he'd last made love to his wife. "Secrets are walls." And then with a smile: "And I'm all out of beer."

He felt good, jaunty almost, as he left the house to walk up to Eagle Liquors. It was a gorgeous day, the sun flooding the street. When they'd been kids, the el tracks used to run down here, splitting Crescent in the center and piling it with soot and blotting out the sky. It only added to the sense one got of the Flats as a place cloaked from the rest of the world, tucked under it like a banished tribe, free to live any way it chose as long as it did so in exile.

Once they'd removed the tracks, the Flats had risen into the light, and for a while they'd thought that was a good thing. So much less soot, so much more sun, skin looked healthier. But without the cloak, everyone could look in on them, appreciate their brick row houses and view of the Penitentiary Channel and proximity to downtown. Suddenly they weren't an underground tribe. They were prime real estate.

Dave would have to think about how that had happened when he got back home, formulate a theory with his twelve-pack. Or he could find a cool bar, sit in the dark on a bright day and order a burger, chat with the bartender, see if the two of them together could figure out when the Flats had started slipping away, when the whole world had started revolving past them.

Maybe that's what he'd do. Sure! Take a leather seat at a mahogany bar and while away the afternoon. He'd plan his future. He'd plan his family's future. He'd figure out each and every way in which he could atone. It was amazing how friendly three beers could be after a long, hard day. They were taking Dave by the hand as he walked up the hill toward Buckingham Avenue. They were saying, Hey, ain't it great to be us? Ain't it just the flat-out balls to be turning a new leaf, shedding yourself of soiled secrets, ready to renew your vows to your loved ones and become the man you always knew you could be? Why, it's just terrific.

And look who we have ahead of us, idling at the corner in his shiny sports car. He's smiling at us. That's Val Savage, smiling away, waving us over! Come on. Let's go say hi.

"Dandy Dave Boyle," Val said as Dave approached the car. "How they hanging, brother?"

"Always to the left," Dave said, and squatted down by the car. He rested his elbows on the slot where the window had descended into the door and peered in at Val. "What're you up to?"

Val shrugged. "Not much, man. Was looking for someone to grab a beer with, maybe a bite to eat."

Dave couldn't believe this. Here he'd been thinking the same thing. "Yeah?"

"Yeah. You could go for a few pops, maybe a game of pool, right, Dave?"

"Sure."

Dave was a bit surprised, actually. He got along with Jimmy and Val's brother Kevin, even sometimes with Chuck, but he never remembered Val showing anything but complete apathy in his presence. It must be Katie, he figured. In death, she was bringing them all together. They were united in their loss, forging bonds through the sharing of tragedy.

"Hop in," Val said. "We'll hit a place I know across town. Good bar. A buddy of mine owns it."

"Across town?" Dave looked back up the empty street he'd just come down. "Well, I'll have to get home at some point."

"Sure, sure," Val said. "I'll take you back whenever you want. Come on. Hop in. We'll have ourselves a boys' night in the middle of the day."

Dave smiled and took the smile with him as he walked around the front of Val's car toward the passenger door. Boys' night in the middle of the day. Exactly what was called for. Him and Val, hanging like old pals. And that was one of the great things about a place like the Flats, the thing he feared would be lost—the way old feelings and entire pasts could be laid to rest with time, as you aged, once you realized that everything *was* changing and the only things that remained the same were the people you'd grown up with and the place you'd come from. The neighborhood. May it live forever, Dave thought as he opened the door, if only in our minds.

25

TRUNK BOY

WHITEY AND SEAN had a late lunch in Pat's Diner, one highway exit down from the barracks. Pat's had been around since World War II and had been a hangout for the Staties so long that Pat the Third liked to say his may have been the only family of restaurateurs to go three full generations without getting robbed.

Whitey swallowed a hunk of cheeseburger and chased it with his soda. "You don't think for a second the kid did it, do you?"

Sean took a bite of his tuna sandwich. "I know he was lying to me. I think he knows something about that gun. And I think—just possibly now—that his old man's still alive."

Whitey dipped an onion ring in some tartar sauce. "The five hundred a month from New York?"

"Yeah. You know what that adds up to over the years? Almost eighty grand. Who's going to send that if it ain't the father?"

Whitey dabbed his lips with a napkin and then dove back into his cheeseburger, Sean wondering how the guy had managed to dodge a heart attack so far, eating and drinking the way he did, pulling seventy-hour weeks when a case sank its teeth into him.

"Let's say he is alive," Whitey said.

"Let's."

"What's this, then—some grand mastermind plot to get back at Jimmy Marcus for something by wasting his daughter? What, we're starring in a movie now?"

Sean chuckled. "Who would play you, you think?"

Whitey sucked his soda through a straw until it slurped against the ice. "I think about that a lot, you know. It could happen, we bust this case, Supercop. Phantom from New York kinda shit? You *know* we'd be up there on the big screen. And Brian Dennehy would be all over the chance to play me."

Sean considered him. "That's not entirely insane," he said, wondering how he'd never seen it before. "You're not as tall, Sarge, but you got the gut."

Whitey nodded and pushed his plate away. "I'm thinking one of those *Friends* pussies could play you. You know, guys look like they spend an hour every morning clipping their nose hair and plucking their eyebrows, get pedicures once a week? Yeah, one of them would do just fine."

"Jealous."

"That's the thing, though," Whitey said. "This Ray Harris angle is such a curve. It's got a probability quotient of, like, six."

"Out of ten?"

"Out of a thousand. Backtrack, okay? Ray Harris rats out Jimmy Marcus. Marcus finds out, gets out of the stir, puts a hit on Ray. Harris, what, he gets away somehow, goes to New York, finds a steady enough job to send five bills home each and every month for the next thirteen years? Then one day he wakes up and goes, 'Okay. Payback time,' and gets on a bus, comes here, and smokes Katherine Marcus. And not just in the regular everyday kinda way, but he smokes her with extreme prejudice. That was psycho rage in that park. And then, old Ray—and I do mean old, he's gotta be forty-five, humping through that park after her—he just gets on a bus and goes back to New York with his gun? Did you *check* New York?"

Sean nodded. "No matches on the social, no credit cards in his name, no employment history for a guy with his name and age. NYPD and State have never arrested anyone matching his prints."

"But you think he killed Katherine Marcus."

Sean shook his head. "No. I mean, not for sure. I don't even know if he's alive. I'm just saying I think he *could be*. And it's real likely that the murder weapon was his gun. And I think Brendan knows something, and he definitely has no one who can confirm that he was home in bed when Katie Marcus was murdered. So I'm hoping he spends enough time in that cell, he'll tell us a few things."

Whitey let out a burp that ripped the air.

"You're a prince, Sarge."

Whitey shrugged. "We don't even know that Ray Harris held up that liquor store eighteen years ago. We don't know if that was his gun. It's all conjecture. It's circumstantial at best. Never hold up in court. Hell, a good ADA wouldn't even present it."

"Yeah, but it feels right."

"Feels." He looked over Sean's shoulder as the door behind Sean opened. "Oh, Jesus, the moron twins."

Souza came around the side of their booth with Connolly a few steps behind.

"And you said it was nothing, Sarge."

Whitey put a hand behind his ear, looked up at Souza. "What's that, boy? My hearing, you know?"

"We ran the tow records from the parking lot of the Last Drop," Souza said.

"That's BPD jurisdiction," Whitey said. "What I tell you about that?"

"We found a car ain't been claimed yet, Sarge."

"And?"

"We had the attendant go out to double-check it was still there. He came back on the phone, said the trunk's leaking."

"Leaking what?" Sean said.

"Don't know, but he said it smelled awful ripe."

THE CADILLAC WAS two-toned, a white hardtop over a midnight blue body. Whitey bent by the passenger window, his hands on either side of his eyes. "I'd say that's a suspicious-looking brown smear by the driver's door console."

Connolly, standing by the trunk, said, "Jesus, you smell this shit? It's reeking like friggin' low tide at Wollaston."

Whitey came around the back just as the tow lot attendant put the lock-puncher into Sean's hand.

Sean stepped up beside Connolly, moving the man out of the way as he said, "Use your tie."

"What?"

"Over your mouth and nose, man. Use your tie."

"What are you using?"

Whitey pointed at his own shiny upper lip. "We put Vicks on during the ride over. Sorry, boys, all out."

Sean positioned the rim at the end of the lock-punch. He slipped it over the Cadillac's trunk lock and drove it home, felt the metal slide over metal and then catch, grip the entire lock cylinder.

"We in?" Whitey said. "First try and everything?"

"We're in." Sean pulled back hard, taking the lock cylinder with him, getting a glimpse of the hole he'd left behind before the latch clicked free and the trunk lid rose up and that low-tide smell was replaced by something worse, a combined stench of swamp gas and boiled meat left rotting in a pile of scrambled eggs.

"Jesus." Connolly pressed his tie over his face and stepped back from the car.

Whitey said, "Monte Cristo sandwich, anyone?" and Connolly turned the shade of grass.

Souza was cool, though. He stepped up to the trunk, one hand pinching his nose, and said, "Where's the guy's face?"

"That's his face," Sean said.

The guy was curled in a fetal position, his head tilted back and to the side as if his neck were broken, the rest of his body curled in the opposite direction. His suit was top-shelf, his shoes, too, and Sean guessed his age at around fifty after a glance at his hands and hairline. He noticed a hole in the back of the guy's suit jacket, and he used a pen to lift the fabric away from his back. Sweat and heat yellowed the white shirt underneath, but Sean found a match for the hole in the jacket, halfway up the back, the shirt puckered into the flesh there.

"Got an exit wound, Sarge. Definite gunshot." He peered into the trunk for a bit. "I can't find the shell, though."

Whitey turned to Connolly as the man started to sway. "Get in your car and head back to the parking lot of the Last Drop. Inform the BPD first thing. We don't need a fucking turf war. Work your way out from where you found the majority of the blood in that parking lot. There's a good chance there's a bullet there somewhere, Trooper. You got me?"

Connolly nodded, gulping air.

Sean said, "Bullet entered the sternum through the lowest quadrant, almost dead center."

Whitey said to Connolly, "Get CSS down there and as many troopers as you can without pissing off the BPD. You find that bullet, and you personally accompany it to the lab."

Sean craned his head into the trunk and took a good look at the pulverized face. "Judging by the amount of gravel, someone rammed his face off the pavement until they couldn't ram no more."

Whitey put his hand on Connolly's shoulder. "Tell BPD they're going to need a full Homicide crew down here—techs, photographers, the on-call ADA, and the ME. Tell them Sergeant Powers requests someone who can give me a blood type on-scene. Go."

Connolly was elated to just get the hell away from the smell. He ran to his cruiser, had it in gear and fishtailing out of the lot in under a minute.

Whitey shot a roll of film around the outside of the car and then nodded at Souza. Souza slid on a pair of surgical gloves and used a slim jim to pop the passenger door lock.

"You find any ID?" Whitey asked Sean.

Sean said, "Wallet in his back pocket. Take some shots while I get my gloves on."

Whitey came around and photographed the body, then let the camera hang from the strap around his neck as he scribbled a crime-scene diagram in his report pad.

Sean pulled the wallet from the corpse's back pocket and flipped it open as Souza called from the front of the car: "Registration's in the name of August Larson of Three-two-three Sandy Pine Lane in Weston."

Sean looked down at the driver's license. "Same guy."

Whitey looked over his shoulder. "He got an organ donor card in there, anything like that?"

Sean searched through credit cards and video club cards, a health club membership ID, AAA card, finally found a Tufts Health Plan ID. He held it up so Whitey could see it.

"Blood type, 'A.'"

"Souza," Whitey said. "Call Dispatch. Put out an APB on David Boyle, Fifteen Crescent Street, East Buckingham. White male, brown hair, blue eyes, five-foot-ten, a hundred-sixty-five pounds. Should be considered armed and dangerous."

"Armed and dangerous?" Sean said. "I doubt it, Sarge."

Whitey said, "Tell that to trunk boy here."

BPD HEADQUARTERS was only eight blocks away from the tow lot, so five minutes after Connolly had left, a battalion of cruisers and unmarked cars came through the gates, followed by the City Medical Examiner's van and a CSS truck. Sean took off his gloves and stepped back from the trunk as soon as he saw them. It was their show now. They wanted to ask Sean any questions, fine, but otherwise, he was out of it.

The first Homicide dick out of a tan Crown Vic was Burt Corrigan, a warhorse from Whitey's generation with a similar history of blown relationships and bad diet. He shook Whitey's hand, the two of them Thursday night regulars at JJ Foley's and members of the same dart league.

Burt said to Sean, "You ticket this car yet? Or you going to wait till after the funeral?"

"Good one," Sean said. "Who writes them for you these days, Burt?"

Burt slapped his shoulder as he came around the back of the car. He looked in, took a sniff, and said, "Funky."

Whitey stepped up to the trunk. "We think the murder took place in the parking lot of the Last Drop in East Bucky on early Sunday morning."

Burt nodded. "Didn't one of our forensic teams meet your guys out there Monday afternoon?"

Whitey nodded. "Same case. You sent guys over today?"

"Few minutes ago, yeah. Supposed to meet a Trooper Connolly and search for a bullet?"

"Yup."

"You put a name out on the wires, too, right?"

"David Boyle," Whitey said.

Burt looked in at the dead guy's face. "We'll need all your case notes, Whitey."

"No problem. I'll hang with you for a bit, see how it plays out."

"You bathe today?"

"First thing."

"All right then." He looked over at Sean. "What about you?"

Sean said, "I got a guy in holding I want to talk to. This is yours now. I'll take Souza back with me."

Whitey nodded and walked with him toward their car. "We tie Boyle to this, might turn him on the Marcus murder. Get ourselves a twofer."

Sean said, "A double homicide ten blocks apart?"

"Maybe she walked out of the bar and saw it."

Sean shook his head. "Timeline's all fucked-up. If Boyle killed that guy, he did it between one-thirty and one-fifty-five. Then he'd have to drive ten blocks, find Katie Marcus just driving down the street at one-*forty*-five. I don't buy it."

Whitey leaned against the side of their car. "Yeah, I don't either."

"Plus, the hole coming out of that guy's back? It was small. Too small for a thirty-eight, you ask me. Different guns, different doers."

Whitey nodded, looking down at his shoes. "You're going to take another run at the Harris kid?"

"Keeps coming back around to his father's gun."

"Maybe get a picture of the father? Have someone do an age-progression, float that around. See if someone's seen him."

Souza came around and opened the passenger door. "I'm with you, Sean?"

Sean nodded, turned back to Whitey. "It's a little thing."

"What's that?"

"Whatever we're missing. It's a minor detail. I figure it out, I'll close this."

Whitey smiled. "What's the last open homicide you got on your plate, kid?"

The name popped off Sean's tongue. "Eileen Fields, eight months cold."

"They can't all be dunkers," Whitey said, and started walking back toward the Cadillac. "Know what I mean?"

BRENDAN'S TIME in the holding cell hadn't been kind to him. He looked smaller and younger, but meaner, too, as if he'd seen things in there that he'd never wished to know existed. But Sean had been careful to have him tossed in an empty cell, away from the dregs and junkies, so he had no idea what could have been so horrible for him, unless he really couldn't handle isolation.

"Where's your father?" Sean said.

Brendan chewed a nail and shrugged. "New York."

"Haven't seen him?"

Brendan went to work on another nail. "Not since I was six."

"Did you kill Katherine Marcus?"

Brendan dropped the finger from his mouth and stared at Sean.

"Answer me."

"No."

"Where's your father's gun?"

"I don't know anything about my father having a gun."

There was no blinking this time. He didn't avert his eyes from Sean's. He stared into Sean's face with a kind of cruel and beaten fatigue that allowed Sean to sense a potential for violence in the kid for the first time since he'd met him.

What the hell had happened in that holding cell?

Sean said, "Why would your father want to kill Katie Marcus?"

"My father," Brendan said, "didn't kill anyone."

"You know something, Brendan. And you're not telling me. Tell you what, let's see if the polygraph's free right now. We'll ask you a few more questions."

Brendan said, "Let me talk to a lawyer."

"In a minute. Let's—"

Brendan repeated it. "Let me talk to a lawyer. Now."

Sean kept his voice level. "Sure. You got anyone in mind?"

"My mom knows one. Let me make my phone call."

Sean said, "Look, Brendan—"

"Now," Brendan said.

Sean sighed and pushed his phone across the desk. "Dial nine first."

BRENDAN'S LAWYER was an old Irish blowhard who'd been chasing ambulances since the days they'd been drawn by horses, but he'd been around enough to know Sean didn't have the right to hold his client on lack of alibi and nothing else.

Sean said, "Hold him?"

"You put my client in a cell," the lawyer said.

"We didn't lock it or nothing," Sean said. "Kid wanted a look."

The lawyer made a face like Sean had disappointed him and then he and Brendan walked out of the squad room, not looking back once. Sean read through some case files, the words making no impact. He closed the files and leaned back in his chair, shut his eyes, saw his dream Lauren and his dream child in his head. He could smell them, he really could.

He opened his wallet, pulled out a slip of paper with Lauren's cell phone number on it, placed it on his desk, and flattened the creases with his hand. He'd never wanted kids. Outside of priority boarding on an airline, he couldn't see the upside to them. They took over your life and filled you with terror and weariness and people acted like having one was a blessed event and talked about them in the reverent tones they once reserved for gods. When it came down to it, though, you had to remember that all those assholes cutting you off in traffic and walking the streets and shouting in bars and turning their music up too loud and mugging you and raping you and selling you lemon cars—all those assholes were just children who'd aged. No miracle. Nothing sacred in that.

Besides, he wasn't even sure she was his. He'd never taken the paternity test, because his pride said, Fuck that. Take a test to prove I'm a father? Could it get any more undignified? Uh, excuse me, I need to get some blood drawn because my wife was fucking another guy and got pregnant.

Fuck it. Yeah, he missed her. Yeah, he loved her. And yeah, he'd dreamed of holding his child. So what? Lauren had betrayed him and then she'd abandoned him and she'd had a baby while she was gone, and still, she'd never apologized. Still, she'd never said, Sean, I was wrong. I'm sorry I hurt you.

And had Sean hurt her? Well, yeah, of course. When he first found out about the affair, he'd come damn close to hitting her, pulling back his fist at the last moment and putting it in his pocket, Lauren seeing the urge in his face, though. And all those things he'd called her. Jesus.

But still, his anger, his pushing her away was *reactive*. He had been wronged. Not her.

Right? He gave it another few seconds of thought: Right.

He put the number back in his wallet and closed his eyes again, drifted off in his chair. He was woken by steps in the hallway and opened his eyes as Whitey rolled into the squad room. Sean could see the booze in his eyes before he smelled it on his breath. Whitey dropped into his chair and threw his feet up on the desk, kicked aside the box of miscellaneous evidence Connolly had dropped off early this afternoon.

"Long fucking day," he said.

"You find him?"

"Boyle?" Whitey shook his head. "No. Landlord said he heard him go out about three, never came back. Said the wife and kid ain't been around in a while either. We called his work. He works a Wednesday-through-Sunday rotation, so they ain't seen him." He belched. "He'll turn up."

"What about the bullet?"

"We found one at the Last Drop. Problem is, it hit a metal post behind where the guy was shot. Ballistics said maybe they can ID it, maybe not." He shrugged. "The Harris kid?"

"Lawyered up."

"Did he now?"

Sean came over to Whitey's desk, started sifting through the box. "No footprints," he said. "Fingerprints don't match anyone on file. Gun was last used in a robbery eighteen years ago. I mean, what the fuck?" He dropped the ballistics report back into the box. "The only guy without an alibi is the only guy I don't suspect."

"Go home," Whitey said. "Really."

"Yeah, yeah." He took the 911 cassette tape out of the box.

"What's that?" Whitey said.

"Snoop Dogg."

"I thought he was dead."

"That's Tupac."

"Hard to keep up."

Sean placed the tape in the recorder on the corner of his desk and pressed play.

"Nine-one-one, police services. What is the nature of your emergency?"

Whitey stretched a rubber band over his finger and fired it at the ceiling fan.

"There's like this car with blood in it and, ah, the door's open, and, ah—"

"What's the location of the car?"

"In the Flats. By Pen Park. Me and my friend found it."

"Is there a street address?"

Whitey yawned into his fist and reached for another rubber band. Sean stood up and stretched, wondered what he had in the fridge for dinner.

"Sydney Street. There's blood in there and the door's open."

"What's your name, son?"

"He wants to know her name. Called me 'son.' "

"Son? I said your name. What's *your* name?"

"We're so fucking outta here, man. Good luck."

The connection broke and then the operator placed his call to Central Dispatch, and Sean shut the recorder off.

"I always thought Tupac had more of a rhythm section," Whitey said.

"It was Snoop. I told you."

Whitey yawned again. "Go home, kid. Okay?"

Sean nodded and popped the tape out of the recorder. He slid it back into its case and tossed it over Whitey's head into the box. He took his Glock and holster out of his top drawer and snapped the holster onto his belt.

"Her," he said.

"What?" Whitey looked over at him.

"The kid on the tape. He said, '*her* name.' 'He wants to know *her* name.' Talking about the Marcus girl."

"Right," Whitey said. "Dead girl, you refer to her as a 'she.' "

"But how the hell's he know that?"

"Who?"

"The kid who made the call. How's he know the blood in that car came from a woman?"

Whitey's foot came off the desk and he looked at the box. He reached in and took out the tape. He flicked his wrist and Sean caught the tape in his hand.

"Play it again," Whitey said.

26

LOST IN SPACE

DAVE AND VAL passed through the city and drove over the Mystic River to this dive bar in Chelsea where the beer was cheap and cold and there wasn't much of a crowd, just a few old-timers who looked like they'd worked the waterfront their whole lives and four construction workers who were having an argument about someone named Betty who apparently had great tits but a bad attitude. The bar was tucked under the Tobin Bridge with its back against the Mystic, and it looked like it had been there going back several decades. Everyone knew Val and said their hellos. The owner, a skeletal guy with the blackest hair and the whitest skin, was named Huey. He worked the bar and gave them their first two rounds on the house.

Dave and Val shot pool for a while, and then settled into a booth with a pitcher and two shots. The small square windows fronting the street had turned from gold to indigo, the night having dropped in so quickly, Dave felt almost bullied by it. Val was actually a pretty easygoing guy when you got to know him. He told stories about prison and thefts that had gone awry, and they were all kind of scary, actually, but somehow Val made them funny, too. Dave found himself wondering what it must be like to be a guy like Val, utterly fearless and confident, and yet so damn small.

"This one time, back in the day, right? Jimmy's been sent up and we're still trying to hold our crew together. We haven't figured out yet that the only reason any of us are thieves is because Jimmy planned everything for us. All we had to do was listen to him and follow his orders and we'd be fine. But without him, we were morons. So, this one time, we take off this stamp collector. He's tied up in his office and me and my brother Nick and this kid Carson Leverett, who couldn't tie his own fucking shoes you didn't show him, we're going down in this elevator. And we're cool. We're wearing suits, looking like we fit in. This lady gets on the elevator and she *gasps*. Loud, too. And we don't know what's going on. We're looking respectable, right? I turn to Nick and he's looking at Carson Leverett because the fucking bonehead's still wearing his mask." Val slapped the table, laughing. "You believe that? He's got a Ronald Reagan mask, the big smiley one they used to sell? And he's wearing it."

"And you guys hadn't noticed?"

"No. That's the point," Val said. "We walked out of the office, and me and Nick took ours off, just assumed Carson did, too. Little shit happens like that on jobs all the time. 'Cause you're jumpy and you're stupid and you just want to get in the clear, and sometimes you miss the most obvious detail. It's staring you in the face, you can't see it." He chuckled again and threw back his shot. "That's why Jimmy was so missed. He thought of every detail. Like the way they say a good quarterback sees the whole field? Jimmy saw the whole field on a job. He saw everything that could possibly go wrong. Guy was a fucking genius."

"But he went straight."

"Sure," Val said, lighting a cigarette. "For Katie. And then for Annabeth. I don't think his heart's ever been in it, between you and me, but there you go. Sometimes, people grow up. My first wife said that was my problem—I couldn't grow up. I like the night too much. Day's just something you sleep through."

"I always thought it would be different," Dave said.

"What's that?"

"Being grown-up. You'd feel different, right? You'd feel grown-up. A man."

"You don't feel that way?"

Dave smiled. "Sometimes maybe. In glimpses. But most of the time I don't feel much different than I did when I was eighteen. I wake up a lot going, 'I got a *kid*? I got a wife?' How'd that happen?" Dave could feel his tongue thickening with the booze, his head getting that floating feel because he never had gotten that bite to eat. He felt a need to explain. To make Val see the guy he was and to like that guy. "I think I always figured one day it would be permanent. You know? One day you'd just wake up and *feel* grown-up. Feel like you had a handle on things the way fathers always did in those old TV shows."

"Ward Cleaver, like?" Val said.

"Yeah. Or even like those sheriffs, you know, James Arness, guys like that. They were men. Permanently."

Val nodded and sipped some beer. "Guy in prison says to me once, he says, 'Happiness comes in moments, and then it's gone until the next time. Could be years. But sadness' "—Val winked—" 'sadness settles in.' " He stubbed out his cigarette. "I liked that guy. He was always saying cool shit. I'm going to get another shot. You?" Val stood.

Dave shook his head. "Still working on this one."

"Come on," Val said. "Live it up."

Dave looked into his scrunched, smiling face and said, "Okay, fine."

"Good man." Val slapped his shoulder and walked up to the bar.

Dave watched him standing up at the bar, chatting with one of the old dockworkers as he waited for his drinks, Dave thinking the guys in here knew what it was to be men. Men without doubts, men who never questioned the rightness of their own actions, men who weren't confused by the world or what was expected of them in it.

It was fear, he guessed. That's what he'd always had that they didn't. Fear had settled into him at such an early age—permanently, the way Val's prison friend had claimed sadness did. Fear had found a place in Dave and never left, and so he feared doing wrong and he feared fucking up and he feared not being intelligent and he feared not being a good husband or a good father or much of a man. Fear had been in him so long, he wasn't sure he could remember what it had felt like to live without it.

A passing headlight bounced off the front door and flashed white directly in his face as the door opened and Dave blinked several times, caught only the silhouette of the man who came through the door. He had a bulky frame and what could have been a leather jacket on. He looked a bit like Jimmy, actually, but bigger, wider at the shoulders.

In fact it was Jimmy, Dave realized as the door shut again and his eyes began to clear. Jimmy, wearing a black leather jacket over a dark turtle-neck and khakis, nodding at Dave as he stepped up to Val at the bar. He said something in Val's ear and Val looked back over his shoulder at Dave and then said something to Jimmy.

Dave started to feel woozy. It was all the booze on an empty stomach, he was sure. But it was also something about Jimmy, something about the way he'd nodded to him, his face blank and yet somehow determined. And why the hell did he look bulked up, as if he'd gained ten pounds since yesterday? And what was he doing over here in Chelsea, the night before his daughter's wake?

Jimmy came over and slid into Val's seat, across from Dave. He said, "How's it going?"

"Little drunk," Dave admitted. "You gain some weight?"

Jimmy gave him a quizzical smile. "No."

"You look bigger."

Jimmy shrugged.

"What're you doing around here?" Dave asked.

"I come here a lot. Me and Val have known Huey for years. I mean, going way back. Why don't you drink that shot, Dave?"

Dave picked up the shot glass. "I'm feeling a bit hammered already."

"Who's it hurt?" Jimmy said, and Dave realized Jimmy held a shot of his own. He raised it and met Dave's glass. "To our children," Jimmy said.

"To our children," Dave managed, really feeling out of sorts now, as if he'd slid out of the day, through the night, and into a dream, a dream in which all the faces were too close, but their voices sounded like they were coming from the bottom of a sewer.

Dave downed the shot, grimacing against the burn, and Val slid into the booth beside him. Val put his arm around him and took a drink of beer directly from the pitcher. "I always liked this place."

"It's a good bar," Jimmy said. "No one bothers you."

"That's important," Val said, "no one bothering you in this life. No one fucking with you or your loved ones or your friends. Right, Dave?"

Dave said, "Absolutely."

"This guy's a hoot," Val said. "He can get you going."

Jimmy said, "Yeah?"

"Oh, yeah," Val said, and squeezed Dave's shoulder. "M' man, Dave."

CELESTE SAT on the edge of the motel bed as Michael watched TV. She had the phone in her lap, her palm flexing over the receiver.

During the late afternoon hours she'd spent with Michael by the tiny swimming pool in rusted chairs, she'd gradually begun to feel tiny and hollow, as if she could be seen from above and she looked discarded and silly and, worse, unfaithful.

Her husband. She'd betrayed her *husband*.

Maybe Dave had killed Katie. Maybe so. But what had she been thinking when she told Jimmy, of all people? Why hadn't she waited, thought some more on it? Why hadn't she considered every other conceivable alternative? Because she was afraid of Dave?

But this new Dave she'd seen in the last few days was an aberration, a Dave produced by stress.

Maybe he hadn't killed Katie. Maybe.

The point was, she needed to at least give him the benefit of the doubt until the matter was ironed out. She wasn't sure she could live with him and put Michael at risk, but she knew now she should have gone to the police, not to Jimmy Marcus.

Had she wanted to hurt Dave? Had she expected something more to come from looking into Jimmy's eyes and telling him her suspicions? And if so, what? Of all the people in the world, why had she told *Jimmy*?

There were a lot of possible answers to that question, and she didn't like any of them. She picked up the receiver and dialed Jimmy's home. She did so with tremors in her wrists, thinking, Please, someone, answer. Just answer. Please.

THE SMILE on Jimmy's face was sliding now, back and forth, up one side, back down, and then up the other, and Dave tried to focus on the bar, but that was sliding, too, as if the bar were on a boat and the sea was getting pissed.

" 'Member we took Ray Harris here that one time?" Val said.

"Sure," Jimmy said. "Good old Ray."

"Now Ray," Val said, and slapped the table in front of Dave, "was one hilarious son of a bitch."

"Yeah," Jimmy said softly, "Ray was funny. He could make you laugh."

"Most people called him Just Ray," Val said as Dave tried to concentrate on just who the fuck they were talking about. "But I called him Ray Jingles."

Jimmy snapped his fingers, pointed at Val. "That's *right*. 'Cause of all the change."

Val leaned into Dave, spoke into his ear. "This guy, right? He carried like ten bucks in change in his pocket on any given day. No one knew why. He just liked having a lot of change in his pocket, case he had to make a phone call to Libya or some fucking place, I guess. Who knows? But he'd walk around with his hands in his pockets and just jingle that change all day long. I mean, the guy was a thief, and it was like, 'Who *wouldn't* hear you coming, Ray?' But apparently, he left the change at home during jobs." Val sighed. "Funny guy."

Val took his arm off Dave's shoulder and lit another cigarette. The smoke climbed up into Dave's face, and he felt it crawl all over his cheeks and burrow through his hair. Through the smoke, he could see Jimmy watching him with that flat, determined expression, something in Jimmy's eyes he didn't like, something familiar.

It was the cop's look, he realized. Sergeant Powers. The sense that he was peeking directly into Dave's mind. The smile returned to Jimmy's face, riding up and down like a dinghy, and Dave felt his stomach go with it, bouncing as if riding a wave.

He swallowed several times, and took a deep suck of the air.

"You all right?" Val said.

Dave held up a hand. If everyone would just shut up, he'd be fine. "Yeah."

"You sure?" Jimmy said. "You're looking green, man."

It surged up inside of him and he felt his windpipe close like a fist and then pop back open and beads of sweat explode across his brow. "Oh, shit."

"Dave."

"I'm going to be sick," he said, feeling it beginning to surge again. "Really."

Val said, "Okay, okay," and slid out of the booth fast. "Use the back door. Huey don't like cleaning it off toilet rims. Got it?"

Dave pushed out of the booth and Val gripped his shoulders and turned them so that Dave could see the door at the far end of the bar past the pool table.

Dave walked toward the door, trying to keep his steps straight, one foot in front of the other, one foot in front of the other, but the door listing a bit anyway. It was a dark door and small, the oak painted black and scarred and chipped over the years. Dave could feel the heat in this place suddenly. It was clammy and thick and it blew on him as he lurched toward the door, reaching out for the brass knob, grateful for how cool it felt in his hand as he turned it and pushed the door open.

The first thing he saw were weeds. Then water. He stumbled out, surprised at how dark it got back here, and as if on cue, a light over the door snapped on and bathed the cracked tar directly in front of him. He could hear the traffic honking and banging away on the bridge above him, and suddenly he felt the wave of nausea pass. He might be all right after all. He took a deep gulp of the night. On his left someone had piled stacks of rotting wooden pallets and rusted lobster traps, some of them with ragged holes as if they'd been attacked by sharks. Dave wondered what the hell lobster traps were doing so far inland and on a river, then decided he was too drunk to figure out the answer anyway. Beyond the piles was a chain-link fence, as rusty as the lobster traps and strangled in weeds. A field of weeds taller than most men stood to the right of him, going back through the torn and cracked gravel for a good twenty yards.

Dave's stomach lurched again, and the new surge was the strongest yet, punching its way up through his body. He stumbled to the water's edge and got his head down just as the fear and the Sprite and the beer poured out of him into the oily Mystic. It was pure liquid. There was nothing else in him. He couldn't honestly remember the last time he'd eaten. But the moment it cleared his mouth and hit the water, he felt better. He felt the cool of the dusk in his hair. A slight breeze rose up off the river. He waited, on his knees, to see if he'd heave up any more, though he doubted it. It was as if he'd been cleansed.

He looked up at the underside of the bridge, everyone battling to either get into the city or out of it, everyone in an irritated rush, probably half aware that they wouldn't feel any better once they got home. Half of them would go right back out again—to the market for something they'd forgotten, to a bar, to the video store, to a restaurant where they'd wait in line again. And for what? What did we line up for? Where did we expect to go? And why were we never as happy as we thought we'd be once we got there?

Dave noticed a small boat with an outboard to his right. It was tied up to a flat plank so tiny and sagging you couldn't justifiably call it a dock. Huey's boat, he figured, and smiled at an image of the deathly looking stick of a guy rolling out into these greasy waters, the wind in his pitch-black hair.

He turned his head and looked around at the pallets and weeds. No wonder people came out here to puke. It was completely isolated. Unless you were on the other side of the river with binoculars, you couldn't see this spot. It was blocked on three sides, and it was so quiet, the sound of the cars overhead having a muffled distance to them, the weeds blocking out everything but the caws of the gulls and the lap of the water. If Huey was smart, he'd clear the weeds and pallets, build a deck out here, attract some of the yuppies moving into Admiral Hill and trying to turn Chelsea into the next battleground for gentrification once they got done with East Bucky.

Dave spit a few times and then wiped his mouth with the back of his hand. He stood, deciding he'd have to tell Val and Jimmy that he'd need to get something to eat before he had another drink. It didn't have to be great food, just substantive. And when he turned around, they were standing by the black door, Val to the left of it, Jimmy to the right, the door shut tight, Dave thinking they looked kind of funny, like they were here to deliver furniture, couldn't see where they were going to drop it in all those weeds.

Dave said, "Hey, guys. Come to make sure I didn't fall in?"

Jimmy came off the wall and walked toward him, and the light that hung over the door snapped off. Jimmy, gone black in the dark, approached slowly, his white face picking up some light from the bridge and moving in and out of shadow.

"Let me tell you about Ray Harris," Jimmy said, talking so quietly that Dave had to lean forward. "Ray Harris was a buddy of mine, Dave. He used to come and visit me when I was in prison. He used to check up on Marita and Katie and my mother, see if they needed anything. He did these things so I'd think he was my friend, but the real reason was guilt. He felt guilty for getting his balls caught in a vise and ratting me out to the police. He felt real bad about it. But after he'd been coming by the prison for a few months, a weird thing happened." Jimmy reached Dave, and he stopped, looked into Dave's face with his head slightly cocked. "I discovered I liked Ray. I mean, I honestly enjoyed the guy's company. We'd talk about sports, about God, about books, about our wives, our children, the politics of the day, what have you. Ray was the kinda guy, he could talk about anything. He had an *interest* in everything. That's rare. Then my wife died. You know? She died and they sent some guard into my cell to say, 'Sorry, convict, your wife passed last night at eight-fifteen. She's gone.' And the thing was? What killed me about my wife dying, Dave? It was that she had to go through it completely alone. I know what you're thinking, we all die alone. True. That last stage when you've slipped away, yeah, you're alone. But my wife had skin cancer. She spent the last six months dying slow. And I could have been there for that. I could have helped her with the dying. Not the death, but the dying. I wasn't there, though. Ray, a guy I liked, robbed me and my wife of that."

Dave could see an ink-blue slice of river—lit by the bridge lights and shining—reflected in Jimmy's pupils. He said, "Why you telling me this, Jimmy?"

Jimmy pointed over Dave's left shoulder. "I made Ray kneel down right over there and I shot him twice. Once in the chest, once in the throat."

Val came off the wall by the door and walked over to Dave's left, taking his time, the weeds rising up behind him. Dave's throat closed up and his insides went dry.

Dave said, "Hey, Jimmy, I don't know what—"

Jimmy said, "Ray begged. He said we were friends. He said he had a son. He said he had a wife. He said his wife was pregnant. He said he'd move away. He said he'd never bother me again. He begged me to let him live so he could see his child being born. He said he knew me and he knew I was a good man and he knew I didn't want to do this." Jimmy looked up at the bridge. "I wanted to say something back to him. I wanted to say I loved my wife and she died and I hold you responsible and, besides, on general principle, you never rat out your friends if you want to live a long life. But I didn't say anything, Dave. I was crying too hard. That's how pathetic it was. He was blubbering, I was blubbering. I could barely see him."

"So why'd you kill him?" Dave said, and there was a desperate keen in his voice.

"I just told you," Jimmy said, like he was explaining himself to a four-year-old. "Principle. I was a twenty-two-year-old widower with a five-year-old daughter. I'd missed the last two years of my wife's life. And fucking Ray, he damn well knew rule number one of our business—you don't rat out your friends."

Dave said, "What is it you think I did, Jimmy? Tell me."

"When I killed Ray," Jimmy said, "I felt, I dunno, I felt the complete *lack* of myself. I felt like God was staring down at me as I weighted him down and rolled him into that water. And God was just shaking his head. Not mad, really. He was just disgusted but not all that surprised, I guess, the way you'd get when a puppy shits on your rug. I stood right there behind where you're standing now, and I watched Ray sink, you know? His head going under last, and I remember thinking how when I was a kid I used to think that if you swam to the bottom of any body of water, you'd push through the floor and your head would pop out into space. I mean, that's how I pictured the globe, you know? So there I'd be, my head sticking out of the globe, and all that space and stars and black sky around me, and I'd just fall. I'd drop into space and float away, keep floating for a million years, out in all that cold. And when Ray went under, that's what I thought of. That he'd just keep sinking till he popped out through a hole in the planet and sank through a million years of space."

Dave said, "I know you're thinking something here, Jimmy, but you're wrong. You think I killed Katie, don't you? Is that it?"

Jimmy said, "Don't talk, Dave."

"No, no, no," Dave said, noticing the gun in Val's hand suddenly. "I didn't have *anything* to do with Katie's death."

They're going to kill me, Dave realized. Oh, Jesus, no. This is something you have to be able to prepare for. You don't just step outside a bar to throw up and turn around to realize it's the end of your life. No. I'm supposed to go home. I'm supposed to make things right with Celeste. I'm supposed to eat that meal.

Jimmy reached into his jacket and came back out with a knife in his hand. His hand was trembling a bit as he pulled the blade open. So was his upper lip and part of his chin, Dave realized. There was hope. Don't let the brain freeze up. There's hope.

"You came home the night Katie died with blood all over your clothes, Dave. You told two different stories about how you fucked up your hand, and your car was seen outside the Last Drop around the time Katie left. You lied to the cops and you've been lying to everyone else."

"Look, Jimmy. Please look at me."

Jimmy kept his eyes on the ground.

"Jimmy, I had blood on me, yeah. I beat someone, Jimmy. Beat him bad."

"Oh, is this the mugger story?" Jimmy said.

"No. He was a child molester. He was having sex with a kid in his car. He was a vampire, Jim. He was poisoning that kid."

"So it wasn't a mugger. It was some guy who, I get it, was molesting a kid. Of course, Dave. Sure. You killed this guy?"

"Yeah. Well, me . . . me and the Boy."

Dave had no idea why he'd said that. He'd never spoken of the Boy. You didn't do that. People didn't understand. Maybe it was the fear. Maybe it was a need for Jimmy to see into his head, to understand that, yes, it was a mess in there, but see *me,* Jimmy. Realize I'm not the kind of man who'd kill an innocent.

"So, you and the molested kid went and—"

"No," Dave said.

"No what? You said that you and the boy—"

"No, no. Forget that. My head gets fucked up sometimes. I say—"

"No shit," Jimmy said. "So you killed a child molester. You're telling me this, but you don't tell your wife? I would think she'd be the first person you'd tell. Particularly last night, when she told you she didn't believe the mugger story. I mean, why *not* tell her? Most people don't really mind when a *child molester* dies, Dave. Your wife was thinking you killed my daughter. And you'd have me believe that you'd have preferred she thought *that* than think you killed a pedophile. Explain that to me, Dave."

Dave wanted to say, I killed him because I was afraid I was turning into him. If I ate his heart I would subsume and submerge his spirit. But I can't say that *aloud*. I can't speak *that* truth. I know I swore today that there'd be no more secrets. But, come on, *that* secret has to stay one—no matter how many lies I have to tell to keep it buried.

"Come on, Dave. Just tell me why. Why couldn't you tell your own wife the, ah, truth?"

And the best Dave could come up with was "I don't know."

"You don't know. Okay, so in this fairy tale, you and the kid—what's he supposed to be, you when you were a kid?—you and him go and—"

"It was just me," Dave said. "I killed the faceless creature."

"The fucking *what*?" Val said.

"The guy. The molester. I killed him. Me. Just me. In the parking lot of the Last Drop."

Jimmy said, "I didn't hear of any dead guys found near the Last Drop," and looked over at Val.

Val said, "Letting this bag of shit *explain,* Jim? What're you kidding me?"

"No, it's the truth," Dave said. "I swear on my son. I put the guy in the trunk of his car. I don't know what happened to the car, but I did, I swear to God. I want to see my wife, Jimmy. I want to live my life." Dave looked up at the dark underside of the bridge, heard the tires slapping away up there, the yellow lights streaming home. "Jimmy? Please, don't take that from me."

Jimmy looked in Dave's face and Dave saw his death there. It lived in Jimmy like the wolves. Dave wished so hard that he could face this. But he couldn't. He couldn't face dying. He stood here now—right now with his feet on this pavement, his heart pumping blood, his brain sending messages to his nerves and muscles and organs, his adrenal glands open wide—and any second, it could be the very next one, a blade would plunge through his chest. And within all that pain would come the certainty that this life—his life and his vision and his eating and lovemaking and laughing and touch and smell—would end. He couldn't be brave to that. He'd beg. He would. He'd do anything they wanted if they just didn't kill him.

"I think you got in that car twenty-five years ago, Dave, and someone else came back in your place. I think your brain got fried or something," Jimmy said. "She was nineteen. You know? Nineteen and she never did nothing to you. She actually *liked* you. And you fucking killed her? Why? Because your life sucks? Because beauty hurts you? Because I didn't get in that car? Why? Just tell me that, Dave. Tell me that. Tell me that," Jimmy said, "and I'll let you live."

"Fuck no," Val said. "Jimmy? No. Come on. You're feeling *pity* for this fucking turd? Listen—"

"Shut up, Val," Jimmy said, pointing across the tar at him. "I handed you a fucking *machine* when I went in the joint and you ran it into the ground. Everything I gave you, and the best you can do is run muscle and sell fucking *drugs*? Don't you give me advice, Val. Don't you fucking think of doing that."

Val turned away, kicked at the weeds, talking fast to himself in a whisper.

"Tell me, Dave. But *don't* give me that child-molester bullshit because we're not purchasing bullshit tonight. Okay? Tell me the truth. If you tell me the lie again, I'll open you the fuck up."

Jimmy took a few breaths. He held the knife up in front of Dave's face and then he lowered it and slid it between his belt and pants over his right hip. He held his empty hands wide. "Dave, I will give you your life. You just tell me why you killed her. You'll go to jail. I ain't bullshitting you there. But you'll live. You'll breathe."

Dave felt so grateful he wanted to thank God aloud. He wanted to embrace Jimmy. Thirty seconds ago, he'd been filled with the blackest despair. He'd been ready to fall to his knees and beg and say, I don't want to die. I'm not ready. I'm not ready to leave. I don't know what's out there beyond me. I don't think it's heaven. I don't think it's bright. I think it's dark and cold and an endless tunnel of nothing. Like your hole in the planet, Jim. And I don't want to be alone in nothing, years of nothing, centuries of cold, cold nothing and only my lonely heart floating through it, alone and alone and alone.

Now he could live. If he lied. If he bit the bullet and told Jimmy what he wanted to hear. He would be reviled. He would probably be beaten. But he would live. He could see that in Jimmy's eyes. Jimmy didn't lie. The wolves had gone away and all that was left in front of him was a man with a knife who needed closure, a man who was sinking under the weight of all this not-knowing, grieving for a daughter he would never touch again.

I will come home to you, Celeste. We will make that good life. We will. And then, I promise, no more lies. No more secrets. But I think I need to tell this one last lie, the worst lie of my lying life, because I can't tell the worst truth of my life. I'd rather he think I killed his daughter than know why I killed that pedophile. This is a good lie, Celeste. It will buy us our lives back.

"Tell me," Jimmy said.

Dave told as close to the truth as he could. "I saw her in McGills that night, and she reminded me of a dream I've had."

"About what?" Jimmy said, and his face crumbled, his voice cracked.

"Youth," Dave said.

Jimmy hung his head.

"I don't remember having one," Dave said. "And she was the dream of it, and I just snapped, I guess."

It killed him to say this to Jimmy, to tear him with this, but Dave just wanted to get home and get his head right and see his family, and if this was what it took, he was going to do it. He was going to make things right. And a year from now, when the real killer had been caught and convicted, Jimmy would understand his sacrifice.

"Some part of me," he said, "never got out of that car, Jim. Just like you said. Some other Dave came back to the neighborhood in Dave's clothing, but he wasn't Dave. Dave's still in the basement. You know?"

Jimmy nodded, and when he raised his head, Dave could see that his eyes were damp and shiny and filled with compassion, maybe even love.

"It was the dream, then?" Jimmy whispered.

"It was the dream, yeah," Dave said, and felt the cold of his lie spread through his stomach and grow so cold that he thought it might have been hunger, having emptied his insides just minutes before into the Mystic River. It was a different cold, though, different than any he'd ever felt before. A freezing cold. So cold, it was almost hot. No, it was hot. It was on fire now and licking its way down through his groin and up through his chest, sucking the air out of him.

Out of the corner of his eye, he saw Val Savage jump in the air and shout, "Yes! That's what *I'm* talking about!"

He looked in Jimmy's face. Jimmy, his lips moving too slowly and too quickly at the same time, said, "We bury our sins here, Dave. We wash them clean."

Dave sat down. He watched the blood leak out of him and onto his pants. It was pouring from him, and when he put his hand to his abdomen, his fingers touched a crevice that ran from one side to the other.

He said, You lied.

Jimmy bent down over him. "What?"

You lied.

"See his fucking lips moving?" Val said. "He's moving his lips."

"I got eyes, Val."

Dave felt the knowledge sweep over him then, and it was the ugliest knowledge he'd ever faced. It was mean and indifferent. It was callous, and it was merely this: I am dying.

I cannot come back from this. I cannot cheat or slide away from this. I cannot beg my way out or hide behind my secrets. I cannot expect a reprieve based on sympathy. Sympathy from who? No one cares. No one cares. Except me. I care. I care a lot. And this isn't fair. I can't handle that tunnel alone. Please don't let me go there. Please wake me up. I want to wake up. I want to feel you, Celeste. I want to feel your arms. I'm not ready.

He forced his eyes to focus as Val handed Jimmy something and Jimmy lowered it to Dave's forehead. It was cool. It was a circle of cool, of kindness and relief from the burning in his body.

Wait! No. No, Jimmy! I know what that is. I can see the trigger. Don't, don't, don't, don't. Look at me. See me. Don't do this. Please. If you get me to a hospital I'll be all right. They'll fix me up. Oh God Jimmy don't you do that with your finger don't you do that I lied I lied please don't take me away from this please don't I can't prepare for a bullet in my brain. No one can. No one. Please don't.

Jimmy lowered the gun.

Thank you, Dave said. Thank you, thank you.

Dave lay back and saw the shafts of light streaming across the bridge, cutting through the black of night, glowing. Thank you, Jimmy. I'm going to be a good man now. You've taught me something. You have. And I'll tell you what that something is as soon as I've caught my breath. I'm going to be a good father. I'm going to be a good husband. I promise. I swear . . .

Val said, "So, okay. It's done."

Jimmy looked down at Dave's body, the canyon he'd cut in his abdomen, the bullet hole he'd fired through his forehead. He kicked off his shoes and took off his jacket. Next, he removed the turtleneck and khakis he'd stained with Dave's blood. He shed the nylon running suit he'd worn underneath and added it to the pile beside Dave's body. He heard Val place the cinder blocks and length of chain in Huey's boat, and then Val came back with a large green trash bag. Underneath the running suit, Jimmy wore a T-shirt and jeans, and Val pulled a pair of shoes from the trash bag and tossed them to him. Jimmy slid them on and checked the T-shirt and jeans for any blood that might have leaked through. But there was none. Even the jogging suit was barely stained.

He knelt by Val and stuffed his clothes into the bag. Then he took the knife and the gun to the edge of the wharf and threw them one at a time out into the center of the Mystic River. He could have placed them in the bag with his clothes, tossed them off the boat later along with Dave's body, but for some reason he needed to do it now, to experience the motion of his arm as it shot out into the air and the weapons spiraled, arced, plummeted, and sank with soft splashes.

He knelt over the water. Dave's vomit had long since floated away, and Jimmy plunged his hands into the river, oily and polluted as it was, and washed his hands of Dave's blood. Sometimes, in his dreams, he was doing this very thing—washing himself in the Mystic—when Just Ray Harris's head would pop back up, stare at him.

Just Ray always said the same thing. "You can't outrun a train."

And Jimmy, confused, said, "No one can, Ray."

Just Ray, starting to sink again, smiled. "You in particular, though."

Thirteen years of those dreams, thirteen years of Ray's head bobbing on the water, and Jimmy still didn't know what the hell he meant by that.

27

WHO DO YOU LOVE?

BRENDAN'S MOTHER had gone out to Bingo by the time he got home. She left a note: "Chicken in fridge. Glad you're okay. Don't make a habit of it."

Brendan checked his and Ray's room, but Ray was out, too, and Brendan took a chair from the kitchen and placed it down in front of the butler's pantry. He stepped up on the chair and it sagged to the left where one of the legs was missing a bolt. He looked at the ceiling slat and saw the smudge marks of fingers in the dust, and the air directly in front of his eyes began to swim with tiny dark specks. He pressed his right palm against the slat, lifted it slightly. He brought his hand down, wiped it on his pants, and took several breaths.

There were some things you didn't want to know the answers to. Brendan had never wanted to run into his father once he was grown because he didn't want to look in his father's face and see how easy it had been to leave him. He'd never asked Katie about old boyfriends, even Bobby O'Donnell, because he didn't want to picture her lying on top of someone else, kissing him the way she kissed Brendan.

Brendan knew about the truth. In most cases, it was just a matter of deciding whether you wanted to look it in the face or live with the comfort of ignorance or lies. And ignorance and lies were often underrated. Most people Brendan knew couldn't make it through the day without a saucerful of ignorance and a side of lies.

But this, this truth had to be faced. Because he'd already faced it in the holding cell, and it had sliced through him like a bullet and lodged in his stomach. And it wasn't coming out, which meant he couldn't hide from it, couldn't tell himself it wasn't there. Ignorance was not a possibility. Lying was no longer an accessible part of the equation.

"Shit," Brendan said, and pushed the ceiling slat aside and reached back into the darkness, his fingers touching dust and chips of wood and more dust, but no gun. He felt around up there for another full minute, even though he knew it was gone. His father's gun, and it wasn't where it was supposed to be. It was out in the world, and it had killed Katie.

He put the slat back in place. He got a dustpan and swept up the dust that had fallen to the floor. He took the chair back to the kitchen. He felt a need to be precise in his movements. He felt it was important that he remain calm. He poured himself a glass of orange juice and placed it on the table. He sat down in the chair with the sagging leg and turned so that he was looking at the door in the center of the apartment. He took a sip of his orange juice and waited for Ray.

"LOOK AT THIS," Sean said, pulling the latent prints file from the box and opening it in front of Whitey. "That's the cleanest one they pulled off the door. It's small because it's a kid's."

Whitey said, "Old Lady Prior heard two kids playing on the street just before Katie banged her car up. Playing with hockey sticks, she said."

"She said she heard Katie say 'Hi.' Maybe it wasn't Katie. A little kid's voice could sound like a woman's. And no footprints? Of course not. What do they weigh—a hundred pounds?"

"You recognize that kid's voice?"

"Sounded a lot like Johnny O'Shea's."

Whitey nodded. "The other kid not saying anything at all."

"Because he can't fucking speak," Sean said.

———

"HEY, RAY," Brendan said as the two boys entered the apartment.

Ray nodded. Johnny O'Shea waved. They started heading back toward the bedroom.

"Come on in here a sec, Ray."

Ray looked at Johnny.

"Just a second, Ray. I got something I want to ask you."

Ray turned and Johnny O'Shea dropped the gym bag he'd been carrying and sat on the edge of Mrs. Harris's bed. Ray came down the short hall into the kitchen and held out his hands, looked at his brother like "What?"

Brendan hooked a chair with his foot and pulled it out from under the table, nodded at it.

Ray's head tilted up as if he smelled something in the air, a scent he wasn't fond of. He looked at the chair. He looked at Brendan.

He signed, "What did I do?"

"You tell me," Brendan said.

"I didn't do anything."

"So sit down."

"I don't want to."

"Why not?"

Ray shrugged.

Brendan said, "Who do you hate, Ray?"

Ray looked at him like he was nuts.

"Come on," Brendan said. "Who do you hate?"

Ray's sign was brief: "Nobody."

Brendan nodded. "Okay. Who do you love?"

Ray gave him that face again.

Brendan leaned forward, his hands on his knees. "Who do you love?"

Ray looked down at his shoes, then up at Brendan. He raised his hand and pointed at his brother.

"You love me?"

Ray nodded, fidgeting.

"What about Ma?"

Ray shook his head.

"You don't love Ma?"

Ray signed, "Don't feel one way or the other."

"So I'm the only person you love?"

Ray thrust his small face out and scowled. His hands flew. "*Yes*. Can I go now?"

"No," Brendan said. "Have a seat."

Ray looked down at the chair, his face red and angry. He looked up at Brendan. He raised his hand and extended his middle finger, and then he turned to walk out of the kitchen.

Brendan didn't even realize he'd moved until he had most of Ray's hair in his hand and was pulling him up off his feet. He pulled back with his arm as if he were pulling the cord on a rusty lawn mower, and then he opened his fingers and Ray flew backward out of his hand and over the kitchen table. He hit the wall and then dropped onto the table, brought the whole thing crashing to the floor with him.

"You love me?" Brendan said, not even looking down at his brother. "You love me so you kill my fucking girlfriend, Ray? Huh?"

That got Johnny O'Shea moving, as Brendan had figured it would. Johnny grabbed his gym bag and bolted for the door, but Brendan was all over him. He picked the little prick up by his throat and slammed him against the door.

"My brother never does anything without you, O'Shea. Never."

He pulled back his fist and Johnny screamed, "No, Bren! Don't!"

Brendan punched him so hard in the face he heard the nose break. And then he punched him again. When Johnny hit the floor, he curled into a ball and spit blood on the wood and Brendan said, "I'm coming back. I'm coming back and I just might beat you to death, you piece of fucking garbage."

Ray was standing on wobbly feet, his sneakers sliding on broken plates when Brendan came back in the kitchen and slapped him so hard across the face he knocked him into the sink. He grabbed his brother by the shirt, Ray looking into his face with tears streaming from his hate-filled eyes and blood smearing his mouth, and Brendan threw him to the floor and spread his arms and knelt on them.

"Speak," Brendan said. "I know you can. Speak, you fucking freak, or I swear to God, Ray, I'll kill you. Speak!" Brendan shouted, and brought his fists down into Ray's ears. "Speak! Say her name! Say it! Say 'Katie,' Ray. Say 'Katie'!"

Ray's eyes went foggy and dull and he spit some blood up onto his own face.

"Speak!" Brendan screamed. "I'll fucking kill you if you don't!"

He grabbed his brother by the hair along his temples and pulled his head off the floor, shook it from side to side until Ray's eyes focused again and Brendan held his head still and looked deep into those gray pupils, saw so much love and hate in there that he wanted to rip his brother's head clean off and throw it out the window.

He said it again, "Speak," but this time it came out in a hoarse, strangled whisper. "Speak."

He heard a loud cough and looked behind him, saw Johnny O'Shea on his feet, spitting blood down onto the floor, Ray senior's gun in his hand.

SEAN AND WHITEY were coming up the stairs when they heard the racket, someone screaming in the apartment and the unmistakable snaps of flesh hitting flesh. They heard a man scream, "I'll fucking kill you!" and Sean had his hand on his Glock as he reached for the door-knob.

Whitey said, "Wait," but Sean had already turned the knob, and he stepped into the apartment and saw a gun pointed at his chest from six inches away.

"Hold it! Don't pull that trigger, kid!"

Sean looked into the bloody face of Johnny O'Shea and what he saw there scared the shit out of him. There was nothing there. Probably never had been. The kid wouldn't pull the trigger because he was angry or because he was scared. He'd pull the trigger because Sean was just a six-foot-two video image, and the gun was a joystick.

"Johnny, you need to point that gun at the floor."

Sean could hear Whitey's breathing from the other side of the threshold.

"Johnny."

Johnny O'Shea said, "He fucking punched me. Twice. Broke my nose."

"Who?"

"Brendan."

Sean looked to his left, saw Brendan standing in the kitchen doorway, hands down by his side, frozen. Johnny O'Shea, he realized, had been about to shoot Brendan when Sean came through the door. He could hear Brendan's breath, shallow and slow.

"We'll arrest him for that if you want."

"Don't want him fucking arrested. I want him dead."

"Dead's a big thing, Johnny. Dead's never coming back, you know?"

"I know," the kid said. "I fucking know all about that. You going to use that?" The kid's face was a mess, blood pouring from that broken nose and dripping off his chin.

Sean said, "What?"

Johnny O'Shea nodded at Sean's hip. "That gun. It's a Glock, right?"

"It's a Glock, yeah."

"Glocks kick ass, man. I'd like to get me one of those. So you going to use it?"

"Now?"

"Yeah. You going to draw on me?"

Sean smiled. "No, Johnny."

Johnny said, "The fuck you smiling for? Draw on me. We'll see what happens. It'll be cool." He thrust the gun out, his arm straight, the muzzle maybe an inch from Sean's chest now.

Sean said, "I'd say you got the drop on me, partner. Know what I mean?"

"Got the drop, Ray," Johnny called. "On a fucking cop, dude. Me! Check it out."

Sean said, "Let's not let this get out—"

"Saw this movie once, right? Cop's chasing this black guy on a roof? Nigger threw his ass *off*. Cop's like all 'Aaagh' and shit the whole way down. Nigger's so bad-ass he don't *care* the cop got the wife and little shits at home. Nigger's that cool, man."

Sean had seen this before. Back when he was in uniform and sent as crowd control on a bank robbery gone bad, the guy inside gradually growing stronger for a two-hour period, feeling the power of the gun in his hand and the effect it had, Sean watching him rant and rave over the monitor hooked up to the bank cameras. At the start, the guy had been terrified, but he'd gotten over that. Fell in love with that gun.

And for one moment, Sean saw Lauren looking over at him from the pillow, one hand pressed to the side of her head. He saw his dream daughter, smelled her, and thought what a shitty thing it would be to die without meeting her or seeing Lauren again.

He focused on the empty face before him. He said, "You see that guy to your left, Johnny? The one in the doorway?"

Johnny's eyes darted fast to his left. "Yeah."

"He *doesn't* want to shoot you. He doesn't."

"Don't care if he does," Johnny said, but Sean could see it got to the kid, his eyes getting rabbity now, jerking up and down.

"But if you shoot me, he has no choice."

"Ain't afraid of dying."

"I know that. Thing is, though? He won't shoot you in the head or nothing. We don't kill kids, man. But if he shoots you from where he's standing, you know where that bullet's going to go?"

Sean kept his eyes on Johnny, even though his head seemed to be magnetized to the gun in the kid's hand, wanting to look down on it, see where the trigger was, if the kid was pulling on it at all, Sean thinking, I don't want to get shot, and I definitely don't want to get shot by a *kid*. He couldn't think of a more pathetic way to go. He could feel Brendan, ten feet to his left and frozen, probably thinking the same thing.

Johnny licked his lips.

"It's going to go through your armpit and into your spine, man. It's going to paralyze you. You'll be like those kids on those Jimmy Fund commercials. You know the ones. Sitting in the wheelchair, all frozen up on one side, head hanging off the chair. You'll be a drooler, Johnny. People will have to hold the cup up beside your head so you can suck from the straw."

Johnny made up his mind. Sean could see it, as if a light had clicked off in the kid's dark brain, and Sean felt the fear seize him now, knew this kid was going to pull the trigger if only to hear the sound.

"My fucking *nose*, man," Johnny said, and turned toward Brendan.

Sean heard his own breath pop out of his mouth in surprise, and he looked down to see that gun sweeping away from his body, as if revolving on top of a tripod. He reached out so fast it was as if someone else was controlling his arms, and closed his hand over the gun as Whitey stepped into the room, Glock pointed at the kid's chest. A sound came out of the kid's mouth—a gasp of defeated surprise as if he'd opened a Christmas present to find a soiled gym sock inside—and Sean pushed the kid's forehead back against the wall and stripped the gun from him.

Sean said, "Mother*fucker*," and blinked at Whitey through the sweat in his eyes.

Johnny started to cry the way only a thirteen-year-old could, as if the whole world was sitting on his face.

Sean turned him to the wall and pulled his hands behind his back, saw Brendan finally take a deep breath, his lips and arms trembling, Ray Harris standing behind him in a kitchen that looked like it had been hit by a cyclone.

Whitey stepped up behind Sean, put a hand on his shoulder. "How you doing?"

"Kid was going to *do* it," Sean said, feeling the sweat that drenched every inch of his clothes, even his socks.

"No, I wasn't," Johnny wailed. "I was just kidding."

"Fuck you," Whitey said, and leaned his face into the kid's. "Nobody cares about your tears but your mommy, little bitch. Get used to it."

Sean snapped the cuffs on Johnny O'Shea and took him by the shirt, led him into the kitchen, and dropped him in a chair.

Whitey said, "Ray, you look like someone threw you from the back of a truck."

Ray looked at his brother.

Brendan leaned against the oven and his body was sagging so bad, Sean figured he'd fall over in a light breeze.

"We know," Sean said.

"What do you know?" Brendan whispered.

Sean looked at the kid sniffling in the chair and the other kid, mute, looking up at them like he hoped they'd leave soon so he could get back to playing Doom in the back bedroom. Sean was pretty sure once he got a sign language interpreter and a social worker and questioned them that they'd say they did it "because." Because they had the gun. Because they were there on the street when she drove up it. Maybe because Ray had never really liked her. Because it seemed like a cool idea. Because they'd never killed anyone before. Because when you had your finger curled around a trigger, you just had to pull it or otherwise that finger would itch for weeks.

"What do you know?" Brendan repeated, his voice gone hoarse and wet.

Sean shrugged. He wished he had an answer for Brendan, but looking at these two kids, nothing came to mind. Nothing at all.

JIMMY TOOK A BOTTLE with him to Gannon Street. There was an assisted-living home for the elderly at the end of the street, a chunk of 1960s limestone and granite that was two stories tall and ran half a block down Heller Court, the street that began where Gannon ended. Jimmy sat on the white front steps and looked back down Gannon. He'd heard they were kicking the old people out of here, actually, the Point having grown so popular that the owner of the building was going to sell to a guy who specialized in starter condos for young couples. The Point was gone, really. It had always been the snobby sister of the Flats, but now it was like it wasn't even in the same family. Pretty soon, they'd probably draw up a charter, get the name changed, carve it off the Buckingham map.

Jimmy took the pint from his jacket and sipped some bourbon, looked at the spot where they'd last seen Dave Boyle that day the men had taken him, his head looking back through the rear window, covered in shadow, gone soft with distance.

I wish it hadn't been you, Dave. I really do.

He raised the pint to Katie. Daddy got him, honey. Daddy put him down.

"Talking to yourself?"

Jimmy looked over and saw Sean climbing out of his car. Sean had a roadie beer in his hand and he smiled at Jimmy's pint. "What's your excuse?"

"Tough night," Jimmy said.

Sean nodded. "Me, too. Saw a bullet with my name on it."

Jimmy slid to the side, and Sean sat down beside him. "How'd you know to look for me here?"

"Your wife said you might be here."

"My wife?" Jimmy had never told her about his trips here. Christ, she was a real piece of work.

"Yeah. Jimmy, we made a bust today."

Jimmy took a long pull from the bottle, his chest fluttering. "A bust."

"Yeah. We got your daughter's killers. Got 'em cold."

"Killers?" Jimmy said. "Plural?"

Sean nodded. "Kids, actually. Thirteen years old. Ray Harris's son, Ray junior, and a kid named Johnny O'Shea. They confessed half an hour ago."

Jimmy felt a knife enter his brain through the ear and push toward the other side. A hot knife, slicing away through his skull.

"No question?" he said.

"None," Sean said.

"Why?"

"Why'd they do it? They don't even know. They were playing with a gun. They saw a car coming, and one of them lay down in the middle of the street. The car swerves, clutch kicks out, and O'Shea runs up to the car with the gun, says he just meant to scare her. Instead the gun went off. Katie hit him with the door, and the kids say they snapped. They chased her so she wouldn't tell anyone they had a gun."

"And the beating they gave her?" Jimmy said, and took another drink.

"Ray junior had a hockey stick. He wouldn't answer any questions. He's mute, you know? Just sat there. But O'Shea said that they beat her because she'd made them mad by running." He shrugged as if the utter wastefulness of it surprised even him. "Little fucking kids," he said. "Afraid they'd get grounded or something, so they killed her."

Jimmy stood. He opened his mouth to gulp some air and his legs gave way and he found himself right back on the step. Sean put a hand on his elbow.

"Go easy, Jim. Take a few breaths."

Jimmy saw Dave sitting on the ground, fingering the slice Jimmy had drawn from one end of his abdomen to the other. He heard his voice: Look at *me*, Jimmy. Look at me.

And Sean said, "I got a call from Celeste Boyle. She said Dave's missing. She said she went a little crazy the last few days. She said you, Jim, might know where he is."

Jimmy tried to speak. He opened his mouth, but his windpipe filled right up with what felt like damp cotton swabs.

Sean said, "No one else knows where Dave could be. And it's important we talk to him, Jim, because he might know something about a guy who got killed outside the Last Drop the other night."

"A guy?" Jimmy managed before his windpipe closed up again.

"Yeah," Sean said, something hard finding his voice. "A pedophile with three priors. Real piece of shit. The theory at the barracks is that someone caught him in the act with a little kid and canceled his fucking ticket. So anyway," Sean said, "we want to talk to Dave about it. You know where he is, Jim?"

Jimmy shook his head, having trouble seeing anything out of his peripheral vision now, a tunnel seeming to have formed in front of his eyes.

"No?" Sean said. "Celeste says she told you that Dave killed Katie. Seems to think you believed the same thing. She got the feeling you were going to do something about it."

Jimmy stared through the tunnel at a sewer grate.

"You going to send five hundred a month to Celeste now, Jimmy?"

Jimmy looked up and each of them saw it at the same time in the other's face—Sean could see what Jimmy had done, and Jimmy could see that knowledge appear in Sean.

"You fucking did it, didn't you?" Sean said. "You killed him."

Jimmy stood up, holding on to the banister. "Don't know what you're talking about."

"You killed both of them—Ray Harris and Dave Boyle. Jesus, Jimmy, I came down here thinking the whole idea was nuts, but I can see it in your face, man. You crazy, lunatic, fucking psycho piece of shit. You did it. You killed Dave. You killed Dave Boyle. Our friend, Jimmy."

Jimmy snorted. "Our friend. Yeah, okay, Point Boy, he was your good buddy. Hung with him all the time, right?"

Sean stepped into his face. "He was our friend, Jimmy. Remember?"

Jimmy looked into Sean's eyes, wondered if he was going to take a swing at him.

"Last time I saw Dave," he said, "was at my house last night." He pushed Sean aside and crossed the street onto Gannon. "That's the last time I saw Dave."

"You're full of shit."

He turned, arms wide as he looked back at Sean. "Then arrest me, you're so sure."

"I'll get the evidence," Sean said. "You know I will."

"You'll get shit," Jimmy said. "Thanks for busting my daughter's killers, Sean. Really. Maybe if you'd been a little faster, though?" Jimmy shrugged and turned his back on him, started walking down Gannon Street.

Sean watched him until he lost him to the darkness under a broken streetlight right in front of Sean's old house.

You did it, Sean thought. You actually did it, you cold, cold-blooded animal. And the worst part of it is that I know how smart you are. You won't have left us anything to go on. That's not in your nature, because you're a detail guy, Jimmy. You damn prick.

"You took his life," Sean said aloud. "Didn't you, my man?"

He tossed his beer can into the curb and walked to his car, called Lauren from his cell phone.

When she answered, he said, "It's Sean."

Silence.

He knew now what he hadn't said that she'd needed to hear, the thing he'd refused to say in over a year. Anything, he'd told himself, I'll say anything but that.

He said it now, though. He said it seeing that kid pointing the gun at his chest, the kid reeking of nothing, and seeing, too, poor Dave that day Sean had offered to buy him a beer, the spark of desperate hope he'd seen in Dave's face, the guy probably never believing, truly, that anyone would want to have a beer with him. And he said it because he felt it deep in his marrow, a need to say it, as much for Lauren as for himself.

He said, "I'm sorry."

And Lauren spoke. "For what?"

"For putting it all on you."

"Okay . . ."

"Hey—"

"Hey—"

"You go ahead," he said.

"I . . ."

"What?"

"I . . . hell, Sean, I'm sorry, too. I didn't mean to—"

"It's okay," he said. "Really." He took a deep breath, sucking in the soiled, stale-sweat stench of his cruiser. "I want to see you. I want to see my daughter."

And Lauren answered, "How do you know she's yours?"

"She's mine."

"But the blood test—"

"She's mine," he said. "I don't need a blood test. Will you come home, Lauren? Will you?"

Somewhere on the silent street, he could hear the hum of a generator.

"Nora," she said.

"What?"

"That's your daughter's name, Sean."

"Nora," he said, the word wet in his throat.

WHEN JIMMY GOT home, Annabeth was waiting up for him in the kitchen. He sat in the chair at the table across from her and she gave him that small, secret smile he loved, the one that seemed to know him so well he'd never have to open his mouth for the rest of his life and she'd still know what he meant to say. Jimmy took her hand and ran his thumb along hers and tried to find strength in the image of himself that he could see in her face.

The baby monitor sat on the table between them. They'd used it last month when Nadine had come down with a bad case of strep, listening to her gurgle as she'd slept, Jimmy picturing his baby drowning, waiting for the sound of a cough so ground in glass he'd have to leap from bed and scoop her up, rush her to the emergency room wearing only boxers and a T-shirt. She'd healed quickly, though, but Annabeth didn't return the monitor to its box in the dining room closet. She'd turn it on at night, listen to Nadine and Sara sleep.

They weren't sleeping now. Jimmy could hear them through the small speaker, whispering, giggling, and it horrified him to picture them and think of his sins at the same time.

I killed a man. The wrong man.

It burned in him, that knowledge, that shame.

I killed Dave Boyle.

It dripped, still burning, down into his belly. It drizzled through him.

I murdered. I murdered an innocent man.

"Oh, honey," Annabeth said, searching his face. "Oh, baby, what's wrong? Is it Katie? Baby, you look like you're dying."

She came around the table, a fearsome mix of worry and love in her eyes. She straddled Jimmy and took his face in her hands and made him look in her eyes.

"Tell me. Tell me what's wrong."

Jimmy wanted to hide from her. Her love hurt too much right now. He wanted to dissolve from her warm hands and find someplace dark and cavelike where no love or light could reach and he could curl into a ball and moan his grief and self-hatred into the black.

"Jimmy," she whispered. She kissed his eyelids. "Jimmy, talk to me. Please."

She pressed the heels of her hands against his temples, and her fingers dug through his hair and against his skull and she kissed him. Her tongue slid into his mouth and probed him, searching deep for the source of his pain, sucking at it, capable of turning into a scalpel if necessary and cutting away his cancers, sucking them back out of him.

"Tell me. Please, Jimmy. Tell me."

And he knew, looking into her love, that he had to tell her everything or he'd be lost. He wasn't sure she'd be able to save him, but he was positive that if he didn't open himself to her now, he would definitely die.

So he told her.

He told her everything. He told her about Just Ray Harris and he told her about the sadness he'd felt anchored inside of him since he was eleven and he told her that loving Katie had been the sole admirable accomplishment of his otherwise useless existence, that Katie at five— that daughter-stranger who'd needed and mistrusted him at the same time—was the scariest thing he'd ever faced and the only chore he'd never run from. He told his wife that loving Katie and protecting Katie were the core of him, and when she had been taken, so had he.

"And so," he told her with the kitchen gone small and tight around them, "I killed Dave."

"I killed him and buried him in the Mystic and now I've discovered, as if that crime weren't bad enough, that he was innocent.

"These are the things I've done, Anna. And I can't undo them. I think I should go to jail. I should confess to Dave's murder and go back into jail, because I think I belong there. No, honey, I do. I'm not fit for out here. I can't be trusted."

His voice sounded like someone else's. It sounded so far from the one he usually heard leaving his lips that he wondered if Annabeth saw a stranger before her, a carbon Jimmy, a Jimmy vanishing into the ether.

Her face was dry and composed, though, so still she could have been posing for a painting. Chin tilted up, eyes clear and unreadable.

Jimmy could hear the girls on the monitor again, whispering, the sound like a soft rustle of wind.

Annabeth reached down and began unbuttoning his shirt, and Jimmy watched her deft fingers, his body numb. She opened the shirt and pushed it halfway off his shoulders and then she placed her cheek to it, her ear over the center of his chest.

He said, "I just—"

"Ssshh," she whispered. "I want to hear your heart."

Her hands slid along his rib cage and then up his back, and she pressed the side of her head tighter against his chest. She closed her eyes, and a tiny smile curled up her lips.

They sat that way for a while. The whispering on the monitor had changed to the hushed rumble of his daughters' sleeping.

When she pulled away, Jimmy could still feel her cheek on his chest like a permanent mark. She climbed off him and sat on the floor in front of him and looked into his face. She tilted her head toward the baby monitor and, for a moment, they listened to their daughters sleep.

"You know what I told them when I put them to bed tonight?"

Jimmy shook his head.

Annabeth said, "I told them they had to be extra-special nice to you for a while because as much as *we* loved Katie? You loved her even more. You loved her so much because you'd created her and held her when she was tiny and sometimes your love for her was so big that your heart filled like a balloon and felt like it was going to pop from loving her."

"Jesus," Jimmy said.

"I told them that their Daddy loved *them* that much, too. That he had four hearts and they were all balloons and they were all filled up and aching. And your love meant we'd never have to worry. And Nadine said, 'Never?' "

"Please." Jimmy felt like he was crushed under blocks of granite. "Stop."

She shook her head once, holding him in her calm eyes. "I told Nadine, 'That's right. Never. Because Daddy is a king, not a prince. And kings know what must be done—even if it's hard—to make things right. Daddy is a king, and he will do—"

"Anna—"

"—he will *do* whatever he has to do for those he loves. Everyone makes mistakes. Everyone. Great men try to make things right. And that's all that matters. That's what great love is. That's why Daddy is a great man."

Jimmy felt blinded. He said, "No."

"Celeste called," Annabeth said, her words like darts now.

"Don't—"

"She wanted to know where you were. She told me how she'd mentioned her own suspicions about Dave to you."

Jimmy wiped his eyes with the back of his hand, watched his wife as if he'd never seen her before.

"She told me that, Jimmy, and I thought what kind of *wife* says those things about her husband? How fucking gutless do you have to be to tell those kinds of tales out of school? And why would she tell you? Huh, Jim? Why would she run to you?"

Jimmy had an idea—he'd always had an idea about Celeste and the way she looked at him sometimes—but he didn't say anything.

Annabeth smiled, as if she could see the answer in his face. "I could have called you on your cell. I could have. Once she told me what you knew, and I remembered seeing you leave with Val, I could guess what you were doing, Jimmy. I'm not stupid."

She was never that.

"But I didn't call you. I didn't stop it."

Jimmy's voice cracked around the words: "Why not?"

Annabeth cocked her head at him as if the answer should have been obvious. She stood, looking down at him with that curious glare, and she kicked off her shoes. She unzipped her jeans and pulled them down her thighs, bent at the waist and pushed them to her ankles. She stepped out of them as she removed her shirt and bra. She pulled Jimmy out of his chair. She pressed him to her body, and she kissed his damp cheekbones.

"They," she said, "are weak."

"Who's they?"

"Everyone," she said. "Everyone but us."

She pushed Jimmy's shirt off his shoulders and Jimmy could see her face down at the Pen Channel the first night they'd ever gone out. She'd asked him if crime was in his blood, and Jimmy had convinced her that it wasn't, because he'd thought that was the answer she was looking for. Only now, twelve and a half years later, did he understand that all she'd wanted from him was the truth. Whatever his answer had been, she would have adapted to it. She would have supported it. She would have built their lives accordingly.

"We are not weak," she said, and Jimmy felt the desire take hold in him as if it had been building since birth. If he could've eaten her alive without causing her pain, he would have devoured her organs, sunk his teeth into her throat.

"We will never be weak." She sat on the kitchen table, her legs dangling off the side.

Jimmy looked at his wife as he stepped out of his pants, aware that this was temporary, that he was merely blocking the pain of Dave's murder, ducking from it into his wife's strength and flesh. But that would do for tonight. Maybe not tomorrow or in the days to come. But definitely for tonight, it would provide. And wasn't that how all recoveries started? With small steps?

Annabeth placed her hands on his hips, her nails digging into the flesh near his spine.

"When we're done, Jim?"

"Yeah?" Jimmy felt drunk with her.

"Make sure you kiss the girls good night."

Epilogue

JIMMY FLATS

SUNDAY

28

WE'LL SAVE YOU
A PLACE

JIMMY WOKE UP Sunday morning to the distant sound of drums.
Not the rat-a-tat and cymbal clash of some nose-ring band in a sweaty
club, but the deep, steady, tom-tom thump of a war party encamped just
on the outskirts of the neighborhood. Then he heard the bleat of brass
horns, sudden and off-key. Once again, it was a distant sound, riding the
morning air from a distance of ten or twelve blocks away, and it died
almost as soon as it had started. In the silence that followed, he lay there
listening to the crisp quiet of a late Sunday morning—a bright one, too,
judging by the hard yellow glow on the other side of the closed shades.
He heard the cluck and coo of pigeons on his ledge and the dry bark of a
dog down the street. A car door snapped open and shut, and he waited
for the gun of its engine, but it never came, and then he heard that deep
tom-tom thumping again, steadier, more confident.

He looked over at the clock on the nightstand: 11 A.M. The last time
he'd slept this late, he'd been . . . He couldn't remember the last time
he'd slept this late, actually. Years. A decade, maybe. He remembered the
last few days' exhaustion, the sensation he'd had that Katie's coffin rose
and fell like an elevator car through his body. And then Just Ray Harris

and Dave Boyle had come to visit as he'd sat drunk on the living room couch last night, a gun in his hand, watching them wave to him from the backseat of the car that had smelled of apples. And the back of Katie's head stretched up between them as they drove off down Gannon Street, Katie never looking back, and Just Ray and Dave waving like mad, grinning like fools, as Jimmy felt the gun itch against his palm. He'd smelled the oil and thought of putting the barrel in his mouth.

The wake had been a nightmare, Celeste showing up when it was packed at eight in the evening and attacking Jimmy, hitting him with her fists, calling him a murderer. "You have her *body!*" she'd screamed. "What do I have? Where is he, Jimmy? *Where?*" Bruce Reed and his sons pulled her off him and carted her out of there, but Celeste still screamed full throttle: "Murderer! He's a murderer! He killed my husband! Murderer!"

Murderer.

Then there'd been the funeral, and the service at the grave site, Jimmy standing there as they lowered his baby into the hole and hit the coffin with piles of dirt and loose rock and Katie faded away from him under all that soil as if she'd never lived.

The weight of all that had found his bones last night and sunk in deep, Katie's coffin rising and falling, rising and falling, so that by the time he'd put the gun back in the drawer and flopped into bed, he'd felt immobilized, as if his bone marrow had filled with his dead, and the blood was clotting.

Oh, God, he'd thought, I have never been so tired. So tired, so sad, so useless and alone. I'm exhausted from my mistakes and my rage and my bitter, bitter sadness. Wiped out from my sins. Oh, God, leave me alone and let me die so I won't do wrong and I won't be tired and I won't carry the burdens of my nature and my loves anymore. Loose me of all that, because I'm too tired to do it on my own.

Annabeth had tried to understand this guilt, this horror at himself, but she couldn't. Because she hadn't pulled the trigger.

And now, he'd slept until eleven. Twelve hours straight, and a dead sleep, too, because he'd never heard Annabeth wake.

He'd read somewhere that a hallmark of deep depression was a consistent weariness, a compulsive need to sleep, but as he sat up in bed and listened to the thump of drums, joined now by the blasts of those brass horns, almost in tune, too, he felt refreshed. He felt twenty. He felt wide, wide awake, as if he'd never need sleep again.

The parade, he realized. The drums and horns came from the band prepping to march down Buckingham Avenue at noon. He got up and went to the window and pulled up the shade. The reason that car hadn't started out front was because they'd blocked off Buckingham Avenue from the Flats straight up to Rome Basin. Thirty-six blocks. He looked through the window and down onto the avenue. It was a clean stripe of blue-gray asphalt under the bright sun, as clean as Jimmy could remember seeing it. Blue sawhorses blocked access at every cross street and stretched end-to-end along the curbs as far as Jimmy could see in either direction.

Folks had just begun to come out of their homes and stake out their places on the sidewalk. Jimmy watched them set down their coolers and radios and picnic baskets, and he waved to Dan and Maureen Guden as they unfolded their lawn chairs in front of Hennessey's Laundromat. When they waved back, he felt touched by the concern he saw in their faces. Maureen cupped her hands around her mouth and called to him. Jimmy opened the window and leaned into the screen, got a whiff of the morning sun, bright air, and what remained of the spring's dust clinging to the screen.

"What's that, Maureen?"

"I said, 'How you doing, hon?' " Maureen called. "You okay?"

"Yeah," Jimmy said, and it surprised him to realize that, in fact, he did feel okay. He still carried Katie in him like a second stricken and angry heart that would never, he was certain, stop beating its mad beat. He had no illusions about that. The grief was a constant now, more a part of him than a limb. But somehow during his long sleep, he'd gained an elemental acceptance of it. There it was, part of him, and he could deal with it on those terms. And so, under the circumstances, he felt far better than he would have expected. "I'm . . . all right," he called to Maureen and Dan. "Considering. You know?"

Maureen nodded, and Dan asked, "You need anything, Jim?"

"We mean *anything,*" Maureen said.

And Jimmy felt a proud and everlasting surge of love for them and this whole place as he said, "No, I'm good. But thanks. Very much. It means a lot."

"You coming down?" Maureen called.

"I think so, yeah," Jimmy said, not knowing for sure until the words left his mouth. "We'll see you down there in a bit?"

"We'll save you a place," Dan said.

They waved and Jimmy waved back and then left the window, chest still filled with that overwhelming mixture of pride and love. These were his people. And this was his neighborhood. His home. They'd save a place for him. They would. Jimmy from the Flats.

That's what the big boys had called him in the old days, before he'd shipped out to Deer Island. They'd take him to the social clubs on Prince Street in the North End and say, "Hey, Carlo, this is that friend of mine I was telling you about. Jimmy. Jimmy from the Flats."

And Carlo or Gino or one of the O's would widen his eyes and go, "No shit? Jimmy Flats. Nice to meet you, Jimmy. I admired your work a long time now."

The jokes about his age would follow—"What, you crack your first safe with your diaper pin?"—but Jimmy could feel the respect, if not a kind of minor awe, these hard guys felt in his presence.

He was Jimmy Flats. Ran his first crew at seventeen. *Seventeen*—you believe that shit? A serious guy. Not to be fucked with. A man who kept his mouth shut and knew how the game was played and knew how to show respect. A man who made money for his friends.

He was Jimmy Flats back then, and he was Jimmy Flats right now, and those people beginning to gather along the parade route—they loved him. They worried about him and shouldered a modicum of his grief as best as they could. And for their love, what did he give them in return? He had to wonder. What, really, did he give them?

The closest thing this neighborhood had to a governing presence in the years since the Feds and RICO had busted up Louie Jello's gang had been—what?—Bobby O'Donnell? Bobby O'Donnell and Roman Fallow. Pair of bantamweight drug dealers who'd moved into the protection and shylock rackets. Jimmy had heard the rumors—how they'd forged some kind of deal with the Vietnamese gangs up in Rome Basin to keep the gooks from muscling in, carved up the territory and then celebrated the alliance by burning Connie's Flower Shop to the ground as a warning to anyone who refused to pay their insurance premiums.

That's not how you did it. You kept your business out of your neighborhood; you didn't make the neighborhood your business. You kept your people clean and safe and they, in gratitude, watched your back and became your ears to whispers of trouble. And if occasionally their gratitude came in the form of an envelope here, a cake or a car there, then that was their choice and your reward for keeping them safe.

That's how you ran a neighborhood. Benevolently. With one eye on their interests and one on your own. You didn't let the Bobby O'Donnells and the slant-eyed tong wannabes think they could just stroll the fuck in here and take whatever they desired. Not if they wanted to stroll back out on their God-given limbs.

Jimmy left the bedroom and found the apartment empty. The door at the end of the hall was open, and he could hear Annabeth's voice from the apartment upstairs, could hear his daughters' small feet scampering across the floorboards as they chased Val's cat. He let himself into the bathroom and turned on the shower, stepped in when it got warm, and raised his face to the spray.

The only reason O'Donnell and Farrow had never bothered Jimmy's store was because they knew he was tight with the Savages. And like anyone with a brain, O'Donnell was afraid of them. And if he and Roman feared the Savages, then that meant that, by association, they feared Jimmy.

They feared him. Jimmy from the Flats. Because, on his own, Lord knows, he certainly had the brains. And with the Savages watching his back, he could have all the muscle and balls-to-the-wall, batshit fearlessness he'd ever need. Put Jimmy Marcus and the Savage brothers together for *real,* and they could . . .

What?

Make the neighborhood as safe as it deserved to be.

Run the whole damn city.

Own it.

"Please don't, Jimmy. Jesus. I want to see my wife. I want to live my life. Jimmy? Please, don't take that away from me. Look at me!"

Jimmy closed his eyes and let the hard, hot water drill his skull.

"Look at *me!*"

I'm looking at you, Dave. I'm looking at you.

Jimmy saw Dave's pleading face, the spittle on his lips not much different than the spittle on Just Ray Harris's lower lip and chin had been thirteen years ago.

"Look at me!"

I'm looking, Dave. I'm looking. You never should have gotten back out of that car. You know that? You should have stayed gone. You came back here, to our home, and there were crucial pieces of you missing. You never fit back in, Dave, because they'd poisoned you and that poison was just waiting to spill back out.

"I didn't kill your daughter, Jimmy. I didn't kill Katie. I didn't, I didn't."

Maybe you didn't, Dave. I know that now. It's starting to look like you actually had nothing to do with it. Still a small chance the cops got the wrong kids, but I'll admit, all in all, it looks like you may have been guilt-free on the Katie account.

"So?"

So you killed *someone,* Dave. You killed someone. Celeste was right about that. Besides, you know how it is with kids who get molested.

"No, Jim. Why don't you tell me?"

They turn into molesters themselves. Sooner or later. The poison's in you and it has to come out. I was just protecting some poor future victim from your poison, Dave. Maybe your son.

"Leave my son out of this."

Fine. Maybe one of his friends then. But, Dave, sooner or later, you would have shown your true colors.

"That's how you live with it?"

Once you got in that car, Dave, you should never have come back. That's how I live with it. You didn't belong. Don't you get it? That's all a neighborhood is—a place where people who *belong together* live. All others need not fucking apply.

Dave's voice fell through the water and drummed into Jimmy's skull: "I live in you now, Jimmy. You can't shut me off."

Yes, Dave, I can.

And Jimmy turned the shower off and stepped out of the tub. He dried off and sucked the soft steam up his nostrils. If anything, it left him feeling even more clearheaded. He wiped steam off the small window in the corner and looked down into the alley that ran behind his house. The day was so clear and bright that even the alley looked clean. Christ, what a beautiful day. What a perfect Sunday. What a perfect day for a parade. He would take his daughters and his wife down to the street and they would hold hands and watch the marchers and the bands and the floats and politicians stream by in the bright sunlight. And they'd eat hot dogs and cotton candy and he'd buy the girls Buckingham Pride flags and T-shirts. And a healing process would begin amid the cymbals and drumbeats and horns and cheers. It would take hold of them, he was sure, as they stood on the sidewalk and celebrated the founding of their neighborhood. And when Katie's death pressed in on them again during the evening hours, and their bodies sagged a bit with the weight of her, they would at least have the afternoon's entertainment to balance their grief a little bit. It would be the start of healing. They would all realize that, at least for a few hours this afternoon, they'd known pleasure, if not joy.

He left the window and splashed warm water on his face, then covered his cheeks and throat with shaving cream, and it occurred to him as he began to shave that he was evil. No big thing, really, no earthshattering clang of bells erupting in his heart. Just that—an occurrence, a momentary realization that fell like gently grasping fingers through his chest.

So I am then.

He looked in the mirror and felt very little of anything at all. He loved his daughters and he loved his wife. And they loved him. He found certainty in them, complete certainty. Few men—few people—had that.

He'd killed a man for a crime the man had probably not committed. If that weren't bad enough, he felt very little regret. And in the long-ago, he'd killed another man. And he'd weighted both bodies down so that they'd descended to the depths of the Mystic. And he'd genuinely liked both men—Ray a bit more than Dave, but he'd liked them both. Still, he'd killed them. On principle. Stood on a stone ledge above the river and watched Ray's face turn white and sagging as it sank beneath the waterline, eyes open and lifeless. And in all these years, he hadn't felt much guilt over that, although he'd told himself he did. But what he called guilt was actually a fear of bad karma, of what he'd done being done to him or someone he loved. And Katie's death, he supposed, may have been the fulfillment of that bad karma. The ultimate fulfillment if you really looked at it—Ray coming back through his wife's womb and killing Katie for no good reason *except* karma.

And Dave? They'd wrapped the chain through the holes in the cinder block, tied it tight around his body, and locked the two ends together. And then they'd struggled to lift his body the nine inches it needed to clear the boat, and they'd tossed him over, Jimmy having a distinct image of the child Dave, not the adult, sinking to the river floor. Who knew exactly where he'd landed? But he was down there, at the bottom of the Mystic, looking up. Stay there, Dave. Stay there.

The truth was, Jimmy had never felt much guilt for anything he'd done. Sure, he'd arranged with a buddy in New York to have the Harrises sent five hundred a month over the last thirteen years, but that wasn't guilt so much as good business sense—as long as they thought Just Ray was alive, they'd never send anyone looking for him. In fact, now that Ray's son was in jail, fuck it, he could stop sending the money. Use it for something good.

The neighborhood, he decided. He'd use it to protect his neighborhood. And looking in the mirror, he decided that that's exactly what it was: his. From now on, he owned it. He'd been living a lie for thirteen years, pretending to think like a straight citizen, when all around him he saw the waste of blown opportunities. They were going to build a stadium down here? Fine. Let's talk about the workers we represent. No? Oh, okay. Better keep a close eye on your machinery, boys. Hate to have a fire on something like this.

He'd have to sit down with Val and Kevin and discuss their future. This town was waiting to be opened up. And Bobby O'Donnell? His future, Jimmy decided, wasn't looking all that bright if he planned on sticking around East Bucky.

He finished shaving, looked one more time at his reflection. He was evil? So be it. He could live with it because he had love in his heart and he had certainty. As trade-offs went, it wasn't half bad.

He got dressed. He walked through the kitchen feeling like the man he'd been pretending to be all these years had just gone down the drain in the bathroom. He could hear his daughters shrieking and laughing, probably getting licked to death by Val's cat, and he thought, Man, that's a beautiful sound.

OUT ON THE STREET, Sean and Lauren found a space in front of Nate & Nancy's coffee shop. Nora slept in her carriage and they placed it in the shade under the awning. They leaned against the wall and ate their ice cream cones and Sean looked at his wife and wondered if they'd make it, or if the yearlong rift had done too much damage, squandered their love and all the good years they'd had in their marriage before the mess of the final two. Lauren took his hand, though, squeezed it, and he looked down at his daughter and thought she did look a little bit like something to be adored, a small goddess, perhaps, filling him up.

Through the parade streaming in front of them Sean could see Jimmy and Annabeth Marcus, their two pretty girls sitting atop the shoulders of Val and Kevin Savage, the girls waving at every float and open convertible that passed by.

Two hundred and sixteen years ago, Sean knew, they'd built the first prison in the region along the banks of the channel that ultimately bore its name. The first settlers in Buckingham had been the jailers and their families and the wives and children of the men housed in the prison. It had never been an easy truce. When the prisoners were released, they were often too tired or too old to move very far, and Buckingham soon became known as a dumping ground for the dregs. Saloons sprouted up along this avenue and its dirt streets, and the jailers took to the hills, literally, building their homes up in the Point so they could once again look down on the people they'd corralled. The 1800s brought a cattle boom, the stockyards springing up where the expressway was now, a freight track running along the edges of Sydney Street and unloading the steers for the long walk up to the center of what was now the parade route. And generations of prisoners and slaughterhouse hands and their offspring pushed the Flats all the way down to the freight tracks. The prison closed in the wake of some forgotten reform movement, and the cattle boom ended, and the saloons kept sprouting. The Irish immigrant wave followed the Italian wave in twice the numbers, and the el tracks were built, and they streamed into the city for jobs, but always back here when the day closed. You came back here because you'd built this village, you knew its dangers and its pleasures, and most important, nothing that happened here surprised you. There was a logic to the corruption and the bloodbaths and the bar fights and the stickball games and the Saturday-morning lovemaking. No one else saw the logic, and that was the point. No one else was welcome here.

Lauren leaned back into him, her head beneath his chin, and Sean could feel her doubt, but also her resolve, her need to rebuild her faith in him. She said, "How scared were you when that kid pointed the gun in your face?"

"The truth?"

"Please."

"Close to losing bladder control."

She craned her head out from underneath his chin and looked at him. "Seriously."

"Yeah," he said.

"Did you think of me?"

"I did," he said. "I thought of both of you."

"What'd you think?"

"I thought of this," he said. "I thought of now."

"The parade, everything?"

He nodded.

She kissed his neck. "You're full of shit, honey, but it's sweet of you to say."

"I'm not lying," he said. "I'm not."

She looked down at Nora. "She's got your eyes."

"And your nose."

She was staring at their baby when she said, "I hope this works."

"Me, too." He kissed her.

They leaned back against the wall together, a steady stream of people passing by along the sidewalk in front of them, and then Celeste suddenly stood before them. Her skin was pale and her hair was speckled with dandruff and she kept pulling on her fingers as if trying to pop them from the sockets.

She blinked at Sean. She said, "Hey, Trooper Devine."

Sean held out his hand because she looked like she needed contact or she'd float away. "Hi, Celeste. Call me Sean. It's okay."

She shook his hand. Her palm was clammy, her fingers hot, and she let go almost as soon as they'd touched.

Sean said, "This is Lauren, my wife."

"Hello," Lauren said.

"Hi."

For a moment, no one knew what to say. They stood there, stilted and untethered, and then Celeste looked across the street and Sean followed her gaze to Jimmy, standing there with his arm around Annabeth, the two of them shining as bright as the day, surrounded by friends and family. They looked like they'd never lose anything again.

Jimmy's eyes swept past Celeste and met Sean's. He nodded in recognition and Sean nodded back.

Celeste said, "He killed my husband."

Sean felt Lauren freeze up against him.

"I know," he said. "I can't prove it yet, but I know."

"Will you?"

"What?"

"Prove it?" she said.

"I'll try, Celeste. I swear to God."

Celeste looked out on the avenue and scratched her head with a lazy ferocity, as if digging for lice. "I can't seem to put a finger on my mind lately." She laughed. "That didn't sound right. But I can't. I just can't."

Sean reached out and touched her wrist. She looked at him, her brown eyes wild and aged. She seemed sure he was going to slap her.

He said, "I can give you the name of a doctor, Celeste, someone who specializes in those who've lost loved ones to violent crime."

She nodded, though his words didn't seem to provide any consolation. Her wrist fell away from his hand, and she tugged at her fingers again. She noticed Lauren watching her, and she looked down at her fingers. She dropped her hands, then raised them again and crossed her arms over her chest and tucked her hands under her elbows as if trying to keep them from flying away. Sean noticed Lauren giving her a small, hesitant smile, one of abject empathy, and he was surprised to see Celeste

respond with a tiny smile of her own and an acknowledgment of gratitude in the blink of her eyes.

He loved his wife then as deeply as he ever had, and he felt hum-
bled by her ability to convey instant kinship with lost souls. He was
sure then that it was he who had wronged their marriage with the emer-
gence of his cop's ego, his gradual contempt for the flaws and frailty of
people.

He reached out and touched Lauren's cheek, and the gesture caused
Celeste to look away.

She looked out onto the avenue as a float in the shape of a baseball
glove drifted by, ringed on all sides with Little Leaguers and T-ball teams,
the kids beaming and waving and going crazy with the adoration.

Something about the float chilled Sean, the way the baseball glove,
maybe, seemed less to be cradling the kids and more on the verge of
enveloping them, the kids oblivious, smiling like mad.

Except for one. He was subdued and he looked at his cleats, and Sean
recognized him immediately. Dave's son.

"Michael!" Celeste waved to him, but the kid didn't look back. He
kept his eyes down even though she called his name again. "Michael,
honey! Sweetie, look! Michael!"

The float kept drifting along, and Celeste kept calling, and her son
refused to look her way. Sean could see a young Dave in the kid's shoulders and the droop of his chin, his almost delicate good looks.

"Michael!" Celeste called. She pulled her fingers again and stepped
off the curb.

The float passed them, but Celeste kept following it, moving through
the crowds, waving, calling her son's name.

Sean felt Lauren idly caress his arm, and he looked across the street at
Jimmy. If it took him the rest of his life, he was going to bring him down.
You see me, Jimmy? Come on. Look over again.

And Jimmy's head swiveled. He smiled at Sean.

Sean raised his hand, the index finger pointing out, the thumb cocked
like the hammer of a gun, and then he dropped the thumb and fired.

Jimmy's smile broadened.

"Who was that woman?" Lauren said.

Sean watched Celeste as she trotted along the line of parade watchers, growing smaller as the float continued up the avenue, her coat flapping behind her.

"Somebody who lost her husband," Sean said.

And he thought of Dave Boyle, and he wished he'd bought him that beer like he'd promised on the second day of the investigation. He wished he'd been nicer to him when they were kids, and that Dave's father hadn't left him, and his mother hadn't been nuts, and that so many bad things hadn't happened to him. Standing along the parade route with his wife and child, he wished a lot of things for Dave Boyle. But peace mostly. More than anything, he hoped Dave, wherever he was, got a little of that.